ALSO BY DAVID POYER

FIRE ON THE WATERS

A NOVEL OF THE CIVIL WAR AT SEA

DAVID POYER

SIMON & SCHUSTER

NEW YORK   LONDON   TORONTO   SYDNEY   SINGAPORE

SIMON & SCHUSTER
Rockefeller Center
1230 Avenue of the Americas
New York, NY 10020

SIMON & SCHUSTER and colophon are registered
trademarks of Simon & Schuster, Inc.

Book design by Ellen R. Sasahara

Manufactured in the United States of America

1 3 5 7 9 10 8 6 4 2

Library of Congress Cataloging-in-Publication Data
Poyer, David.
Fire on the waters : a novel of the Civil War at
sea / David Poyer.
p. cm.
1. United States—History—Civil War, 1861–1865—
Naval operations—Fiction. I. Title.
PS3566.O978 F5 2001
813'.54—dc21
2001020307

ISBN 0-684-87133-5

For information regarding special discounts for bulk purchases,
please contact Simon & Schuster Special Sales at 1-800-456-6798
or business@simonandschuster.com.

ACKNOWLEDGMENTS

———◆———

Ex nihilo nihil fit. For this book I owe thanks to Chuck Antony, Miles Barnes, Bill Black, Mike Cobb, William B. Cogar, Jean Coleman, John Coski, Harry Crandall, Michael Crawford, Alice Creighton, John P. Cummings, Karl Dillmann, Stefan Dulcie, Clyde Edgerton, John Ellis, Ed Finney, Alan Flanders, Lynne Foley, Tom Freeman, Heather Freidle, Doris and Noel Galen, Herb Gilliland, Frank and Amy Green, Tom Haas, Sloan Harris, Jean Hart, Lenore Hart, Mark Hayes, Alice Haynes, Glenn Helm, Mark Hugel, Jeff Johnston, Bob Kelly, Bert and Lanny Lasky, Joe M. Law, Hunt Lewis, W. R. McClintock, Paula Mills, Steve Milner, Ben Allston Moore Jr., Allen Mordica, Sarah H. Morgan, Gail Nicula, Caroline Orr, Tara Parsons, Janet Perry, Libby Phillips, Duff Porter, John V. Quarstein, David Rosenthal, Tim and Cheryl Scheib, Sandra Scoville, Craig Symonds, Marysue Rucci, Bill Whorton, and Paul Wilson.

Thanks also to "Bunky" Wichmann of *Mobjack,* Captain Ivan T. Luke Jr. and the officers, crew, and cadets of the United States Coast Guard barque *Eagle,* the National Archives, the New-York Historical Society, Portsmouth Naval Shipyard Museum, the Naval Historical Center, Norfolk Naval Shipyard, the Eastern Shore Public Library, the Navy Department Library, the United States Naval Academy Library, the Virginia War Museum, the Museum of the Confederacy, the Mariner's Museum, the Valentine Museum, the Armed Forces Staff College Library, and the New York Public Library.

As always, all errors and deficiencies are my own.

CONTENTS

———◆———

PART I

PART I

New York, April 6–9, 1861.

1

THE black ship's wedge of bow split hammered-iron river from
a galvanized sky. Her topmasts tilted above a spiky under-
growth of spars and shears. Smoke streamed from her single
funnel off over the gray-green flatness of the East River, merging at
last with the sooty pall from the thousands of other ships and homes
and factories of Manhattan.

As Elisha Eaker dropped his boots into trampled mud, the smells
of horse dung and coal ashes bloomed in his nostrils. He paid the
hack off with a red-dog note, then stood coughing, holding a handkerchief to his lips as its wheels ground away.

Was it wise, to venture this? Was it really a way out? Or was all
pride and folly, the disordered imaginings of a feverish brain?

Eli was tall and young, with pale, smoothly shaven cheeks. A
sword tilted awkwardly at his side. He'd put on the regulation full
dress for the first time that morning. Epaulettes from Warnock and
lace from Tiffany's; a cocked hat and silk stock and gold-striped pan-
taloons.

Marine sentries in pomponed shakos and white gloves snapped to present arms as he reached the gate. He expected them to ask for a password, given the unrest in the city and, indeed, throughout the Republic this apprehensive spring. But they neither questioned nor hindered him, and after a moment he walked on, into the Brooklyn Navy Yard.

The sloop's masts loomed against the smoldering sky as he headed downhill past foundries and shops echoing with the clang of iron and the shouts of workmen. Her black sides towered from the murky bay. Even immobile, she looked somber and intimidating.

But did he belong here? Or was he only fooling himself?

He hesitated again, then pushed doubt away and marched up the gangway. His boot caught, and only the manrope saved him from flinging himself into the dark water that sloshed and bumped a frowsy lumber of dead rats and waterlogged dunnage. At the top he drew in a deep first breath of her, of the curious, deep, peculiar ship-redolence mingled and amalgamated of tar and brass polish, coal dust and slowly mortifying oak, of old food and the damp reek of packed-in men; and beneath it all the sweet, smoky cured-tobacco aroma of the hempen rigging that lifted above him like a frozen whirlwind up into the murky sky.

A stocky, bullet-headed petty officer aimed him a questioning scowl. Eli saluted him and said, —Good day. My name is Elisha Eaker, and I am here to join your ship.

Lieutenant Ker Claiborne, U.S. Navy, first lieutenant and acting executive officer of U.S.S. *Owanee*, had slept for three hours out of the last forty-eight. Two days before, the yard commander had ordered her coaled and provisioned to sail at short order, and her just-dismissed crew remustered from the concert saloons, cider stubes, and panel houses of Five Points and the Bowery. Captain Trezevant had passed the command along with an ironic twist of the lips—a sardonic humor Ker would have shared, if he had not been so disquieted of late.

He was in the teak-paneled wardroom, going over a bill of lading by the light of a gimbaled lamp, when one of the ship's boys, looking, as usual, as if he expected to be caned, rapped at the jamb.

—What is it, Jerrett? Another of our lads back aboard drunk?

—No sir. Gunner Babcock's compliments, and there's a gen'lman on the quarterdeck to see you.

A caulking hammer tapped somewhere. Ker dipped the pen; held the back of his wrist against his pointed beard, pondering; then etched a line in firm Spencerian. He glanced at the card the boy laid on his desk. —Tell the gunner I will be up directly. Then carry this to Mr. Glass, if you please.

The boy vanished, and Claiborne rose, head brushing the varnished beams. He buttoned his coat and took his service cap off a peg. He studied a curved glass tube on the bulkhead. Then turned the lamp down, and went up the companionway.

The air on deck felt bracing after twenty-four months off West Africa. He'd contracted the fever of the country off the Guinea coast, and it came calling with chills and ague when he drove himself too hard. As he most likely was just now.

He touched his beard again, looking across the water not at the tropic continent but at his own country; but instead of comfort, memory and apprehension chilled his heart. When *Owanee* had deployed, two years before, the nation had been quiet. But since she'd returned, it seemed men had gone mad, lost their senses or been mastered by demons.

Like the Gadarene swine, he thought, we stampede blindly toward an infinite and fatal abyss.

Forward on the main deck, the gunners were scraping an amber paste of grease and varnish off the Dahlgren, flinging each bladeful into a tin bucket. A few yards aft, the boatswain was supervising a party swaying up the fore-topmast. At a pipe of his silver whistle the hoistlines tautened. The mast stood upright, then lifted its heel just clear of the deck, searching in the wind like an old man's uplifted and uncertain cane. Ker ran a critical eye over the rigging. He'd apprenticed to the art at Annapolis. The old school ship *Preble* had been just seaworthy enough to jog about the Chesapeake, but her sail plan and fitting out had been classic sailing navy. Summer cruises to the Caribbean and Mediterranean on the *Plymouth* added experience of levanters and hurricanes, but it was off the coast of Africa that he'd become a master. Coal was scarce and dear, and *Owanee* had sailed through most of her service there.

A curious tableau awaited him on the quarterdeck. A fair-haired young fellow, not badly made, but whose pale face and slack posture gave the impression of a life spent at ease, stood beside the ship's gunner. He was in full dress, but wore no insignia of rank. Ker made him the abbreviated bow one gives a stranger of whose intention one is uncertain. —Lieutenant Ker Claiborne, at your service.

—My name is Elisha Eaker. Late of the firm of Eaker and Callowell, of Manhattan.

—Did you wish to see the purser, sir? If it is a matter of business.

Eaker hesitated, then drew a document from his sleeve.

Ker was pondering it when a hoarse snort bellowed from the smokestack. A black cloud shot up, then hovered between mainmast and mizzen like a cloud of summer midges. Greasy flakes fluttered down like black snow.

—That turd Hubbard's doing, no doubt, and without the least concern for us topside, said the gunner angrily.

Eaker glanced around, at the morose-looking seamen, the rows of heavy guns that lined the waist. He flicked a flake of soot from his sleeve. —Could we perhaps . . . ?

And Ker said, —Certainly, sir. If you'll accompany me below?

Eighty feet aft, a scraping clang sounded from within a well of darkness. A moment later a little man in grease-stained denims and a cap with a broken bill emerged headfirst from beneath an iron casting that extended from the shadowy bilges to thick glass skylights thirty feet up. Their pearly glow illuminated a firm chin, determined lips, and deep-set eyes that peered from a face so sooted he resembled a blackface minstrel.

Theodorus Hubbard, *Owanee's* engineer, wiped his hands on a twist of cotton and pitched it overhand into a bucket. He braced his diminutive frame against a massive door. It slowly gathered momentum, then slammed shut with an iron boom that traveled the length of the space, dying away along catwalks, pumps, copper-shining piping, gutta-percha hose, glass tube-gauges of foaming water the color of melted opals. He said in a Connecticut twang, —Pappy, what I want to know is, how you let everything go to hell in just two weeks.

The burly man above him growled, —Well, last I heard was they was going to jerk this heap o' junk out of her and install one of them new Isherwoods. Never thought to be takin' her back to sea.

—Get them stokers on the rails. Watch the gauge when you cut in the crossover. Let's fire her up, see if she holds.

MacNail's shout echoed above the inhaling roar of fans and the slap of leather blower belts. Two huge men with Irish faces ran toward them, boots hammering the limber boards laid over bilges black with a slurry of coal dust, ash, and seawater. They seized fascines of kindling, heaved them into the furnace, and tossed bucketfuls of kerosene after. MacNail hastily seated twelve huge iron nuts on the man-cover from which Hubbard had emerged, then began torquing them down with a wrench as the stokers snatched shovels off iron clips and threw coal like men possessed, raising a fine choking dust of black anthracite.

Eli followed Claiborne down a shoulder-wide ladder into a low cabin that smelled of segar smoke, spar varnish, and the rotten-egg stench of sulphur fumigant. The lieutenant pointed to a chair. Eli aligned his cap on his knees and cleared his throat. —Are you the master of this vessel?

—The captain, you mean? No. I am the first lieutenant and executive officer. Just appointed as Captain Trezevant's second in command.

—Might I see the captain?

—He is not aboard at present. Nor would it be proper for me to intrude your presence upon him without ascertaining your business here, and that in considerable detail.

The lieutenant looked tired. Eli noticed he wore no sword, and began to doubt whether his own was not out of place. He nudged it around out of sight behind him as Claiborne said, —Well, sir, let's have another look at those papers.

As he leafed through them, Eli found his glance arrested by two small gleaming eyes that stared back at him from a fiddle-boarded bookcase. In the dimness he gradually made out that they were set in a tiny wizened face. He stood to examine what he took for a stuffed curio, then put out a hand. And staggered back a moment later, gripping his finger and stifling a scream.

—His name's Auguste, said Claiborne as the monkey hopped out, drawing a minuscule paw across its mouth and chattering angrily at the New Yorker. —Monsieur C. Auguste Dupin, to give him his complete honors. We took him and a few of his compatriots aboard at Porto Praya. As the days passed they gradually grew fewer, but we were hard put to tell where they'd gone. Finally we discovered this fellow here was pitching the smaller ones overboard at night to watch them swim.

The animal leapt to the floor and scrabbled up the companionway. Claiborne turned the documents over, scanning each with every appearance of interest. Finally he cleared his throat. —I hope you will not take it amiss if I observe I have never heard of the New York Naval Militia.

—Not at all. Eli wrenched his mind away from the ape, how disturbingly its shadowy leer had parodied a human smile. —It's a volunteer body, recently organized among the better sort of the city. Those who wish to step forward, should the slavocratic conspiracy put our temper to the test.

—Should the what?

—The renegade Carolinians who feel disposed to insult our flag.

Claiborne said gravely, —You must pardon me; I have been absent the country, and am unfamiliar with the political cant of the moment.

—You must know that the Deep South states have rejected all compromise, and set up a rump legislature at Montgomery.

—I read the journals, sir; and as far as I know, no offer of concession has been tendered them as yet. But let us lay that difficult topic aside. Your purpose in visiting *Owanee*?

Eli felt steadily less comfortable. The gravely courteous officer before him was plainly from south of the Mason-Dixon. The fellow's eyes, too, were unsettling, the same pale bleached blue as the noon sky in August. —I'm here to help in any way you may find convenient. I won't require pay.

—No pay, eh? It's true we're shorthanded just now. Claiborne examined the letters again. —These reflect attendance at Harvard University. What degree did you take?

—I was permitted to withdraw after two years, for reasons of health.

—You appear robust enough to me.

Eli said carefully, —Just now I feel well.

—Do you have anything resembling experience at sea?

—My family's been in shipping for three generations. I've also spent some considerable time aboard Mr. Cornelius Vanderbilt's private yacht.

Claiborne's eyebrows rose. —I see. Aboard his private yacht. You know Mr. Vanderbilt intimately, I take it?

—Not intimately, but well enough to speak to.

The exec mused over this for a moment more, then reached for a bell. —Ask the bo's'n to step in, he said to Jerrett's apprehensive countenance. —Your qualifications would not go so far as a mate's ticket, would they, Mr. Eaker?

—I'm afraid not. I'm willing to learn, though. And as I said, I will be happy to serve without emolument.

A tap at the doorjamb, and the exec motioned in a spare, spry old warrant with a furrowed brow, bright black eyes, and a preposterous forked gray-and-tobacco beard that hung below his waist. Claiborne introduced him as Josiah Girnsolver, *Owanee*'s boatswain. He told Girnsolver their visitor had alluded to experience in yachts, and that his qualifications as a sailing officer were under discussion.

The old man turned his head slowly to the left, then to the right, as if easing a stiff neck. He pulled up a trowser-leg, revealing the top of a prickly-looking red wool sock. Then said in a Down East accent, scratching his ankle thoughtfully, —Wal, let's say the cap'n tells ya to furl sails. What d'ya say to carry that out, now, sor?

Eli cleared his throat, calling on Mnemosyne to assist him. —To furl sails. Well, first I should call away the men. Um, then, command them to go aloft.

—"Aloft t'gallant and royal yardmen?" Girnsolver suggested.

—Quite so. When they have gained the rigging, get the topmen aloft; then man my clew jiggers—

—Buntlines and clew jiggers?

—I was about to say, buntlines as well. When all men are in position, I tell them to furl away. Then when all is complete, to lay down from aloft, I suppose.

Claiborne prompted, —And the downbooms?

—I should tell them to lay in the downbooms.

They regarded him noncommittally. The warrant fingered his whistle, which hung from his neck on a lanyard of ornately embroidered marline. He said, —Say ye're under way by the wind on a starboard tack, under all sail. What d'ya do if the wind hauls aft, as the officer of the deck?

Eli coughed into his fist, fighting both nervousness and the familiar rising tickle in his throat. —Maintaining the same course? I should first ease off sheets. Get a pull of the braces. Man the halyards on deck, then haul taut and hoist away. And make sure, ah, make sure the boom, I forget the name of it, but make sure it's ready for coming back in.

Claiborne asked him, —How many pieces of gear does a fully rigged ship need?

He sat struck dumb. There would be hundreds, no, thousands of fittings and parts from truck to keel. Then he smiled.

—Why, none, of course. If she needed any, she would not be fully rigged.

The first officer favored him with a lifted eyebrow. —He's got that right, at least. Well, Boats?

—'E don't know the commands, sor.

—Granting that, his unfamiliarity with service phraseology.

—Well, he's sort of got the idear. We maught could train him up, if he was willing to work. But a verbal examination ain't no proof of his effectiveness on deck. And a yacht ain't no warship.

The exec turned to Eli and cleared his throat. —Well, you have heard your judgment rendered. A segar, sir?

—Thank you, no. Feel free, if you like.

—Bo's'n?

—Thanks, sor, b'lieve I will indulge.

The two navy men lifted the globe of the lamp to light their cheroots. The lieutenant settled back on the settee, puffing out a cloud of rum-cured Cuban as the clank and drag of a massive chain reverberated through the overhead. —Are you certain you wish to subject yourself to sea-discipline, Mr. Eaker? The rigors and subordination of a man-of-war are quite a comedown from the leisure of civilian existence.

—I shall endeavor to do so to the best of my ability.

—So you present yourself as a gentleman volunteer, is that what we are to understand? Serving on a pro bono basis, with no allowances of any sort?

—That is correct, sir.

The exec cleared his throat. —An irregular mode of proceeding; but these seem to be irregular times. The final decision must be the captain's. Still, it's true we're very shorthanded. I will propose this: you take over the Forecastle Division; and since our gunnery officer has left for Mississippi, assume that position as well, at least temporarily. I'll ask Mr. Duycker to be your bear-leader. That is, to break you in on deck, and give you such guidance as you may need to find your footing.

Eli recalled the black weapons couched on the deck above, the half-naked men slaving over them like acolytes of a heathen temple. He had not anticipated quite so responsible a task so soon. But this did not seem to be the time to offer demurrals. Claiborne waited, then went on, —Bo's'n, have him put into Mr. Minter's stateroom, if you please. Then bring him back for luncheon, and we'll take his measure in the mess.

His cabin was soberingly small, dark, and dank, so much so he suspected he was being shown a punishment cell by way of further test; but he said nothing, simply nodded to the old man. Girnsolver was leading him down a narrow passageway when a smear-faced little fellow in dirty clothes shoved past. Eli started to protest, then closed his mouth again. He brushed smut off his coat and continued after Girnsolver, who was rambling to the end of what was obviously a well-worn tale about Captain Porter and the old *Essex*'s battle with the *Cherub* and *Phoebe* off Valparaiso in March of '14.

—Y're joinin' a good ship here, sor. Not tae much Andrew Miller and sichlike pimpiness, and the prog's first-rate. We're supposed to go inta ordinary, after this long trick in Africky, but scuttlebutt is they're sending us down to deal with these here *se*-cessionists. Since we're about the only steamer left around.

—The rest of the fleet's overseas, I understand.

—Yes sor, in the Med or off Brazil. If something goes to pop, we're the ones t'will have to pull the chestnuts. Girnsolver opened another door, gestured him through. —Mind you use the right fork, sor, and good luck.

Claiborne introduced him simply as a Manhattan gentleman, interested in joining the sea service. Mindful that his stay was uncertain, Eli merely bowed as, one after the other, the exec introduced the men around the dining table.

The paymaster and purser was a supercilious-looking Israelite named Judah Glass. The smutty boy who'd jostled Eli in the corridor had become a small-framed but fully grown man, face scrubbed, reattired in a civilian sack coat and tie. He was introduced as Mr.

Theodorus Hubbard. A magnificently mustachioed officer in a blue army-style uniform and gold shoulder knots was presented as Lieutenant Robert Schuyler, commanding *Owanee*'s detachment of marines.

Nicholas Duycker was a lean, graying master; he favored Eli with a Voltairean smirk as they shook hands. Eli recognized the man Claiborne had appointed to "bear-lead" him.

A corpulent, brandy-breathed fellow well past youth rose grudgingly to the name of Doctor Alphaeus Steele. There remained two very young midshipmen, Eddowes and Thurston, and three empty places. When the proprieties were satisfied Claiborne took the head of the table and led them in a short grace.

—Well, and what is the mood of the city today? Dr. Steele asked Eli as an aged, bent Negro in a rusty frock coat slowly passed from one to the next, pouring out a tablespoon of claret to each glass.

He noted the others awaiting his lead as guest. He raised the glass to his lips, though he did not actually drink. Instead of answering he said, —And this man? Has he a name?

Claiborne looked puzzled. —I believe I have introduced everyone.

—Not our sable friend here, said Eli, turning in his seat to face the Negro.

The table quieted. The old man had stopped short, on his way out with the carafe, but did not speak. Looking up, Elisha saw the far orb turned on him now. A silver-filmed sphere, immobile, obviously blind, it yet gave the impression of præternatural observation. An elderberry mark was tattooed on each temple in the shape of a shark's fin. The front teeth were filed, not to points, but successively, long yellow teeth alternating with mere pegs. A chill hackled Eli's spine.

—We call him Uncle Ahasuerus, said Claiborne quietly. —He does not answer you because he cannot speak. He was mutilated some years ago by the Kroomen, his own tribe. Why, we do not know. When we took him off a Brazil-bound slaver he indicated his desire to stay with us, in the capacity wherein you see him. He is Commander Trezevant's—is the phrase *fidus Achates*?

Eli nodded. The reference was to Vergil; Achates had been the faithful companion who accompanied Aeneas on his wanderings.

The steward left, vanishing into some back pantry. Dr. Steele rumbled his throat free and said again, —What news from the city? Is the mayor still offering to secede, along with his friend Jeff Davis?

A chuckle ran around the table. Eli flushed, reminded of the corrupt Fernando Wood's proposal that New York should leave what he called a "dismembered government," the better to retain its hundreds of millions in Southern business. —The city's overwhelmingly loyal. My father says the price of gold has found its level—

An etheric current seemed to run around the table, as at the séances popular in some circles. Duycker drawled, —Your father wouldn't be—

—He is Micah Eaker.

—Who is . . . ? said Claiborne, looking from one to the other.

—A Manhattan financier, Hubbard said darkly, helping himself to a tureen of Lynnhaven oysters. Eli caught his glance; the envy in it was unmistakable.

Steele hoisted his eyebrows. —Not merely a "financier," my dear Hubbard. Micah Eaker sitteth at the right hand of Vanderbilt and Astor.

—One fellow who won't cavil at the mess bill, at least, Glass muttered.

—Moreover, he is one of the leading lights of Republicanism in the Empire State. And you, sir? Do I sense you too worship at that dusky shrine?

Eli helped himself to the stewed oysters, trying to keep his sangfroid. The room was warm, and the hot food didn't help; he felt sweat break under the heavy wool uniform. —I am a Republican. Not from any sense of righteousness, I am afraid. My grandfather traded to Africa and, I regret to say, trafficked in helpless men and women, stolen from their homes.

—A trade which has not yet ended, Glass put in. —We have just returned from a long patrol on the Gulf of Guinea, and had several encounters with illegal blackbirders. Most of whose masters, interestingly enough, hail from New England.

Steele pressed. —You are a Lincolnian, sir?

—Since hearing him, yes, I number myself among those friendly to him.

—You've met the president? Schuyler said. The marine had a scratchy, damaged-sounding voice, and touched his collar as he spoke.

—I heard him speak at Cooper Union, when he began his quest for the nomination.

Duycker said contemptuously, —You support the man who's destroying the Union? Does he really resemble what Mr. Darwin would style—how would you put it, Hubbard—our "anthropoid cousins"?

Claiborne cleared his throat in warning. But Eli replied, as coolly as he could, —Not at all. It's true he's taller than the average, but he's not the outlandish character such pandering rags as the *Herald* make him out to be.

Duycker smiled loftily, started to respond, but the exec said sharply, —Politics are out of order in the mess, gentlemen. Find some other topic.

—Such as the impossibility of putting to sea with these wretched boilers, the engineer said.

The others sighed. Eli essayed a chuckle. —We can still sail, can't we?

Hubbard glared. —Useless top-hamper, and a lot of useless hands to pull it about. Throw it all overboard, and fill the hull with coal.

—Mr. Hubbard is a mechanical enthusiast, Claiborne explained.

—But sails do not break down, Theo. Should a mast go to smash, we simply jury-rig a spar. But when her engine breaks down, a steamer is helpless.

—A ship should have two, then.

—That really is going beyond the bounds of good taste, said Glass silkily. —We should be manned with nothing but grease monkeys and Paddy stokers, and sleep with lumps of bituminous stuffed into our ticking.

They chortled as the ancient Negro, glaring out from his un-clouded eye, took off the soup plates and brought baked cod in thin, flaky crust, asparagus, hot scones and sweet butter, and sliced burga-loos for dessert. By the time they sipped hot coffee ground from beans purchased in the Bay of Benin, Dr. Steele was dilating on a re-markable flower that he had observed in Martinique. —The mere scent of which can induce vomiting. If inhaled in a closed room, I was told, it would induce death in persons of weakened constitution; by reason of which, it has been implicated in numerous mercy mur-ders of the aged and infirm.

And the unpleasant topic of disunion had been banished from the speech, if not the thoughts, of all.

After luncheon Claiborne put him together with the gunner, one Thomas Babcock, a heavyset, saturnine, bald-headed warrant, or sen-ior petty officer, old enough to be his father, if not his grandfather; in fact the same man Eli had first saluted on stepping aboard. Babcock, who seemed to be in a bad humor, carried a colt, a short length of braided manila that he continually slapped against his thigh. He led Eli on a tour of their demesne. *Owanee* carried five guns. To port and starboard midships crouched four old-style thirty-two-pounders, grim Jaganaths on oaken carriages with lignum vitae trucks. The largest, though, was the single huge nine-inch Dahlgren. It was mounted forward, but iron racers on deck made it trainable to either broadside. The gunners were working on it, scraping off the last of a greasy coating. Babcock explained that they were preparing the metal for varnishing. Gradually Eli noted that their apparent leader was a huge man with enormous shoulders.

He muttered to the gunner, —Is *he* a member of the crew?

—Hanks! Stand to attention.

The sailor froze, half turned at the warrant's peremptory sum-mons. For the merest fraction of a second Eli caught a red-eyed gaze, direct and full of what looked very much like hatred. Then, quick as the snap of a caplock, a blank mask took its place. The sailor laid aside an iron handspike, straightened from his work, and came to attention in front of them.

—Calpurnius Hanks, sir.

—Mr. Eaker didn't address you, boy, said Babcock threateningly.
—You keep that mouth shut till you hear an order, or you and me are going to have a falling-out. The sailor blinked; his mouth compressed, then sank back into a quiescent line.

Eli did not count himself as a small man, but Hanks looked twice as wide. He examined the rounded head, the small, protruding ears, curled as if they'd been given a hard twist in infancy. His beard was tightly curled, as if twisted back into the skin. His lips were fleshier than a white man's and, with the heavy, outthrust jaw, projected the lower half of his face forward. Deep brown irises deepened to a black pool, the whites like old ivory. Eli's glance dropped to large, curled hands, then to big, blacked, square-toed boots.

—He calls himself a freedman, said Babcock, slapping the colt into his palm. Eli noted a tattooed American flag on the back of his hand. —But I think he's an escaped slave.

He tried to imagine the black in rags, fleeing, the way Liza jumped across the ice floes in Mrs. Stowe's play. He could not catch the man's gaze. It floated beyond him, fast to the distant line of river and bay.

—Your position aboard, Hanks? Eli asked him.

The wide lips hesitated. —Second gun cap'n on numbah one, sir.

—Are you truly an escaped slave?

—Fugitive slaves not permitted to enlist in the navy, sir.

He nodded. A good answer to a question he realized now he should not have asked. —Very well, Hanks. You can go back to your work.

They descended from there to inspect the magazines, arms lockers, and departmental records. Eli insisted on an inventory. Two hours later, he realized it was well he had. Eight of the ship's revolvers were missing.

—Mr. Minter *did* leave with a heavy carpetbag, Babcock said darkly.

—I had best report this loss to Mr. Claiborne.

—You think he'll mind?

Eli frowned. —What do you mean by that?

Babcock met his eye, glowering. —Sir, we enlisted men can't resign. That'd be desertion. But the officers are let to walk off whenever they like. If I might speak frankly, there's others still aboard more secesh than otherwise.

—I will not countenance criticism of the officers, Eli said stiffly. —Excuse me.

Neither gun room nor wardroom held Claiborne. Only when Eli came out onto the main deck, now cooler beneath the threat of a squall, did he see him by the gangway, peering through a telescope. When he came up the first lieutenant clapped it shut.

—A word, sir.

—Your servant, Mr. Eaker.

He explained about the revolvers, and Babcock's suspicion as to their fate. Claiborne's lips tightened, but he said only, —I will enter that information in the log. Now, if you please, stand away from the quarterdeck.

Two men were walking toward them down the pier. One was in undress uniform, a lean aristocrat with a raptorial nose and weatherbeaten complexion. The other was stouter, black bearded, in a steel-pen coat and top hat. He gestured expansively with both arms as they paused at the brow.

The boatswain's pipe shrilled. —*Owanee,* arriving, Midshipman Thurston shouted to the quartermaster. A pendant snapped down from the leaden sky, leaving the Stars and Stripes to rustle and flap alone in a sudden cold breeze.

The officer paused as he stepped aboard, sweeping a keen glance aloft, then down the main deck. As he returned Claiborne's salute his gaze marked Eaker, then returned to his companion as the latter resumed speaking.

—That's the captain? Elisha asked, when the new arrivals had vanished below.

—Commander Parker Bucyrus Trezevant, *Owanee*'s commanding officer.

—And the other?

—A Mr. Fox, a former naval man who I understand now runs a woolen mill. He is connected with the Blairs. Something of a politician, I suspect.

Eli said, —I'd like to step ashore now, if no one minds. Is that all right?

—That is generally phrased in the service, "Request permission to go ashore, sir." Claiborne smiled, making a jest of it rather than a rebuke, and Elisha found himself liking the Southerner. —You will not stay the evening? Theodorus is not a bad hand at the harmonium, and the captain carries a baritone. We also play various and beautiful but somewhat uncertain games of cards. But perhaps you have a rendezvous with one of the softer sex.

Eli flushed, recalling who actually waited for him, and what he had to tell him. The thought made his palms sweat. For a moment he was tempted to confide in Claiborne, perhaps ask his advice. But at last all he said was, —I'm expected home.

Facing the old flag, he contemplated its bloody scarlet and empyrean blue, the scatter of stars, each separate, yet conveying in their massed ranks power and unanimity. Could it be possible that the "mystic chords of memory," as the new president had styled them in his inaugural address, could be sundered? He could not believe it. The erring sisters would return, once a firm hand was shown. But by then he'd be free. One way or another, surely he would be free.

Descending the gangway, he vanished into the blue evening.

2

The Music Ride ♦ Reaction to the Playing of "Dixie" ♦ An Evening at the Eaker Town House ♦ The Sumter Dilemma ♦ Mr. Seward's Plan for Peace and Union ♦ A Hostile Fleet Off New York ♦ A Final Solution to the African Problem ♦ Embrace on the Back Stairs

T HE evening sky was charcoal outside lofty arched windows. But within the Reitclubb, an artificial glare held night at bay. It blazed from gas globes studding the walls, and from a huge cast-iron gasolier suspended above the sand. The long hall reverberated with the stamp and jangle of a hundred horses and riders, trotting in step to the rising and falling bows of violins in the balcony, to the darting, swooping strains of the *Valse Impromptu*.

Four places back from the van, a slim dark girl rose to the trot, gripping the reins cavalry fashion. A black ostrich plume dipped and shook. Black riding skirts fell to her boots. Her mount was a Lusitaner stallion, glossy as polished jet. As she passed beneath a gaslight her forehead shone out pale and rounded, and large, dark, slightly protruding eyes flashed out, fixed with a nervous alertness on the rider ahead.

Araminta Van Velsor had drilled herself and El Cid mercilessly for the last music ride of the season and, she suspected, her last at the Reitclubb. She wasn't sure why she felt that way. In two months she'd be married. True, but many of the riders about her were married women. For some time now, though, she'd felt a period in her life drawing to an end, to be succeeded by something as yet shadowy as the distant roof beneath which the cream of New York society promenaded in an enormous wheel.

At the center of the ring the scarlet-coated *Reitmeister* rose in the saddle as his Austrian stallion lifted into a levade. He swept a supercilious glance about the spinning zoetrope of Morgans and Arabs, fine flashy Spanish and Portuguese bloods. In the balcony the waltz rose to its climax, the arms of the violinists whipping as if intent on kindling their instruments into flame, and at last crashed to a halt.

He raised his whip, and brought it down.

With a thump and a skirr the band broke into the strains of "Dixie." Araminta no more than brushed him with her heel beneath her skirt, and the stallion moved without hitch or hesitation into a canter.

> *Oh, wish I was in the land o' cotton,*
> *Old times there are not forgotten,*
> *Look away! Look away!*
> *Look away!*
> *Dixie's Land!*

Her consciousness merged with that of the beast beneath her. The heavy sharp hooves of the horse ahead sliced the air inches from Cid's breast, yet the stallion maintained his dress and interval without the least pressure on the reins. Riding him was the closest she'd ever felt to another living being, and she felt a sudden bittersweet regret the moment could not last forever. From about her at the same instant came a curious vox humana through the jingling thunder of moving horseflesh, the jaunty lilt of the minstrel tune, the burst of applause from the spectator boxes. It was made of murmurs from between mustached lips, protests at the choice of music; and along with them, cheers, hurrahs, and even a curious, high, yipping cry.

Two hours later she hunted through the first floor of her uncle's house, eye roving each room, missing nothing, taking nothing for granted.

Number 372 Fifth Avenue had been built in the teens, and the parlor had always seemed dingy and old-fashioned to her as a child. She'd redecorated two years ago, when Micah had given her official management. Out went the old klismos chairs and the creaky re-camier. Now lavender moiré draperies puddled to a figured carpet. Gold-on-cream de Fossé wallpaper glowed beneath Italian glass torchères. A black leather settee stood between the front windows, and a fireplace mirror in a rococo frame reflected a fauteuil, comfortable bergères, and prints of the Hudson Valley. The thick stone walls muted traffic roar to a distant grumble so faint she could hear the hiss of the gas and an occasional thump from the basement.

Her uncle was upstairs dressing. She had finished her own toilet quickly, brushing her hair straight back and binding it with a fillet of paper roses. Her dress was a pale blue *crêpe lisse*. She wore her favorite black lace shawl draped about her arms, but no jewelry. Micah considered it inappropriate.

She went through the other rooms, making sure Maire and Roberta had attended to the cleaning, that the windows were tuned to let air flow through the house. She fanned a glow away and turned a page on the Schomacker grand, running her fingers absently along the gadrooning as she reviewed the lied she'd sing after dinner. Paused again in the dining room, before a portrait of a woman. Then pushed open a door, twitched up her skirts, and went swiftly down into an upwelling of food smells and the chatter of the cooks as once again 372 Fifth prepared to host those who still steered the ship of state and finance, even in this most democratic of all nations and all centuries.

The man who headed the table could not quite be called elderly yet, but his silvery hair and pouchy eyes attested him in the waning years of middle age. Micah Adolphus Eaker's somber, intent features and luxuriant mane had been compared by the *Times* to those of

Beethoven. Fresh white linen showed at cuffs and collar, and at the moment, two days past his last attendance by a barber, a silvery sparkle glittered on his cheeks.

The men around the table, all men except for Araminta, were soberly dressed, as if in mourning. They were Ellery Phelps, a thirty-ish political man associated with the former Empire State governor and secretary of state in the new cabinet, William Seward; Hinton Helper, a North Carolina writer whose book had been banned throughout the South; and Horace Greeley, the editor of the *New York Tribune.*

Greeley was the most remarkable looking, she thought, with his round cherub's face wreathed by white whiskers, collars barely re-strained by a large black silk neckerchief, and light, vague blue eyes behind glittering spectacles. He looked rumpled and countryish, but this was the man whose cunning praise had so increased suspicion of Stephen Douglas in the South it had split the Democratic Party, and whose machinations in Chicago had cost Seward the nomination by swinging the Bates delegates to Lincoln.

Two English servants attended them at table, supervised by Parkinson, the butler. As the soup was served Helper nodded toward the portrait. —They tell me you're a widower, Mr. Eaker. Would that lovely lady have been your wife?

—That was my wife, my absent son's mother and Araminta's aunt.

—A true beauty.

The old man inclined his head. —She was the angel in my house.

Greeley said, in a weak, husky voice, —Yet I see she has been suc-ceeded by another. You will forgive me, but when I saw your niece, long-forgotten lines came to mind.

> *But lady! In that mild, soul-speaking glance,*
> *Those lustrous orbs, returning heaven its hue,*
> *I greet an earlier friend—forgive the trance!*
> *'Tis Nature only, imaged her so true*
> *That, briefly, I forgot the Printer's art*
> *And hailed the presence of a Queenly Heart.*

She dropped her eyes and summoned a blush. She'd found she could do this in the dramatic group. Her color deepened as she remembered how her uncle had stormed into the rehearsal, cursed her friends for pansy boys and loose women, and pulled her from the room. Well, they'd take it as modesty, so long as she kept her anger screened from her voice and smile.

She kept the conversation light, inquiring whether any of them had heard the Havana musical troupe at Castle Garden. The main course was being served when Elisha came in, unhooking a sword and handing it, and his gloves and cocked hat, to the butler.

She mouthed her knuckles, staring. After a moment Micah snarled, —What costume ball do *you* come from, boy?

—I joined the navy today, Father. Elisha bowed to the others. —My apologies for being delayed. May I join you?

She turned fascinated back to her stepfather, bracing herself for the explosion. But to her surprise his face was bland. Then she recognized the pursed lips, the noncommittal eyebrows. He would reveal nothing until it was time to strike.

Only then, as the talk resumed, did she suddenly wonder what her cousin's act meant to her own future.

As the ninth stroke of the clock died away she folded her napkin. The gentlemen pushed back their seats, but Micah remained sitting. —Leaving us so soon, Araminta?

—I thought I would sing some Schubert for you.

—No, no. We have serious matters to discuss. You'd better go to bed.

She almost objected, she'd practiced for hours; but she held her tongue. She made her good-nights and bent to kiss her uncle. As her lips brushed his hair she smelled his pomade, and the familiar scent made her stiffen and edge away.

The library was dominated by a huge fireplace, the mantel of which was supported by carved Indian warriors. A coal fire glowed and flickered as Micah took a chair near an inlaid smoking cabinet, waving his guests to seats. Eli, Helper, and Phelps made themselves comfortable near him. Greeley took a seat a few paces from the smokers. The white-haired butler set out whiskey and lucifers, then brought the editor the milk and sugar he'd asked for.

Micah said angrily, —The navy, is it? You could have done me the courtesy of notice.

Eli smiled nervously. —I'm sorry, Father; I thought you'd be pleased.

—Thought I'd be *pleased*? Micah said to the others, —He's found things too difficult at Harvard, gentlemen. Well, no surprise there! This is just the latest hobbyhorse.

Eli bent his head silently. Micah went on, tone heavy with contempt, —Like the girl; she had delusions of being a playactor. The both of them, worthless as a customhouse oath! So now you're running off to sea?

He'd prepared a ringing declaration on the cars home; noble words about defending the flag. Face-to-face with his father, though, he couldn't remember them. He mustered a weak smile. —Oh, I don't know. I just thought . . . improve my health. . . .

—The sea's a manly calling, said Greeley, thin voice compassionate.

Micah smiled frostily. —You support him in defying me? No doubt he knows better than his father. Very well, sir, pray tell us then, as the voice of the rising generation, what our course should be in regard to this imbroglio over Sumter.

Phelps put in, —Do you see the political dilemma Sumter represents, Eli?

He cleared his throat. —I think so. If Lincoln gives it up peacefully, no one will believe he means to maintain the Union. But if we fight our way into the harbor, the North becomes the aggressor.

Greeley said, —The South will respond to a firm hand. "No concessions to traitors." That's how I've advised Mr. Lincoln from the start. But he's in the web of some cunning spiders.

—You don't mean Governor Seward? said Phelps.

The editor returned a benevolent smile. —I was thinking more of Mr. Weed, and of course Simon Cameron, though he's more interested in just getting the till jimmied open.

Micah snorted. He poured out the barest suggestion of whiskey, the single drink he'd allow himself tonight. Phelps and Helper selected cheroots. Eli refused the decanter with a shake of his head, and let the tobacco pass as well.

Greeley set down his jaggeried milk, leaving a chalky shadow on his upper lip. —No, the hootings and posturings will quickly cease once they see we won't yield to threats. Or would you disagree, Mr. Helper?

The Carolinian murmured, —We may differ in important points, sir.

Micah turned to Phelps. —We're interested in your views, Ellery. Especially as they reflect Mr. Seward's.

The politician crossed his boots. —We can still reach some accommodation. Above all, we must take no irretrievable steps.

—But listen to this, said Greeley, pulling a scrap of newsprint from a hidden pocket. —The telegraphic report of a speech Mr. Stephens just made. After excoriating our old Constitution, he says their new one "rests upon the great truth that the Negro is not equal to the white man; that Slavery, subordination to the superior race, is his natural and normal condition. This, our new Government, is the first in the history of the world, based upon this great physical, philosophical, and moral truth."

A gust of wind flattened the dancing flames, and sent a smoky whiff of coal gas into the room. Micah coughed; the other men shielded their segars and held their breaths for a moment.

Helper said, —His conclusions are end about. The Negro's not a source of wealth, but our primal curse. Hamitic slavery has reduced our working whites to poverty, imprisoned our women, and subjected us to the narrow interests of an oligarchy. The Southland's got to throw off both yokes. That of the niggers, and of the planter aristocracy.

—I am always . . . *refreshed* to see a man of opinions, Hinton, said

Greeley. —Your courage in maintaining yours in your homeland is evident.

Phelps said, —As a statesman, Governor Seward understands compromise is the only course between Scylla and Charybdis. If I may lay out his reasoning?

The others nodded. The politico said, flourishing his cheroot as if addressing a convention, —First principle: that the greatest of all evils is civil war. For such an enmity would be *perpetual,* once the two sections faced each other in battle. To avoid it, we should accept a constitutional amendment protecting slavery forever. Thus, to Sumter. We will renounce it, in proof of our good faith.

—But what then? said Micah, frowning. —If they agree to return?

—The governor's design is to forge a new coalition, North and South, in a common policy of support for the Union. Slavery will not be mentioned. This new party will dominate American politics for the next twenty-five years.

—Just the sort of abomination Seward would stitch together, Greeley growled. —A Frankenstein's monster of Whigs and Know-Nothings, galvanized by cotton money.

Phelps said tolerantly, —Horace, your radical locofocos will never command the support of the American people. Garrison and Lizzy Stanton have been vaporing about abolition for thirty years. They're not one inch closer to their goal.

—We've made enough concessions to traitors, Greeley growled. —The compromise of 1820! The compromise of 1850! Now 1861, and then—1880? 1910? 1963? I see you smiling, but will not the same issue recur down through the generations? My conclusion grieves me, for I am a peaceful man. But if the question must be settled by military means, so be it.

—General Scott's a Virginian himself.

Phelps said, —As are most of our best officers, unfortunately. We must also beware the English and French, both of whom may favor a dismembered Union as advancing their positions in the New World. If war comes I should not be surprised to find this city under military control within a month, or at the very least, with a hostile fleet off the Battery.

—They may be there already, said Greeley. —Trustworthy sources have reported a fleet off Sandy Hook.

Eli sat up. —A foreign fleet? British?

—They flew no flag. It may be the Spanish.

As Eli tried to fit this news together with the preparations for war aboard *Owanee,* Phelps drawled, —All right, mine host, enlighten us. I know you can't speak for Daniel Drew and Commodore Vanderbilt, at least not directly; but can you outline the position of the financial element?

Micah's face closed. —I haven't seen as much raw fear on the Street since '57. The loss in securities is over three hundred millions. The South owes us another hundred and fifty million in crop loans. If they repudiate, things will be desperate indeed. Shipowners, cotton export, textile concerns, railroad stocks have all dropped fifty percent or more. As you know, I manage the issues of several concerns. Half will face default if this crisis is not brought to a speedy resolution. This waiting policy is crushing us, Ellery. I share Horace's concern for the suffering black man. But if compromise will bring peace, for God's sake let's compromise now.

Parkinson returned with another glass of jaggery on a tray. He poked up the fire, setting free a few flakes of gray ash. They circled in the warm air, then settled to the carpet. He emptied the ashtrays into a scuttle, then left again.

Greeley sucked greedily at the sugared milk. —But why must *we* always give way to these slave breeders? The entire South has less manufacturing capacity than New York City. Why, just look at their railroads. Every state has a different gauge. They can't afford to fight. The fools in Montgomery know that as well as we do. A firm stand at Sumter will end this foolishness.

—I'll take issue with you on that, sir, said Helper, and he spoke still courteously but now with a dark seriousness that sobered them. —You deceive yourself if you think we'll come back with our hats in our hands once blood is spilled. If we are lacking in the sinews of war, we can buy those overseas. The crux of the matter is the colored question.

Micah said, —Indeed, what is to be done with the Negro? Lincoln wants to ship him back to Ethiop. Others suggest the unpopulated West.

Helper said, —My book gave my answer. If this undesirable population cannot be deported, we must find a way to stop it reproducing. Under a properly conducted system, but a few years would be required to make it vanish.

Phelps clicked his watch open and suddenly sat up. He threw his segar into the fire and clapped his hands on his knees. —I must thank you all for your views. But you may depend on this: there will be no war. It requires both flint and steel to strike a spark. Governor Seward will not commence his administration with bloodshed. The Sumter garrison will be withdrawn.

Eli got up. —It's been a long day for me, gentlemen. If you will permit me to withdraw.

The others nodded, but his father did not deign to notice his departure. As the door closed behind him he heard one last remark in Greeley's squeaky voice. —I believe we can all be easy on one point, gentlemen.

—And that is?

—That one way or another, things will come to a head very soon.

He was climbing the stairs when he saw her hugging her knees on the landing. Her dark hair was loose, falling like a schoolgirl's about her shoulders. A candle burned on the step above, throwing a brightness around her.

Araminta watched the man she was expected to marry come up the stairs, carrying his sword. His face was troubled, and his breathing rasped in the stairwell. She wondered what had happened in the library, whether Micah had shouted at him, threatened him. He hadn't said anything about the navy to her.

Eli came up the last few steps, hesitated, then bent, and kissed the crown of her head. Her hair smelled of patchouli. —Waiting for me?

—Is he very angry with you?

He studied the side of her face. Her thin neck, her all too prominent eyes and nose. A rush of pity and guilt shuddered through him, as if through a bottleneck too narrow to let all his feelings pass. Micah had made it plain over the years that he expected them to marry when they were both of age. He'd accepted that as destiny; accepted that their lives in the house would go smoothly on together. But now he had to tell her. He lowered himself awkwardly.

Araminta felt herself stiffen, feeling his bulk pressing in on her. She and Eli had played together, known each other since she'd come to live here as a child. She'd always known he loved her. And she loved him, but . . . as a cousin, not as one betrothed.

His face approached, white as wax in the candle dimness. She let him kiss her cheek. His lips felt like ice.

—I'm sorry, Ara.

—For what offense, dearest cousin?

He cleared his throat, trying to speak blithely. —I have something not entirely pleasant to tell you.

—You'd better do so right now, then.

—Well, you remember I've had this plaguey cough. And I was going to see the other doctor, after Dr. Wetmore blistered me. He said, this other doctor . . . I may have a slight oppression of the lungs.

—Oh, Eli. She covered her mouth with her hand, horrified. —You don't mean . . . not like your mother?

—No, no, not that. Not at all! He said it quite certainly wasn't. Simply a little fever now and then.

She stared at him still, hardly believing what he was saying. —But, but, your lungs? Eli, how? We've always had a good fire, a warm house.

—I don't know; but I'm afraid it's so. He turned to her, and she saw with new eyes the burning intentness of his gaze, the hollowness of his cheeks compared to their boyish plumpness when he'd left for Cambridge. —I was studying too hard, most likely. But the upshot is, I need a change of air. I could go to California or the Rockies, but a sea voyage would do just as well. And I thought with the way things are now with the country . . .

She said slowly, trying to think it out, —But Eli, won't it be dangerous? Mightn't there be war? I could never live if you came to harm.

—Oh, not a bit of it. Mr. Phelps says this whole secesh nonsense will be over in a month or two.

He rubbed his hand over his face. This was the part he'd been dreading. He only hoped she didn't cry. He said in a rush, —But considering all that, being out of sorts, and having to go away for a time, well, I don't think it would be fair to hold you to our understanding. At least not until I get myself built up again.

Her heart leaped up, but she let nothing show but a catch of the breath. Was it possible, *was* there a way out? She didn't want to marry him. She wasn't sure she wanted to marry anyone.

Then she swallowed, elation succeeded by a rush of guilt. He was her all-but-brother, he was ill, and all she could think of was herself. She laced her hands together and bent her head, the attitude of Resignation. —Eli, Eli. Of course I cannot object, if you think that the wisest course. She put the back of her hand to her brow. Or was that too self-consciously thespian? She lowered it quickly. —My happiness must come after yours. May you come home restored to radiant health. And may our government lay low the nefarious schemes of the devil traffickers in human flesh.

He studied her, relieved she wasn't too upset, but at the same time puzzled. —You really believe in that, don't you, Araminta? In abolition?

Despite herself, emotion fired her voice. —I do, Elisha. Ever since I heard that Sojourner woman speak. Buying and selling men and women . . . I admit it, we're not stainless. But they've learned nothing. I don't see why we *want* union with those monsters!

—Dearest Ara. How good you are. How understanding. And how little I deserve you.

She felt his lips touch her forehead, and gasped at both fear for him and a dark rush of something even more terrifying. She couldn't name it, but it made her knees draw suddenly up beneath the bone and steel of her crinoline, into the pit of her stomach. She felt his fingers on her back, a tentative caress.

—One last thing, my love.

—Yes, Elisha.

—Don't tell Micah this, about my indisposition. He thinks me weak and useless already. I would like very much indeed to prove him wrong.

—Of course, I will not. With all my heart.

—Good night, my love and cousin.

—Good night, Elisha. She caught his hand, squeezed it, and guided it deftly aside. The next moment she had picked up her skirts and glided up the stairs, till she vanished into the darkness.

He looked after her, the flash of a momentarily revealed ankle ineradicable in his mind; and for a moment salt stung his eyes, regret and sadness. She wasn't beautiful. But she was so alive! Those great eyes were dark as forest pools, but close up they reflected each passing feeling so clearly, so honestly.

He only wished he could love her the way she deserved of a husband. But he couldn't.

—Elisha, said a familiar voice from below.

He flinched, called back unwillingly. For a moment he debated sneaking up to his room on tiptoe, sliding into bed, pretending sleep. It had never saved him from a beating, or a lecture, but still the fatal cowardice in his soul urged him to flight. But then Micah's head poked around the corner of the stairwell. His father's mouth was a white line. Eli picked up the candle and went down, feeling sick with fear.

Micah's first words were, —You fatuous mooncalf! Do you want to break Ara's heart? She's been planning this wedding for months.

—I know that, sir. If it could be otherwise—

Micah smiled fiercely. —Oh, it can! And it will! I warn you, don't jar me, Elisha. We both know you're a good-for-nothing beetlehead, agreed? *Agreed?*

He couldn't face him; he couldn't. He dropped his head and muttered, —Yes sir. You're right. I'm sorry—

—Enough; show the virtue of obedience, at least. Return this ridiculous uniform, wherever it came from. I'll hear no more of this stupidity.

He took a deep breath, and said, —Sir, it's not just a matter of returning something to the tailor. I signed aboard ship today. If I don't show up tomorrow, they'll take me up for desertion.

This shot, though not precisely veracious, took effect. He saw Micah thinking it over, and pressed home. —Perhaps it was impulsive. But to withdraw could turn out to be even less well advised, if events proceed to open hostilities.

—Oh, it won't come to that. This secession talk's just bluff.

—Mr. Greeley doesn't think so.

Micah eyed him contemptuously. Eli felt disgusted with himself, hiding behind Greeley, but he'd never been able to face his father down. A cough scratched at his throat like an impatient cat. —The Union's in danger, Father. There's a duty there too, it seems to me.

Micah shook his head slowly. —You want to be your own man? he said at last. —Very well. You'll do it without a dollar from me, however. And you will explain to Araminta why your marriage will have to be put off.

He turned on his heel, returning to the library. Leaving Eli pressing the handkerchief to his face, shaking, trying helplessly to muffle the coughs that tore out of his chest like clawed, wild creatures determined to be free.

3

THE man his shipmates knew as Calpurnius Hanks hiked steadily down Water Street, striding through the falling darkness with the lurching roll of the deep-sea sailor man.

Here, as full night descended, gas lamps guttered between long pools of darkness. By harsh white case-oil brilliance women stood languidly at cellar doors. Bedraggled whores in jangling jewelry screamed at one another, grabbed at his blues as he passed. Thighs cocked in bright-lit doorways; hands reached out to proffer wineglasses, rum bottles, opium pipes with flat disc bowls.

He kept his eyes ahead, square boots tapping in the crisp evening air. He didn't mind walking. He'd grown up south of Atlanta, red clay country, where worn rounded hills lay like sleeping women with a fine hovering mist tucked between their breasts. He'd lived and labored there for twenty-three years. Till one day he began walking toward the North Star, and never stopped till he reached it.

All day he'd felt a shadow riding his back. It was like the cheesy stink of an overseer behind him. As its icy finger traced his back again he reached inside his jumper to grip the linen pouch of juju.

At last he paused at the sounds of shouting, singing, the clink and clatter of cheap ware. He looked over his shoulder once more, then pushed his way through the swinging doors.

Into smoke and noise, the smells of yeast and wet wool and sweat. A drunk was bawling out "Mother Machree." Others were howling, arguing at the cracking extremes of whiskey-sawed voices. The men and women who stood at the bar or sat at tables, or lay on the spit-smeared sawdust, were white and black, mulatto, and quadroon.

Hanks relaxed. This obscure and wretched neighborhood was the only place in America men were truly equal. He stood by the door, fists cocked in his pea jacket, till a laborer shoved away from the bar and staggered into the dim rear.

He ordered a penny beer. It was flat and stale but before he finished it a woman put her hand on the nape of his neck. She had brown dirty hair and patches of scarlet rouge on a worn face. Her languorous look seemed to have been pressed into it with metal type. — You gon' stand me to a sheoak, honey?

He snapped down a nickel as the man next to them slid to the greasy floor. The woman kicked him aside with her gaiter and took his place. She said her name was Jossalyn. She was Cuban, and she used to dance at Harry Hill's. He nodded and she told him above the din, —Honey, you don't need to spend yer time in here. You got you a dollar? I got a bottle of Monongahela at my place, got everythin' a man needs. Oh, you are a sailor! She put his cap on her head and mocked a salute. —You have got the cutest little ears.

He leaned back against the bar, surveying the turbulent dark through slitted eyes. —How long that dollar buy me?

—Oh, honey, I didn't have you figured for a haggler. You can rest wit' me all night if you want. Show me that dollar. You don't got to gimme it now, but lemme lamp it. Oh, yeah. I swear to God, you are so good lookin' I'd take you there for nothin', but the rent's due and that sonofabitch Jew already give me warning.

He grinned bitterly. —You sure about that?

She drew a fingernail slowly down the buttons of his trowsers.

—Honey, all mens is the same to me. Longs they got somethin' tween they legs needs lovin'.

Outside, the night breeze was loaded with the dead smell of river like a broached cask of salt horse. He slid his hands into his reefer pockets. Felt the heavy compactness of the lead strap, and in the other, the knife. He felt the evil hovering just behind his head, but when he turned only the slow uncoiling of coal smoke and blowing dust rode the night.

—Now, where you goin'? My room's this way. Or you rather go in this alley?

—Neither, he said. He took the silver dollar from his pocket and held it out to her. —I just wants to rent your services for a hour. And you won't even have to take off your slops.

The office was in a block of swaybacked clapboard, not far from the mills and granite dumps at Corlear's Hook. He stood in a doorway for some minutes, examining the light that burned upstairs, watching those who passed on the street.

At last he crossed, and took the creaking paintless steps up the piss-smelling stairwell two at a time.

A colorless stringy woman was copying a document beneath a shaded lamp. Bare boards, strewn with sand, grated under his boots. Ceiling-high cabinets stuffed with yellowing bundles smelled of old ink and slowly decaying paper. A letterpress hulked in the corner. He took off his flat hat.

She turned over a page. —Yes?

—To see Mr. Fort.

—Name?

He hesitated again. Then muttered, —Verity. Caesar Augustus Verity.

She rose with a sigh of skirts and fetched a portfolio, then swept into an inner office. He stood motionless, head lifted, waiting for some signal from the shade that had dogged his consciousness all day. But nothing came, and after a few minutes the copyist returned.

—Counselor Fort will see you now.

The inner office was tighter and darker than the outer, lined with high mahogany bookcases filled with heavy black-bound volumes. It held the same smell, but boiled down, concentrated, desiccated into a close stench of time and the law.

Ira Fort was hunched, with a beaked nose and a flat forehead as if he'd grown up with it pressed against a wall. His frock coat was of an antique cut, and his linen was greasy at cuffs and neckline. —Good evening, he said, unfolding in abrupt jerks from behind his desk as Hanks came in. —Take a seat, please. We are keeping late hours these days, as you see.

—Thanks, sir. Means a lot to us, having white folks who labor to set us free.

—The Lord's work, I'm sure. You're here to enquire about your case, I understand.

—That's right, sir. Been some months since I heard from you.

Fort had sunk back behind the desk; his eyes seemed to pass beyond, looking at something behind him. Hanks twisted, but saw nothing but the shadows. —Well, the lack of action was not on our side, Caesar. When we last met, it was explained to you that to serve the writ of mandamus on the state of Georgia would require an application fee of two hundred dollars. Not having received that wherewithal, the writ has not been applied for.

The cloth-wrapped wad jingled as he set it down. He'd gone without tobacco, without cards, without jam or the other little shipboard luxuries, to accumulate this sum. It wasn't just his pay, either; it included what he'd gotten for the revolvers he'd stolen and sold in Brooklyn. He knew this was ungrateful. But he'd done it, and he'd do more.

He'd do whatever he had to, to see them free.

Fort's hand crabbed forward, taut joints wrapped in yellowing flesh. The bell's silvery note still lingered when the copyist rustled in and swept the money off the table and left.

He looked after her. —Will I gets a receipt, sir?

—As I recall, you could not read it if you did, my friend. We must operate on a basis of mutual trust. Fort reached a printed form from a stack and dipped his pen into a well crusted with ink so ancient it had turned to verdigris. He cocked his head as if listening. —Let us proceed to cases. The name of the first party, please.

—That be my big-un brother, Hanks said. —His name Andrew.

A little woolly-headed boy running through the woods. Ducking under branches and leaping with unimaginable speed and skill across fallen trees, across stumps. And you pelting behind him, both yelling in sheer mortal terror. You could never remember what you saw up there, at the top of the hill that rose from the orchard behind Mister Ingram's farm. Only that you'd both fled screaming from it as fast as your legs could carry you.

A childhood in Georgia . . . Mama leaving in the cold gray but you got to stay snuggled close to Baba. Then later pone and water and the sizzle of fat meat, and life was magic, and you watched hungry till Baba swept off the ground by the cook pot and dumped out the peas in a fragrant mass, and the kids squatted naked and ate with their hands till nothing was left but a damp spot. And hoecakes raked out from the coals, gray, hot, and teeth-gritty with the ashes. And at Christmas the Junkanoo men singing from door to door, and the children laughing and shouting behind them.

Didn't know then you was owned, that you yourself nor your mother nor brother nor none of those child faces around you belonged to the white-faced ghosts that lived in the dark house by the running stream.

—The next party, said the attorney, and the only sound in the room was the clawing scratch of his pen. —That would be your mother, am I correct? Her name?

Eyes first; hard eyes set in a tired face, running with sweat and dust when evening come. Then one day she gone and Andrew and you alone.

Then later, a lapse of time unknowing before one image, one memory; of a side of meat; at least that was what you thought; then saw as a length of naked back, bucked up by the wrists to a beam in the smokehouse. The smells of salt meat and grease and blood. The whistle and crack of the cowhide. Staring from the doorway, you watching a rusty brown seep into the Georgia clay. Mister Ingram sweating, cursing in his bellowing voice. —I told you not to step out with that buck again. Said I'd peel an' pickle you, an' I will.

—Suritah, he muttered. —Her name Suritah.

One by one he named those left behind. Two younger sisters who came coffee-an'-cream, but slaves just the same. The babies, they'd be talking by now, Aeleen and Jim that they called Lil Jake. He knew their father but his he did not know. Most likely just a field hand out in the long miles of sunlight heat and dust where hundreds moved slowly along the rows of shining blossoms that stretched down to the river.

—Very well, the attorney said when the forms were sprinkled with sand and laid aside. He laced his fingers and leaned back with a creak. —Now let us discuss how we will pay for your family, once we have identified and located them.

Hanks went quiet inside, listening to the shadow close behind him now, near enough to whisper into his ear. —Pay for 'em?

Fort steepled his fingers. —Current prices are from one to three thousand dollars for a healthy male, such as you describe your elder brother to be. We can often purchase a family for somewhat less per head, particularly if we find them in the employ of one predisposed to liquidate. Still, I should reckon at least five thousand dollars in toto. Can you raise that sum?

—You didn't say nothing 'bout buying them last time, Mr. Fort. You told me you get them out for two hundred dollar. I thought this association you with, that was what it was for, to help Negroes get out—

—Oh, my friend, you have sadly misunderstood me. Would that we could liberate our sable brethren so easily! I said the *writ* would cost two hundred. The lawyer's tired smile moved from shadow to lamplight. —Have you no one who can loan you a sum of that magnitude? Kind friends? Someone who owns land, perhaps?

A tap at the door, and the plain woman put her face in. —Your next are here.

Fort waited, shadowed eyes deep with compassionate sorrow.

—Come, Caesar, think. Perhaps we could secure them for somewhat less. Could you raise three thousand, say?

He shook his head, dazed by unimaginable numbers. Surely Fort had said they could be freed. Some paper he could write, once he knew his true name, and the address of his master.

The attorney rose and sidled toward the door. —If you will excuse me.

—Where you going? We ain't got this settled yet, he said. The feeling was on him now, cold and menacing as a thunderhead squall. He splayed big hands across the desk. —Wait, Mr. Fort. You said, I bring you two hundred dollars and you could get them out. Now you need thousands. Why you tell me to come back, did you know you couldn't do what you said?

Fort stood bent by the door, hands locked behind him. He said in a grave tone, —Do you really wish to be reunited with your family?

—That's why I come here. Say you helped 'scaped slaves—

—You'd give up whatever you have, to that end?

—'D give up anything, but I just ain't gots that kind of money. Done things I shouldn't ought to have to get this much. Don't the association have money, Mr. Fort?

Fort called through the door, —Show them in, Miss Holdt.

Two unfamiliar white men entered, immediately separating to face him from both sides of the room. They were in rough, worn suits, and their immobile faces bore no expression. They carried leather-covered bars in gloved hands. The attorney jerked a Deringer from inside his frock coat and cocked it.

—Careful with that Goddamn thing, Fort. This the one? said the larger of the man hunters. He had a small, grimy blue ribbon fraying at one lapel.

—I give you Caesar Augustus Verity, to be returned to the bosom of his family. The reward to be delivered at this address.

—You, there. The smaller man, who wore a grimy Panama, pulled a pair of wrist irons from his coat. His grin lacked upper teeth. —You had a good run, boy, but you're caught fair and square. Put out your hands.

He faced them, fists clenched at his sides. —You calls yourself an abolitionist, he told the attorney. —But you turns us in to the slave catchers.

—The laws of my country require me to return fugitives to the rightful owners. I personally believe such ordinances contrary to natural law and divine justice. But it is still my duty to obey the statutes of the United States.

—C'mon, boy, said Panama, taking a step closer. —I know this here's a blow to the head. Your master, he says he don't bear you no ill will. He moved warily, eyes on Hanks's shoulders. He held out the irons, like a tidbit extended to tempt a wary dog.

Hanks looked around the room but made no move toward him. Instead he backed away. At the window he stood for a moment looking down, toward the dark street below. Then turned and lifted his arms slowly and said, —I wants my money back. I gave you two hundred dollars.

The small man said instantly, —He had money? If he come in here with ary, it belongs to us. Hand it over, Fort.

—It's a nigger lie. The rascal gave me nothing. You'll have to be on your toes with this one.

—Them as makes it this far is ginrally pretty sharp. But they still gets cotched, said the bigger catcher. —You, there! Time to get these irons on. Come easy, we won't have to brash you none. But we'll drag you back if you want. Don't make no never mind to us.

Hanks backed against the desk. His pursuers drifted closer.

A sudden commotion in the outer office, then a woman's scream. —What the devil? said Fort.

The screaming approached. The words became clearer. Someone was shouting "fire" in the stairwell.

The copyist appeared in the doorway, face white as cotton. —My gosh, Mr. Fort, she says the downstairs is on fire.

—My God, said Fort. —This whole place will go up. Get the receivables, Flora. I will secure the strongbox.

She vanished, and a clatter came back up from below. The man catchers wheeled, momentarily forgetting Cal. —There a back way out of here?

—There's no other way out. We got to go down the front.

—Come on out of here, boy. You go with us or be—

The slave catcher with the ribbon gaped at him. Then he lowered his eyes, slowly, to stare down at the heavy seaman's blade buried between his dirty lapels.

It stayed there only an instant before Hanks jerked it free, smashing him across the face with a lead-bound fist, and advanced on his suddenly rooted partner.

The second manhunter jumped back, but crashed into one of the cabinets. The Panama spun off and fell to the floor. He drew a huge bowie. Hanks stepped on the hat as he went in toward him, his blade weaving, and it skidded under his boot and he went down on one knee.

—Shoot the sumbitch, Fort, shouted the little man, and the lawyer thrust the Deringer out and closed his eyes and pulled the trigger. The cap cracked but the charge didn't go off.

The catcher man came at him, aiming the bowie at his eyes. He scrambled to his feet and knocked the knife aside. Then his blade whipped in. A scarlet gush jetted out like a fire pump, splashing across the wall. The slave catcher fell to his knees, gripping his throat. He looked pleadingly at them. The blood pulsed, rolling out to soak the scattered papers in a dark pool. He stretched out full length, slowly, on the bare wood.

Fort stared as Hanks approached. The useless pistol drooped in his hand. He closed his eyes. A sob caught in his throat.

Then he opened them again. The big arms circled him. But the massive hard hands had not closed around his throat, but on the bookcase behind him.

They were face-to-face, inches apart. —Spare me, Fort whispered. —Mr. Verity. I beg you.

He couldn't answer. Couldn't speak. If the copyist had stayed, he'd have killed her. If a child had been in the office, he could not have stopped himself, as long as its face was the pasty fish belly of the race that had destroyed his family, made his life a hell of hunger and rage and endless fear. He choked through a constricted throat, —Spare you? I won't dirt my hands with you. I'll leave you to the law.

—To the law. Thank you. You have a forgiving heart! I have often said it, of people of color. Thank the living God—

Hanks took a step back, braced himself, and with a tremendous jerk brought ten feet of solid oak and heavy law books down with a thunder like a frigate's broadside on the attorney's head. The tumbled heap surged once, then subsided. From beneath it came a grunting cry. It came again faintly, then fell silent.

He looked around the office, panting. He'd never killed before. He'd never thought he could. But now, looking on his handiwork, he did not regret any of it.

He found the strongbox, and took from it the rag-wrapped bundle he'd given Fort. He looked at the rest, gold and silver and banknotes. Then took that too, thrusting handfuls into his blouse. When it was empty he crossed the room once more, stepping over the bodies, and backhanded the lamp to the floor. A ripple of fire ran across it, then flared up to throw his shadow against the dingy ceiling.

He stared up for a moment watching it, as it hesitated too, a black distorted giant looking down at him.

Seconds later he was on the street again, merging with the shouting crowd a fire always gathered. He passed through them like an errant spirit, and melted once more into the sheltering dark.

4

ELI boarded the next morning behind a returning tar. Jack sported a travesty of naval uniform, with trowser-cuffs flared waist wide, silver tape glittering on his collar, huge floppy cap cockbilled over one eye. He hauled himself up the brow as if up a crag, trailing a reek of rum. Nick Duycker stood at the top, in discussion with the boatswain. The master glanced over as the sailor saluted, reeled, and tripped over a gun truck. —Hopwood, good to have you back with us.

—Was benderin' with Sammy Plummer last night, sir, down at Allen's dance house, an' he said we're remusterin' for a job of work down south.

—Lay below, I think your old mess still has room for you. Duycker's eye fell on Eli and grew cold. —Mr. Eaker. It pleases you to grace us with your presence.

—Good morning. I trust you slept well—

—Not another word, sir. *You* will stand by in the wardroom. Bo's'n, we'll need thrum mats in the rigging. Chafing gear on the stays and shrouds and topping lifts.

Girnsolver looked at Eli sympathetically, but all he said was, to Duycker, —Rig the preventer backstays, sor?

—Make it so. Caulk the port shutters, and make sure the jack-asses are greased. He threw a glance aloft, and Eli followed his look at the hurtling clouds.

Duycker added, —I imagine we're going to see a breath of wind.

—What in the Christ's name do you think you're playing at? said Duycker a few minutes later.

—I'm sorry, said Eli, holding a position of respectful attention in the wardroom. He'd felt well this morning, strong and eager, at least until now. —I didn't realize that—

The master reached out suddenly and tore a button off his blues. He put his hand to the violated area, too startled even to protest. Duycker snarled, —I don't want to hear your rich man's excuses! If you want to lie abed, stay home. The navy's not the place for you.

So that was it. The maid had tapped at his door at seven, just as he'd told her. A reasonably timely breakfast, then into the barouche, and it was just now nine o'clock, an hour he'd reckoned reasonable for a gentleman to apply himself to military business. He said carefully, —What time should you prefer me to be aboard?

Duycker told him reveille for the crew was at five. They turned to with hose and holystone, then breakfasted at seven-thirty, by which time the captain expected his officers back aboard. —Today'll be busy. Quarters for inspection at four bells aforenoon—that's ten o'clock. Have your men ready a quarter hour ahead. If they're not, you lose another button.

—I am beginning to understand.

—You had better. The master reached down a black-bound book from a fiddled shelf. —These are the ordnance instructions. Pay particular attention to the powder regulations; we're loading ammunition tonight. Any questions?

—Only one.

—Only one, *sir.* You're junior to me, Eaker, so shit-all junior as far as I'm concerned you rank below the ship's black bugs.

—Black bugs? He frowned. —We have roaches aboard?

Duycker's eyes widened, and the venous lace in his cheeks took on a darker hue. Eli added quickly, —Junior to you, yes, I understand. Sir, it sounds as if we're getting under way to meet the enemy fleet. Is that the correct inference to make from these preparations?

The master frowned. —Enemy fleet? What enemy fleet?

—Mr. Greeley of the *Tribune* dined with us last night. He said unknown sail have been sighted off the coast.

Duycker snorted and turned away. —You will learn that at sea, we make preparations for many eventualities that don't pan out. You will not discuss such matters ashore, sir, or anything else of Captain Trezevant's intentions or orders which you happen to overhear.

Eli thought of the drunken tar, how the fact *Owanee* was regathering her crew seemed to be common gossip about the stews of New York; but held his tongue. He just stood waiting until Duycker, looking disgusted, flapped a hand for him to go.

He sat in his cabin sucking a pastille and reading the ordnance instructions until fifteen minutes before the hour. Then straightened, ducked under the jamb, and went topside.

The thirty men of the Forecastle Division toed a seam between the forward pivot and the starboard bulwark. Aft and to port the rest of the crew bustled about, some laying out cables, others dragging up masses of blocks, yard irons, and other tackle he could not even identify as to purpose, let alone put a name to. Shading his eyes aloft, he saw that the t'gallants, *Owanee's* loftiest sails, were being bent on foremast and main.

Babcock, trig in flare-legged blues, neckerchief, and black straw hat; Eli noted the gunner was not carrying his colt today, but his expression was just as sour. —Forecastle Division ready for inspection.

He returned the salute and began at the tall end. Lofty bearded Yankees with faces like battered boots and huge, scarred hands stared beyond him as if he were not passing eighteen inches before their face. The ratings wore dark blue wool trowsers and blue flannel shirts, with black jackets, the big gold buttons unfastened. Some wore the flat cloth hat, the rest straws like the gunner's. He finished the front rank, began on the second. He examined one man, shoes to cap, then stepped to the next. It was the big Negro he'd spoken to at the forward pivot. His expression was even more closed and emotionless than that of the others. What went on behind such a face? Eli wondered. Certainly it could not be the same process as that of the more advanced race.

He moved to his right, and confronted the air.

His glance dropped to a little chap with round red cheeks and a lock of fair hair escaping his hat. He wore the same uniform as the others, but in a pocket edition, with silver-thread fancywork on his blouse. As he stared in astonishment the lad's lip began to tremble.

—What is this child doing here, Gunner?

—This here's one of our monkeys, sir. Billy Ripley.

—Monkeys? He recalled a wizened face, eyes full of hate. He hadn't seen Auguste since their encounter in the gun room.

—Our powder boys. When we beat to quarters, those twisting ladders, you get some fallen spars, why, a grown man won't get about at all. Smaller they be, livelier they scamper. Isn't that so, Sugar-drawers?

—Aye, Gunner, Ripley said in a frightened voice. By his glance Eli saw it was not he the boy feared, but Babcock.

—How old is this child?

—Twelve, sir, said Ripley firmly. Eli saw he was lying; there was no possible way he could be more than ten. After considering the matter, though, he decided it was too early for him to take issue with enlistment policy.

Instead he paced around to the front again. The men, his men, stared back, faces as uncommunicative as they could well be. He ought to say something inspiring and martial on the occasion of his first meeting them. Don't Give Up the Ship. I Have Not Yet Begun to Fight. He searched for words, but instead began to cough. He placed his handkerchief to his lips as they watched. At last, when he was able to wipe his mouth, he was out of breath and the moment had slipped past. Then their eyes snapped past him, and he turned to see Clai-

borne's slim elegant form bearing down, and he brought his hand up.
—Gun Division, ready for your inspection, sir.

—Very well, Mr. Eaker, the exec said coolly. —Fall in behind me, and let's have a look at them.

The officers were standing behind their chairs when Eli let himself into the wardroom. He nodded to those he recognized: Duycker; Dr. Steele; Midshipman Thurston; Glass, the paymaster; Schuyler, the marine officer.

—Good day, gentlemen. A murmur met Claiborne. This time, though, the Virginian did not take the head of the table, but the first seat to the right. For nearly a minute no one spoke. Then the exec straightened as the after door opened. —Attention on deck.

Captain Trezevant entered. He took the principal place without a word, and the rest followed with a scrape of chairs. He nodded to Ahasuerus, who had been hanging back by the galley door, and the servant began bringing out a clear soup that smelled of asparagus.

The chatter and counterpoint of yesterday was missing now. Not a man spoke save for the please-pass-me's. Eli examined their commanding officer with short glances. His physical type was not unlike that of Mr. Lincoln. A crease like a bloodless knife cut catenaried beneath each eye socket. The skin was weather-beaten and darkened. Eli felt the heavy inhibition of the commander's presence but could not help remarking to Schuyler in an undertone that he believed there were fewer present than yesterday.

—Right, muttered the marine. —Two more Southrons packed their traps and went ashore last night. Certain members waxed sentimental at the parting. *I* was not among them.

Eli looked up to meet Trezevant's eye. —This is our new officer, I take it? the captain said.

The first lieutenant napkined his beard. —May I present Mr. Elisha Eaker, sir?

—Mr. Eaker. Welcome aboard.

—Thank you, Captain. A server appeared in front of him, and he helped himself to a slice of deviled goose. A spoonful of broth from a ladle added the scents of thyme, pepper, mustard, and a faint taste of what might be strawberry preserves.

—The exec informs me you are a New Yorker, joining us on a volunteer basis.

—Sir, that is correct.

—I assume you have seen considerable merchant service?

—I have passed time at sea, sir. I can see naval procedures differ, however.

Trezevant said austerely, —I will be frank, sir. I am not certain you are fit for your place aboard. Thus, I have not yet entered your name on the muster roll.

He bit back his first response, which was to ask who would fill this emptying wardroom, unless it was volunteers such as himself. He was given a moment to consider his response by the presentation of a dish of rice bread. He helped himself, then said, as blandly as he could manage, —You're the captain.

Napkins came up, and Dr. Steele burst into a guffaw like that of a startled donkey. Trezevant cleared his throat, fixing Eli with a sharp glance.

The disturbance ebbed and the commander turned to Claiborne. —Mr. Hubbard's repairs to the boilers. I expect them to be completed by eight tomorrow morning.

—Sir, if it can be done, Theodorus and his boys will carry it through. I will keep a close eye on the work.

—Unto, unto, I will discuss it no further here. My cabin, sir, after this meal is concluded.

A small black boy came out from the galley. Ahasuerus hovered, watching as the lad silently served each officer a dish of what Eli found to be peach sorbet. When the captain's was half consumed the old Negro made a writhing motion of his forearm. Trezevant nodded, and added aloud, —Leave us until it is prepared. Take Shippy with you, and slide that galley door to. No, wait; send for Mr. Eddowes and Mr. Hubbard; I will have them here for this as well.

The servers glided quietly out in what Eli saw now were buckskin slippers.

When the midshipman and the engineer had been located, the commander touched his lips gently. Claiborne pushed back his chair. The captain's gaze flicked to the closed doors, then around the table. —This will be a confidential discussion, gentlemen.

—As you all know, South Carolina and several other states have moved the dissolution of their bonds with the rest of the nation. They are merging their militias into a confederate army, commanded by a new government at Montgomery.

—However, federal forces remain in occupation of strong points. The most delicate situations are Fort Sumter, dominating Charleston harbor, and Fort Pickens, off Pensacola. Major Anderson commands Sumter. I know him, we met at Molino del Rey during the war. He is of the chivalry of Kentucky, ever ready to join a friend at the festive glass or to face an enemy at ten paces. However, he has reported his supplies are running out. He cannot hold beyond April 15.

The captain signaled Claiborne with an impatient gesture, and the exec passed the wine carafe. —Mr. Fox has imparted to me that Mr. Lincoln has ordered a joint army-navy mission to relieve the fort. It will consist of *Owanee* and *Powhatan,* from New York, together with the revenue cutter *Harriet Lane. Pocahontas* will join us from Norfolk. We will escort the Aspinwall liner *Baltic,* carrying army troops, and three chartered tugs.

—*Powhatan* has already sailed, sir, said Duycker.

—That is correct, Master. We will follow her at dawn tomorrow, as soon as coaling is complete, and make all possible speed to Sumter.

Hubbard looked up from wedging navy cut into his pipe. —What precisely are we to do when we arrive, sir?

—The troops will not be landed unless the supply of provisions is interfered with. That is, we are to provision the fort, but not reinforce it unless it is attacked.

Dr. Steele rumbled, —They fired on the other supply ship. This is a clever cat's-paw, to place the onus of opening hostilities upon the Palmetto State.

———

Ker sat with fingers to his lips, considering the matter as the captain had just laid it forth. Old Pills was right: it was a real Tom Cox's traverse. Lincoln had turned his own Hobson's choice—withdraw, and suffer political embarrassment, or mount a massive invasion—into a move that wedged Davis and Beauregard in the forks of a dilemma. To reprovision starving men could not be considered a hostile act. To fire on the ship that carried the food, however, would be of necessity a casus belli.

He said softly to Trezevant, —Sir, you do not seem overpleased.

—I am not, Mr. Claiborne. According to the telegraphic reports, the harbor is heavily fortified by now.

—Can we fight our way in? Hubbard asked. Possibly alone of the wardroom, he sounded eager at the prospect. The others looked at him with varying degrees of hauteur and suspicion.

Ker stroked his beard, adding up numbers of guns. He came up with only twenty-eight: *Owanee,* five; *Pocahontas,* six; *Harriet Lane,* four; *Powhatan,* fourteen. Further weighting the scales against them was the dictum that one gun ashore was considered equivalent to three afloat. Aloud he said, —It could be, as Lord Wellington said of Waterloo, a "damned close-run thing."

—Would we have surprise? the marine officer asked. It was the first time he had spoken. He massaged his throat, as if the effort of speaking hurt.

The captain said, —Unfortunately, Mr. Fox tells me Mr. Seward insisted on informing Governor Pickens a resupply expedition was under way.

—I assume there are only a few routes into the harbor. If they cover those with fire—

Trezevant slammed his hands down and hoisted his length abruptly to his feet. —Unto, unto, unto. I am pleased neither with the plan nor with the intent of the thing. I will do my duty, and shall insist every man do the same. But my heart is not in this act of coercion.

The others rose as well. The galley door opened and the boy reappeared, carrying a steaming urn. —I will take my coffee aft, the captain said, and left.

Ker scanned their faces. Some looked troubled, others with a bit of the wind up. Hubbard was eager as a boy. The only one who looked unaffected by the news was the new fellow, Eaker. His pale visage was the epitome of unconcern.

—Very well, Ker said, taking their attention back. —We have a great deal yet to do. Each man to his division, and I will take reports this afternoon at eight bells.

The powder began coming aboard late that afternoon. In a blustering wind and occasional drizzle, each crewman stepped up to the wagons on the pier and was handed down one of the sealed metal tanks, about three feet long, which he cradled carefully in both arms. One after another, like ants raiding a sugar bowl, they carried their burdens up the brow, across the space of brown water, then down the ladder and forward along the orlop.

Eli watched them pass the cylinders through a scuttle. Then, pockets emptied on a green baize cloth, feet cased in india-rubber slippers, he pushed his way through leather curtains into a dim space walled with row on row of them.

The closed-in air smelled like urine and alcohol. The only illumination came from a lantern hung just outside a square of thick glass. In its yellow gleam the gunners' mates opened each cylinder as it slid in, inspected the charge, and resealed it. The hinged tank lids were distinguished by color: white for distant firing, blue for ordinary ranges, red for near firing. He found Babcock far back in the magazine. The old warrant did not look pleased to see him, but on Eli's questioning grumpily explained the stowage arrangements. The ordinary charges had to be ready to hand, closest to the scuttles, and the musket powder, saluting charges, signal rockets, and flares for the life rings were stowed separately along the narrow alleys.

When he was satisfied he went aft to the shell room. The projectiles came aboard not in tanks but as filled shells, fuzes already screwed in by the armorers at the yard. When he lifted one the enormous weight of hollow iron packed with high-velocity musket powder dragged at his arms. After a moment he set it down again, feeling the men's eyes on him. Beyond thick glass he saw more, in carefully stacked ranks. There lay *Owanee*'s claws: enough power to devastate a fleet or level a city.

For the first time he sensed the real meaning of war.

At seven that night they finished loading. Rather apprehensively—it was the first time he'd spoken to the captain alone—he reported to Commander Trezevant's cabin with a statement of what they'd taken aboard. The captain conned it silently, then looked up. —I see no mention of small arms. Were we not missing some?

—Revolvers, sir. Apparently Mr. Minter made off with them.

Trezevant looked shocked, then lofty. —You do very wrong to assume Lieutenant Minter took them. One does not speak such things of any gentleman, unless the case be proved beyond doubt.

—Yes sir.

—Now, as to these arms, we must have them for the boarding party. You will have to go ashore and secure replacements. Apply to the armorer of the yard.

Outside the captain's cabin, he glanced out a porthole at the rapidly advancing night. He'd hoped to get home this evening, as they were to sail at dawn. He frowned out, puzzled by his own fickle desires. Now that he'd put off the wedding, he was wondering if he'd done right.

The first man he saw on deck was the Negro from the forward pivot. He was carrying a tompion over his shoulder, rather, Eli thought, like Ulysses' oar. He said peremptorily, —You there. Hanks, was it? Do you know where to find the yard armorer?

The sailor gazed at him blankly. Finally he said, —You means de armorer o' the yard, sah? Yassah, I knows can fin' him.

—Take me to him.

The enlisted man wrung his hands deliberately into a large rag. —
You finish up, he said to the man working with him. —Make sure
that tallow goes all the way down the bottom of the bore. Then he
said to Eli, —Follow me, sah.

It was raining in earnest by the time they got back, blown along the
pier by a gusty wind more like February than April. The armorer had
been extremely hard to deal with. He had insisted on a written sum-
mary of the investigation into the loss, which Eli had sat down and
more or less made up on the spot. Keeping the captain's admonition
in mind, he mentioned no names, referring only to "numerous resignations from the Service" and "personnel departing the ship with
weighty baggage, uninspected due to presumption of honorable conduct." Hanks had stood by watching his pen scratch, face inscrutable
as basalt. In the end they got eight antediluvian horse pistols that
looked more dangerous to the firer than to anyone in front of the
muzzle. On Hanks's advice he made sure bullet molds, caps, and a
tool kit were included.

—*There* you are, said Claiborne as he pulled himself up the gangway once again. —I've been looking for you all over the ship. Where
have you been?

This time he couldn't suppress it. He doubled over, holding the
handkerchief close against his mouth. When he could speak, he explained, and stepped aside to let Hanks carry the heavy chest past.

Claiborne looked at him with a mingling of alarm and concern.
—Quite a raw cough you have there, Mr. Eaker.

—I've been breathing powder fumes all day, sir.

The exec nodded at that and told him he had a visitor waiting
outside the yard gate. She'd been there for some time, sending notes
in by means of the sentries. —You had better go out and see her,
Claiborne finished. —But I want you back aboard in half an hour, no
longer. And instruct your fiancée, if that is what she is, in the patience required of a navy wife.

—Aye aye, sir. He turned to go.

—Wait, wait. You're wet through. Don't you have a waterproof?

He said he didn't, but was still startled when the lieutenant stripped off his own mackintosh and handed it to him without another word.

The misty rain sifted down. The sentries had taken shelter in the gatehouses, shadowy monitors in the unlit interiors. Gas flames shone on the roof of a closed cabriolet. A chestnut mare, dark with wet, tossed her head as he came up. He nodded to the cabbie and rapped. The door cracked, and Araminta peeped out.

—Eli. Get in.

—It wouldn't be suitable. I'll stand out here.

—Get *in,* you foolish boy. You'll catch your death.

He hesitated, glancing around. But the street was empty and the hour late. At last he grasped the frame and swung himself in, but left the door open. The mist blew in and he shivered. —What is it, darling? We are rather busy aboard ship.

—It's all over the city that you're going to Charleston. I didn't want us to part, perhaps forever, with last night between us.

Araminta peered toward him. His face looked drawn in the wind-flickering gaslight. He was wearing some sort of waterproof but she could smell wet wool beneath it.

She wasn't sure what had driven her out on this windy night. She'd never been out after twilight before, not alone. The cabdrivers' expressions, the remarks of loungers on the ferry made it plain what they took her for. She'd pretended she didn't hear, though one Bowery rough had been most explicit. It gave her a delicious shiver to be taken for one of Dumas *fils's dames aux camélias.* But the sense of adventure had faded as she'd waited in the cab, its closed interior smelling of segar smoke and cologne and the hundreds of others who'd used it before her. She'd visualized a romantic farewell, but seeing his weariness she recognized her fantasy as tawdry and adolescent. He might well be sailing into danger. The Carolinians had already fired on one ship.

Another scenario limelighted in her mind. Herself dressed in black, devoted to the memory of one beyond the grave . . . She shook the thought off like a wasp from her glove, and shoved the box into his hands.

—What's this?

—I'm afraid I have misused my household money.

When he lifted the lid he found a boxed Colt's revolver, so new it smelled of oil and steel. He said softly, —Thank you, Ara. I will try my best to carry it honorably.

—Eli. Listen to me. If you want to resume our understanding, I will do so.

He didn't answer, just stared out at the falling rain with the gun on his lap. —I won't ask you to do that, he said at last.

—Why not? If I make a free offering of my heart?

Looking on her, he was tempted. For a moment she was almost beautiful. But instead he said, —If there's a fight over Sumter, it won't stop there.

—What are you saying?

—If war comes, we may be parted for a long time. I don't want you bound to a choice you might regret.

She clenched her fists around her *porte-monnaie.* —I wish I could go with you, she whispered.

He chuckled. —That'd be a sight. Crinolines and petticoats during gun drill. You can help by being brave, Ara. Staying home. Writing to me.

—I want to do more than that. I want to fight too.

He cleared his throat—she was talking nonsense now—and swung himself out. He looked back at her pale face, framed by the cabriolet's window, and felt his heart tear as he looked on what he could neither summon the resolution to take nor bear to leave. He wanted to stay with her, and he wanted to sail away.

He remembered now the day at divine service he'd really listened to the hymn the congregation was singing, "Praise to the Lord, the Almighty," and the words had struck to his soul.

> *Hast thou not seen*
> *How thy desires e'er have been*
> *Granted in what he ordaineth?*

He accepted that now, and confessed his sin and faithlessness. He was confused and imperfect. But God realized that, and cared for his creatures. Yes, even for him.

Knowing his days might be short, he was discovering the inestimable sweetness of each one, letting it go slowly through his fingers, slipping like drops of honey into the fire of eternity.

—Good-bye, Ara, he whispered as the cab disappeared into the rain.

5

U.S.S. *Owanee,*
Brooklyn N. Yd.,
April 8, 1861.

Dearest Catherine—

Your sweet letter of the 2nd instant came this morning. After our time in Norfolk it is doubly hard to find our bodies though not our spirits separated again. At any rate there are not nearly so many miles which part us now, and hardly any degrees of longitude! But still you and Rob.t are there, I am here, with the uncertainties of the future before us.

I owe you an apology for the remarks you took such exception to. To the effect that much as we love a child we should not permit ourselves too great an attachment. This was an oft-repeated advice of my Father, who as you know lost three in infancy. Your response was the right one. We cannot waive or evade the promptings of Nature, especially those of your Sex. If the worse occur we must bear it as best we can with the aid of Faith that we shall be reunited in a sunnier Land beyond the grave. As I most faithfully believe.

I was glad to read that you are seeing Mrs. Farragut. Her

husband is one of the most distinguished officers of the navy, and of the highest sense of Honor. Please convey to them both my profound respects.

We are still lying to at Brooklyn but are no longer scheduled for ordinary. The crew is being recalled but we have not a complete manning. There is much uproar and turmoil here although it does not seem to be bent on any well-concerted purpose.

Powhatan sailed on the 6th although I may not say where bound. There was some contretemps at the last minute. Capt. Mercer, you met him at Mrs. Allston's, was treated shamefully. I encountered him at the headquarters and he told me he had been relieved by telegram by Lieutenant Porter, such telegram signed by the Rail-Splitter himself. (This is the David D. Porter son of old Commo. Porter of 1812 fame. He is very old for a Lt. but is rumored to have political connexion with the new Secy. of Navy.) At any rate Mercer reluctantly yielded, disembarking as she passed Staten Island. He barely got back in a leaky boat when he finds a new telegram directing Porter give the ship back to him, this one signed—Seward. A perfect muddle as it always seems to be in home waters, but I hope it is not the beginning of something ominous for our suffering Country.

I have just been called to the deck.

Resuming later. Dr. Steele is as ever and the remaining members of the wardroom the same, though we are sadly few since Mssrs. Watkins and Minter and the others whom I told you had gone South. I cannot say it operates well for our Performance and we are increasingly shorthanded, with little prospect of relief save for one Yankee volunteer.

It would at first seem you and I would have little sympathy with what seems to be the matter most at issue in this secession agitation as neither holds any servants save Betsey. Having witnessed the horrors of the Coromandel Coast, I am no fervent supporter of the institution of Hamitic Slavery. Mr. Minter and I had an exchange before his departure. He attempting to shew me bondage justified both by the Constitution and by Holy Writ. My demurring, he became agitated and asked me if I did not believe Southrons such as he and I could whip Yankees five to one. I expressed doubt on that point too, the Northern men with whom I have served being on the whole excellent seamen if not overpunctilious about courtesy, etc., etc., as well as an eleven-inch shell not taking much account of breeding or lack of same of the fellow it makes cat's meat of.

I myself sincerely hope our sacred Union may be preserved, and if not, a pacific secession may preserve the amicability of the Sections and avert the horrors of internecine War.

In case the worst comes to pass, however, the only other course would be to request service in California. The which is being taken by the Bureau as tantamount to an admission of Southern sentiment if not of attempting to skirt one's obligations, which of course as an officer is to fight. I do not think that route would be honorable for me to take if the conflict thus opened, and Honor being the only sure guide, it should certainly be consulted as well as the advice of such intimate Friends as yourself.

To my mind my obligation is to the old Flag, under which I have served her in very many "Hot" situations in Africa. It does seem that to wantonly dissolve the best government under which human beings ever lived is an error not readily equaled in History. Yet still the Old Dominion is my home.

It is in short a quandary so cruel to contemplate that the business of the ship is a relief to me. One whom I intend to consult is Capt. Trezevant, who has thus far made no pronouncement except to bar political discussions from the mess, which is a wise order. I will say I am very bitter at this moment against those who have driven us to this point, and I include not only the radical Abolitionists but also those mooncalf Charlestonians who seem to be burning for bloody war.

I will close now to make evening's post, but to repeat what

I said our last time together, that you are the Star I steer by and my anchor to windward as the storm comes upon us. Yet the simile is not perfect, for there is no night that can blot out your dear image and that of our infant son, two beings more precious to me than my own life. I pray we will be reunited soon and if we are ordered south I will immediately send word in advance if I can come home. Though we are so shorthanded we have only two qualified watch officers besides myself. I do not like to ask for leave at such a time but still may do so.

I will write more tomorrow if only a short note as we get under way.

Your loving Husband,
Ker

6

T HE bunker was black save for the faraway safety lamps, darting and hunting in the far-stretching gloom. It boomed and
rattled with the scraping roar of tons of coal rocketing down
iron chutes.

Theo Hubbard thought suddenly that it was exactly like a mine,
save that here, in a mocking reversal of human effort, the coal was being packed with great toil back into tightly compacted seams. Its
choking grittiness filled the air, and he pulled the neckerchief tighter
over his mouth as he reflected the atmosphere he breathed probably
held deadly firedamp as well.

Coaling had begun just after dark, and now, at four in the morning, it was still coming aboard. At a little after midnight he'd crawled
into his bunk with his grimy clothes on for three hours' sleep. Waking,
he'd checked on MacNail in the boiler room, then come down here.
Now he raised the safety lamp and scrambled forward a few more feet,
the jagged anthracite biting his knees through worn denim.

Gradually, as if he swam toward them deep underwater, the
heavers came into view. A pulsing stream thundered steadily from the
chute. As fast as it hit the deck, Hart and O'Kennedy's heavy shovels

sent it clattering into the recesses of the bunker. Thus far they were working on their feet, but the most wrenching and awkward labor would come as the level mounted toward the overhead. The heavers would have to work bowed over, and at last wield their shovels stretched full length beneath the down-pressing beams of *Owanee's* gun deck.

He reminded them to use plenty of dunnage, then crab-scuttled out into more breathable air. He stooped for a quick dust-off, signed the safety lamp back in, then ran up the engine room companionway to the spar deck.

A fresh breeze swept in off the East River. He leaned on the bulwark, inhaling gratefully. He noticed the officer of the deck watching him. The greenhorn, the volunteer, Eaker. What did he want? Oh, of course. He was leaving sooty footprints, and his hands would leave greasy stains on the brightwork.

To hell with him, Theo thought. To hell with all the braiders. He stared back at Eaker till the fellow looked away.

Dawn was still an hour distant. Only the lanterns swaying from the rigging and along the gangways cast a flickering yellow over the two hundred men who formed an endless belt from shore to ship and back again. Most were *Owanee's*, but the shipyard had sent laborers too. Dozens of patient dray horses stood on the pier, wagon after wagon drawn up in line. They came from Tilton, Wheelwright & Company, and each wagon held four tons of number 27 Pennsylvania anthracite. The men were as much beasts of burden as the horses. Once his canvas sack was shoveled ninety pounds full from a wagon, each hoisted it by a chest band and lugged it up the fore gangway, where he upended it into the chute, sending the coal below and a gritty cloud across the deck. Then headed aft, canvas dragging like a struck sail, to descend the stern gangway and begin again.

Visualizing the whole laborious process, from coal yard to pier to shipboard to bunker to furnace, made Theo's blood boil. A fluid fuel would eliminate 90 percent of the labor, dirt, and wastage. Lay tracks on the pier, run a trainful of tank cars out on it, and gurgle kerosene aboard through a gutta-percha hose. The wells in Pennsylvania—Titusville and Pithole and Bradford—were producing so much "petroleum" its price had crashed to pennies a barrel.

He slumped against the bulwark as he pondered the filters and valves and burners such a system would require. There'd have to be tanks belowdecks, and pumps to move it from the bunkers to the fire room. . . .

Mind a thousand miles from his diminutive body, Theodorus Hubbard dreamed.

He'd been born in Connecticut, on a farm in Weatogue. He'd left his parents and gone to Hartford at the age of twelve, signing on as a machinery oiler at the Hanbury cotton mill. As a result of hard work, respectful address, and natural ability, he was an assistant foreman at fifteen, a foreman at sixteen, and a journeyman machinist and head of the loom maintenance gang at seventeen. On his eighteenth birthday he quit and applied to the best school he could afford, using his savings to live on as he completed his education.

When he graduated, the largest machine tool company in Hartford hired him as a master machinist. But the company failed in '55. He could have found employment at another local mill or factory. But he wanted to see the world. He was considering a position as a locomotive engineer for the Hartford and New Haven when a notice in the *Courant* of vacancies for steam engineers in government service caught his eye.

The oral board had been in Washington. He took a morning train, changing at New Haven, New York, and Philadelphia, sitting up all night on a hard bench seat barely ameliorated by a thin cushion rented from the conductor for a nickel. The questions were practical ones, easily answered by anyone who'd run a modern stationary engine. He was assigned as third assistant engineer in the old paddle wheeler *Susquehanna*. He went from there to first assistant in the *Mississippi* after her return from her shelling of the Chinese forts at Pei Ho. He had been aboard *Owanee* for a little less than two years.

Theo was twenty-six now, and more than a little world-weary.

The Mediterranean and West Africa had sated his wanderlust. He was disgusted with the navy's studied indignities toward its engineering personnel, such as ranking them "with" but not "as" commissioned officers, restricting them to the warrants' mess, and assigning them all the Irish recruits. He had nothing against the Irish, so long as they could read, but in this expectation he was so often disappointed he'd bought seven McGuffey *Readers* and applied himself to teaching the heavers the alphabet during the long ocean crossings under sail.

He'd enjoyed his time at sea, but he could see that the future was being built on land. Clever men with vision, like Drake and Morse and Rockefeller, were changing the face of the country. America would bring the world wheels of steel and wings of bronze, nerved by electricity and powered by superheated steam. On landing in New York, he'd called on Mr. McLeod at the South Brooklyn Steam Engine Works, the result being an offer of employment in the engine design loft. His letter of resignation from the service had followed, effective once *Owanee* paid off.

He wanted to contribute to the great work of the world. He wanted to invent, and profit from his inventions, maybe even become a famous name like Cyrus McCormick or Eli Whitney or Joseph Henry. He wanted these things with the desperation of a man born poor and nearing thirty.

He had one more reason for bidding farewell to the ocean wave. Sea service had offered no opportunity to remedy what he now felt as a decided lack. There were no candidates for the position at present, but he had no doubt of his eligibility for marriage should a suitable opportunity present itself.

Theo's reverie was interrupted by a drawn-out twitter of pipes, and the boatswain's bawl.—Reveille, reveille, heave out and trice up.

On the pier a draft of seamen was reporting for duty under an ashy dawn. He watched Girnsolver send them to join the human chain that still toiled at the coaling. He stared, restless brain buzzing, until he smelled coffee on the wind.

The wardroom was chilly and dirty. The black dust had filtered even down here, making filthy shadows in the corners. He only glanced in. He was not welcome in the officers' mess unless invited, as he'd been by Claiborne two nights before. He thrust his head into the galley. As he'd hoped, a pot bubbled on the red-hot caboose. Ahasuerus, unspeaking, pushed a steaming cup toward his hand, with the usual two lumps of sugar on the saucer.

He preferred a mug to cup and saucer, it was more efficient, but he took it uncomplaining out into the passageway and stood musing how to burn a thousand pounds of kerosene an hour. Wicks were out of the question. There'd have to be some kind of special burner . . . He burned his tongue on the coffee and muttered a curse. Hadn't da Vinci designed something of the sort?

A brown paw plucked the sugar lumps from his saucer. He raised his eyes to a wrinkled, malevolent child's face. The ape was hanging upside down from a speaking tube on the overhead. It tucked the sugar inside its mouth pouch and gesticulated angrily for more.

—Mr. Hubbard, said the exec for the second time, before Theo realized he was being spoken to.

—Yes sir?

—I was enquiring as to the progress of coaling.

—On the last bunker. Two more hours and we'll break down the chutes.

—The captain intends to get under way at noon, unless the weather should deteriorate further.

—Aye aye, sir.

Claiborne reached up to the monkey, and it spun itself around the brass tube and dropped to his shoulder. It blinked at Hubbard disdainfully, scratching beneath its tail, then inspecting something interesting it had found. A moment later, whatever it was, was in its mouth. Theo looked away, wishing he had not seen that. He counted himself as an evolutionist, but having sailed with this beast, he could sympathize with those who preferred to disown their relatives of the lower orders.

—One other thing. Mr. Eaker will be standing deck watches when we get under way. I should like you to take a few minutes to explain your machinery to him after we cast off, at some time convenient to you both.

He said he'd do that, and the exec nodded and went on into the wardroom. He didn't ask him to come in. Theo smiled contemptuously. "Take a few minutes." "Explain your machinery to him." Oh certainly, sir. Eaker was nothing more than some big bug's son who wanted to play about with boats, but the braiders welcomed him. No question about *him* eating with them. Hell, the fucking *monkey* was in the wardroom now. Well, at least he was drinking their coffee. It wasn't the corpse-waking fluid his boys brewed with live steam, but even without sugar it tasted sweeter.

A few minutes later he was at the desk, tucked into a corner of the engine room that served him as an office. Its surface was stained with rings of paint. He sighed and passed a filthy hand over his face, knowing he was making himself a mess but not caring. He pressed the lever on a patent inkwell, dipped his pen, and began rapidly signing coaling receipts, leaving a black smudge on each one.

Then he tensed, looking blankly at the gray blurred print. He held his breath, suspended like a man advancing his cupped hand slowly above a fly.

Then pounced, and the idea wriggled in his grasp. He swept the receipts to the deck and jerked a pen scroll from a pigeonhole.

He'd forwarded his other ideas to Washington, but not this one. He'd never mentioned it to another human being. Erased and redrawn many times, the paper was a muddy palimpsest. It showed a long tapered outline, with hand-lettered call-outs to various mechanical details. He looked at it for a long moment. Then put the pen aside, staring at the design, and picked up a pencil.

Back bent, the little man erased furiously; then began drawing, intent, withdrawn, absorbed, and all alone.

7

KER was on the forecastle, inspecting the forebrace with Duycker and Girnsolver, when he noted a marine trotting down the pier at trail arms. The leatherneck ran up *Owanee*'s brow and disappeared from view.

Not many minutes later a shadow fell on the edge of Ker's vision, anchored by the shiny toes of brass-capped brogans. He finished the inspection, then nodded to Ahasuerus. —His cabin, I presume?

He paused at the top of the companionway to examine the sky once more. Its darkness worried him. The wind was from the southeast at near gale force. The barometer had dropped sharply over the last forty-eight hours. Even in the shelter of Wallabout Bay, with the low stone island of the cob dock between them and the river, the gusts rocked the sloop-of-war. Not that he was worried about her. She could make her way in dirty weather, and he'd seen a bit of it himself.

No, what he couldn't shake from his mind was where they were going, and what might happen when they got there.

He smoothed his beard and went down the ladder. A moment later and forty feet aft, he knocked at a paneled door.

Commander Trezevant was at his sea desk in the stern gallery, writing in his remark book. He was in undress uniform, and his lean neck disappeared into an unbuttoned collar. His long legs lay tumbled under the table like logs left by a receding flood. His silvering hair stuck up in back. One of the portlights was open, and the wind stirred the drapes. A slip of paper fluttered desperately, pinned to the desktop by a jagged fragment of Johannesburg quartz. Ker listened to the pen scratch, like the frantic scrabble of some chitinous insect, and inspected the telltale compass that hung from the overhead.

Finally Trezevant held the book to the portlight, letting the wind dry the ink. He closed it and reached it into a fiddle-boarded shelf. Corked the inkwell and wiped the pen and said in his deep baritone, without looking up, —Take a seat, Exec. Are we ready to get under way?

—Yes, sir. Mr. Hubbard reports coaling complete and heavy-weather dunnage in place. Mr. Glass reports stores and comestibles accounted for. Mr. Eaker reports all ammunition aboard and stowed. Mr. Duycker and the bo's'n have made preparations for high winds and heavy seas. I have not yet heard from the pilot, however.

—Draft?

—Eleven feet two inches by the marks forward, twelve feet one inch aft.

—How do you judge the weather?

—Wind's from the southeast at about twenty knots here, sir. It'll be stronger outside. The barometer's still dropping.

Trezevant nodded. —Due to the sea conditions reported outside Sandy Hook, Captain Fox has advised me to delay our sailing twenty-four hours. We'll go out on the tide tomorrow.

—Aye aye, sir. He felt relieved rather than otherwise; no seaman looked forward to bad weather. But Trezevant looked like he had something more to say.

Instead of going on, though, the captain pushed his seat back and peered out of the portlight. A minute passed before he said, —Do you recall the discussion we had at Christmas, Claiborne? When we first heard this Black Republican had been elected?

—I've thought of little else since, sir.

—It's placed those of us who hail from our part of the world in a devilish awkward position. The hawk profile came round, stony eyes fixed on him for a moment before turning again, always moving, and the long fingers picked up a pair of dividers and turned the sharp points glittering to and fro like questing bayonets. —Can you spare a moment?

—Yes sir. Should I just let Nick know sailing's been postponed—

—This won't take long.

He lowered himself again. —I'm at your disposal, sir.

—I'll hew to the point, First Luff. After so long in suspension, events have begun moving with great speed. The cruise we are about to depart on will bring matters to a head. Virginia has not yet gone out. Nor has my state. Yet both may declare themselves outside the Union within days.

Trezevant waited, then added softly, —In such a situation, where would your loyalties lie?

He took a deep breath. —Sir, I have always been loyal to the flag. I hope the seceded states will still return, if some adjustment can be made to accommodate them.

Trezevant looked away. —I share your feelings about the flag. I went into battle beneath it, in Mexico. I have devoted my life and all my holiest hopes to its service. But I fear South and North have at last reached the parting of the ways. Insofar as loyalty goes . . . have we not also a duty to our states? Our homes?

—Yes sir; both call to us. But we've sworn an oath. It seems to me this is the very time we should not falter in obeying it.

The captain paced around the cabin. His grizzled cowlick brushed the overhead. —I have a letter from Franklin Buchanan. Old Buck. You were at the Academy when he was superintendent, as I recall.

—Actually, shortly thereafter, sir, but I have the pleasure of his acquaintance.

—I do not believe I would be violating his intention in writing me when I share part of it with you. He writes that most of our best officers are going South, but more particularly, he explains their reasoning. They say theirs is *not* a rebellion against the old flag.

—It isn't?

—No. Washington has fallen into the hands of radicals. Their rallying cry is the presumed plight of the colored race, but their true program is nothing less than the subordination of the South to the money interests of Boston and New York. Thus, this is less a rebellion than the frank and manly recognition that sectional conflict has begun between North and South.

He sat conning it over. —You're saying the *meaning* of the flag has changed, sir?

—That is their argument. The North, not we, tore it from above us by breaking solemn agreements. We are thus absolved from our oaths, and must cast our lots with that section to which we owe natural allegiance.

Ker said dryly, —But how precisely is one "absolved" from an oath, sir? I fear my education has rather glossed over that point.

—In their view, the resignation of their commissions absolves them from any special obligation. They thus return to the class of private citizens.

He saw the reasoning, but he wasn't sure it was as convincing as the captain seemed to find it. —So far they've made no move to violate our rights.

—Is resupply of a federal fort in South Carolina's territory an abrogation of that state's rights?

—I'll have to leave that one to the politicians and newspaper editors, sir.

Despite himself, it seemed, Trezevant's weather-beaten face split into a smile. —Very well, then. You deny the commodore's reasoning.

—Sir, I do not. Captain Buchanan is an honorable man. As for myself, I am acquainted with another Southerner who is a staunch Unionist.

—Captain Farragut. A Tennesseean, if I recall correctly.

—Yes sir, by birth, though we're neighbors now in Norfolk. My wife is intimate with his, and our families have had much friendly intercourse. If the commonwealth secedes, he'll go North. He hesitated, unsure what he wanted to say. —When I ponder that two such men can differ so far, what light have the rest of us on our path? Yet there must be an honorable way through. It is up to us to discover it.

Instead of replying, Trezevant took another turn around the cabin. A minute passed and he did not speak. Ker began to feel uncomfortable having the captain on his feet when he was not. He stood, but the older man gestured him back down impatiently.

Finally the captain nodded heavily, as if reaching a decision. He seated himself and pulled an envelope from his desk. Held it up. —Stephen Mallory has been appointed secretary of the navy in Mr. Davis's government. He has offered me a commission in the grade of commander.

—Are you leaving us too, sir?

The knife cuts beneath the captain's eyes deepened. —I hope North Carolina doesn't secede. But if she does, I can't fight my brothers and neighbors. I pray Lincoln lets us depart peacefully.

—I feel the same way, sir. I mean, about withdrawing peacefully.

—But if Buck's correct, if this will be a sectional conflict, there are larger questions than one's personal fate. For example: what is the disposition of our mutually held national property?

He wasn't sure he followed. —Of what property, sir?

—Of government property. This ship was paid for by citizens of the South as well as those of the North.

Ker studied the gaunt face. What did the captain mean? A ship could not be divided, like a bequest after the reading of a will. Or was he suggesting part of the fleet, as well as of the officers manning it, should go South, the rest North? He decided to miss the point. —Sir, if you're sounding me as to my readiness to obey orders, let me reassure you. If we should be attacked on our way to Sumter, or in the process of resupplying it, I am still an officer of the United States Navy.

—Unto, unto; as am I, sir; as am I.

—Yes sir. Ker stood. —Will that be all, sir?

—I believe so. Yes, said Trezevant, reaching again for the remark book. —That'll be all. Inform the officers we'll sail tomorrow, and keep all hands aboard again tonight.

8

Under Way from Brooklyn ♦ A South Street Farewell ♦ The Saluting Gun ♦
Matched Against the Sea

ER didn't like the looks of the approaching tug. It wasn't just
late; he suspected its master was inebriated. It had entered
the slip aimed straight at *Owanee,* and sheered off only at the
last moment, side wheels thrashing full aback and stem yawing like a
biter-bitted horse.

The ninth of April, 7 A.M., and the East River was so cloaked with
mist and coal smoke one could no longer be certain God had created
light. Hubbard had reported steam up in both boilers at midnight.
He'd been on deck since then, overseeing preparations for getting under way. At 4 A.M. Trezevant had come aboard in a sealskin coat that
looked as if it would be right comfortable in a winter gale. Which,
judging by the whitecaps in the river, they might soon be in, outside
Sandy Hook.

The crew stood to the lines. The captain had come on deck at the
pipe call, taking his habitual position forward of the wheel, Girnsolver awaiting deck orders a few paces away. He stared aloft as Ker, a
few feet away, watched him unobtrusively.

He and Parker Trezevant had shared the deck so many times off
Africa, in storm and heat and long stern chases. Sometimes the
slavers had fired back. More than once there'd been action inland,

87

along the slow broad fever-gripped rivers. He'd thought he knew his commander. But this tense, closed man, peering to seaward with his hands locked together, was not the one he'd sailed with through the bright seas off the Guinea coast.

The tug arrowed in again. The captain looked around questioningly, and Ker roused himself with a start. He sometimes forgot, since Mr. Watkins had gone South, that he was the ranking officer on deck now. He told Duycker, —Make her up to starboard, just aft of the fore shrouds. Give her plenty of cable on the tow.

The master passed the order to Girnsolver. The boatswain knew what to do, he could have gotten the ship under way without officers at all, but the chain of command had to be preserved. As strong as an anchor cable, and just as essential when the strain came.

He leaned back to look aloft. Main, top, and t'gallants all bent on, but not yet set, of course. The captains of the fore and main waiting for the word up there in their skyscraping aeries. Above them the low sky was a dirty beggar's blanket patched with black scraps of rain wrack. The wind was from due south, tearing the smoke off the stack. He'd hoped all night it would haul around, but they'd be steaming directly into it headed out, dependent on the engine and the towboat for motive power.

Two piers over he caught a glimpse of another black hull sliding into the stream like a birthing porpoise. The Stars and Stripes flamed in the steady wind. Smaller than *Owanee* and more lightly armed, *Harriet Lane* would make southing with her until the rendezvous off Charleston. He noted with professional jealousy that the gunboat had gotten under way without the assistance of a tow.

Duycker fingered his cap. —Tug fast at short stay, sir.

—Very well. He threw a glance over his shoulder. The new officer, Eaker, stood gripping the pull rope to the engine bell.

Ker took a last look at the smoke. In the growing light it streamed off over the cob dock, over the lead-colored river, over the piers and shipping and the city. The wind would push them off the pier . . . Very well, it was time. To see what waited for her, and for the country, and for them all, over the curve of gray sea.

—Take in forward spring. Take in after spring . . . take in all lines. Mr. Eaker, one bell astern, if you please. He crossed to port, aiming the speaking trumpet and pitching his voice above the hoarse chuffing of both ships' engines across to the towboat, —Take a strain and put us in the river.

A moment later the boatswain's pipe shrilled again, sending the message all over the ship that the last line had left the shore.

Owanee was under way.

By the mast, Eli pulled the cord in a quick jangle to signal the next order would be astern, then sounded one bell for "Slow." A rush of steam and smoke burst from the funnel over the homes and church spires of Brooklyn. As the gap widened between ship and pier he searched the waterfront for Araminta. Then remembered: she didn't know they were leaving.

Setting her free had been the most difficult thing he'd ever done. Yet now he felt at peace, as if the last line securing him to his old life had been taken in, and that life was drifting off like the departing waterfront. As they backed slowly, the towboat splashing and hissing beside them, the faces of the few spectators—the line handlers, a few yardbirds and officers who had emerged from the bureaus and workshops to see them off—dwindled, till the piers themselves were lost in the jumble of boat sheds and warehouses.

Behind him the exec bawled at the tug, his normally cultivated voice peremptory, and the land fell back on either hand as *Owanee* emerged from Wallabout into the open river. The low dark hills of old Breuckelen fell back, and the brick fortifications on Governors Island came into view. As they emerged the city spread until it seemed to extend forever. He gazed on the familiar riverfront, the gray sky punctured by needling church spires, and closer in the spiky bristle of masts and spars. One of those gray slate roofs was Eaker and Callowell's, but he couldn't tell which from here. Above all the vast mass of stone and brick floated a smoky brown coal pall, no sooner spun out above the million-souled habitation than it was swept away by the steady wind, no sooner swept away than renewed from below. A steady roar came across the water from it as if from the ceaseless revolution of some vast engine.

Duycker, close behind him. —Eaker. Eaker! Pay attention, Goddamnit! Mr. Claiborne asked for two bells, ahead.

Flushing, he jerked at the cord. A moment later a tremor came through the wood beneath his feet. Gulls swooped down from the lightless sky, their despairing shrieks cutting the heavy thump of machinery as they crossed and recrossed the road of disturbed water *Owanee* creased through the leaden river.

Two decks below, Theo stepped beneath one of the ladders. The draft of the furnaces sucked air down it. The breeze, already cold, felt freezing after the buildup of heat as the sloop sat pierside that morning.

Lighting off was a slow process, and he had taken each step deliberately, sparing the hastily patched boilers any strain due to uneven heating. It began with a layer of Southern pitch pine on the grate bars, covered with four inches of powdery coal sweepings. On top of this the stokers scattered larger chunks of anthracite, and on top of that, several editions of the *Herald* and the *Times,* well crumpled, to start the draft. Meanwhile the boiler men were letting in water through the blowoff pipe, opening the blowoff cock and lifting the safety valve so that the river water came flooding up into the boilers from beneath the hull. A half barrel of rags well soaked with pine tar, pushed back under the grates, completed the preparations.

He checked the water gauge and told MacNail to close the dampers. Then scratched the lucifer and tossed it in. Thin white smoke filled the furnace, gradually rising as the heated air began pushing upward. The wind helped the draft; even down here they could hear it howling, weirdly magnified by hollow iron as in a massive pipe organ. As the paper writhed into black tissues of char he flicked a second locofoco under the grate. The rags blazed up instantly, yellow flames daggering up into the pitch pine, and in seconds things were well started and O'Kennedy clanged the door shut.

By five o'clock the mercury gauge showed five inches of pressure. He blew off two inches' worth of steam to get rid of the last air in the boiler and held pressure there as he clambered and swung round the casings, tapping and listening, alert for any sign of leakage. He flinched at a sudden sharp bang from deep within "B" boiler. But it wasn't repeated. Probably just an old zinc letting go as the shell expanded.

He signaled Hart and O'Kennedy to stoke up, and opened the blow-through valve to start warming up the condenser and the engine. At seven inches he cut in the blowers. The gauge immediately responded, steam pressure rising swiftly and the water level falling so suddenly the waterman reacted too late. Theo steadied him with a word, but felt uneasy. If the water dropped too low, pressure skyrocketed. That was when you got boiler explosions, scalded men and wrecked ships . . . A thread of sweat broke down his back. The fire room was noisy now, with the scrape and clank of shovels as the stokers ran from coalhole to the boiler fronts. The fans were roaring, the flames were roaring, the raucous shouts and curses of the Irish added to the clamor. He sent word up that the engines were ready, and hooked on. The great pistons eased into motion, the rockshaft began nodding, and soon steady thunder like an iron avalanche and the acrid smell of hot steel filled the long shedlike compartment. When the first bell came down, its tinny clang barely penetrating the din, he signaled "Back slow" to MacNail, who stood by at the long iron lever that worked the steam valves.

And now the bell for two-thirds ahead. He stood back, letting Pappy stop engines and ease them into motion again. The iron walls rolled around him, and he selected a handhold amid the maze of bare piping, one that wouldn't burn him. They'd be in the stream now, likely passing down Buttermilk Channel headed for the Narrows. He flicked his watch open and checked the time, absentmindedly wiping his forehead as the heat grew steadily in the enclosed space.

———

On the far side of the river, Araminta looked over the swirling water beneath the South Street pier. Underneath the iron sky the river seemed narrow enough to leap. It sloshed loudly beneath the pilings. The cold wind whipped fish stench along the waterfront, where the Fulton Market teemed with the early-morning crush. She'd stopped at Williams & Co. to look over their tea selection, then paid a breakfast call on Harriet Lispenard, an acquaintance from the dramatic society. Picking her way back along the cobbled street, she'd heard schoolgirls chanting the rhyme that had begun circulating when Anderson moved from Moultrie to Sumter in the middle of the night.

> *Bob Anderson my beau, Bob*
> *When we were first aquent,*
> *Ya were in Mexico, Bob*
> *Because by order sent;*
> *But now ya are in Sumter, Bob*
> *Because ya chose to go*
> *And blessings on ya anyhow, Bob*
> *Anderson, my beau.*

Now she pulled her shawl tight as she watched the black ships emerging from the jumble of piers and buildings across the river. A few others, waterfront loungers but also gentlemen from the commission merchants and chandleries, ship-bread bakers and block makers that lined the riverfront, had stopped as well to watch the minuet of masts. One fellow dilated on how quickly the Southrons would come to terms once they faced ships' guns. His acquaintance ridiculed him, describing in terms she found chilling how rapidly forts would dispose of a sloop and a gunboat. Her stomach cramped, as if her corset were laced too tightly.

—Pray, do you know which is the *Owanee?* she asked them.

They stared, taken aback at being addressed by a lady. One swept off his hat, unplugged his segar, and bowed. —I believe it is the larger of the two, miss. A sloop of war—yes. The other is the *Harriet Lane,* which rates as a gunboat, I believe. Have you an acquaintance aboard?

She turned back to the river, not responding to his impertinent query. A white cone burst from the lead ship, followed a few seconds' remove by a scream that echoed back from the walls behind her. What she had at first taken for part of it separated from it. The tug yawed alarmingly, nearly colliding with the warship, then cut away lightly as a water skimmer, a white flutter showing at its wheels like lace trim beneath a lifted skirt. She noticed scraps of colored bunting being hoisted into the rigging of the larger warship as it gathered way.

—A naval signal, said a voice at her elbow, and she whirled furious to rebuff the fellow, only to find, lifting his hat to her, the gracefully inclined form and elegant mustache of Mr. Ellery Phelps. —In the naval code, but I should guess, most likely simply advising the consort to fall in astern. I trust I am not intruding, Miss Van Velsor? I observed you out alone, and wondered if I might be of assistance.

—I was simply observing the view, thank you.

—We are witnessing a historic event. Phelps smiled. —The departure of the heroes under sealed orders, off to relieve the beleaguered fortress.

She said sharply, —I do not know about you, sir, but I am seeing my cousin off to war.

—I sincerely hope not, said Phelps. The politico was faultlessly dressed, she noted, in a fine gray coat perfectly cut and a spanking pair of kid gloves. Most men in her uncle's circle adhered to a drabber sartorial style. —The governor has arranged matters such that a peaceful outcome is assured. His quick eye must have caught demurral in her face; he added swiftly, —I assume that is what you too had hoped for. Since Eli has taken it upon himself to join the republic's defenders.

—I should not like to expose any young man to the hazards of battle, sir. Yet it seems more and more inevitable.

—My dear young lady, one could discourse for hours about such

matters. I would not weary you with the sordid details of our duplic-
itous profession. He captured her glove and pressed his glossy mustache to soft kid. —I can only say Eli's a fortunate young fellow,
sharing his home with such a beauty.

—You are forward, Mr. Phelps.

In fact, his attentions were not improper for a male acquaintance
encountered in a public way. Yet he was a married man, and his reputation was whispered about. Not that she was afraid; it was exciting;
but with such men, one had to be on one's guard.

—I shall beg your pardon, then. He bowed again and withdrew. A
pace down the pier he turned. —May I hope to see you when I call
upon your father? Perhaps tomorrow?

She turned her back and did not reply. Shading her eyes, she
searched again for the departing vessels. They were far downriver
now, and she realized the tide was with them, carrying them away
even in the teeth of the wind. She was straining her eyes after them
when a sudden jet of white smoke was followed by a curiously dead-
sounding *thud.*

—Ready. *Fire,* bellowed Babcock, and a dart of orange flame and a
clap of thunder were succeeded instantly by a sulphurous cloud. The
powder smoke whirled down the deck as little Billy Ripley dashed
up, presenting the bucket with the next charge, but the warrant gunner knocked him back with a sweep of his arm. —Not till she's
sponged, Babcock shouted.

Cal Hanks leaned forward, but did not advance till the command
"Serve vent and sponge." He stopped the vent, and the sponger
rammed the wet mass home on the end of its staff. He twisted it several times, then hauled it out, struck the staff three sharp raps under
the muzzle, and handed it to another crewman, who examined it and
cleared the worm.

—With powder and wad only. *Load.*

Billy jumped forward again. The number three man positioned

the charge in the muzzle, seam down, small end in, and started it down the bore with a shove of his arm. Hanks had the rammer now, and with a powerful yet precisely measured thrust ran it in till the painted mark on the rammer staff met the muzzle. Hand over hand out, and the saluting wad, a plug of sand wrapped in bagging, went home in its turn.

—Run out!

He stepped back to pass off the rammer to number six, bent to pull out the truck quoin, then laid his shoulder to the gun with the others. He yanked the hempen breeching up with his right till it was clear of the fore trucks, then with powerful thrusts of his legs ran the gun squealing over the deck till the side tackle two-blocked to the eyebolts.

—Prime, yelled the gunner, and the second captain thrust in a friction primer, then sprinkled a few grains of gunpowder in the vent and stepped back, shaking out the lanyard with an easy freeing motion.

—Aim!

The men stood fast. Cal relaxed, knowing from the way the gunner stepped back the final command would not come immediately. He stood swaying as the sloop pitched, and his gaze ran out over the green carpet of river. A small crowd was gathered at Peck slip. A few waved handkerchiefs and top hats. The rest stood immobile as the sailors about *Owanee*'s deck.

His face betrayed nothing. A slave learned that skill early: to make his manner do his bidding, though in everything else he was his master's. For if his face was as others wanted it, smiling or uncomprehending or obedient, his mind might yet remain his own.

He'd stayed close aboard ship since the night at Corlear's Hook, not going on deck unless duty called him topside. It wasn't guilt. He'd thought about what he'd done, and decided not to mourn. The man hunters, they deserved it. Nor, if he'd been the instrument of God's vengeance in regard to Fort, was that call for remorse. He saw now what a stult he'd been. The attorney must have been preying on fugitive slaves for years, wringing cash out of them with legal mumbo jumbo, then selling them to the slave catchers.

The North was a hard land. No milk and honey, like he'd dreamed following the drinking gourd. He knew now there was no such paradise. Even in Liberia, the lighter-skinned, American-born emigrants lorded it over the darkies from the interior. He'd thought he was an African, till he saw Africa. He didn't know what he was now. The flag that snapped above him now was made of lies and blood. He served it, yet it kept him a slave. It boasted freedom to all, yet each dawn could be the last of his uncertain and limited liberty.

—Look up, Hanks, Babcock said from behind him, and he raised his head, which had gradually sunk in thought. He heard the heavy tread on the deck behind him, then felt him close behind. He kept his gaze ahead, seeing now the bowsprit come left like a huge compass needle as the ship swung past the three-tiered brick of Fort Columbus. The engine thumped beneath their feet, and the shore marched swiftly along.

The gunner stepped around in front of him. Studied him for a long second, drawing the colt slowly through his fingers, then shifted his quid in his cheek and spat over the side. —You salvaged them tackles, like I told you?

—Done that yesterday, Gunner.

—Don't talk back to me, boy. You want to pick a crow, I'll give you a Goddamned passage to Hells a-poppin, you coal-colored son of a bitch. We got one more salute, at the Narrows. Then you wash this here gun down and sponge it out, make sure it's dry before you reload. Make up some blacking and do all the gear. We're going to be usin' these guns when we get down to Charleston.

He stood silent. The pivot was his gun, not this one. —I gave you an order, the petty officer reminded him.

—Aye aye, he said, and the warrant squinted at him for a time and then, at last, walked away. He relaxed again, looking across as the river broadened and the distant woods of Bayonne came into view, here and there a white house standing out on a headland like a lookout on the bow of a vessel headed out to sea.

———

Eli left the engine bell, standing a few respectful paces back from the captain as mud flats moved rapidly down their port side. Tangled mounds of snags and lumber logs from the Hudson timber rafts were shoaled up on the Bay Ridge like the shattered remnants of ship-wrecks. Claiborne alternately bent over a chart, then put his sextant to his eye, holding it parallel to the deck. Trezevant stood watchful behind him.

Once past Governors Island *Owanee* angled out to bisect the line between Bedloe's and Red Hook. The deck quivered. Smoke whipped off the stack and blew aft, dropping like a funeral veil over their seething wake. A schooner ran past, foresails braced round and jibs sheeted out. Her hatches were covered with a deckload of white pine, the barked trunks shockingly pale, like stripped corpses picked up from a battlefield. She flew blue and yellow, Swedish colors. Claiborne called out, —Answer the dip, quartermaster. The sails swayed against the sky, bowsed to their yards like closed chrysalides. The wind was dead in their teeth. The pitching grew, and Eli braced a hand on the bulwark. At least he'd never suffered from mal de mer.

A report from the headland, and he made out the low brick pile of a fort. Seconds later the dull concussion of *Owanee*'s returned salute rebounded from the palisades. The gun crew were already bent furi-ously in their reloading drill. A live projectile, this time, to match the other loaded guns ranged fore and aft along the deck.

Ker kept looking aloft, then out to eastward. Fort Hamilton passed down their port hand, the sloop accelerating as the Race grabbed her. Norton Point fell astern in its turn. The wind threw the leadsman's cry back to them. —And a quarter, five. Three fathoms clear under *Owanee*'s whirling screw, enough but not overmuch with shoals and banks crowding the channel out.

Now the Lower Bay dawned ahead, bleached with whitecaps un-der the pewter sky and streaked with the egg-white foam that meant the wind had reached thirty knots. A cable's length astern *Harriet Lane* dipped her martingale to slice translucent jade. She was pile-driving already. —Going to be heavy outside, Ker shouted to Trezevant.

—Daresay we'll chase no flying fish. The captain pursed his lips, then added, —I expressed my doubts the tugs could get under way in this. But Mr. Fox insisted we put out. Are we coming left, sir? Make sure we have enough windage to pass clear of the East Bank.

He took a last sight on Coney Island, making certain he had the lighthouse and not one of the white-shingled cottages that had begun to dot the shore. He crossed that with Breezy Point, a blue line to the east, and a third bearing on Crooks. The fix placed them six thousand yards south of Coney Island, with half a mile of sea room to leeward. He picked up the Staten Island range and yelled to the helmsmen, two seamen clinging like twin Ixions to the man-high wheel, —Starboard your helm; southeast by east.

—Southeast by east, sir.

—Bo's'n: make all secure for sea. Secure anchors and boats.

Trezevant's voice pitched above the wind. —I believe it is time to make sail, if you please. You'll have to close-jam her in this sea, see how well you can do.

Ker studied the wind, holding his beard as if it might blow off. It was generally best to set sail from fore to aft, to maintain control, but in this case, with the wind from forward and engine power available, he ordered main and top, main and mizzen, close haul, sharp up, taut bowlines.

—Lay aloft, sail loosers! T'gallants and tops'l yardmen! bawled Girnsolver in his shrill old voice, and two dozen boys and men scrambled into the converging shrouds and clawed their way upward with astonishing rapidity. —Lay out and loose! And below them as they cast off the gaskets the buff canvas spun out from its tight smooth harbor furl, gradually papering over the sky. —Sheet home and belay. Topsail halyards! Girnsolver cried, and as the hands on deck bent and hauled, the spars rose slowly, the still-slack canvas cracking and flailing in the gusts till sheet and spar took strain and drew cloth tight over the curved wind.

—Sheet home, tops'ls! Mains'l halyards, take a strain! Sheet home there, close aft, you damned soldier! Sheet in on that spanker! Take the slack out o' that line afore ye foul it! Now man the braces, brace her up!

The quartermaster, cradling the case that held the brass fish: —Patent log, sir? Claiborne told him to pay out slowly to avoid fouling the screw.

As the braces came in the yards pivoted. The big square topsail and main caught and bellied taut with a thundering crack. A slack clew jigger caught a boy on the side of the head; he cried out and fell to his knees, fair locks darkening with blood. Men staggered as the deck heeled, heaving in hand over hand with reddened streaming faces, bracing each yard around and blocking each sheet till each sail was trimmed precisely to the wind. Ker planted his seaboots wide as the ship yawed, then gathered herself and leapt forward like a frightened doe. A blue-green surge rose along the rail, and the wind tore its head off and flung its salt blood over the bulwarks. The first slash of icy spray caught the breath in his throat.

He grinned suddenly under its whip. They were under way again, and the stays were whining and the clouds scudded close overhead like gray-hulled pilot boats racing for a homebound liner. The jib went up, cracking and battering about, and staysails clawed into the lurching sky and the sloop began driving.

Ahead lay the open Atlantic, its mood deadly in an onshore storm. This wouldn't be easy, a run south against stream and wind with a gale in the offing. He didn't know what lay at their destination. But he knew Parker Trezevant. Whatever his views on the crisis that was tearing the navy apart like a ship with a rotten keel, given an order the captain would pursue it into the jaws of the devil himself. Bow high or blow low they would go south, or go down. It would test them all, old hands and new blood alike.

Two steps away Eli stood with one hand still gripping the bell rope, the other clinging to the fife rail as he stared openmouthed across the waste of water. A roaring white tumult bleached the sky on either side of their narrow path to the open sea. A steel curtain of squall blew toward them, its blast flattening the waves under a reflectless luminescence before it struck with a shriek of stinging rain that blotted out all vision, all voice, all sight. The storm erased the sea, the swaying masts, extinguished everything around them, leaving only the dimly lit spike of the crazily bobbing compass card, pointing out to them all their inescapable and fated destination.

PART II

Sumter, April 10–13, 1861.

9

ELI came awake with the darkness groaning around him, water
rushing close past his ear, and someone or something standing silently over him. He flung his arm up instinctively, and
the shadow stepped back a pace.

—It's Rapp, sir. The quartermaster. You've the midwatch. Got a
stub?

—A what?

The petty officer didn't answer, just pulled a candlestick from its
wedging in the overhead and touched it to the glowing wick of his
lantern. —It's raining and blowing out there, he said, and pulled the
grate to behind him.

When his bare feet touched the wet planks Eli shivered. There
seemed to be a leak in the overhead of his cabin. He shook his head
to clear it, and looked around the tiny space that walled him. Above
his head someone was shouting, —A-a-all out the starboard watch.

What went by the name of "stateroom" aboard a sloop of war was
just long enough for him to stretch out at full length, but not high
enough to stand up without crouching. If one outstretched hand
touched the door, the fingers opposite brushed the inner hull. His
berth, a wooden trough with a cotton-ticking pad an inch thick, con-

sumed half the space. Above it, cunningly positioned to catch his forehead if he sat up too quickly, a bookshelf was jointed into the ship's timbers. The candle flame swayed and glowed on a minuscule bureau. A washstand stood in the after corner, contents gurgling and sloshing at each heave of the deck.

He coughed for several minutes, then forced himself up. His chest felt as if worms were gnawing it from within. He threw water on his face, steadying himself against the motion with a trembling hand. He put on the same salty-damp socks and uniform he'd worn for the past three days, and over that storm clothes that smelled of mildew and rancid linseed oil. As he was struggling with the heavy sou'wester the deck tilted up into a savage incline, making him reel into the door and bark his face on the transom. The candle stub flew off the bureau. It hit a soaked towel wadded up in the corner and went out with a sizzle, plunging the room back into darkness.

The wardroom was cold and unlit and deserted. It stank of the bilge and the remains of dinner. His boots discovered the slickness of a patch of vomit, too late to avoid tracking it along with him. He couldn't help remembering the quiet cleanliness, the luxurious appointments of Mr. Vanderbilt's yacht. He'd stretched the truth, describing his sea service to Claiborne. In point of severe fact he had been aboard it only twice, and in neither outing had they ventured beyond the Narrows. He headed aft, the bulky mackintosh snagging on each lashed-down chair and table corner, and fought his way up a slick-treaded ladder and through a tarp-covered hatch out onto the weather deck.

Icy rain slashed his face, and darkness covered the face of the deep. He clung to a shroud, coughing, as the oncoming crew pushed and blundered past him, cursing and muttering. The sky was totally lightless. Even if it hadn't been overcast, they were in the dark of the moon till the thirteenth.

Dark of the moon. But clinging to the shroud, feeling it go steel hard as the mast leaned into it, he knew true darkness lay within. He pressed his face to the icy strapping of a horse block, willing his lungs to stop convulsing and simply breathe. The block smelled of the sea and of dank iron, like old blood.

—Mr. Eaker? That you?

He couldn't answer. Pressing his face into the rough metal, he breathed deep, then coughed into the endless wind. Tears tided in his eyes and slid down his cheeks, mingling with the running spray. A hook twisted deep in his chest. He felt it there, the inevitable, growing thing that, unless he could conquer it, would make him one with the darkness.

Its grip lessened after a time, and slowly his sight returned. He sensed the black-on-black of the sails and the towering loft of stay and shroud, the hell glow of engine fire reflected off the wind-flattened main. A lantern reeled on the mainstay, striking green flame off passing crests black and gleaming as wet flint. His lips moved soundlessly as he recalled lines of Coleridge's.

> *About, about, in reel and rout*
> *The death-fires danced at night.*

Relinquishing his handhold at last, he forced himself grimly forward along cold soaked oak.

A carefully shielded whale-oil wick illuminated the binnacle. The faint golden compass-gleam lit the broad back of one helmsman and the down-bent face of the other. It limned the childish features of Midshipman Thurston, mustering the oncoming watch from a wheel book. Beyond this tiny flickering circle stretched the looming darkness of the trysail, sheeted close to squeeze the last ounce of driving force from the gale.

He noticed another glimmer, jagged and instantaneous, to the westward. Passing them by, he hoped. He didn't like lightning, particularly at sea.

Duycker's voice from the dark. —That you, Eaker? Ready to relieve?

—Guess so.

The old master's voice turned scornful. —Well, sir, I hope it pleases you to let us know when you decide.

The raw wind caught in his raw throat, and Eli swallowed and said hoarsely, —I'm ready. What's our course?

—South by southeast, as before. Wind's off a point. We braced around about an hour ago. Everything's snug aloft.

—She surely rolls.

—Ship that don't roll's a ship that's ready to go down. Get your sea legs on an' you'll hardly call this a roll at all. She *is* a bit wet, though. Not like your typical rich man's yacht.

He ignored the gibe, peered around in the dark. —Where's *Lane?*

—Haven't seen her all this watch. First luff last sighted her off the starboard quarter, just after dark. Duycker's voice turned brisk. —O.K., we're on the port tack, as you can tell, with the first reef in the courses and tops. Stays'l forward. Trys'l on the main. Spanker aft. T'gallant yards on deck. Running into head seas at seven and an eighth by the log with two bells rung up. Captain's night orders are to crowd sail and maintain a sharp lookout.

Eli cast a wary eye aloft. It seemed like a great deal of sail to be carrying for the weather, but he had too few buttons left to argue the point. —May I see the chart?

—The chart? Think, Eaker! Keep a chart on deck, some fool will let it blow overboard. We're off Virginia, eighty miles out, all you need to know.

The rain came harder, driving straight across the sea into their faces. Water trickled down his neck inside his oilskins. Lightning flicked again, like God's flint and steel, closer, brighter, making the seas instantaneous tilted mirrors of polished lead, lighting for one flickering flash the web of shrouds and ratlines stretching upward above him, the board-flat tautness of the main trysail stiff as a sheet of rolled iron. Through the drone of stays and shrouds and the grumble of thunder came shouts. —Starboard cathead. —Port cathead. —Starboard gangway. —Port gangway.

—Life buoy! roared Duycker past the helm, and a scared boy's voice from the obscurity aft piped, —Life buoy, aye sir.

Eli looked once more at the great shadowy masses above, at the vertical blackness of the smoke pipe. The wind and seas rolled steadily in from the dark. The sloop chiseled into them at an angle. As each crest crashed into her hull the whole frame shook. He could see nothing on the heaving deep except whitecaps floating over the sprit seconds before they hit. He yelled to the men struggling with the wheel, —What sort of helm's she carry?

—A trifle to weather, sir.

—Quartermaster? Where's Rapp?

—I'm here, sir, said the quartermaster. Eli told him to make sure the helm was properly relieved. He reeled across the deck, checking the weather and lee braces by feel. At least, he thought they were the braces.

—I relieve you, he said, and touched the great floppy hood of the oilskins.

Duycker handed over the speaking trumpet, the scepter of authority on deck. —You might want to keep an eye to weather, he said, and vanished.

Eli shaded his eyes against the rain, attempting to see what he meant, what if anything lay to windward. Was that a deeper darkness, an even more somber quarter of the night?

Then a white-hot river of lightning illuminated the welded seams of the storm, and above it a looming blackness so huge and lightless it stopped his breath. A massive avalanche of thunderhead, already toppling down to crush them.

Damn the old bastard, *damn* him! The lightning etched the black with white fire again, and he saw the wind-line on the waves. A mile away? Less? If that gust hit with all sail set, she'd go over like a falling tree.

At his near scream the captain of the watch materialized like a ghost. Gripping a shroud as the ship rolled, Eli sucked a deep breath and gave his first command. —Uh —hands to the main! Reefs, d'you hear? The man did not move, and he shouted, —What are you waiting for? Damn your eyes, *bear a hand!*

—Helm first, said a voice close beside him, and he snapped his head round to see Claiborne in the binnacle light. The exec met his eye calmly. —Lively, isn't she? When you must shorten sail, first get your helm over to weather, then attend to your tops. Brail your mizzen first; you need to reduce sail aft to make sure you can fall off once you're reefed.

He forced calm he didn't feel, and gave the helmsman south by southwest. The wind howled even more insanely as they came around, but the men seemed unfrightened; they went aft as the exec talked him through the spanker reefing procedure. He felt more confident too with the Virginian next to him now, close enough to touch. Claiborne said, cupping his hands to shout into his ear, —That's it. Very well done, actually. Now the main. Throw off the braces, and haul around till your yards are in the wind's eye. Send no one aloft till your yards are laid. Start a brace with men out on the spar and you'll hear them screaming as they fall.

He passed the order in as loud a shout as he could send against the wind, then fumbled his way forward toward the mainmast. He felt as much as saw the men lined up along the bulwark, hoped rather than knew they had the right line in their hands. —Stand by to brace around —stand by —heave away, *oh!*

—That's fine; you are doing very well, said the exec. —Leave the rest to the captain of the watch. *Now* attend to your clew garnets and buntlines.

The buntlines hauled up the foot of the sails, spilling the wind out of them as a woman hikes her skirts to step into a muddy street. The clew garnets pulled the lower corners up and inboard.

—Who wouldn't sell a farm and go to sea, eh, Mr. Eaker? Very well, get your topmen aloft now, and start bracing around the fore.

—Maintop stand by to lay aloft —two reefs in the topsail and main —lay aloft!

The boatswain's pipe keened. Men scrambled upward in the rain-lashed dark. Clinging to the horse block, he was glad it wasn't he climbing the wet ratlings in this shrieking, slanting madness. He couldn't see them up there, but their cries fell faintly through the black whining air as they fisted in the wind-bellied canvas, the men clinging by feet and upper arms to yardarm and footrope, swept through the lightless night in great dizzying reels.

When the main was reefed he ran off and sent them up for the fore and jib, triggering more shouted orders in the dark, more hammering heels along the deck, more crack and thunder of wind-maddened canvas. In the middle of it the squall hit in earnest. The ship staggered over. Spars groaned. The rigging sang like an iron lyre plucked by a giant. The rain bucketed down; he had to hide his head to breathe. Lightning burned from cloud to cloud as if Zeus were battling the Titans above *Owanee's* tilting trucks. But they'd reefed her in time. Heeled to her bulwarks, the reduced sails turned the gale's power into driving force that sent tons of glowing foam shooting up over the weather rail and plunging down on them in great cold drenching sheets. Into the howl and whine Eli yelled, —Pipe down now. All hands lay in—down booms—lay down from aloft.

The squall crescendoed, then swept past. The wind and then the rain slacked off gradually, till he could see again. But the exec was gone like Banquo's ghost, leaving him to the deck and the deck to him. Through his relief, through his anger at Duycker's trick, Eli recalled the night orders: keep all sail he could. The pipe sent the men aloft again, to shake out the reefs they'd just put in. When they stumbled back down, exhausted, he made sure the rigging was made up as well as they could in the dark, and not many minutes later the watch was flaked out along the weather bulwarks, heads down, hard asleep in the blowing rain.

When reveille went, the eardrum-drilling keen of the boatswain's pipes cutting through the crash and rush of the sea against the side, Eli was still awake. Try though he might, he hadn't regained the black surcease of sleep. Sheer terror kept him wide awake, still in his wet clothes, fingers taloned into his pallet, imagining what might have happened. He could not do this. He could not endure these elemental conditions, these rough men, most of all this endless hammering motion. Just clinging to his bunk frame took all the strength he had.

He'd simply tell them that. Ask to be put off in Charleston, or wherever they touched first, and make his way home.

Then he thought about how his father would take it. He opened his eyes and looked for a long time at the shadows moving on the overhead. His lips lifted from his teeth in an animal-like snarl.

Finally he rolled himself out and forced himself back to his feet.

Breakfast was beef and bread and strong coffee, hastily consumed off a slanting table. From above came bangs and the thunder of boots as the "on" watch retrimmed sails, hauled taut the weather braces, and squared away the snakes' honeymoon of line the decks became at night.

—Mr. Eaker, said Claiborne as Shippy cleared. —A word with you.

—Your servant, sir.

—You reacted well this morning. I think you'll make a seaman.

Eli felt a warm rush; he could not meet the other's eyes. He said, —Thank you, sir.

—With a bit of art and the merest breath of wind, one can do anything with sail one can do with engines. And they can take you around the world, not simply from one coaling port to the next. Watch Mr. Duycker closely, how he handles the ship. Observe me, and the captain. Then make your own experiments; that is how one learns. At any rate. Let's have a look at the battle bill.

He unfolded a sheet of foolscap inked with lines and penciled with names. It assigned each man aboard his several duties. Deck watches, general quarters stations, boat stations, landing parties. At the foot were the "idlers," Dr. Steele, Mr. Glass, and so forth.

Claiborne said, —General quarters stations column, under the designation "forward pivot." Our previous gun captain has frenched it.

—Sir?

—He never returned from the stews of Hunter's Point. Have you a suggestion for his relief? A steady man will be required. The bow pivot is a most responsible position, especially in a stern chase, or putting a shot across someone's bow.

—I'll have to ask the gunner. I don't know the men that well yet.

—By all means. Take this along. Make certain I have listed your other positions correctly. Let me have it back by ten o'clock. The captain wishes to exercise the guns then.

—In this weather? Eli had a sudden image of one of the thirty-two-pounders breaking loose, careering across the reeling deck. —Is that wise?

—Not a question usually posed in regard to orders, Mr. Eaker. But Claiborne accompanied the rebuke with a quirk of the lips Eli was beginning to understand as what in another man might be a poke in the ribs. The first lieutenant rolled the bill up with a snap and handed it to him. —Has Mr. Hubbard taken you in hand yet?

—He said you wanted me to see the engine spaces.

—Right. I should like you to know what his machinery is capable of, and not, before we reach our destination.

—Aye aye, sir. I'll see him directly after I attend to this.

He found Babcock drinking a mug of beer in the cramped low warrant officers' mess forward. The senior petty officers cut their eyes at him as he stood in the doorway. Hubbard was there too. Eli nodded to the engineer, but he just looked back insolently, not returning the greeting. He dismissed it and said to the gunner, —About the battle bill.

—Thought we had that settled. Babcock didn't look at the paper he held out.

—We have *not* settled it, Eli said, more sharply than he meant to; but Babcock's sullen, close to contemptuous dismissal of his question could not be let to pass.

The gunner sighed, lifting his eyebrows significantly at the others. He hitched up his jumper and rose. Jerrett quickly removed his tin plate. Babcock smoothed his bald head, domed and shining like a fresh-cast minié ball, exactly as if there were hair on it, and thrust a quid into his cheek like a cartridge into a Sharps. —Let's go up on deck, then, sir, get this done once and f'r all.

—Very well. Mr. Hubbard, the first luff has been at me again to get with you.

The engineer sprawled back in his chair. He drawled, —I'll be in the fire room this morning. If you want me, you can find me there.

The wind was still fierce on deck, cold and fresh and clean. The morning light seemed to pierce Eli's eyes and drive on into his brain like shards of gray glass. He followed the gunner forward, past barefoot crewmen sloshing buckets of sea on the already shining-wet deck and dragging heavy slabs of grit stone into place. Boatswain Girnsolver was on the forecastle, pointing up the Irish pennants and hangjudases left from the toils of the night. Babcock stopped at each thirty-two-pounder to tug on the tompion line, pull on the lock cover, and lean his weight on the securing tackle. Eli followed him, nearly losing the billeting list to the wind. He held it out, but again the gunner did not favor it with a glance. It struck him then that the man could not read. He thrust it inside his jacket. —Let's discuss the forward pivot, Gunner.

Babcock nodded, and having reached that gun, bent to check the trucks. The gun crew was engaged about the muzzle but he ignored them. The big Negro, Hanks, seemed to be in charge. The mass of iron gleamed in the silver light, trained dead ahead on the bowsprit. Water droplets quivered on its black lacquered barrel, shiny as a freshly polished boot toe. Unlike older guns, Dahlgrens had no ornamentation, no cast-in dolphins or eagles or lion's heads. From a flared muzzle the tube widened gradually to the trunnions. From there aft its diameter was double that at the muzzle, ending in a smooth curved bell. The outline was not unlike that of a soda bottle, which he'd heard the men call them. The gun crew were drawing the charge, extracting the solid shot and powder with which the piece had been loaded before putting to sea.

—Something wrong? he asked. —Why are they unloading?

—The powder sucks wet from the air. We're sendin' it below to dry out.

—I see. All right, we're short a number one up here. Who shall we place in charge?

—This elevating screw wants more grease, Hanks. After you're done reloadin'.

Eli began to suspect the man was ignoring him. —Babcock? I asked you a question.

—Sorry, what was it? A bit deef on that side.

—Whom do we wish for gun captain on this position? The previous one not having returned.

—I was considerin' that matter.

—Who's the second captain?

—That'd be our black buck here.

Eli said, watching the ball come slowly out of the barrel and drop into the big man's waiting hands, —He seems to understand what he's about.

—The nig can do what he sees the others do.

He felt awkward discussing this in earshot of the gun crew, but it didn't seem to bother the petty officer, so he pressed on. —Well, does he know the drill?

Babcock went to leeward and relieved his cheek over the side. He came back wiping his chin with the back of his hand, and Eli noticed another tattoo, of a naked woman whose legs were the gunner's thumb and forefinger. He wondered what the rest of the petty officer's body looked like, then decided he did not want to know. He was reaching the point where the less he had to do with this dour and uncivil man, the better he liked it. —There's to be any biz when we get there, we'll need a good hand up here. He knows the drill well enough, I 'knowledge that. But the boys wouldn't stand for it, to work for one of 'em.

—They could stand him as second captain, but not as first? I'm not sure I follow.

—They won't eat with 'em. Colored got their own mess. But they'll work alongside, long as one's not put over them. See the deestinction?

Eli glanced at the gun crew. They were loading a fresh charge now. He said reluctantly, —I suppose so. Very well, then, whom would you suggest?

—Archbold's captain on number five aft. I'd move him forward to captain of the pivot Dahlgren here. Move his number two up to gun

captain back there, leave Hanks here forward as second under Archbold. Babcock cleared his throat, raised his voice to the seaman as the
latter extracted the rammer. —You understand us, here, Hanks?

The massive ebony face didn't alter. —Yassuh. I unnerstands dat,
Gunner. I's to stay second captain. Archbold, he's coming forward to
take charge over me.

Eli penciled in the change on the bill. At that moment the bell
struck through the roar of the wind, and he turned to see the quartermaster at the mast. Five bells of the forenoon watch. He'd be due
back on deck at noon.

If he wanted time to eat, he'd best go below and seek out Hubbard
at once.

10

Designed Against the Chinese ♦ Impossibility of an Explosion ♦
A Drumroll to General Quarters

THEO was standing in the store spaces, watching two of the firemen ransack through the hastily laden crates and barrels, when the volunteer came down the passageway. He felt his temper heat like an empty boiler. No doubt the greenhorn expected him to drop everything and attend to him, show him around with his hat in his hand, just because of the bit of braid on his cap.

Instead he turned away, watching his gang burrow like demented rats. The narrow passageway was stacked with casks of flour, cases of coffee, turgid sacks of beans, barrels of sugar and hardtack and molasses. Somewhere in here was a crate of packings for the condenser head. MacNail swore he'd seen it come aboard, in those frantic last hours before sailing, but it had gone adrift between the gangway and the engine room.

Seeing Eaker lounging in the doorway of the warrant officers' mess had simply underlined that this newcomer was welcomed into the wardroom, adopted into the brotherhood of deck officers, while he himself was not. The damned "gentlemen" and their disdain for real work. Not to mention their contempt for anything that smacked of progress.

—Mr. Hubbard? Do you have a moment for me?

He threw over his shoulder, rather curtly, —Just a moment, just a moment. Can't you see I'm busy?

—I'll wait.

He thawed a bit. Braider he might be, but Eaker didn't seem to have caught their arrogance just yet. Perhaps he could be saved, or at least brought to understand the ship was not moved by magic. He watched MacNail for a few more seconds, just to make his point, then said, —Got rather a unique craft here. Though I imagine the first luff told you that.

—No, he's been busy, and I've been trying to learn the ropes on deck. She certainly rolls, doesn't she? I know she's shallow draft.

The passageway lifted and slammed down around them. Both men grabbed for handholds. Theo said, —She was designed to fight the Chinese. That's why she only draws ten feet, to be able to go up the Yang-tze. Ever heard of John Griffiths?

—The clipper ship designer. *Rainbow. Sea Witch.*

—That's right, he said, surprised. Maybe Eaker wasn't so green. —Griffiths was trying for a shallow-draft ship with clipper lines. Below water she's very fine. Sharp fore and aft. A hard turn at the bilge and nearly flat bottom.

They paused at an iron-framed door in a massive wall of black metal. —This bulkhead's watertight.

Eaker rapped a fist on the bulkhead. —Iron?

—The decks are braced with it. Properly protected, it'll never corrode or rot. Far stronger than the best live oak. Watch your head.

A roar of furnaces, and a gust of heat that soaked both men instantly with sweat. Theo led the way through the fire room. Shouting against the roar of blowers, he pointed out the massive Martin boilers, rattling off the statistics: three furnaces per boiler, total grate surface two hundred square feet, heating surface six thousand square feet, fuel consumption 2.9 pounds of coal per horsepower per hour.

—How much do we carry? Eaker asked.

—A hundred and forty tons. We can burn anything, but she likes a good grade of anthracite. This donkey boiler powers the fans and two auxiliary pumps. Now, careful on the catwalk. Duck your head.

Beyond speech, beyond hearing, they gripped a brass handrail as they stared across the width of the hull. A gigantic mass of black-painted cast iron stirred and pulsed beneath the iron-plate overhead, relieved here and there with the gold glint of brass and the slick shining silver of oiled steel. Within it great levers rose and fell to alternating blasts of steam. Oil-shining rods extended and retracted. Huge castings shuttled back and forth, nodding and plunging with such swiftness the eye could barely follow. Oilers picked their way along flimsy catwalks, ministering to the laboring beast. At each revolution a thud and a hiss succeeded, and plumes of mist sprayed up, invisible at first, condensing into an opal mist as they touched the atmosphere.

He bent beneath the vibrating handrail, swung from a handgrip, and dropped to a perch atop a huge curved cast-iron tube. He balanced there as the ship rolled around him, as on either side great masses of metal flung themselves out and retracted, flung themselves out and retracted. He cupped his mouth to bellow, —This is a Reanie and Neafie direct-acting condensing engine. The engine has two cylinders of sixty-five inches bore, with a stroke of thirty-six inches. At full steam it makes thirty-six revolutions per minute, producing seven hundred and eighty horsepower. Remember when you're on deck yellin' orders, it takes time to stop all this metal, more time to make it go in the opposite direction.

Eaker leaned over the rail. —What exactly goes on here? I don't know much about engines.

This question pleased Theo enormously. Most of the deck officers didn't give a plugged nickel for what went on belowdecks; they rang the bell and that was the end of their knowledge or any wish for it. He yelled, —Well, I said this was a direct-acting engine.

—But what does that mean?

—Means the pistons lead directly to the crankshaft through connecting rods and crankpins. You've seen the engines on paddle-wheel ferries?

—The beam that goes up and down?

—Correct. If the piston rod connects to something like that, a beam or a crosshead, then the crosshead takes power to the crankshaft. That's a non-direct-acting engine.

As he warmed to his explanation he jumped from one casting to the next, bending to point as he explained each component's function. A machinist watched them from across the compartment. —This is Pirsson's patent double-vacuum condenser. We pump seawater through it to cool the exhausted steam.

—It seems to be leaking.

—It sure does. And we've got to fix it pretty soon or we're going to lose vacuum. Then all this iron's going to stop going back and forth. This evaporator makes all the water we need . . . Crankshaft's geared through the wheel aft of the engine. Right, the wooden one. That turns a pinion at a rate of nine to four. So, if at full speed the pistons turn the crankshaft at thirty-six revolutions per minute, how fast does the propeller shaft turn?

—Sixteen times a minute?

—Mr. Hubbard, a thunderous voice yelled. He turned to see MacNail hefting a huge wrench.

—Your arithmetic's fast but backward; the correct answer is eighty-one revolutions per minute. Come around this way and you can see the propeller shaft. —Yeah, Pappy?

McNail ignored the deck officer, addressing himself to Theo. —Sir, we've got that feed pump back together but there's still a shimmy in to her. Want me to take it down again?

—No, see how long it runs. Fix it when it stops. This is Pappy MacNail, my assistant engineer. Mr. Elisha Eaker, a volunteer officer.

—Hullo. Well, we found the packings.

—Where were they?

—Under a wagonload of desecrated vegetables.

—Secure steam to the condenser. Advise the captain we'll be at one-third power for about two hours during repairs.

MacNail nodded and rolled away. Theo cleared his throat, conscious he was lecturing, but not caring. —Now where were we? The screw has four blades. It is eighteen feet in diameter. New, with a clean bottom, this ship made thirteen and a half knots at full steam.

—Can we hoist it? To make better sail?

—No, but we have a clutch coupling controlled by this lever. That lets it spin when the engines are not in use.

Hubbard looked across the compartment, inhaling the astringent smells of grease, sperm oil, and steam. Someday he might marry, but these were his true loves now, the towering masses of machined metal that in their unending motion gave wings to the ship.

Yet they were only a crude glimpse of what they might one day become. A perfectly efficient engine was possible, one that translated all the caloric in fuel into useful work. Iron must give way to steel, and copper to bronze or even tougher compositions. Steam and the telegraph would weld the world together. Progress would subdue Nature, and those who designed its machines would receive the respect that was their due.

—I heard our engines were not in good condition, said Eaker, puncturing the bubble of his thought.

—We've been two years off Africa. Of course things aren't in their best shape just now. Crankshaft's out of line, for one thing. Valve gear's got to be refitted. But the boilers are my main worry.

—What's wrong with them?

—We've just steamed them to death. The riveting's loose. The iron's corroded from the saltwater feed. Leaks keep opening up, and we lose pressure.

MacNail came back with more tools. Theo flicked his watch open. —Well, that's about it, Mr. Eaker. No doubt you have matters to attend to topside.

—They aren't going to explode, are they?

—Explode? Hardly. Most of the boiler explosions you read about are from fools tying down the safeties. We won't be doing any racing, Mr. Eaker, and I will most definitely not be tying down any safeties. So don't lose any sleep over that.

A drumroll burred through the overhead, and both men stiffened.

—General quarters, said Eaker. —We're firing the guns this morning. Thanks for the tour of your Plutonian realm, Mr. Hubbard.

—Why, you're quite welcome, Mr. Eaker. Come back anytime at all.

When he was gone Theo looked after him, then at MacNail.

—Any hope?

—He's not got his head stuffed full of nonsense yet, at any rate.

—They'll soon see to that. You want to give me a hand here?

—Certainly, he said, forgetting the volunteer instantly as his mind moved forward to sealing the condenser. He put his hand on MacNail's shoulder, and jumped down into the bilges to help.

11

Landfall at Dawn ♦ Proper Attitude of Officers Toward the Possibility
of Action ♦ A Quarrel During General Quarters ♦ The Red Ensign
Allowed to Pass Unmolested ♦ The Hanging Man ♦
A Proposal from the Lieutenant of Marines

T HE indigo line had floated there since the first hint of light,
emerging gradually from the darkness like a residue of that
darkness undissolved by day. A thin, lowering shadow,
slightly heavier where trees presumably marked higher ground. But
this far off no sign of human presence marked the distant coast. Only
faintly fading hues, like those of an old aquarelle, that traced the
more distant variations of the low-lying shore, till at last they faded,
to north and south, into the rose mist of early morning.

Ker leaned at the port cathead, glassing for marks. He'd been on
deck since four, when, as navigator, he'd expected to pick up the light
on Sullivans Island. They never had, though they were within soundings. At last, for safety's sake, he'd hauled off, then watched the coast
emerge from darkness into cloudy day. The breeze was easterly with a
heavy swell from the north, a vestige of the gale they'd just struggled
through and a reminder another could be on them at any time.

Trezevant had given Hatteras a wide berth, staying sixty sea miles off the treacherous hook of sand long known as a sailor's graveyard. The sea and wind had dropped after that, and the wind had backed. They ran southwest by west from Diamond Shoals, paralleling the dropping away of bights and bays that ran down the Carolina coast from Lookout to Cape Romain. Then they'd sheered out on Claiborne's watch, feeling their way in from the east to avoid the shoals that barred the entrance to the capacious but shallow harbor within.

Girnsolver, saluting: —Morning, sor. Jack to the foretop, sor?

—Make it so, Bo's'n, but I doubt we'll see a pilot. I believe they have put out the lights as well.

He unrolled the chart and ran his eye over it again. He'd already calculated bearings and headings for the main channels. He went over them again, committing them to memory.

Till a shadow impinged on his attention. He looked up to find the blind silver eye on him, the gaunt frame waiting. Called out to Duycker to take the deck, and silently followed Ahasuerus below.

They'd seen little of the captain since New York. Ker encountered him only occasionally, pacing the quarter deck at night or standing at the stern looking down into the wake. The motionless silhouette spoke of a spirit in trial. When he'd reported noon position or asked for night orders, responses had come slowly, dictated with an absent air he found disturbing in his normally self-possessed commander.

Now he knocked and entered the stern cabin. —Claiborne, sir.

—Come in, Exec.

Trezevant sprawled in his accustomed seat in the quarter gallery. The telltale pendulumed above him like a censer in a Spanish cathedral. His folding table was set out. Fiddle boards anchored a steaming teapot, saucered cups, sugar cruet, jam pot, and a plate of scones melting with butter. He gestured hospitably, and Ker took a seat opposite, noting the hot food with relish. It was definitely time for breakfast.

—Any marks in sight? the captain asked him.

—None yet, sir. By the lead I'd say we're about eight miles off Morris Island. The wind could hardly be better for an entrance.

Trezevant nodded to the table. —Will you partake?

—I have the watch at the moment, sir.

—Who else is on deck?

—Mr. Duycker, sir.

—He will do very well alone. Join me, sir.

He knew the captain didn't like to discuss matters of duty at table, so they confined themselves to generalities. Trezevant reminisced about a visit he'd made to Charleston in '55. When they were done and Shippy had cleared the last crumb of scone and smear of blackberry, the captain folded down the fiddles and drew out a chart. Ker leaned forward, pinning the heavy paper against the lacquered tabletop. Trezevant selected a pencil with maddening calm. He needled the point on a scrap of sharkskin and laid it six miles east of Morris Island. —I presume you have made a study of the entrance?

—I have taken that liberty, sir.

—As you see, we are off the main channel, which runs parallel to the coast south of the geographical entrance before bending west to pass into the harbor proper. The city lies three miles within. You are familiar with its situation?

—I have not had the pleasure of a sojourn.

—The bar prevents direct access to the harbor. There are several smaller channels in, but they are narrow and deceptive. Captain Fox advised me to stand a dozen miles out. About here—to which position I intend to repair, once we've ascertained the lighting and buoying situation. That will be our rendezvous point with the other ships in the expedition.

—Should they not be here already, sir?

—That's been puzzling me as well. *Lane* I do not expect for some time. She was making heavy weather when we lost her. But the others should be here. I hope no misadventure befell *Baltic* en route.

Ker bent over the chart. The one he'd studied was of the approaches and the outer capes. Trezevant's ran from the outer islands all the way in to the city.

Charleston's situation was not unlike that of Manhattan Island. A peninsula, bounded on the west by the Ashley and on the east by the Cooper. Sullivans corresponded to Long Island, to the east; and Morris covered the southern side of the entrance, though thrust down and to seaward like a pugnacious lower jaw, rather as if Staten Island had been rotated counterclockwise and moved east. But the captain did not seem concerned about the city itself. He was pointing to a bone stuck in the craw of the main channel.

—This is Sumter. It's supposed to show a light, but as you have reported, we have observed none.

—I mounted to the crosstrees before dawn, and made a close study with the glass. They've obviously doused the lighthouses. There's no sign of the Rattlesnake lightship, either.

—Let's look at the disposition of the rebel batteries.

This time the unfolded paper was a page from the *New York Tribune,* dated the morning they'd sailed. Trezevant acknowledged his questioning look with a half smile. —That's right. That fool Greeley's sheet. But they have a correspondent reporting sub rosa from the city. He reports a large number of cannon at Moultrie, north of Sumter across the channel. They cover the fort and any approach from the east. Another battery is reported at Fort Johnson, to the west across an area of marsh and tideflat. The final, smaller battery is reported at Cummings Point, less than a mile due south of the fort.

The captain refolded the journal and added in a dry tone, —As you see, if this information is correct, the fort is well covered. We know Mr. Davis sent Beauregard to assume command from the locals. I have no doubt his dispositions are made in a professional manner.

—I see, sir. He considered, then got up. —Your orders?

—We will stay well offshore for now. Trezevant peered at the chart, checking the etched-in numbers that delineated depth. —You may heave to, or sail on and off at your discretion. The engines may be secured, to conserve fuel, but do not draw fires under the boilers.

—The guns are loaded with solid shot, sir. Should I reload with shell?

—No. We do not hold an overplus of fuzes, and I don't see this situation coming to blows. Trezevant let the chart snap shut and slotted it between the deck beams.

—You really do not, sir? I myself am not so sanguine.

The captain said quietly, —But then, you are quite a young man yet, Claiborne.

He stood silent, feeling like a green midshipman who has unwittingly trespassed upon the quarterdeck. Trezevant drummed his fingers, then said abruptly, —I do not relish battle. A disinclination one of our profession hesitates to confess. But given those on whom we would be turning our guns, I trust you will understand my misgivings.

A tap at the door. At a nod, he opened it. Eaker stood there. —Sir, masthead reports a small steamer to the northwest.

—Within the bar, or off?

—I should guess within.

—Is it approaching? Trezevant asked.

—No sir. Seems to be stationary, making black smoke.

—Have you inspected it? Ker asked him. Eaker shook his head. —Then do not "guess," if you please. Go aloft, observe it closely, and report back what you descry.

The Northerner looked around the cabin, as if expecting someone else to be in there with them; hesitated; then left.

—A picketboat, I should think, Trezevant said.

—Most likely, sir. Set to observe our movements. He thought a moment, then added, —We might attempt to capture it, and ascertain the state of events ashore.

—Unto, unto, Lieutenant. One "captures" an enemy. No war has been declared, nor do I propose to begin it. We will stand by out here until the responsible authority arrives.

—Aye aye, sir.

—Drill at the guns this morning. And keep the men occupied, especially the waisters. A certain slackness has overtaken them. I should like to see the ground tackle overhauled. Have Mr. Schuyler drill the marines as well. Keep them up to the mark, sir, to the mark. Have we any cases for mast?

—The master at arms has two or three names on his list, I believe.

—We will make an example of them at noon.

—Aye aye, sir. Ker stood for a moment longer, wondering if there was not something unsaid. Trezevant had already remarked that his heart wasn't in this mission. Now he had confessed to an unwillingness to give battle. What yet lay buried in the captain's soul? Or had he shared it all?

But the captain had returned to his pondering study of the chart, and his gloomy expression did not invite further questioning. Ker stood for a moment longer, still waiting, still wondering; then silently took his leave.

Topside again, Ker took the deck back from Nick Duycker. Trezevant came up shortly thereafter. When the captain nodded he gave the word to beat to quarters.

When the tattoo sounded, a quick rattle from the marines' drums, a rumble of boots and port tackle, shouted commands, and grating gun trucks filled the ship. The topmen raced for the yards. The boys ran water tubs and fire buckets up from below. Lieutenant Schuyler loped past carrying his naked saber point down. Ker cast a glance round the horizon, making certain any maneuvers would not embarrass them with shipping. He was also hoping to see *Pocahontas* or *Baltic* or the black heavy hull of *Powhatan.* But the open sea, still lumpy with a heavy swell, lay empty. Only the indigo line to the west interrupted it, and no word came from the lookout aloft.

—Port Division manned and ready.

—Starboard Division manned and ready.

—Captain of the tops reports manned and ready.

—Marine detachment ready for action.

Ker turned and saluted. —Captain, all hands are at quarters. The guns are run out and we are ready for action.

Trezevant was nodding acknowledgment when a disturbance from forward distracted his attention. He frowned. —Mr. Claiborne, would you attend to that?

He found a knot of seamen gathered around the forward pivot. One of the gunners lay on his back. The Negro stood with hands dangling.

—What's going on. Archbold. Archbold! Get up.

The pivot captain flinched and sat up. He rubbed his jaw, then spat blood and tobacco juice onto the deck. —The bumbo here's gone mad, sir. 'E struck me.

He turned to the black man. —Hanks, what have you to say? Did you strike the gun captain?

The big man's face was still suffused with blood. He didn't answer, or look at any of them around him, and Ker was about to speak again when he said slowly, —He use provokin' words.

—I see. What sort of words, Hanks?

—Say we don't know how to handle the gun.

—Archbold? Get up from there, man. What about it?

The petty officer rose slowly, looking at Hanks with a sort of wary vicious gloating. —'E's not goin' by the drill, sir. Got some tricky-clever way 'e's frictioning 'is carriage. I told him we wasn't having none of his nigger riggin', we was doin' things navylike. Got to have discipline 'ere, sir. Can't be lettin' a man blow down his gun captain.

Ker looked around for Babcock, but instead saw Eaker pushing through the throng. The gunnery officer would do. He said coldly, —The rest of you, back to your posts. We are still at general quarters. Mr. Eaker, do you need assistance maintaining order among your men?

The volunteer looked around. —What's the trouble here?

—It seems one of your men resents being corrected by his superior, Ker told him. —The captain does not look lightly at quarreling among the crew, especially when we are standing to the guns. You will place him on report at once with the master-at-arms, for captain's mast at noon.

Eaker did not reply, only stared at the silent Negro.

Ker exercised them for two hours, drilling the gun crews at ricochet firing, then reloading before calling away repel boarders and then the boarding party. For the latter evolution he took command of the forecastle, leading the mock attacks with saber and pistol. At last the boatswain passed "Secure from general quarters." Ker hung his side arms in his cabin, bathed his face, and was back on deck when the lookout called down a sail to seaward. He swung the telescope in that direction, to be rewarded with a buff speck against the shining hemisphere of sea and sky.

The sail closed over the next hour as *Owanee* made easy easting under courses and topsails. Studying it through the glass, Ker made it as a small brig or snow. He could not make out her flag. Given the storm, she was most likely from Europe or England. Her course would bring her close aboard.

He stroked his beard, mulling over his options. A sea officer had to be something of a diplomat, and something of a lawyer as well at times. The problem reminded him of the Napoleonic-era cases they'd studied at the Academy. Under normal conditions, a warship meeting a merchant on the high seas would simply return the latter's courtesies and sail on. But conditions were not normal. The Charlestonians had closed the port, if not officially, then de facto, through dousing the lights and removing the entrance buoys.

If the tariff could not be collected, then, as an agent of the federal government, Captain Trezevant could deny entrance to foreign commerce. As far as Ker personally was aware, however, the general government still considered Charleston to be within the Union and the port still open. Turning away a foreign flag would thus be tantamount to admitting rebellion had begun, and not only that, might be construed as an unfriendly act by the country whose ship was refused entry.

It was a nice quandary and at last he decided it was one the captain should resolve. He sent Midshipman Eddowes below to present his respects and to ask him to step on deck. To be forehanded he told Rapp to make up the hoist "Heave to and await boarding," but not to break it yet; and sent Jerrett to tell Mr. Eaker to man the forward pivot. The crew were still on deck, securing tackle from the drills, and within a minute or two the New Yorker reported ready.

When Trezevant came up he listened soberly to Ker's explanation. He placed the glass briefly to his eye to conn out the other ship. By now it had hoisted the Red Ensign.

—Shall we order her to heave to, sir? I've manned the forward pivot in case she needs a shot across her bow.

Trezevant said slowly, —I do not believe it is my place to do so. I will permit her to proceed.

He chewed on this for a moment. —Should we not at least inspect for contraband, sir? I believe that would lie within our purview, under the Treaty of Paris.

The captain clapped the deck glass shut, handed it back, and turned for the companionway. —No, we will not. I have said we are not in a blockading situation.

When he was gone below, Ker stood troubled, watching the brig close. She didn't dip, but then, it was possible she didn't recognize them as a man-of-war. Nor did she bear off, which would have been common courtesy in a vessel running downwind. But he wasn't really thinking about her. He was thinking about Trezevant. For there it had been again, that curious passivity in the man he'd always thought of as the most active and pertinacious officer he knew.

The flutter of scarlet nodded, and he started, recalled to the deck. —There's the dip. Return it, Rapp, return it.

The quartermaster shouted, and *Owanee*'s big ensign aft slid downward, paused, then lofted again. The brig's colors climbed once more, two-blocked, and she glided rapidly down their port side a cable's length off. As she showed her quarter gallery he put the glass to his eye again. Seamen stared back. A fellow in a dark coat raised his cap from near the wheel. A stern board gave her name, but too distant now for him to make it out. He told Eddowes to log her as a British merchant bound for Charleston. Then watched her sail on, the broad path of smoothed water under her counter disturbing to him somehow, suggesting unwelcome thoughts.

———

They reached the rendezvous a little after seven bells, to find only empty sea. At local noon he took his sun sight, then put them on a northerly tack with orders to the officer of the deck to run six miles north, then twelve miles south. He calculated the distance of the horizon in his head. Given the height of *Owanee*'s crosstrees, the lookout should see the topgallants of a full-rigged ship twenty miles off. The sky was still overcast but the atmosphere clear. If *Pocahontas, Baltic, Harriet Lane,* or *Powhatan* showed, they could not miss one another.

The boatswain's pipe sounded for mast a little after noon. Ker had arranged the cases in rough order of heinousness. The most serious seemed to be Hanks's, so he retained it till last.

As always at captain's mast the proceedings were swift and the red tape minimal. A marine with a loaded and bayoneted rifle stood by as the accused's division officer brought each miscreant forward. The subject of the proceedings listened at rigid attention while the master-at-arms read whatever the charge was: bringing liquor aboard, committing a nuisance on the berthing deck, using insulting language, et cetera. Trezevant asked for any explanations or circumstances, then awarded punishment.

Hanks had no better response at mast than he'd had on deck, and the captain awarded him to be hung from the spanker boom. Suiting the action to the sentence, the gunner was stripped to the waist and led aft. His wrists were triced behind him, and a quickly knotted hempen bight looped round his neck. A line party of a dozen hands took their places at the downhaul.

As his division officer, Eaker had followed his man aft to witness punishment. They were standing together, awaiting the master-at-arms's return with Dr. Steele, when he touched his cap to Ker. —A word, sir?

—What is it, Mr. Eaker?

—Is this not an extreme punishment?

Ker raised his eyebrows slightly. —For striking a petty officer in the performance of his duties? I should think not. Ask your warrant how many lashes he'd have gotten in the old days.

—But to be hung for it?

—Ah. He placed a hand on the other's shoulder and walked him a little distance away. —I forget, you are as yet unused to naval custom. We are not putting your man to death. Merely teaching him a lesson, by a short suspension by the neck. I emphasize short. The master-at-arms has gone to find the minute glass.

—I see.

—Congress has abolished flogging, but specified no acceptable punishment in its place. Thus leaving such corrections as are necessary to the individual commander's imagination. Hanks is fortunate. I have seen men branded aboard other ships, but Captain Trezevant considers permanently disfiguring punishments barbaric.

—I'm glad he's so enlightened.

He studied Eaker's expression, unsure whether the remark was meant in irony. But aside from a faint flush, he could read nothing into the other's visage.

The master-at-arms returned, set the minute glass on deck, and glanced aloft. Steele waddled to the bulwark and leaned against it with a grunt. He looked bored and hot, which made Claiborne wonder what he'd been doing. He took out his own timepiece and flicked the cover open. Beside him Eaker stared at the black man. Hanks stood with hands lashed together behind him, immobile and expressionless.

—Stand to the line. Stand by . . . heave away.

The line drew straight, and Hanks's feet left the deck and he soared a full twelve feet into the air. Twice the height of a man he dangled in the wind, and his back arched and his feet kicked as he wheeled in the sky. The hemp sank into his dark flesh like string into a soft cheese. As his back rotated toward them the marks of old scars came into view. They were darker than the flesh around them, which was cruelly knotted and drawn. Ker thought they looked like the multiple strokes of a lightning storm. They arced and twisted from a thick central root, splaying apart up his back and around his shoulders.

———

Four, Hanks thought, fighting not to shit himself, fighting not to struggle.

He dangled helplessly by his neck, and the heavy rope stopped his breath and blood. The pull of it was tremendous, drawing him apart, as if someone were hanging on his legs, dragging down on him.

When they'd pulled him up off the deck he'd had a moment as close to screaming in terror as he'd ever come. But he couldn't scream, because he couldn't breathe. He tried not to fight the rope. If you fought it, the sharp-edged hemp tore the flesh open like a whip. He'd seen it happen to other men.

Five.

He was counting so as not to think. He was thinking so as not to panic. The officers had to let him down before he died. He could go without breathing for a minute. Anyone could. But his body did what it wanted. It wasn't listening to him anymore.

Six. Please, Lord, how much longer? He was losing count.

Flashes of light started burning through his head, as if the top of it were coming off and the sun were pouring in through an empty hole. His hands began to work. He couldn't stop them trying to get free, trying to break the ropes.

Six. Six. What came after six?

He could not remember, and he could not breathe.

Ker turned his head slightly. Beside him the new officer stood tensely erect, holding a handkerchief to his mouth. His normal pallor was now perfectly paper white.

—Are you quite well, Mr. Eaker?

—It is nothing, sir.

He said softly, —We might disagree about the method. But surely you see some form of discipline is necessary. We cannot countenance division in a world as small as a ship.

Hanks's legs drew up, then straightened. Dangling on the line, he whirled slowly to face forward. The wind fluttered the cuffs of his trowsers. His eyes were squeezed closed, and a livid hue suffused his face. A strawy liquid ran from one dangling heel.

—For God's sake, he heard Eaker whisper.

—Another half minute. He blinked, swallowing; kept his eye firmly fixed on his watch.

Fifteen feet above them, Hanks had passed beyond counting, beyond struggle, beyond thought itself, into a place where bloody lightning crashed through him. He no longer felt his body dangling. He had left it. Floated somewhere beyond it, out in the darkness of infinite night. Like the black of a moonless night at sea. But beyond the darkness was another place. He moved forward, in what, he could not tell; for he was not in a body. He knew he was not the body, he was something else; something free of the body. And now he moved forward again, away from the light, away from life, maybe, but toward what, he did not know.

Then he looked past and through the darkness into a blacker darkness not only beyond form and void but possessed of a quality that was opposed to all light. It was like a cave in the darkness; it opened, welcoming, inviting him as he moved toward it.

He couldn't see anything. But he could tell, somehow, that something was waiting for him in there. Something that knew him and expected him. Something bad, something dangerous. But try as he might he couldn't call its face or what it wanted.

The bundle swinging above them made a choking sound. His great arms bulged, but the line at his wrists held against the strain. The ship rolled, and the gaff halyard and its dark burden pendulumed far out over the wake and then back again, wheeling over the men who watched beneath it. Gulls screamed, hovering, bright black eyes darting hopefully.

—Time, Ker said simultaneously with the master-at-arms. The

line handlers walked slack into the line, then paid out hand over hand.

The hanging man descended. When his feet hit the deck Ker stepped up to him and pulled the noose off. The gunner buckled at the knees, staggered, and then, incredibly, found his balance. He stood upright. His lids flew open, and bright-red eyes stared round at the faces that watched him curiously around the afterdeck. Tears ran down from them, and the tears too were red with blood.

—Get that line off him. Off his wrists, too.

Hanks blinked and shook his head. He could not think straight. He'd been somewhere dark . . . someone had been talking to him . . . then he'd jerked his eyes open suddenly, to find light in them and his feet on deck and his trowsers wet and the curious hard faces of the white officers all around. He wanted to let go and fall down. But he mustered all his fainting strength and somehow he didn't. He swayed, but he didn't fall.

Ker looked at the man curiously. For a moment he had seemed about to speak. But then his puffy lips relaxed. The master-at-arms loosed his wrist lashings, then knelt to cut free his feet. The gunner reeled with the roll of the stern, rubbing his wrists as he looked vacantly about.

The doctor stepped up. Steele thumbed his lids open, then thumped him in the chest. The black man did not react or even look at him. —Observe, said the medico sententiously, throwing his arm out with a gesture of demonstration. —Some hæmorrhaging of the sclera, or white matter of the eyeball; but it is minor and will not affect his sight. A bit of bruising about the neck. But aside from that, he is fit for duty. The more animal natures are less affected by trauma than those of more finely tuned constitution.

Hanks looked around. The blood-flecked, blood-weeping eyes peered into each of their faces. But still he did not speak. He took a step, and then another, shuffling his feet forward over the deck.

He walked slowly and heavily to the companionway, where a visage of scarified ebony waited. Ahasuerus put his arm around him, the serving boy took his other. They supported him on either side as he groped his way below.

The captain wanted all officers at dinner that evening. Ker checked that the wardroom was swabbed and polished and the lampglobes washed, that Uncle Ahasuerus understood a special effort was required, and Shippy was in a clean shirt. They sat down at seven with the last of the African Madeira, and passed from that to a baked ham. The last courses were dishes of Spanish raisins and French bonbons. When the table was cleared and the port broached, when cheroots and pipes had been lit, Trezevant cleared his throat. —Gentlemen, if you will favor me?

They ranged themselves in listening attitudes, except Steele, who lunged forward to replenish his glass yet again. Ker signaled the servers to withdraw, and permitted himself the liberty of crossing his legs as he lit one of the Havanas he'd replenished in New York.

—Gentlemen. My career in the employ of the United States dates from April of 1821. Thus, forty years this month. By no means the longest term of service in the navy, but long enough to teach me, as you too will learn, that one is occasionally sent on a mission that has not been carefully thought through.

The captain glanced at the overhead as he outlined, in briefer terms, the situation as he'd laid it out to Ker that morning. Claiborne followed his glance to where the gun-deck skylight was a black square grated against the night. A saffron blur beyond it might be the face of the helmsman, lit by the binnacle. The fabric of the sloop creaked as oak and spruce and white pine accommodated themselves to the sea.

Trezevant continued, —We are therefore in the situation of being ordered to relieve a position which cannot be relieved without triggering war. In effect, we will force the rebels to begin hostilities. I do not gainsay the political cunning of such a maneuver, but I see little possibility of tactical success. Certainly *Owanee* alone is not possessed of sufficient fighting power to force a passage. In view of which, I have determined to take no rash action.

—Sir, if I may venture a word.

—Certainly, Mr. Schuyler.

The marine lieutenant rasped in his damaged voice, —Sir, I have given much consideration to this matter since you spoke to us before getting under way. You're right, it'd be rash to go directly at Sumter. However, we could land a party on Morris Island, to the south of the inlet. Between my boys and the landing party, we could muster eighty men. If we spiked the guns at Cummings Point, you could run in to Sumter with less chance of damage.

—That is a small force with which to assault a position.

—Small forces daringly led have won victories, sir. In case of need, the ship's guns could back us up.

Steele cleared his throat. —But the captain's point, that he didn't want to initiate hostilities. Such an attack would clearly do so.

Trezevant said, —Exactly, Doctor. I appreciate that counsel, Mr. Schuyler. But our orders do not direct us to open the ball; and I shall endeavor with all my power not to do so. We are here to peacefully succor a garrison which, in my view, if the radicals in Washington do not succeed in pressing to an open break now, will most probably be withdrawn once the South's secession is officially recognized. Therefore, I will proceed according to the letter of my orders, rather than what we all recognize as their spirit.

Ker was startled when the next voice was that of the new man, Eaker. —Sir, on what do you base your understanding of the "spirit" of your orders? It seems to me that they mean exactly what they say, and that the administration is simply determined to maintain the national position.

Trezevant looked taken aback to be challenged at his own table. —Politicians follow, sir, they do not lead.

—Then should we not show them the way, by determined action? Or shall we too play upon the lyre as Rome kindles about us?

The others stirred, glancing at the young man who sat slouched in their midst. Ker hitched his chair forward, about to silence him, but

Trezevant nodded to the company and rose. Taken by surprise, they started to their feet. Chairs clattered down. —You have fire, Mr. Eaker. But zeal must be tempered with caution. Exec, would you join me in my cabin?

—Yes sir, he said, stubbing his cheroot out and rising quickly. The others stood in silence. Reaching for his cap, he followed the captain out. They were entering his cabin when Trezevant asked him to send back for Eaker as well.

12

ELI closed the captain's door. He wasn't sure yet when one
should come to attention, so he simply stood. Trezevant and
the exec were seated before a small table. A Betty lamp oscil-
lated above them with the roll and pitch of the gun-deck beams. And
it came to him how this bare, tight, warm compartment with its pine
paneling and smell of bilge and mildew held just now more power
more tightly concentrated than even his father's richly appointed office in Manhattan.

—You called for me, sir?

The captain said angrily, —I did, Mr. Eaker. Your remarks this
evening struck me as close to insolence.

He lowered his head, wondering what had possessed him to speak
out. He had no official place here. Trezevant could put him off the
ship in a rowboat, if he desired. —I meant no offense, sir. I simply
felt we were sent here to take action.

—Unto, sir, unto; and so we shall; but I cannot run a gantlope
with nothing more than the *Tribune* to guide me. Trezevant leaned
forward, and the buttery light from above threw his face into jagged
relief, like the moon's terminator seen through a telescope. —I will

forgive your outspokenness once, sir, on account of your newness to the service. But not again.

—Yes, sir.

—Now, sir, I understand you are "well acquent" with Charleston, as Robert Burns would say.

The sudden change of direction took him by surprise. He cleared his throat. —Ah, I visited for my father's firm, sir.

Claiborne said, —The harbor, Mr. Eaker; how familiar are you with it?

He pulled out his handkerchief and blotted his brow, his lips, searching for time to think, trying to concentrate on the question. The room seemed close and far too warm. He felt eddies of heat from the circling lamp. Or maybe he was feverish again. *Owanee* had no quarter gallery proper, as a ship of the line or frigate had. But there was a large outward sloping window that stood open. Through it came the rush and murmur of the sea. The question, the question, they were waiting for him to answer. In point of fact he'd hardly glimpsed the harbor. He'd arrived by rail, taken a brougham to his father's factor at Broad and King, and departed the same way, without venturing seaward of the Battery promenade. But instead of explaining this he said, for some reason he himself was not sure of, —Well, I should say tolerably familiar.

—Excellent. Trezevant pulled a paper tube out of the overhead. —Join us, please, and refresh your memory with this chart. Whiskey?

—I don't indulge, thanks.

—I've asked the first luff to ready the cutter for a pull in to Sumter.

Eli felt a coolness move over him like an advancing cloud, or like the enveloping mist from a fountain on a hot day. —And you have me in mind for this expedition?

—If you should feel moved to back your fiery words this afternoon.

And there was nothing else for him to say to that but, —I do, sir. If those are your orders.

Trezevant nodded, and flattened the chart where it had sprung up

into a tight recoiling. —We are on a westerly heading just now, showing no lights. I have asked Mr. Claiborne to run us within the main
bar and proceed as far north as is consistent with our not being seen
from shore. You will have two miles to row to reach the channel entrance, at which point the making tide will set you into the harbor.
You know where Sumter is. A light burns on the fort. You will not be
armed. This is not a warlike foray, merely a communication with the
garrison. I have prepared a note for Major Anderson. You will destroy
it if intercepted by local forces.

Eli shifted in his chair, feeling slightly disoriented. They were
both looking at him, so he said, —Yes sir, go on.

—Should the written message be lost or destroyed, simply inform
the major that I am here in *Owanee,* that at present forces outside the
bar are insufficient to come to his aid, but that additions are expected
hourly. The tide will turn at two o'clock. We will stand by within the
bar until you return, showing a blue light. I should very much prefer
that you return before dawn.

—I will do so if physically possible, Captain.

Claiborne said, —I must tell you that when Captain Trezevant in-
formed me of his intent I was most insistent that I be permitted to
command the boat. I was told in no uncertain terms that my place
was aboard.

Eli nodded, already starting to wonder why the captain hadn't let
Claiborne go, had chosen him instead of the exec or Master Duycker.
Trezevant said, —The boatswain will second you in the cutter with a
picked dozen of our best oarsmen. Take a compass, and a dark
lantern in case you have to signal. Do you have any questions, sir?

He couldn't think of any. The captain rose and they stood as well,
and after a word or two further he showed them to the door.

Eli went below and changed his smallclothes. He put the blue undress uniform back on. He wound his watch and wrapped it in oilskin, and pulled on his reefer jacket. Then he went up on deck.

The cutter, an open longboat that normally resided capsized on the spar deck, had been righted and hoisted out to the rail. It swung there, snugged close by tending lines. Babcock and Girnsolver stood together at the bulwark, watching the men pass tackle and oars up from the deck.

—Gunner. Bo's'n.

Babcock nodded his bald head; Girnsolver quickly put his cap back on and knuckled it. Eli said to the old man, —First luff's going to round up and drop us in the water. After that she's ours. I'm still green at this, Warrant Officer Girnsolver. Have we got everything we'll need?

—Not taking much, sor. Leathers for the oars. Line and anchors. Keg of water and another of salt horse, case we get blown out. Signal flags. Dark lantern. Four rifles, three pistols, and cutlasses and boarding axes.

He blinked. —I understood the captain to say we wouldn't be carrying arms.

Babcock said, —Different orders from Mr. Claiborne, sir.

Girnsolver murmured, —We'll pull 'em out if you want, but 'tis better to have them, sor. I mind when I was on the old *Essex,* with Captain Porter—

—No, no, if he thinks we need them, leave them in.

The Virginian appeared from the darkness. —Are you ready to hoist away, Mr. Eaker?

—I am assured we are, sir.

—Mr. Thurston, lay her into the wind. Make us a lee. Bo's'n, take charge and put the cutter in the water.

The exec stood fast as Girnsolver passed orders, the deck gang casting off tackle and putting their backs to the lines to sway the deadweight of the cutter out over the lightless sea. He said to Eli, —Remember the turn of the tide, which I calculate for between one-thirty and two-thirty or thereabouts. You have your watch and some lucifers, I assume.

Eli said he did, and after a moment added, in a lower tone, —You told Babcock to put arms in the boat?

—Perhaps I misunderstood Captain Trezevant's order. Those you

I should not like you and your men to
extended his hand. —Good luck,

ly. He wasn't sure how he felt. It was all
t chaffering in the wardroom, the next up
to a hostile harbor at night. He still felt
, he told the exec.

thundering, taken aback as she headed up
a few feet apart, watching as the cutter's keel
kissed the   figures appeared atop the bulwarks and then
sank downward. He counted a dozen of them. With himself and
Girnsolver, there'd be fourteen men.

—Off for glory, eh?

It was the voice of the little engineer, dry and sardonic. He faced
the darkness defensively. —I'm not going for "glory," Mr. Hubbard. I
was ordered to, by the captain.

—I'm sure you were. What puzzles me is why they're giving you
the chance to distinguish yourself.

—I've been to Charleston before.

—*They've* all been to Charleston too, Mr. Eaker. That don't wash.
When *they* give people like us something, beware.

—*Timeo Danaos et dona ferentis*, eh?

—What's that?

—I fear the Greeks, even when they bear gifts. The *Aeneid.*

Hubbard was silent, and for a moment Eli feared he'd offended
the prickly little man. It wouldn't surprise him if he took a classical
reference as patronizing. But he said only, —Something like that.
Anyway, be careful.

He felt something poke him in the stomach. It took a moment
before he recognized it as Hubbard's hand, and took it.

—Where's the boat officer? Mr. Eaker, they're ready for you.

He turned away and stumbled toward the bulwark, urged by invisible hands in the dark. The gleam of a momentarily unslotted dark
lantern; Girnsolver, a few feet ahead. He clambered awkwardly up after the old man and found a Jacob's ladder beneath his boots. He got

a few steps down it, then stopped, watching fascinated the surge and leap of the dark mass below him. It slammed against the hull with a crunching boom, as if fighting to get at him, to crush him. When it rose again he closed his eyes and let go. Someone grunted as he slammed into them. He groped for the stern sheets and sat up, struggling against vertigo and nausea as the cutter surged high and then dropped away.

—Cast off the painter, a voice said from above, and he recognized it as Claiborne's and shouted back, —Cutter away.

—Oars out. Dip oars. Give way together, said Girnsolver, who had gained the stern too and settled now beside him, gripping the tiller. —Did ye want the hellum, sor?

—You may keep it, Bo's'n. I imagine you have been on expeditions of this sort before.

—Indeed so, sor, indeed so. I recall back in '38 we had what they called the Mosquito Fleet, we rowed all through south Florida chasin' the Seminoles; and the marines wouldn't bear a hand, they wanted us to do all the dirty work while they kept their white belts clean.

To the accompaniment of muffled shouts, the clack and squeal of blocks, and the shuddering creak of stays under strain, the sloop departed from them. From a looming presence, both menacing and comforting, it began to slip away. When it had melted into the night the universe was totally black. No stars, no moon penetrated the gloom. The cutter danced on the swells. A steady cold wind cooled his cheeks. He opened his eyes wide and after some seconds noticed a disappearing radiance on the horizon. It puzzled him before he decided it must be the luminescent loom of the seceded city. Their direct sight of it was blocked by the Sea Islands, but that glow beyond the darkness was Charleston.

—What's your plan, Boats?

—Heading nor'-n'r'east, sor. Running by the wind, and we'll toss the lead presently.

—Do you think you can steer us to Sumter?

—Can pretty sartin get us around the point. Past that they should be showin' a light to steer on.

The old Yankee sounded like he knew what he was doing. —Very well, carry on, he told him.

The regular thump and swish of the oars went on for an interminable time. He checked his watch, shielding it from the spray that from time to time burst over the gunwale. He licked bitter brine from his lips. They were into the ebb. The black tide around them was moving, and they were moving on its surface. Yet it seemed as if the men pulled without progress, that they labored like Tantalus. Till almost ten, when Girnsolver said in a low voice, —A craft ahead, sor.

—Whereabouts? I don't see it.

—Runnin' dark, a point off to larboard.

—Uh, and which way was larboard, again?

—To port, sor, to port! See her boiler glowin' off the smoke! An' some lubber's got a hatch cracked aft. Shall I alter?

—Yes, do. To landward, if you can.

The tiller creaked and as the bow swung he caught a fiery gleam in the darkness, a fainter luminescence aft of it. It might be the picket steamer he'd glimpsed earlier. If it was, and if it hadn't moved, they must be drawing abreast of Cummings Point. He looked carefully to port, keeping his sight above the line of the horizon. The city glow, closer now, silhouetted a low blackness. He tried to recall the chart, and the depths along the point.

The seas grew more violent, peaking and cresting, it seemed, directly beneath them. He clung to the gunwale as icy water dashed over them. The men pulled grimly, not even bothering to curse.

—By the mark, two, whispered the leadsman. Girnsolver muttered, —We're out the channel. That's why she's so offish here. Might be time to muffle the fins now, sor.

The rowers stopped, and the oars grated inboard. He smelled the greased leather as the men worked it into the oarlocks. When they began rowing again he noticed the glow had shifted. They were headed in now, with the wind nearly at their backs. The sea was behind them too, and from time to time a swell lifted the stern and rushed them forward through the darkness with dizzying speed.

His feet felt cold. He reached down and was startled to find the

bottom of the boat filled six inches deep. He muttered to Girnsolver,
—We took a good deal of water from the last swell.

—That's not spray, sor. We're leaking.

He looked down into the liquid darkness. Now he noticed that
two of the shadows up forward were continually bending and
straightening. —Leaking? he repeated.

The old man muttered, —Yes sor, they was going to survey this
cutter, she was so stove up after Africky, but she got put right back
aboard when we had to shove off so sticky fast.

—I see.

—Now, I don't hear so well these days, sor. Let me know, you hear
surf close.

—I hear something off to port. Where's the fort, do you think?
Close now, I hope?

—It ain't far inside the point. Should pick up its light pretty soon.
We keep off the bottom, we'll be there fast with this breeze an' this
tide behind us.

Eli pressed his bosom gently, where he'd placed the letter from
Captain Trezevant. It was wrapped in oilskin and bound around with
marling. If capture seemed imminent, he decided to go overboard
with it. Try to make land, and find his way to the fort from there. He
could swim well enough, though he wasn't sure how long he'd last in
water this cold.

The men rowed on in uncomplaining silence. He could see their
outlines now against the growing glow. Their backs rose and fell.
They did not seem to tire, though they'd been rowing for nearly an
hour now.

A distinct rushing sound penetrated his consciousness, and he
turned to the warrant. Girnsolver said, —I hear it too, sor. I'll put her
a point or two to starboard, but damn me, we should have seen that
light by now.

He got up and stood in the stern sheets, placing a hand on the
old man's shoulder to steady himself against the pitch and sway, and
looked for a long time off in the direction of the surf. —I see some-

thing white off to port. Long and white and sort of glimmering.

—Swell breakin' on rocks, sure enough.

—We don't want to land there.

—No sor, stove and shiver us for sure. I figure to swing in behind and take her in on the lee side. Shallow there, but we don't draw much. If she takes the bottom, why, then you can walk in with the dark lantern and we'll stand off for ye.

Eli told him that sounded like a prudent plan.

The city crept into view ahead, a prickling of distant lights that wavered and danced in the night wind. To left and right stretched darkness, save for a few scattered lamps far off to the east. Eli huddled in the stern, wishing he'd thought to borrow Claiborne's mackintosh again. The spray had wet him through, his feet were soaked, and he shuddered with the cold.

He realized only gradually that a greater and more profound darkness than that of the night was looming above them. Girnsolver whispered for the men to lay on their oars, and the black wall passed silently down their port side. He heard the seas thundering apart at its base, could see their ghostly glimmer, but strain his eyes as he might could gain no glint from above them. Trezevant had said the fort would burn a beacon. Had it been abandoned? Or perhaps already taken, and within its darkened walls waited not Anderson's troops but those of the secessionists.

—Stand by your oars . . . out oars . . . give way.

The locks creaked again, muffled yet still all too distinct to his pricked ears. The distant city lights swung away, and they rolled, coming beam on, and slammed full tilt into something solid, a piling or marker of some kind, so hard men shot off the thwarts into the ceiling boards, cursing in whispers.

—Where exactly are you heading, Girnsolver?

—Sor, I'm betting there's a pier in here som'urs. Got to have summar for lighters to lie alongside, load out their supplies.

—I don't see any lights.

—Puzzling to me too, sor. Reckon we just go on in and find out what we got. In oars! Boathook, stand by! Bowline, to port!

A dazzling beam suddenly shot out ahead of them. Eli threw up his arm, expecting it to be followed by a fusillade. Instead a challenge rang from the dark. —What boat's that?

—Cutter from U.S.S. *Owanee,* communication for Major Anderson.

He heard shouting, but nothing that sounded like an invitation to land. Till another voice called, —Thank God you are here at last. Throw us your line.

The gunwale grated on granite riprap, and rope rattled as the lines went up. He stood, blinking as the lanterns played on his face and fell to his uniform, then searched among the oarsmen, who were stretching and shaking out their arms as they sat at their places. He still couldn't see anyone behind the lights. —We're navy, he said. Come to deliver a message.

—Come up, sir, come up. We've been waiting for you fellows far too long.

—Good luck, sor, Girnsolver muttered as he placed his boots and stepped across, received by the outstretched arms of several soldiers. They let go as soon as he had firm footing, and he found himself facing two shadows.

—I'm Eli Eaker, from the *Owanee.* He saluted, then found his hand gripped roughly and shaken again and again.

—I am the officer of the guard, Lieutenant Hall. This gentleman is Captain Abner Doubleday, second in command. We certainly are glad to see the navy.

—You say you have a message for the major? Doubleday said.

—From Captain Trezevant, commanding. To be delivered personally.

—Please accompany me, sir.

—Uh, before we do, may my men come up on the pier? I should like them to be able to get out of the boat and rest a bit. They have had a hard pull in here tonight. Oh, and could we borrow a couple of buckets? We've had rather a leaky time of it.

Doubleday said all would be taken care of, and when Eli had passed that word to Girnsolver, turned and led the way down the pier. He followed, guided by a lantern-gleam one of the troops aimed in front of their feet. It suggested rather than illuminated the black cliff that stretched above their heads. It picked out an arched sally port framed in granite. The tunnel echoed to the stamp and click of their boots. The immense weight of stone and brick pressed down above them. Then they were in a central keep, open to the sky, and turned and passed down a line of windows, one of which showed the glow of a candle deep within. Doubleday raised his hand at a door, then hesitated. —Show me the letter.

Eli displayed it, without handing it over. The captain nodded and rapped, then held the door for him to enter.

The room within was bare and dark and cold. A single candle burned on a board table. A smoky fire, evidently just kindled, filled the room with a smell like scorched paper. A gaunt officer with burning eyes and a narrow wedge of face was buttoning his tunic. He had iron gray hair and dark eyebrows, sloping shoulders and a determined chin, and just now, he was smiling broadly.

—May I present Mr. Elisha Eaker, sir, from U.S.S. *Owanee.*

The officer bowed at the introduction. He had the courtly manner, the drawled speech of a border-state man. —Elisha. The double portion of the spirit, if I recall my scripture? With the gift of parting the waters, one hopes, as his master had before him.

—Actually I am a volunteer officer from New York, sir.

—Forgive the pleasantry, sir; forgive us, we are all very pleased to see you. I am Major Anderson, sir. Welcome to Sumter. I trust you had a thrilling run through the guard boats.

—I saw one, Major. Other than that, we had an uneventful passage in.

—You look chilled, sir. I wish I could offer you something refreshing, but we've been restricted as to the essentials of life for some time. And half the time, it is not fit to drink. Anderson chuckled, and Eli forced a smile to acknowledge the joke. —Which situation hopefully will end with your arrival. However, I can manage tea.

—I am a bit damp. Yes, tea, please.

Both officers smiled. —You are a cool customer, Mr. Eaker. Woodson, put on the kettle, if you please. Take a seat, sir. I presume this letter brings good news. I knew my former subordinate would not let me down. Did you know that I recruited Mr. Lincoln for the Black Hawk War?

—I did not, sir. I hope you are pleased at what you read.

Anderson studied the seal, then sliced it open with a penknife. He ran his eyes down the lines. The animation that had quickened his features ebbed. His lips compressed. He handed it to his second in command.

—I don't understand, Mr. Eaker. I know you are only the messenger here, but . . . Trezevant's is the only ship without the bar? And you carry no troops? Mr. Fox told me he was sending a full relief effort, that we'd get provisions and enough troops to hold.

—The weather has been difficult. I know *Baltic* was carrying troops. I can only tell you that as yet we are unaccompanied.

Doubleday put down the letter in his turn. The two officers studied him. But he could see they weren't really seeing him, but something they'd long anticipated and now found it hard to believe he didn't represent.

He cleared his throat. —I'm sorry the news is not what you had wished to hear.

—It is rather a blow. We've been out of supplies and fuel for quite some time now. That's why our beacon isn't lighted.

—It made a ticklish business to approach, sir.

Doubleday said, —We have not the camphene. The authorities ashore, driven by this rascal Pickens, have barred us from the market and impounded our mail.

Anderson got up and checked the kettle, then poured the boiling water into a china pot. Let it steep for a few moments, then continued, as he brought it over, —No milk or sugar, I fear. Mr. Eaker, I have lived my life by the Ten Commandments, the Constitution, and the Army Regulations. The first shot from this fort will ignite a civil war whose flames will convulse the world. Up to now I have managed to pour oil on the waters. But General Beauregard's emissaries called this afternoon. I believe it to be the final communication before they begin their attack.

—What terms did they offer, sir?

—Quite easy, considering our puny band of starvelings. However, I shall not accept, if, as you say, the relief expedition is actually afoot. Or whatever you sailors say. We command the harbor. We have forty thousand pounds of powder and enough guns and shell. All I need is more troops. Which I represented again and again to Mr. Buchanan. If we had had enough men, I could have held Moultrie, Pinckney, and Johnson as well.

Eli sucked gratefully at the hot liquid, shuddering, then cleared his throat. To his surprise he didn't need to cough, hadn't actually needed to all through the wild ride in through the surf. —Sir, my commander's desires are no doubt set forth in the letter. However, I think our greatest uncertainty concerns the location and readiness of the various fortifications with which the disunionists have surrounded you.

—Mr. Doubleday has drawn up a sketch of the redoubts. We will be pleased to furnish this to Mr. Fox. Or to your commander, to be passed on to him.

—Should you like to send one of your officers out to us, sir?

—I do not dare, sir. I have only five, and one suffers so from lung disease that he cannot stand guard. We may need all of them, and that at very short notice. Anderson paused, a little orderly man who gave the impression of resenting the Carolinians mainly because they'd interrupted his routine. Then added, —However, I shall fulfill my orders. Have you time for me to pen a short note? And perhaps enclose a missive for my wife?

—I have to catch the tide, sir, but we have a little time yet.

—Then I shall pen a line or two. In case things do not turn out well for us.

Anderson glanced at Doubleday, who immediately rose and offered a turn around the terreplein. Eli accepted, curious to see the linchpin around which so much might turn. But it was too dark to see much. He could tell, from the distances he was walking, that the fort had been built for a garrison many times the few who manned it at present. They paused atop the gorge wall, looking across to a distant red star Doubleday told him marked Fort Moultrie. Red was appropriate, Eli thought. The color of Mars, the god of war.

—We post double guards these dark nights, Doubleday said. They could drop down with the tide like Indians, land a party, and seize the main entrance; or shoot their way in through the embrasures. They'll get a warm welcome. We mined the wharf, and packed some barrels of powder as makeshift grenades. But they'll win. There are just too few of us.

—Can you hold out under a bombardment?

—With what? We've only got a hundred and twenty-eight people here, and forty-three of those are civilians. Bricklayers and stonemasons, not soldiers. While they have thousands out there. Doubleday looked off into the darkness as a yellow pinprick built gradually into a white flare, swept around the harbor, lighting up the dark waves with astonishing clarity, then slowly faded out.

—What was that? Eli asked him, astonished. He'd never seen an artificial light that bright. In the moment it had pointed directly at them, it had rivaled a tiny sun.

—That's a Drummond light; they mounted it over there last week. No, nobody thought we'd have to defend against land batteries. Our best guns are here on the parapet, where, unfortunately, they'll be swept by enfilade fire. But, again, if we had reinforcements. . . .

—How many would you need?

—With eight hundred artillerymen, adequate supplies, and a firm leader, I could hold this fort forever.

—Are you saying Anderson doesn't have the spine?

The captain's shoulders moved in the darkness. —Not exactly. Robert Anderson's father fought for Washington and was imprisoned by the British here in Charleston. He himself fought Seminoles, Cherokees, Floridas, and Mexicans, and has been brevetted for gallantry. I cannot question his courage. But somehow he's interpreted his orders so as to let the enemy fire on a United States ship before our eyes, to build threatening fortifications within easy gunshot, to insult us and the flag over and over. I would not have stood for a quarter of what he has swallowed.

—You sound chuck-full of fight.

—I'm the only man in this fort who voted for Lincoln. They've told me that if I show my face in Charleston again, I'll be tarred and feathered. I don't intend to accept the invitation.

Doubleday paused, then nodded toward the channel beneath them, running from the invisible sea to the coruscating sparkle of the distant city. —Watch sharp for the guard boats on your way back. If they should catch you, the consequences won't be pleasant.

Eli shuddered suddenly in the searching wind. He thrust his hands deep into his pockets, and his fingers met the hard turnip of his watch. His time was passing. The tide would be turning soon. And another coldness was possessing him, the chill of a more than mortal fear.

—I'll bear that in mind, he said.

The major summoned him back a little after midnight and placed in his hands two sealed letters. One was addressed to Captain Fox, the other to Mrs. Anderson. Eli wrapped them in the same oilskin he'd carried Trezevant's letter in. Anderson shook his hand again, wished him Godspeed, and told the corporal of the guard to show him back to the landing.

The men were sitting and lying about on the pier. As he came up Girnsolver flashed the dark lantern to show him his footing. Then he was aboard, and the men jumped down, and they shoved off quickly and quietly. The sentries called low farewells. The sailors didn't answer, nor did Eli. They bent to the oars, pulling round the jetty and out again into the channel.

He sat huddled in the stern sheets, thinking over what he'd just heard. What he'd just felt, looking out from the terreplein of Sumter.

A garrison too weak to hold. A president who ignored repeated requests for help. A commanding officer who looked on as he was cir-cumvallated. On the secessionist side all seemed fire and daring, spirit and determination. On that of the unionists, acquiescence, concilia-tion, appeasement. Could the Union die without anyone really car-ing? So many seemed lukewarm, even resigned to its passing. And did it really matter if there were four nations on the North American continent instead of three?

The thought called an echo of something Araminta had said, that night on the back stairs when he'd told her their understanding would have to wait. Something about not wanting union—no, she'd said she didn't know why anyone *would* want union with the slave breeders, with the "monsters," she'd called them. He'd chuckled then; but now he'd seen that distant red light, then that slow, sweeping, in-candescent ray moving across the harbor.

They were ready for war. It might be that they would begin it themselves, tonight or tomorrow. What blindness could oppose a whole people, if they had really determined to be separate? If the en-tire British empire had not been able to prevail against the colonies, weak as they were, what chance the North could bend the South to its will? He'd heard Greeley's arguments. He'd read the same twaddle in the *Times*. We have more iron. Our railroads have the same gauge, men like him said.

But war required more than railroads and iron. War took determi-nation, and blood, and skill, and willingness to sacrifice.

That was why he'd shivered, looking out from the ramparts. Nei-ther from the cold nor from fear for himself. But from the realization, belated as it was, of what was so close to beginning.

Much later he made out a hollow sound against the wind, a thud or clank. He wasn't sure what it was, but he passed the word to Girn-solver. The old sailor brought the oars inboard with only the faintest knock, and told the bailers to avast. They drifted on, rising and falling with sickening violence in the spiky, tide-countering chop.

The picket steamer coalesced slowly out of the dark between them and the open sea. It had no lights and now no fires lit, at least that they could see. It might have been anchored. The rowers sat frozen, glancing over their shoulders in its direction. Exposed as they were, with no shelter save the plank sheathing of the cutter, a blast of grapeshot would tear them to pieces. Their few rifles would be useless against even a small deck gun. He whispered, hearing his voice hoarse, hoping it wasn't the beginning of a spasm, —Lie down, all of you. Get down in the bottom of the boat.

Beside him Girnsolver lay back stiffly, hand nailed to the tiller. Eli half turned and lay back with him, but kept his head toward the other craft.

—Ahoy there.

He covered the old man's hand instinctively with his own. Neither spoke. The men on the ceiling boards lay quiet as death.

—Ahoy, I say. Who goes there?

—Not a word, he whispered, thinking, They must have heard the rattle as the oars came in.

They were drifting slowly in on the other craft. They would pass very close indeed, perhaps fifty yards off. He could hear men talking, but the sound of the wind and sea erased the words. Another clank, like the one he'd heard before, as if someone were moving or shifting a heavy chunk of iron.

No one moved in the cutter. Eli lay rigid, holding Girnsolver's hand. No one spoke. They were a boatful of dead men.

The tickle in his chest increased. He swallowed desperately. He couldn't cough now. Not now. He swallowed again, trying to tamp the growing explosion deep in his lungs.

The shadow hovered above them. He smelled coal smoke as the cutter drifted under her bow. She was anchored, then, breasting the tide, her fires banked but still smoldering. The shadow loomed over them. He couldn't imagine anyone not seeing them. He could see the silhouettes of men on deck now, lolled back in the stern boards. A hearty laugh rolled across the water. The strain of a harmonica.

Then, as gradually as it had approached, the picketboat receded, fell astern, melted back into the sheltering dark.

He let five, ten minutes pass, till he felt the tide had carried them well clear. Then he leaned over the side, coughing helplessly into the crook of his pea-jacketed arm. Girnsolver put the men to the oars again, swinging southward, as Eli could tell now, sitting upright again, sweat breaking on his forehead despite the spray and the cold, by the feel of the wind on his cheek. It wasn't magic; the old seaman simply observed everything: the set of the tide, the direction of the wind, even the texture of the surf-roar, whether it broke on rocks or smooth sand.

Behind them as they rowed the long finger of the limelight reached out, fingered across the waves, and lit for a moment the frowning brick of Sumter. He swallowed as he watched it search the harbor, lighting up, for a moment, the anchored picketboat. Then it faded back into its initial pinprick and snuffed out.

When they reached what the old warrant swore was their starting position, *Owanee* wasn't there. They drifted for a time, rocking heavily beam to, until one of the men began retching over the side. At that Eli ordered a slow stroke into the prevailing sea. At last one of the oarsmen pointed out a vanishingly dim will-o'-the-wisp hovering just above the sea some distance to the east. Girnsolver said worriedly, —She's powerful close to the bar, she's over thataway. And that ain't no blue light like the cap'n said he'd burn for us.

—Aground?

—I hope not, sor. God help us in the morning if she is.

But when they made up on the light a strange voice returned Eli's hail. Too late, he realized the dark hull was lower than that of the sloop. Girnsolver gestured silently to the men. They threw back the tarps and seized the rifles. Eli held out a restraining hand. —What ship? he called.

—Revenue cutter *Harriet Lane*.

—Thank God. Have you seen *Owanee*?

—Lying farther out. Steer south by southeast. She's burning a light for you.

When they came alongside at last, under a dim blue lantern riding on the starboard cathead, all seemed normal aboard. Claiborne

stretched a hand down from the top of the Jacob's ladder. A quick report to him, then a fuller one to Trezevant, the captain in nightshirt
and nightcap in his quarters. He handed over the letters. Then a
quick midnight ration of cold salt beef and bread, and he sank back
into his bunk in his little enclosed space of a room, suddenly weary
unto death, too weary even to bring up the choking fullness that lay
ever threatening deep at the base of his throat.

13

ARAMINTA stood on tiptoes in the front parlor, looking out
into the street. Her uncle didn't look back. Today as every day
he simply climbed into the carriage, morning journal tucked
stiffly under his arm, and pulled the door to without farewell or even
a glance around him at a glorious spring morning. Barlow's whip
cracked and the carriage moved off, wheels grating on the cobblestones.

As soon as Micah was out of sight she swept up her skirts, dropped
to the settee, and took out Ellery Phelps's letter.

She'd waited some days after her encounter with him on South
Street, when they had watched Eli's ship get under way, expecting
him to call at the house. But he had not. Till she told herself he'd flat-
tered and then forgotten her. But just now a note had arrived. Taking
up the mail from the front hallway, Maire had brought the cream-
colored envelope to her instead of to her father. The girl had brains,
for a County Cork immigrant with a brogue thick as oat porridge.

Ara sat alone for nearly an hour after reading it, looking out
through the sheer patterned silk of the curtain. Occasionally she

lifted a corner to blink in the sunny, clear light that had come after the storm passed away. Contemplating what she might answer, and if she should answer at all. The clatter and rumble from the avenue continued unendingly, a sound that vibrated the glass but that she no longer heard.

The uneven strains of an itinerant organ-grinder rose above the traffic noise, recalling to her a dark morning that winter. Leaving for the office in the depths of January, Micah had stumbled over a snow-wrapped bundle on their front steps. Summoned down from the carriage to investigate, Barlow had unwrapped the rags to reveal the marble-white face of a small girl. Her dead, frozen fingers still clutched the wooden harp with which she'd been sent forth to cull pennies.

Presently the music faded; the hurdy-gurdy man had moved on. But she pondered on, until at last the maid, coming in, cocked her head and said, —The carriage has returned, miss.

—Very good, Mary. She called this one Mary sometimes instead of Moyra, which was how one pronounced Maire in Gaelic, apparently.

The maid pursed her lips, then pointed to the letter, open on the settee. —Will there be an answer to that, miss?

She stood, threw the sheers aside, and looked out into the hurrying life of the street. —Not just yet, Maire. It's the sort of letter one does not answer without careful contemplation of the consequences.

This was an important day. Not because of Mr. Phelps's letter. That was simply a diversion, a possible adventure she gained as much pleasure in considering, she suspected, as she would have taken in actually meeting him as he proposed.

Today, she and Mrs. Lispenard had decided, she would ask for what was hers.

She'd met Harriet Lispenard at the dramatic society. An older woman, in her thirties, but though no longer quite handsome, Harriet still had a *belle figure*. She had been upon the stage. Now she taught elocution and gesture at a private lyceum, and lived independently of her husband. Even after her uncle forbade her to attend the society, she met Harriet every few days for tea. Once at the office, Micah sent the carriage home; it was hers after that. It was Mrs. Lispenard's she had just left when she had glimpsed the warships getting under way.

The older woman had listened as Ara confided her doubts about marrying Eli, his threatened health, her eagerness to leave the house, but above all her inability to make her uncle tell her what had happened to her mother's money, which she had to have if she was to make her own way. At the end she felt like crying. —I simply wish for what is mine by right, she said.

Harriet half turned away, skirt rustling in the little parlor, and poured more tea. —Have you actually asked him for it?

—Several times.

—But what exactly have you asked? What query, precisely, have you put to your guardian? In my experience, my dear, simple communication is often fraught with the most exquisite difficulties.

—I asked about my mother's money.

—His response?

—That I need not worry about such things.

—Precisely how old are you, Ara? I know you are not yet in your majority.

Araminta told her, and the older woman considered. —I'd say that in some ways you are very mature. But legally, of course, you can't be more mature than your years.

—Do you mean he's right, treating me thus?

—Oh dear, no.

—Then what should I do? I thought of retaining an attorney.

—Against your uncle? No respectable firm would represent you.

She looked down, angrily twisting a handkerchief in her lap.

Mrs. Lispenard said briskly, —Let us not *lasciate ogni speranza.* Your first step must be to approach him in such a manner that he must give a serious answer to a serious question. I can suggest a way, though it might involve a tint of subterfuge. Then you must ask him a series of specific questions. Find out where he's invested those funds, and how much they amount to. Then, and only then, can you clearly and plainly ask for what he's just identified as yours.

And now this was the day, but she had nearly the length of it to get through before approaching him. Micah fortified himself with a chop and coffee each midmorning at an ancient eatery just around the corner from his office. Thus strengthened, he was able to appear at the Exchange during its brief opening hours, after which he took lunch, occasionally with a whiskey, and returned to his office to see clients and transact business until dark.

Her appointment was at two, just after his luncheon.

She rose suddenly, nervous already, and crossed the room to the bellpull. Roberta answered, the second maid. She sounded out of breath. —Yes, miss.

—When Barlow returns, send him out for another newspaper. No, make it both the *Times* and the *Tribune*.

—Not the *Herald,* miss?

—You know I don't permit that filth in the house. And lay out my riding habit, if you would, and the plumed hat and boots.

The light that filtered through the dusty air, that air smelling so wonderfully of straw and horse sweat, manure and leather, was somehow *brighter* than it ought to be, as if it had absorbed a celestial essence from the laundered sky outside the stable window. Or maybe it was her own sense of the importance of the day. So many things went unexpressed at 372. So many things not spoken of. She hadn't realized this when she was a child. Then it had seemed natural that certain events were not referred to aloud, that some things had never happened. Only as she woke to a world outside the servants and the nannies, who came and went, it seemed, nearly every month, had she realized not all families resembled hers.

A snort and the quick thud of eager hooves planted into the peaty floor of the stable. The groom was leading El Cid out. The stallion whiffed her, nostrils flaring and ears pricking up, and snorted his "heh, heh" greeting.

—Are you glad to see me, you wonderful thing? What a delightful morning, Charles.

—So 'tis, miss. And isn't he the handsomest horse who ever stood on iron?

She bent to check the girth, looked at the near fore shoe as the stallion stamped the ground. —I see the farrier took care of things for us.

—That he did, mum, was here yesterday 'n' did him and Mr. Gould's horse too. You do know y'have something black upon your face, mum?

She wiped absently at it with the back of her glove. —It is ink, I am afraid. I cannot get it off.

—Yes, mum. Ready to ride, then, Miss Van Velsor?

She gathered up her skirt and the groom bent, and she stepped into his hands for a leg up. Sitting high up under the heavy iron-bolted beams, she hooked her leg around the pommel beneath her skirt, and he let go the bridle and stepped back, and the stallion whinnied eagerly and trotted out into the cool brilliant air. She dawdled a moment while he mounted one of the club ponies. No lady rode alone. When he was ready she wheeled, and El Cid broke into a canter down the short lane into Central Park.

She loved the Park in spring. At times, when she rode in the afternoon, it was rather a crush, but at this time of day the paths were nearly empty. She turned the horse's nose to the east drive and glanced back. Charles trotted a hundred yards behind. She spurred ahead, past the ponds that glinted in the breeze.

Their ripples made her think of Eli, gone to sea, and she shuddered with a queer intermingled thrill of both fear for him and delight they were no longer engaged. Her impending duty had burdened her for so long that she felt physically lighter without it. He was a good boy. But perhaps that was it, that he was such a boy. Older than she, but still not yet a man, somehow. Or maybe it was what marrying him would mean that she didn't like. Becoming dependent on him, as she'd been forced to play child to Micah. Never being able just to be by herself, for herself, of herself. How sweet such a condition would be! And all she needed was what was already hers.

In the Flower Gardens gangs of Irish laborers were bent on the hillside, doing what, she had no idea. The chunk and ring of shovels floated over the meadows. She loved cut flowers, tulips especially, but she'd never felt any interest in the dull business of growing them. That they existed, and could be bought, was enough.

Sitting in the parlor that morning, she'd read the paper Roberta had brought back. The maid said she could find only the one, the boy had been renting out his last copy, and she'd paid twenty cents for it, ten times its normal price. She suspected she was being cozened for half those pennies, but paid her. Then sat again and followed the columns of print anxiously from head to foot of the still-damp sheets, getting ink in a most annoying way upon her fingers and (she had only noticed too late, after she was dressed) over her cheek and right ear as well.

A general named Twiggs had handed over the entire army in Texas to the seceders. Several more warships had sailed. In contrast, a separate column of telegraphic dispatches headed "Latest from Charleston" boasted about reinforcement of the defenses in the harbor, and a new floating battery being towed into position opposite "Sumpter."

She wished she knew more about money matters. She'd gotten "excellent's" in arithmetic at Miss Bruyenne's. Supposing Micah gave her back her inheritance, how should she invest it? Several of her friends' fathers, experienced speculators, had gone under in '57. Her acquaintances had to leave school and no one knew them anymore. What if she lost it? It did not bear thinking of. Maybe she could ask her uncle for advice. But then, what was the point of getting her money back from him?

She came out of the grove to the east side of the reservoir, where fast riding was permitted, and nudged the big black into a gallop. He needed little urging, as she always galloped on the straight stretches here. One could see an oncoming rider for quite some distance. She'd just missed a smash-up with a carriage when she began riding, long before El Cid, when she was a tomboy and a daredevil and still only half in control of her mount.

She suddenly remembered another event that had taken place not far from this path. The summer she took her first riding lessons. She'd been hanging back from the other girls, who clustered around the riding master, and had seen something moving in the grove. She'd urged her pony closer and glanced ahead. They'd forgotten her, so she'd guided him off onto one of the pathways that branched off the carriage drive.

And discovered a sudden green coolness, a bit of Sherwood Forest in the center of the city. Charmed, she'd drawn the reins, and the pony had slowed to a leaf-padded saunter, shifting its knobby shoulder blades against her knees. Making her progress so silent the half-unclothed couple on the blanket had not heard her approach.

She'd stared, reins pressed to her mouth. A proper young lady would have either fainted or ridden away instantly. But she understood then that no matter how genteel she looked on the outside, she was not a proper young lady. For she'd stayed, and watched. Till finally the pony whinnied, and the man raised himself and looked back at her. Only then had she dragged at the reins and kicked the nag into a reluctant canter, as close to a gallop as it would go.

Remembering that dappled green, the opening of the woman's thighs, white paleness under the man's work-tanned hands, she freed her knee from its awkward crook around the saddle horn and swung her left leg over the pommel and to the other side. She arranged her skirts to conceal this forbidden posture, gripped the massive black's side with her thighs, and spurred him. El Cid shook his head and leapt forward. The bushes and trees and vines around them seemed to accelerate, to blur to a smear of green like a watercolor in the rain. She leaned forward, pressing her groin against the pommel. Her new velvet hat went flying, whipped off by a branch, but still she didn't rein him in. She was fixed on the more precious pleasure, the rhythmic pulse of El Cid's drumming hooves. The heart-racing danger of galloping recklessly down a sedate city path.

Wall Street. The upstairs office of Eaker and Callowell, the smells of leather and cigars and men. The carpet in the receiving room was expensive but filthy, trodden with street dirt. She presented Harriet's card without a word, trusting to her heaviest veil. As she'd hoped, young Reeves, her father's secretary, did not peer too closely. He went into an adjoining room, was gone for a few seconds, then came back in.

—Mrs. Lispenard, he said, and ushered her in.

Micah was standing at his working desk. His spectacles were shoved up and he was rubbing at his eyes. He looked tired and worried. She hesitated, stabbed through her nervousness and anger by something not far from pity. Then he turned, taking them off, and came toward her. A few steps away he slowed, squinting. Then came up and flipped back the veil.

—Araminta? There must be some mistake. Dash it all! Reeves!

—It's not his fault, Uncle. I asked for this interview under an assumed name, to discuss our business relations. Will you invite me to sit?

—What sort of rodomontade is this? We have no "business relations," Araminta.

She unpinned her hat and asked again, pointedly, if she might sit. He cleared his throat and said very well, but only for a moment, he had another appointment.

—No, you don't. Not for half an hour. I scheduled this time so that we could have a thorough talk. The sort we can't seem to have at home.

He looked nonplussed. She noticed, not for the first time, the small red veins at the base of his nose. His hands wandered aimlessly to his vest, touched his watch pocket, explored the lapels of his frock coat. Finally he chuckled and dropped into a wing chair beside his desk, as if to convey his verdict: this was a social call. —Quite a good joke. I suppose it gets a bit dull for you, alone at home. "Mrs. Harriet

Lispenard." Where did you pick up that card? Is there such a person-age?

—I'm not here to joke, Father. I came, as I said, on business.

—Why, honey, of course it's a jest. What possible business could we have?

—I came to ask about Mother's money.

—Oh, my dear. My dear. The tawdry affairs of Mammon are hardly suitable for young ladies to dabble in.

She tried to steady her voice, tried to remember the questions Harriet had told her to ask. —I don't plan to *dabble*, Uncle. I only wish to know what state my affairs are in.

—You're fully invested in safe securities. Nothing more need re-ally be said. He glanced at the doorway, which the assistant had left open. —Reeves!

—May I ask how much my holdings amount to?

—How much? How *much?* Their value fluctuates with the state of the market. As do all investments, including gold.

—My holdings are in gold?

—I did not mean to give that impression. We hold very little gold. Unfortunately, as it's done well of late, given the unsettled con-dition of trade.

Reeves, blinking in the doorway. —Yes, Mr. Eaker?

—My niece is playing a hoax on us. Didn't you recognize her?

The secretary looked alarmed. —I am very sorry, sir. I must per-haps see to getting spectacles.

—Mr. Reeves, will you please leave us alone for a moment? she said, very politely, she thought, but also quite firmly. The interview wasn't going as she'd envisioned it, but she wasn't leaving yet.

He looked to his employer for guidance. Eaker hesitated, then waved him out. Now his frown was set. She thought it made him look like Harriet's Boston terrier. The thought helped. She took a deep breath, and then another.

—Very well; what is it you want?

—As I said, I should like to know the state of my financial affairs.

Where my funds are invested. How much they amount to. I don't need to know to the dollar, just sort of how much generally. That sort of thing. She stopped there, hearing herself start to rattle.

He said ominously, —Are you demanding an accounting from me?

And she said, surprising herself a little at the hardness in her voice, —If you insist upon viewing it in that light. Yes. I demand an accounting.

Rather to her astonishment, he didn't explode. Instead he pushed his pince-nez back and looked at the ceiling. —Your mother's bequest was long ago mingled with the general partnership accounts. Thus, my dear, you share in the general fortunes of Eaker and Callowell. Where we prosper, there prosper you; where we suffer reverse, you also. For an elementary account of the firm's business dealings, see Mr. Reeves for a prospectus. This has not been our most profitable year, I'm sorry to say. However, we're well positioned to take advantage when peaceful conditions are restored.

She sat rooted, uncertain how to respond. —But how much . . . is there stock involved?

He smiled condescendingly. —There is no *stock* in a partnership enterprise, my dear. It's conducted on the word of honor of the gentlemen involved.

—Or some other way of . . . I don't really know how to ask what I want to ask.

He nodded, lacing his fingers comfortably over his belly. —Precisely what I meant when I said you should not concern yourself with such matters.

—But you led me to believe my mother's money was held separately. That the Van Velsor capital would come to me when I grew up.

—Not so, my dear. Let us speak plainly, since that seems to be what you want of me. His tone turned fatherly. —First, your inheritance was not so very large. After all, your mother was only one of four heirs. Through careful husbanding, I have increased its value for you over the years. I may have spoken of it now and then, I was proud to do what I could for you, but I am quite certain I never said you had a separate or reserved accounting. Really, Araminta, there is no cause for upset. Your money is perfectly safe. It is employed in sound investments with excellent long-term prospects. You've always known that all I own will eventually belong to you and Eli. When he returns from his little adventure. I have no other heirs, no other interests. Everything I do is directed toward your security and happiness as a couple.

She wasn't listening to the words so much as she was watching his lips. Thick, fleshy, slowly moving lips. Hands that knitted together over his tightly buttoned coat. When he paused she raised her eyes and said, —I don't believe you. I'm not marrying Eli. And I want my money.

Her guardian's mouth compressed into a pale line, a wintry subtraction mark on the ledger of his face. —I don't see any point in continuing this discussion. Believe or not, as you like. You'll simply have to take my word on the matter.

She didn't answer, she was too angry to answer. Her legs were quivering under her skirt, as if she'd ridden hard all day long. Her uncle rose and came around the desk. She stiffened as he put his arm around her. As his cold dry lips touched her forehead.

Suddenly she couldn't remember what they were arguing about. Her embarrassment and anger snuffed out like a blown-out lamp. In their place was a chill confusion, marbled with something not far from terror. She looked at his face, close above hers. Said, in a voice that trembled like a hurt child's, —You won't give me my mother's money?

—My dear, my dear. He patted her head. —Even if I wished it, I could not do so at present. The condition of the market. To sell now would entail considerable loss. You are well provided for. Are you not? We have not far to look, to find those who are not so blessed.

She closed her eyes, remembering the frozen bundle of rags on the front step. How small it had seemed, cradled in the coachman's arms.

—You're telling me I own nothing whatsoever of my own.

—This sounds not well. You're in the bosom of your family. Have you ever wanted for anything?

—And if I should leave?

—Leave? he repeated.

—If I should leave your house.

He shook his head slowly. —Even the thought is painful to me, Araminta. Who would provide for you? What would happen to you? This world is not kind to unprotected young women.

She sat unable to speak, though her mind supplied words. Placating words, words suitable to a young lady, though beneath that the marbled darkness was still seething. Angry words too, that would cut like a lash. She didn't know which to say! She needed time to think!

He was stroking her shoulder now. —Put these worries from you, daughter. That's how I've always thought of you, Ara. As my daughter. Your future's assured. It will be comfortable and pleasant. You and Eli will see. And don't worry about this naval stupidity. I am bringing that to a speedy conclusion.

She looked at his hand on her arm, and now she could smell him as he leaned over to plant a kiss on her cheek. Segar smoke and hair oil. And through the strange numbness, the confusion, she found at last words something like the ones she wanted. —I told you, I'm not marrying Eli. Not now. Not ever. Nor do I want my future to be "assured" at the price you wish me to pay.

He reared up, and slammed his palm down on the desk so hard and loud right beside her that she flinched and threw up a hand. —Oh. You don't. *You* don't want this. *You* won't have that. Well, *I* won't countenance this foolish and childish outburst! You will be guided by me, as is right and proper! He thumbnailed his watch open, then slipped it into his waistcoat. He took a Havana from a teak box, and she saw with a vindictive pleasure that his fingers were trembling too. As he clipped it he said contemptuously, —I have business to attend to now. I really must ask that you leave. Reeves! Escort her home.

—I don't need an escort. Barlow brought me in the carriage.

—Very well, then. He turned away to light the cigar. —Have dinner ready a bit late tonight. Say, around eight.

Getting into the carriage, giving her hand to the driver, she felt her face burning beneath the resumed veil. She'd expected to be independent one day. Now she knew the truth. He'd never release what was hers. If she left, she'd leave penniless. Unless she could fashion or design some way to get it back from him.

Was there a way? His was a mighty fortress in a high place. She looked up at its walls helplessly, then down at the fists clenched in her lap. At nails too delicate to climb, at soft hands too weak to tear down its stones.

—Yes, Miss Van Velsor, said the Irish maid, lips parted as if expecting a kiss. —It shall be just as ye say, miss.

—You recall the letter which came this morning, Mary? This is my reply. But I do not wish to send it under my name. You will fold it, without reading it, and address it under your own hand.

—Yes, miss.

—Remember you must not speak of it. This must be among the three of us: yourself, myself, and Mr. Phelps. I ask you as a friend; but there will be a trifle for you now and then out of it.

Maire curtseyed, shamrock eyes sparkling with the delight of conspiracy. Turned, nearly tripping on the hem of her work apron, and giggled. She left her mistress once more alone in the parlor before the great front window. Where she stared, lips slightly parted, at the passing bustle outside.

14

Confrontation with Mr. Gustavus Fox ♦ Standing In for Charleston ♦
A Vibration as of Thunder ♦ The Strangely Altered Behavior of
Captain Trezevant ♦ Conversation via Speaking Trumpet

SIX o'clock, of a dark and stormy dawn; and Ker clinging precariously at the t'gallant crosstrees, one arm snap-shackled around the tackle sheet as he glassed sea and coastline with the other. From up here *Owanee* was no larger than a skiff, canted and bucking as she tore through the green water far below. Around him the knitted web of buntline blocks chattered like the *carretillas* and *golpes* of a spirited flamenco, and the gaskets flailed desperately in the steady wind.

From up here, as close, the saying ran, as a sailor ever got to heaven, he could see for many miles beneath the dull gray overcast. Could make out the sand-shrouded batteries inland of the white surf line on Sullivans Island. Could see Sumter, compact and menacing, deep in the harbor. *Harriet Lane* was standing out astern, both men-of-war close-hauled on a larboard tack. With each plunge of the deck the mast whipped through the air. The captain of the maintop balanced a few feet away, one hand to a shroud. He rode his spar as if it were a plunging colt, his beard whipping in the wind.

The lookout had picked up the liner an hour earlier, hull down to the north. Now she was plainly visible. *Baltic* was much larger than the warships, with a sudden straight stem graceful as a meat cleaver and huge paddle-wheel houses shouldering up on either side of a long black hull. But no tugs or other ships accompanied her. She seemed to be alone.

He frowned, and clapped the glass shut. Had they turned back? Given up, faced with the storm? Without the tugs, it would be much harder landing troops. Either the warships would have to tow the landing boats in, hazarding grounding beneath the enemy batteries, or the army would face a long, exhausting row in heavy seas.

He told the lookout to keep an eye to northward, swung around the shroud, and dropped down the ratlings hand over hand, fast and surefooted as a spider.

Trezevant was pacing the quarterdeck restlessly. Ker touched his cap. —It's *Baltic,* sir. Alone.

—Where can the tugs be? Where can *Powhatan* have gone?

They were rhetorical questions, so he didn't answer, simply stood waiting as the captain took another turn around the deck.

—Steer to close her, Trezevant said at last.

—Aye sir. He passed the order to Eaker, who had the deck, and sent Jerrett running in search of Duycker, with word to make ready the gig.

But when they bore up alongside an hour later, both ships altering to run off the wind, they were close enough for the speaking trumpet. Trezevant stayed on the quarterdeck, leaving him to climb a few feet into the rigging and bellow across, —Ahoy the *Baltic.*

—Ahoy the *Owanee.* Where is Captain Trezevant?

—He is listening, sir.

The liner was under power, the big wheels churning out a turbulent trail of cream and mint. The port wheel, the one facing *Owanee,* was nearly out of the water. From his perch he could see the outer rim plunging into the green, and the tips of the paddles, each one cocked into scooping orientation by its rod as it came down. At each revolution the heavier mass of the king rod flashed by. A stain of oily-looking smoke winged toward the violet land. The bearlike figure leaning over the rail was familiar. It was Gustavus Fox.

—I will come aboard you, Fox shouted.

Ker lifted the trumpet. His voice sounded brazen and hollow, confined and altered by the tapered brass. —Shall we send our gig, sir?

—I will use one of our launches. Round up and heave to, if you please.

Trezevant nodded. Ker shouted back, —We're heaving to, and nodded to Eaker to bring her around into the wind.

As she lost way the watch put their backs to braces and sheets, trimming the foremast sails to starboard and the main to port and sheeting out the spanker till she fell off, then steadied, neither driving ahead nor making sternway, only rising and falling uneasily to the seas that came down endlessly out of the northeast, driven by the steady cold wind.

The launch came plowing across, its crew's backs bending and straightening like human pistons. The blunt bow threw spray each time it crashed down. Troops in blue overcoats lined the rails of the steamer. Some watched *Owanee,* others the distant coast.

Girnsolver, fingering his silver pipe beside him: —Honors, sor?

He didn't answer just yet, thinking it over. Certainly if Fox were still in service, they should pipe him aboard. But he wasn't. He glanced toward the quarterdeck, but Trezevant was deep in his brown study. He looked down at the man in the launch, who was gauging his approach to the sea ladder, and finally shook his head. The boatswain dropped his pipe and turned back to the staysails.

—My cabin, called Trezevant, pausing at the top of the companionway.

—Sir, you will not meet him on deck?

But the captain was out of sight, vanished below. Ker mastered his surprise and stepped forward, tucking the long glass under his arm as Fox, stout and rumpled and soaked, black-bearded and scowling, hauled himself up off the ladder and swung dripping boots to *Owanee*'s wet and shining deck.

———

—Trezevant. I'm not surprised to see you here as promised. The non-appearance of *Powhatan,* though, puzzles me most sorely.

Parker Trezevant held up a decanter. —A touch of spiritus frumenti, sir?

—Most gladly. Fox handed his hat to Ahasuerus, drank off the neat whiskey the captain had proffered, and wiped his beard with the back of his hand. He breathed heavily a time or two, then flung himself into a chair with a grunt. —We've got a fair wind. No howitzers and no tugs, but we can't wait any longer. I should like *Owanee* to take the van, *Baltic* the center, leaving *Lane* to cover our line of retreat.

—I regret that I must decline, said Trezevant courteously. He steepled his fingers. —My orders are clear. I'm to stand ten miles off and await *Powhatan.* I am not to engage in adventures, nor to insert myself into a parlous situation and trigger the effusion of blood.

—You had best recur to their main purpose, sir. The entire thrust and weight of our presence here is to relieve and reprovision the fort.

Trezevant nodded, but his eyes stayed flat. —But absent Captain Mercer, I am the senior officer present afloat. Decisions as to how to relieve the fort, if it is possible to do so, are therefore mine. I have not lingered passively at this rendezvous. I have carried out a reconnaissance of the channels. Lights and buoyage have been removed. Pilots are not available, and entrance will be extremely hazardous. I have also sent a boat and officer in to Sumter.

Fox lifted his eyebrows. —Were they peacefully admitted?

—They entered under cover of darkness. Rendering your question moot, I am afraid.

—What word from the garrison?

Trezevant handed him Anderson's letter and Doubleday's sketch of the harbor batteries. —The major also has entrusted me with a letter for his wife.

Fox muttered, —Let me look at this a minute.

Trezevant held up the whiskey decanter questioningly. When the other grunted and shook his head, he put it back into the cabinet and locked it. A minute or two passed.

—Captain, I don't find these batteries so heavy as to preclude an attempt at entry. If they should fire on us, we may sustain damage. However, we will inflict it as well. Don't forget, we'll have the fort's guns behind us.

—And then?

Fox raised his eyebrows. —Sir?

Trezevant got up and crossed the cabin. He came back with a towel and handed it to Fox, who muttered thanks and began rubbing his hair with it. The captain said, —*Powhatan,* our most potent warship, has not yet arrived. As you pointed out, we are also missing the tugs and their launches, which are essential to land the troops safely.

Fox scowled. —They're not *essential.* We can still get reinforcements ashore.

—But with more losses. Due both to the longer exposure to enemy fire, and to the inevitable wastage of landing through surf in small boats. Let us say we throw two-thirds of those troops into the fort. Once Beauregard realizes what we've done, he will assault across these marshes, most likely by night. Trezevant swirled liquor in his glass. —The plain fact is that no position this deep in the South can be held without many thousands of troops and a fleet in support. Without, in a word, full-scale war. I don't want that, Mr. Fox, and I don't think that's what Congress wants either. There's still a chance to resolve these difficulties peacefully.

Fox laid the towel aside, hunched forward over the table. —While I believe that chance is gone, if it ever existed. One last time: will you lead us into the channel?

Trezevant inclined his head with grave courtesy. —For one last time, then, I must decline.

—Then I'll go in without you. I warn you, if you don't follow me, you'll explain it to a court.

—I will gladly hazard court-martial in the cause of peace, Mr. Fox. The captain's voice hardened. —You had best look to your own responsibilities. Is invading a peacefully seceding state, in the absence of any declaration of war or act of Congress, covered by our orders? Is it even lawful?

—Sumter is United States territory. Fox rose then, pointedly did not bow. —I will show myself to my boat.

—Very well, sir.

Trezevant looked after the bearlike form as it left the cabin. He poured himself an additional dram and drank it off, gazing out the quarter window toward the coast. A dark face leaned in at the door, a silent presence he did not have to acknowledge unless he wished.

Ker watched Fox's gig battle its way back toward the liner. The swells heaved it violently into the sky, then sucked it down out of sight. Their visitor hadn't said a word as he emerged from belowdecks, nor had his glower invited queries from a junior officer.

Jerrett darted out of the companionway, collided with him, and shied back, thrusting out a scrap of foolscap as if fending off a blow. —From the captain, sir.

He unfolded it, then turned to Eaker. —Captain's compliments to Mr. Hubbard, and ask him to make steam.

—Aye aye, sir.

Trezevant hadn't mentioned general quarters, nor any preparation for battle, so neither did he. He unshipped the long glass again and steadied it on *Baltic*. Fox's launch had made alongside by now. As he got the lens steady a puff of mingled smoke and steam pushed up from the stacks and the big port wheel, closest to him, started to revolve, spurning out a white foam behind it as the liner began walking toward the distant coast.

Eli stood uncertainly by the starboard cathead, wondering what he should do. He'd watched Fox leave the ship, and *Baltic* steam off. But only for a few miles; the liner had hove to again near the revenue cutter.

Meanwhile *Owanee*, still lying by, had done nothing more than drift downwind. Above the stack a thin brown smoke had paled to a ghost white, then to the thick lightless black of a full-draft coal fire. But he hadn't gotten any course orders, nor had anyone ordered the set of the sails changed.

Now he saw the liner's wheels revolve again, and her stern slew around. A froth showed at her wheelhouses.

Both the liner and the revenue cutter, looking very small next to her, lumbered slowly around till they were stern to *Owanee.* Smoke burst from *Harriet Lane's* funnel as the cutter steered into the liner's wake.

They were headed upchannel, north, toward the inlet. He looked aft, to where Claiborne and Duycker stood looking after the departing ships. Then went toward them, past silent crewmen standing here and there about the deck, and saluted the exec. —Sir, shall I clear for action?

The first luff had been stroking his beard as he came up. He already looked displeased, and frowned even more at the question. —Don't anticipate commands, Mr. Eaker.

—Well, sir, I observe the others heading in for Charleston. Are we to simply stand off here?

Claiborne didn't answer for a moment. Then he said, face hardened and in a tone Eli had not yet heard: —You have a great deal to learn about the service, sir, and about keeping a check on your tongue. We are not your father's employees, as you often seem to think. We will do precisely what Captain Trezevant thinks best, no more and no less, and we will not inflict our opinions on him unless they are invited.

—Sorry, sir. I only felt—

—*Enough,* sir. He beckoned to Jerrett, who had lingered nearby, his usually apprehensive features transformed with delight as he listened to Eli being reprimanded. —Inform the captain *Lane* and *Baltic* are standing in for the bar.

He turned and went to stand behind the wheel. The helmsmen had lashed it with a loop of line, and stood now with their arms folded, watching the departing ships. He took out his handkerchief and touched his brow with it, more out of sheer tension than any need. What the hell were they doing? Anderson needed help. They'd been sent to provision him. Was Trezevant just going to sit out here, while the others went in?

The captain came on deck a few minutes later. He studied the departing vessels through his glass. His swarthy face was immobile and expressionless as oiled teak. Finally he said, and Eli was close enough to hear, —Unto, unto, he is determined to cross the Rubicon. I think he is wrong; but I suppose we must second the attempt. Take us in after them, Exec. But at a distance.

—Aye sir. What distance?

—Give them a mile or two. Perhaps they'll think better of it before it's too late.

—Beat to quarters, sir?

—Not yet. We still have quite a distance to run. But have Mr. Duycker rig for towing, in case one of them should take the ground. And let us have the leadsman begin taking soundings.

The coast rose slowly from the sea, like some primordial land new-created by volcanic catastrophe. Eli saw that the seas had abated during the night, but they were still high, still chaotic, especially here, where the bottom shoaled fast and the inrolling combers piled high. *Baltic* wallowed clumsily, plunging her wheelhouses at each roll. She looked like a fat matron waddling down a church aisle too narrow for her crinolines. Smoke blew toward the white lace that edged the beach. Claiborne was occupied on the port side, taking angles with his sextant. Eli wondered what he could find to sight on, the coast was so featureless. He couldn't see any buildings, just a flat dark cutout of what looked like scrub or low trees.

A faint echo, a disappearing vibration tantalized his ear. He searched the overcast sky for whatever storm was bearing down on them. Yet saw nothing in the iron clouds but the wind-wavering curtain of an approaching squall.

Ker heard the guns, and felt some long-tensioned cord go slack within his chest. Its abrupt release made him feel giddy, as if spun about too rapidly in a parlor game of blindman's bluff. He called to Jerrett, intending to send him below. But the captain was already mounting the companionway steps. He put a hand on the carriage of a thirty-two-pounder and stood looking north toward the sound. Trezevant did not look his way, and quarterdeck etiquette dictated that the commanding officer, like a king or president, could not be addressed first. So he checked his last fix, estimated the direction *Baltic* seemed to be holding, and glanced aloft.

Owanee was under steam now, adding two bells of screw power to the drive of courses and tops rap-full of a hard twenty knots of wind. The Stars and Stripes lashed scarlet furrows across the darkling sky. Inky smoke rolled toward the land, outdistancing the heavy hulls that dragged after it. He glanced over the side, estimated they were making nine knots, and drew out the dead-reckoning line with a pencil slash that ripped the heavy cream chart paper. Oh, God *damn* them all! Fox, Lincoln, Davis, the pride-rotten, vainglorious politicians, the greedy cotton lords, the blind bombastic fire-eaters on both sides. They were too pure to compromise, too fine to suffer differing opinions any longer; and now good men would die.

—Slacken speed, Mr. Claiborne.

—Slacken, sir. He'd started the acknowledgment intending it as a question, but checked himself before the last syllable left his lips. —Aye aye, sir. Mr. Eaker, one bell.

The faint clang was echoed by the tremor of the air. Now the sound was clearer, plainer with every cable's length they pounded to northward. A mist or haze still veiled the land where it opened from the sea. He glanced at the chart again, checked the compass, then extended the glass in one swift motion and leveled it where Sumter should stand.

—What do you observe? Trezevant, just behind him.

—I can't make out the fort yet, sir. But that is the report of heavy guns.

—Unto, unto; do you think I can't hear them? He's still standing in.

—He is indeed, sir.

Before them the liner and the cutter were still heeling and rising to the seas. The swells climbed as they rolled in from seaward, then smashed themselves apart on the bar that lay now between the lead vessels and the open Atlantic. White horses with blowing manes ran along the jade green crests. The wind turned damp against his cheek, freighted with dusty spray, chill as the sea's inmost heart. If it caught the sloop on those shoals, it would hammer her apart and smash her open like a picked crab. He beckoned the gray-bearded boatswain and told him to see to the anchors. Girnsolver said he'd already sent his mates forward to ready for letting go.

—Shorten sail, Mr. Claiborne. And come up a little, we're driving to leeward.

He shouted to Eaker to brace up, letting the wind slip past the sails like a fist off a boxer's greased face, slipping away with only part of its driving power captured.

A rumble, an ominous volcanic muttering, a disquieting vibration of air and sea alike. Even the older men heard it now. They lined the leeward bulwark, staring at the slowly passing coast as if their gazes could penetrate the haze ahead.

—Shall I send them to quarters, sir? he asked the captain again.

Trezevant murmured, his own glass at his eye, —I believe you will see them turning about shortly.

Ker examined the lean familiar face from the side; the hollowed, tropic-darkened cheeks, the set lips, the sleepless, deep-set eyes. And knew that however much his own anguish had harrowed his soul, it had plowed Parker Trezevant's twice as deep.

The captain murmured, —I don't think he'll continue the attempt to reinforce. Not now. However, it might be best to clear for action.

Ker nodded instantly to the boatswain, who'd been shifting from foot to foot and fingering his whistle. The long, dropping keen split the wind and the rattle of blocks as the braces came round. For just a moment it seemed that the ship itself, that the world itself, paused, attending to the piercing call that lifted and dropped, held and drawn out to the limits of an old man's breath.

Then the deck was crowded with running men.

———

When the crew of number one had cleared and cast loose, seen the gun ready for action, and reported manned and ready, Cal Hanks stood waiting on the fo'c'sle, balanced on the balls of his feet in the second captain's position. The handspikemen and train-tacklemen waited around him. Little Billy Ripley stood trembling six steps back, holding the reload cartridge in a bucket with a damp felt over it, as a baker woman covers a hot loaf with a cloth. His freckles stood out dark against his bleached cheeks.

—Stand ready, Archbold snarled. Since their set-to he had avoided Hanks's eye, avoided, where he could, addressing him directly; but of course he had to in line of duty. Now Hanks and the rest of the Dahlgren's crew stepped back warily from the great forward-pointing mass of polished iron. The forward pivot's tapered muzzle frowned over the nodding jibboom at what was either a thunderhead or a slowly climbing mass of smoke on the horizon ahead.

They looked wordlessly toward the thump and rumble of great guns and the slowly rising smoke. He'd heard such guns before, in Africa. Someone was fighting over there, and before too long they'd be in it. For now he stood with hands dangling, occasionally reaching up to rub his neck. It was still sore, not just the skin, where the rough hemp had scraped it to bloody raw flesh, but deep inside.

They'd girdled him like a tree left to die in the woods. But he wasn't going to die. Not for them. He was going to live, for his own reasons, though he wasn't sure yet what those reasons were. Once he'd thought he could save his family. Now they might be gone forever, beyond his reach in a land sundered and closed. Captives forever in the land of Pharaoh, no sea ever to part to let them pass.

He rubbed his neck, face giving nothing to those around him, and watched the distant darkness draw slowly nearer.

———

Ker shouted the discovery without taking the glass from his eye.
—*Baltic*'s coming around, sir. Altering course to port.

—Very well.

The black hull of the liner extended. He watched her prow swinging. Yes, she was coming all the way around. —*Lane* has her rudder over as well. Both ships turning, sir.

—Very well. Four bells, if you please.

Heads snapped round. Duycker, who had taken over the deck as the drums beat to quarters, gaped at the captain. —Full ahead, sir?

Trezevant smiled faintly. —That is what I ordered, is it not? Mr. Claiborne! You will take the batteries on Cummings Point under fire first, passing as close as the lead line permits. Fire out your solid shot and reload with shell.

Ker mastered his surprise and turned to the gunnery officer. —Mr. Eaker.

—Sir.

—Stand your men to the guns. Our target is the fortifications on Cummings Point, to pass down our port side in about twelve minutes. Fire out your solid shot and reload with shell. Ordinary charges will be sufficient. Range will be one thousand yards.

Eaker saluted and he turned back to the captain, wondering what Trezevant could possibly have in mind. The revenue cutter was jibing around now too, topsails swollen and quivering as she swung through the wind. Did the captain plan to steam in on his own, past the retreating vessels, and take on the forts himself?

Trezevant's tight-lipped visage offered no answer. He stood with legs braced apart, swaying to *Owanee*'s roll. A huge jet of smoke vomited from the stack, floated above their quarter, shedding heavy black soot flakes that spiraled down into the waves. The dense puffs that succeeded fled downwind as the engines took on a heavy thump.

Eli faced forward again. *Baltic* had completed her turn and was bow on. *Lane* was still coming around. He could make out Sumter now through the smoke mist. The fort was a squared mass on the horizon, clear of any land, though land reached for it on either hand. A speck above it might or might not be a flag. The smoke towered up from it, then curved over at its apex and streamed off in the direction of the rebellious city. A lower bank of shifting white lay to starboard. Hovering, he supposed, above the guns of Fort Moultrie. Closer at hand, off to port, he could not make out anything yet on Cummings Point that looked like a battery.

The captain said in a detached, almost cheerful tone, —It seems hostilities have begun, Claiborne.

—I find that I agree with you, sir.

—They have fired on the flag. So be it!

He said, looking toward the rising smoke, —It is a great shock to me, sir. I confess, I had hoped it might yet be avoided.

—You have never shown yourself averse to action before.

—I have never faced my countrymen in battle before, sir.

—Nor have I, sir, nor have I. But while we wear this uniform, our duty is quite clear. Trezevant sounded not just relieved, but near to jubilant. Ker realized his old commander was back, as fierce and exultant as the day they took on the *Arachne*. —Well, to the matter at hand. My intention is as follows. I will steam past *Lane* and *Baltic* and rally them. *Owanee* will then lead the way in, suppressing the guns with shell delivered from as close a range as possible. When *Baltic* ranges alongside the fort, we will place our cutter and gig in the water and cover them with fire as the troops land. At that point I shall want grape available to break up an assault.

—Aye aye, sir.

He cracked out orders to Duycker and Eaker, then tried to step back and take stock as *Owanee* thumped steadily nearer to the fleeing ships. They were back in line, steaming to pass down to westward in a port-to-port passage. The disappearing bulwarks dropped away, revealing the green sea foaming and rushing past. The sloop's crew stood ranged along the guns.

The marine officer, Schuyler. A crisp salute to the captain. —Sir, my men are in the tops, ready for battle.

—Bring them down directly, Mr. Schuyler, and kit them out to land. I'll throw them into Sumter along with the troops.

Duycker. —Strike the sails, sir?

—I should rather leave them set, as Mr. Hubbard advises me our engines are not to be depended on.

And as if the mention of the devil had brought him up from the regions below, there the engineer stood, touching his cap in his casual way to Ker. Glancing around, he saw it was because Trezevant had slipped below. —Sir, beg to report steam pressure's dropping.

He rounded on Hubbard instantly. —Damn it, this is not a good time for such news, Chief Engineer.

—They sent us down here without repairs, sir. Can't be helped.

He tried to smooth his voice into a reasonable tone. —We're standing into battle, Mr. Hubbard. Can we run at two bells, say? We're on a lee shore. We must be able to maneuver at the very least.

—We were down to ten pounds when I left the engine room. Hubbard glared at the ascending smoke ahead. —Somebody's got a hell of a wood fire going.

—You are looking at Fort Sumter, into which the rebels are firing. We're leading the force in to the garrison's relief. It is imperative you give us the last ounce of steam you can, Mr. Hubbard.

—We'll do our best, but machinery don't salute. Hubbard watched the smoke a moment more, then trotted back toward the aft companionway.

Trezevant came back up from below. He was in full dress now, tails and epaulettes and the gold-bullioned black cocked hat. His sword swung by his side, the gold-braided knot swinging free. Ker recognized that sword. The Anti-Slavery Society of Boston had awarded it for Trezevant's capture of the most notorious slaver of the Guinea coast. He saluted and relayed the engineer's report. Trezevant only glanced aloft. —Well, so long as the wind blows, we shall not be helpless. Attend to your duty, sir; *Lane* is signaling us.

He broke the signal from the book as the ships tore past. *Owanee's* speed was dropping, but under the spread of canvas she still leapt along, and the liner and then the cutter shot past with a combined speed faster than that of a galloping post-horse. An officer shouted to them as they tore past, but his words were lost in the surge of the wind and sea and the background tympani of the guns, louder now with each yard they advanced.

—Sir, I break that hoist as "Change from the order of sailing to the order of retreat."

Once again, as he studied his commander's expression, he was puzzled. He hadn't understood this headlong charge into the harbor. Nor did he understand, now, as Trezevant struck his hand again and again on the bulwark. —Damn the man. Damn him to hell forever! Well, if he will not charge with us, there is no point in going alone. Come about and range alongside, and let us see what he has in mind now.

Fox's hail came booming across the green riband of sea. Trezevant replied this time himself, stepping up on an ammunition box, then leaping to the taffrail. Babcock moved up, doffing his cap, and the captain steadied himself on the bald gunner's raised arm as he lifted the trumpet. Ker stayed by the wheel, keeping one eye on the compass and the other on the liner that churned along a few yards distant. *Baltic*'s great curved wheelhouses towered above *Owanee*'s main yard. Soldiers looked down at them.

Fox began with, —I am steaming out to the swash channel. Follow me out.

—They're firing on the flag, sir. Will you let that pass? Trezevant bellowed.

—The attack has begun. Our forces are insufficient to force an entrance now.

—Unto, sir, unto! I cannot stand by and let Anderson perish. Do as you wish, sir; I intend to go in.

—I should prefer you not to, Captain. You are a valuable man, and *Owanee* a valuable ship. We need no martyrs.

Ker kept plotting their positions as the commanders argued. The two ships were running southeast on a starboard tack, their course gradually converging on the bar. When the chart showed eight feet half a mile ahead, he stepped up and said boldly, —We're standing into danger, sir.

The captain jerked his head back angrily. —What do you mean?

—We're nearly on the bar, sir. With your permission, I'll slow and let *Baltic* alter course.

Trezevant shouted, —My exec advises we're nearly on the bar.

Fox hollered across, —Will you follow me out, sir? Once again, I wish you to anchor and stand by while I search for the rest of our force. I assure you, I wish to take in some relief as much as you do.

—I will follow you, said Trezevant angrily. He threw the speaking trumpet at Babcock and jumped down from the taffrail. Shot out his sleeves, and cast a swift glance at Ker. —Engine to stop, if you please, and come right a point once we are clear.

He acknowledged the order and passed it on to engine room and helm. The liner walked slowly ahead, *Lane* following her. Trezevant stood fingering his chin, looking after them. Ker glanced at the guns. The men had stood ready by them when she stood toward battle. Now they too looked disappointed as she steamed away. He felt as proud of them as he'd felt ashamed, standing in, of those who had faced them all with this unanswerable dilemma. He moved up to Trezevant's side and cleared his throat. Hot as the captain looked, it would take very little to attract the lightning of his wrath onto himself.

—What is it now?

—Sorry to interrupt, sir. Secure from general quarters, sir?

—That fool. They're all such prudent fools . . . we should have spilt a bit of claret, but we'd have broken through.

—I think you're right, sir. But should we stand the men down now?

—I suppose we might as well. No doubt he wants to *discuss* things some more.

When the pipe shrilled "Secure" the tension broke. Petty officers' shouts broke the men from the guns, sent them to securing the tackle, sent them about their chores. Ker spent a few minutes with

Nick Duycker discussing the sail trim, then strolled aft, to look back down the rocking path of their wake.

The vibrations of the guns had faded but were still perfectly audible: heavy, regular bumps and rumbles that seemed to travel through the sea as much as the gray air. The mass of the fort had sunk beneath the sea, like a disappearing island, but the smoke still hovered above it.

He stood watching it, feeling sick at heart, remembering a pillar of smoke by day, a pillar of fire by night, and wondered where this sign and portent would lead all God's wandering children.

15

THE moment he opened his eyes the next morning, Claiborne saw the smeared gleam of fog through his cabin portlight.

He'd kept the deck till midnight in a steadily increasing wind. Then stayed up past two, muzzy with fatigue but unable to still his whirling mind. Finally he put the latch on and wrote a long letter to Catherine. After that he'd squeezed into his bunk and lain staring at the overhead, which was just visible in the brassy oil-light that bled through the louvers of his door. Thurston and Eddowes had been quarreling in the wardroom. The ship had complained around him, a warped knee joint aft crying out each time she fell into the trough of a sea. And still, though he yearned for sleep, he could not find it.

So that at last he had folded his hands in his narrow bunk and asked for guidance and strength from the source that had never failed him. And that had brought him peace at last.

When he threw the blanket back he found his smallclothes damp with sweat even though the cabin was cold. They smelled of monkey too. Shoving his hand back under the blanket, he felt it gripped by a small paw. Two bright eyes peered out when he lifted it, then Dupin snatched it back down again. The creature detested the cold. He petted it for a few seconds, then gave it a piece of hardtack from his desk.

He washed his face in the corner, pulled on his uniform, and went topside to the little boxed-in officers' head on the quarter.

The sea sloshed beneath the gratings as he squatted in the half-born light. Wind howled in the rigging, driving the fog past at the speed of a fast train. They were anchored a mile east of the swash channel, and the shoaling bottom built steep swells the color of pea soup. He watched a big one take shape from the fog. The sloop bowed to meet it, and it broke green and then white in the head timbers and then blew apart and exploded aft in a cold tumbling flurry of stinging spray.

He got his trowsers up before it reached him. Bending his head under its lash, he ran forward for a word with the anchor watch, who stood like an oilskinned statue with his boot propped on the cable. The fog was so thick that now he couldn't see the stern. Droplets quivered on every exposed surface of wood, soaked every line, and pattered down from the invisible sails furled aloft.

Sitting at the wardroom table alone, waiting for Shippy to bring coffee, he went over the events of the evening before.

After Fox's abortive attempt to enter, the warships had anchored out, while *Baltic* had gone back to the rendezvous point to see if there was any sign yet of *Pocahontas* or *Powhatan,* or of the missing tugs. Coming back, she'd grounded on Rattlesnake Shoal and taken some hours to get off. Later, Fox came aboard for a conference with Trezevant and Captain Faunce, of *Harriet Lane.* Trezevant had asked Ker to sit in.

Fox tried to persuade them to send in their cutters, unescorted, loaded with supplies. Faunce and Trezevant had refused. Lightly loaded and with a seasoned crew, they admitted, a cutter might make it. Eaker had, of course. But beef and beans were a heavy cargo, and would most likely founder a small boat in wind and swells like these; and in daylight, the picket steamers would easily intercept small boats. Throughout the discussion Faunce made it clear that as a Revenue Service officer he was not subject to either Fox's or Trezevant's orders. The captains had eventually agreed, however, to all run the batteries together and try a landing the next morning.

Which was today; but Ker doubted anyone was going anywhere in this weather. Certainly the fog would screen them from the batteries, but without bearings or navigational marks, they'd ground out long before they got anywhere near Sumter.

Late in the previous evening a small schooner had lifted above the curve of sea. *Lane* had hailed her and hove her to before she ran in to capture and confiscation in her happy ignorance. She was out of Maine, laden gunwale-deep with three hundred tons of straw-packed pond ice, to chill the butter and cream of genteel South Carolinians through the summer heat. Trezevant had put a working party aboard with orders to break out her cargo and pitch it overboard.

His musings were interrupted by Eaker, doubled fist muffling his habitual cough. Ker wondered again if he was in the best of health. The volunteer officer looked wan after physical strain or long watches on his feet. —Good morning, sir, the New Yorker said, avoiding his eye, and Ker remembered having had to give him a blowing-up yesterday. Well, the fellow had to learn.

—Good morning, Mr. Eaker. I must say, that cough don't sound very good.

—It's nothing, sir.

—I should advise you to consult Dr. Steele. The *shikko* has helped me a good deal from time to time.

Eaker coughed again as the steward's boy came in. Ker said, getting up to light his first segar of the day from the lamp, —Yes, I shall ask Dr. Steele to take a look down you. Whoa, Shippy! Don't spill that. Carefully, on the table here. Coffee, Eli?

Breakfasted, coffeed, cherooted, he managed a shave without cutting himself, clinging to the washstand with one hand as the ship pitched; then went topside. He lingered on the quarterdeck as the crew stoned the deck and overhauled rigging fore and aft. The sea stayed heavy, but the mist gradually shredded and blew away. The coast emerged from the blind whiteness as if a Japanese screen were being folded away. At seven bells he ordered quarters, then cleared the battery. He canceled "Air bedding" and turned the men out for small-arms and single-stick drill.

In all this time Trezevant still had not shown himself on deck. Not unusual. Ker, as the exec, handled matters of everyday routine, and isolation preserved the commander's dignity. Solitary and separate from the joking, chaffering junior officers, the captain seemed lonely at times; but that, too, was the price of command.

—Sor. Girnsolver, touching his cap. —Masthead lookout reports black smoke from the fort. Also, a small boat comin' in from seaward.

He looked aft. A huge pillar of blackness funneled up from the bearing of Sumter. Now and then a yellow glint darted at its base. Anderson was still firing, but what did all the smoke mean? He turned and followed the boatswain's arm to the boat. The wind was driving it swiftly down on them. It pitched alarmingly in the steep seas, caroming down their sloping faces like a surfboat.

—Stand by alongside. Most likely a message from Captain Fox.

In fact the launch contained the Fox himself. Ker greeted him as he gained the quarterdeck, and escorted him below. He knocked on Trezevant's door. —Sir, Mr. Fox.

—Enter, please.

He stood in front of the closed door a moment, listening to the murmur of voices within. Then turned away. A gentleman did not listen at keyholes, no matter how great his curiosity.

—I do not envy us, sir, said Trezevant over coffee and leftover biscuit. The unlit lamp swayed and clashed overhead. —We are neither of us likely to emerge from this business in good odor with the new secretary.

—I'm more concerned with those men in there. Fox's shambling figure paced across the cabin, hair dragging soot from the smoke-tinted beams. —They're still fighting, but the Carolinians are trying to smoke them out. Either that or the fort's on fire. No matter how straitened our means, we can't stand by and watch.

Trezevant said quietly, —Robert Anderson is a personal friend. But you understand, do you not, that by now ten times our number could not retrieve this situation?

Fox dragged his hands down his face. —Defeat may be inevitable. But not to turn a hand to prevent it . . . He looked at *Owanee*'s commander in appeal.

—You have a plan, no doubt.

—Your engines. Have you succeeded in making repairs?

—Reports from my mechanic are not encouraging.

—Damn it. Well, I have functioning engines aboard *Baltic,* but no seamen. Just the liner's crew and the army. Last night I had their officers organize boat crews. I propose we put your coxs'ns on the tillers, add your cutter and *Lane*'s, and run them into the fort with as many rations and troops as they can hold.

—I believe a larger craft would have a better time of it, in these seas.

Trezevant explained his commandeering of the ice schooner, and his ideas for its employment. Fox listened, scratching his beard and staring out the quarter window. —I doubt we can crowd more than eighty troops into her, Trezevant finished. —But that will double Anderson's effectives. If we run her in under a British flag, they will not fire until they see her actually head for Sumter. At any rate, once her troops are ashore, the schooner is disposable.

—If only we had *Powhatan!* Fox burst out. —I've looked for her all night long. What the hell's keeping Mercer?

The North Carolinian sat back, watching the pacing, raving man. At last he said, —I must tell you I had a note from Sam Mercer.

Fox frowned. —A note? From Mercer? When?

—It was handed me the day we left. *Powhatan* was detached from this force for special duty elsewhere.

Fox blinked, then passed a hand over his face as if brushing away webs. —What're you saying? What special duty? *Who* detached him?

—He may not have been at liberty to say. At any rate, he did not. Simply wrote that on orders of superior authority, he would not be accompanying us to Charleston.

The civilian stared for a second more, then clicked his teeth shut and crossed the cabin with heavy steps. He poured several fingers of whiskey and drained them off. —You should've told me this long since. *Long* since.

—It was not an official communication. I judged my private correspondence should remain so.

Fox slammed his glass down, and now his face was flushed. —That ship had everything we need. Howitzers, to cover a landing. Three hundred sailors. Fighting launches. This is a most serious dereliction on your part.

Trezevant said gently, —Take care what you say, sir.

Fox said angrily, —I'll say what I please. I've had my doubts of you. You're a Southerner. Aren't you? And do you have "other orders" too? Maybe from Montgomery, Alabama?

Trezevant rose, and the two men stood face-to-face in the narrow, pitching cabin. —I remind you, it was not I who diverted her. Your remarks and your tone are offensive, sir. They reflect on my personal integrity.

Fox confronted him for a moment more; then turned away, rolling the tumbler in his palms. —"Superior authority." It's that timid traitor, William H. Seward, playing one of his chess games. Pushing Sumter forward to be sacrificed, and ourselves with it. I don't deserve this, Trezevant.

—Perhaps none of us do. But you have spoken words.

—All right, all right, Goddamnit, I apologize. But my orders are direct from Gid Welles. The only one who could change them's the president—or the secretary of state. That crawling viper! We'll have a reckoning. I won't let this pass.

Trezevant drawled, —If it is meant to be, it will come in good time. I accept your apology, graceless though it was. Now, about the schooner. The only possible time we can throw a party in is at night. They have Drummond lights and picketboats, but one of my officers was able to creep in. A brave fellow, and he knows the harbor like the back of his hand. I propose we make the attempt as soon as dark falls.

Fox looked glumly out of the quarter window. As if without his volition, his hand moved to the decanter once again.

———

Another craft rose slowly into sight at two that afternoon, reefed top-sails and courses a buff patch stitched to the eastern gray. Ker told the quartermaster to send up signal 1116, "Strange sail in sight," to relay the news to the rest of the little flotilla. The men crowded aloft to in-spect her, speculating *Powhatan* had arrived at last, but Duycker guessed her as *Pocahontas.*

He watched her close from the stern, blinking into cold raindrops as another squall brushed by. He wondered how much longer this weather would last. It seemed like weeks since he'd seen the sun. Per-haps he'd become too accustomed to Africa. Could a white man be-come an African? It sounded like a matter for a long wrangle with Steele and Hubbard over brandy and a segar.

The craft drew slowly closer, plunging as the swells passed under her quarter. Gradually he made her out as two-masted, fore-and-aft rather than ship-rigged. Smaller than *Owanee.* It was hard to tell, in this wind, if she was under engine power.

—Pendant ninety-four. *Pocahontas,* all right, the old master said, clapping the glass shut with a serial click. Ker took it from him and studied the closing sail again. For some reason she looked different than when they had sortied from New York together.

—You're sure, Nick?

—It's her all right. Might have some damage aloft, looks like she's made heavy weather of it. Her captain's J. P. Gillis. Not the most dar-ing commander in the navy.

Ker sent Eddowes to the captain with the news. Trezevant came up directly and stood with folded arms watching her near. He'd changed back to service dress, and wasn't wearing a sword. He bit his lip as he watched the gunboat approach, but when he spoke his tone was detached as ever. —Make a signal, Mr. Claiborne. To *Baltic, Poc-ahontas,* and *Harriet Lane:* "Repair on board this ship, officers in command."

Another conference, he thought, and felt like spitting on the deck, though of course he could not set such an example. They should have followed Parker Trezevant's instinct yesterday, rammed their way through full-force or gone down fighting. But he didn't say a word. He clapped the signal together himself, marrying the colorful pendants with the special signalman's knot. Rapp hovered anxiously, as if the flag bag were his only inheritance.

Ker stepped back, and the string leaped off the deck. They were an old set, faded nearly transparent by the Afric sun. The flags climbed jerkily, sucked flat by mainsail backdraft, then snapped to attention, cracking like buggy whips in the fresh wind. *Pocahontas* ran up the "Answering" pendant. *Lane* did so a few seconds afterward. *Baltic* acknowledged by dipping her ensign; he guessed Fox did not have a naval signaler with him, but like most naval officers, he had no doubt memorized most of the code hoists.

Trezevant said gravely, —Mr. Claiborne, no doubt you feel we have had enough palavering.

—I confess the thought had crossed my mind, sir.

—I should like you to be present for this discussion. You will understand why in a few minutes.

—Aye aye, sir.

He'd anticipated another lengthy confabulation, another hairsplitting exchange of views complicated by skirmishing over who was really in charge. Instead, the wet, tired officers who gathered in *Owanee*'s stern cabin were laconic and determined at last. When Trezevant set out his plan to run the icer in as soon as darkness fell, they agreed at once. Captain Gillis felt chance was against it, but that with a bold officer in charge it might succeed. He pointed out that throwing more troops into the fort, however, would not change the tactical situation. Sumter would still lack food and fuel. It could only be reinforced in this way once, before the enemy placed armed vessels within the bar. In short, the position was doomed whatever the forces outside the bar did.

—That's the president's problem. Or General Scott's, Fox said. —They're preparing additional forces, for Sumter and the other forts we still keep, Pensacola and Fort Monroe. We have our orders.

—And I have that brave officer you mentioned, J.P., Trezevant said, and swept his hand around the table and ended pointing at Ker.

—I have another officer making the preparations, even as we speak; but Lieutenant Claiborne here will captain our schooner.

Fox reached out to shake his hand. —Congratulations, Lieutenant. If you should succeed, it will be the exploit of the age.

He said dryly, —I shall do my best, sir.

—A swallow of something strengthening, gentlemen? It promises to be a long night.

Ker contented himself with a sip of the Spanish brandy Trezevant broke out. He kept his voice easy, joking with Fox, shaking hands with the others. He was surprised at how envious they seemed. He was also surprised at how well he could mimic a careless demeanor.

He was trying to come to terms with the likelihood these were his last hours on earth.

The ice schooner was out of New Jersey, three hundred tons burden. Her master, an excitable Portagee, met Eli on deck as he boarded. He had both hands in his beard, knitting at it as if he were making a comforter. Eli told Girnsolver, who had accompanied him with several of *Owanee*'s deck seamen, to prepare to make sail and to receive the troops aboard. To the master he said, —Sir, it is not necessary for you to remain aboard.

—This is my boat.

—The government has commandeered her, sir. The owners will be reimbursed; there's no reason for you to risk your life.

He insisted he would stay. Finally Eli gave in, only asking him to remain below when they began taking fire.

The troops were all seasick, some throwing up, faces as white as if they'd been talced in some ghastly reversal of a Bowery minstrel show. They rowed themselves across in the liner's launches, with maddening slowness. Gradually the little schooner's holds filled with blue-clad men and boxes of hardtack and rifle cartridges, casks of desiccated vegetables, potatoes, and salt pork. As boatload after boatload came aboard he could feel her riding lower in the water. The chilly darkness belowdecks was like the ninth circle of the Inferno, still smelling of ice and straw, echoing with moans, retching, curses.

He straightened, stood for a moment, near to blaspheming himself. Whatever he'd expected from the government service, this makeshift confusion wasn't it. It made him wonder if anyone had really intended to save Sumter at all. If this was the best the Union could manage, it stood no chance against the determined men within the harbor, apparently across the entire Southland. There was no point in fighting at all.

And if no point, why risk the lives of the seamen making up lines and stowing deck gear and shot patches around him? Of the troops battened down below as if they were consignees of the Middle Passage? They were sailing into the jaws of death, like the Light Brigade, and as far as he could see for no better purpose; nothing more than a futile gesture to brighten the smirched honor of those higher up. Those who had so mismanaged this affair as to be too little, too late—

—Ready on deck, Mr. Eaker.

—Very well, Bo's'n. Let us trim up and stand toward *Owanee* again.

Girnsolver told the icer's master, who'd taken the tiller, to go in close. A figure cradling a telescope in the ratlings turned out to be Claiborne. As they slipped down the side Eli called, —Loading's complete, sir, we're ready to go in.

—Stand by, Mr. Eaker. Do not anticipate the command.

Three men came forward to the sloop's bulwarks. One was Trezevant. The schooner was out of shouting range by then. The captain gestured them back. Eli asked the master to heave to a few yards downwind. They tacked clumsily, the draft of navy men unfamiliar with the rig, and ran back under her lee. As they neared again he saw the others were Fox and Gillis. They looked grim enough to preside at an interment.

—Come alongside, Mr. Eaker. Mr. Claiborne will command.

He felt instantly angry, then instantly relieved. The former because he'd been ready to take the schooner in himself. The latter for really the same reason.

—Quickly, quickly, dusk is on us; we have wasted enough time.

The schooner pirouetted about, spinning on her rudder post. As she came into the eye of the wind the jib began to flail, cracking and flapping in the steady wind. She lost way as she coasted in. Claiborne stepped from the Jacob's ladder onto the still-moving quarter rail. He jumped down, staggered at the quick motion of the smaller deck, but caught himself. He crossed to the helm and was opening his mouth when the call of *Owanee*'s lookout fell faintly from the heaving sky.

—Fort—has—struck—her—flag.

Trezevant and Fox craned aloft, as if by looking up they could see what the lookout was reporting. Eli's heart lurched within him, as if it were a suspended weight that had suddenly been tripped. He swung around, trying to see, but Sumter was too distant for him to make out from the low deck of the icer. He glanced at the sloop. The schooner was clear, gathering way only slowly. He grabbed the ratlings next to him and pulled himself up hand to hand.

As he climbed the schooner fell away below him, became a support, a distant deck, then a mere plank tossed on the waves beneath. With each yard gained he felt weaker, his breath came more labored, but with each yard too the horizon pushed away. The enfolding land rose into view, cream-edged, a ribbon of tan, then above that the somberer hues of beach-forest and marsh. At last he had to stop, weakness and fear jelling his arms and legs. He paused there, fingers clawed into the lines, till breath and courage came from some unknown well back to him again; then climbed hand over hand up the last few feet to the gaff jaws, and looked past the black greased spheres of the parral balls.

Sumter lay black against the falling sun, whose rays seeped red as old blood through the streaming pall of smoke. No longer did its guns flash and sparkle against the dark stone. The cannonading was trailing off. Even as he looked on, all firing ceased, the final bumping echoes of the great guns rolling away over the harbor and far inland. An awesome pulsing silence succeeded it, reverberating over the inlet, over the waiting ships without, the flat land, and the rolling sea.

The flag-speck no longer streamed above the battlements. As he saw that, he realized what it meant, the sudden calm, the slowly lift-ing clouds above the shore to his right. The failing light late on a cold spring day, with smoke still streaming up. His breath caught in his throat. He could not credit it. The idea was too painful.

They'd passed through weeks of indecision and bafflement, con-fusion and halfhearted attempts to compromise and placate. Till at last the government had stretched out its hand, and in a hasty scram-ble its servants had attempted a makeshift mission. It had not been well planned. But then, its mission had not been to conquer, destroy, or punish. Only to resupply the last outposts where the flag still flew, preserving a fragile semblance of peace. Now Sumter was the shell of a locust that falls lifeless, its season gone, eaten from within to a hol-low emptiness.

He stared across at a fortress lost, at a city withdrawn. The sun set in flaming glory, sending ruby beams searching upward through the hazy western air. And gradually the entire sky turned bloody, glaring and flickering with russet and copper, as if the whole world had been set aflame.

Part III

Washington, April 16–19, 1861.

16

THE Potomac was yellow and thick as chowder, high and fast and turbulent from the rains of spring. It smelled muddy and cold, like a flooded basement. Ker was standing next to the river pilot, a short, tobacco-chewing, bad-smelling Marylander named Smallwood. Virginia rose on their port hand. The Maryland shore passed slowly down their right. The men stood idle about the decks, or busied themselves blacking blocks or scraping down spars. Girnsolver stood by the ground tackle, sledge to hand in case he had to knock off the stopper at short notice.

The trip upriver had been a frustrating series of breakdowns, anchorings, and occasional driftings with the tide as the engines lost and gained steam. They'd anchored the night before in Occoquan Bay, and gotten under way before dawn. He'd hoisted courses twice this morning, but they were no sooner up than they had to be struck again. They'd touched bottom off Gunston Cove, but he'd rowed out a bower anchor and ordered all the steam Hubbard had and they'd slid back into navigable water at last.

—Captain's on deck.

—Very well, Rapp.

Trezevant nodded distantly at his salute. The captain was hatless, graying hair porcupine-spiky. He greeted the pilot, looked aloft, ahead, aft. The deck quivered to the chuffing steam-thud. Volumes of slaty smoke carried shoreward. Ker watched him, mentally register-ing the calls of the leadsman and the course corrections Smallwood gave the helm between trips to leeward to spit.

Three days before, as *Owanee, Baltic,* and the other warships stood off, Ker had taken the ice schooner into Charleston under a white flag to witness the surrender ceremonies. To everyone's surprise on both sides, not a single man had been killed or even wounded by the furious bombardment. When Sumter's defeated garrison came out to the waiting fleet, the crews had manned the rails for a hearty cheer. Anderson's boys, haggard and exhausted looking, had returned a rather less enthusiastic yell.

Fox had touched at Fortress Monroe for messages, then broken up the relief force. *Baltic, Harriet Lane,* and *Pocahontas* had headed back to Brooklyn, while *Owanee* received telegraphic orders from Wash-ington to proceed up the Potomac to defend the capital.

So now they were at war, war with the South. He understood it intellectually, but he hadn't understood it yet in his guts. They'd missed too much, out on the African station. It seemed so lunatic, so impossible that one half of the nation could be at war with the other, that he literally could not eat. He'd lived on coffee and segars on the transit north, and for most of the workday routine avoided thinking about it at all, as if it were a bad dream that might yet vanish with waking.

Trezevant, beside him. He touched his cap again as the captain said, but not to him, —What do you see as our time alongside, Mr. Smallwood?

—I should estimate about ten o'clock, cap'n. 'F we have no fur-ther trouble with yer fuckin' engines.

—I recall this river as being rather more of a thoroughfare.

—Ain't been much traffic the last few weeks. Now we done showed them what-fer at Sumter maybe things'll liven up again.

Trezevant squinted at the woody shore. Only an occasional plantation house broke the vista of field and forest. —Mr. Claiborne, a word.

Withdrawn to the quarter, out of earshot of the others, the captain propped a boot on a gun truck. Looking shoreward, he said, —I showed you the letter I had. From Mr. Mallory. Offering me a commission.

—Yes sir.

—I am taking my resignation to the Department upon our arrival. Ahasuerus is packing now, as I do not anticipate returning aboard.

Ker put a hand to his beard. Another shock. He really was growing quite tired of them. He cleared his throat. —I regret most keenly to hear that, sir. Most keenly. Do you think they'll accept it?

—Oh, I doubt that very much. The former secretary was gentlemanly about accepting resignations. This new man, Welles, has shown himself vindictive against those of Southern birth. I will be dismissed. But that is neither here nor there. We belong to a new country now, you and I.

He shook his head. —Neither your state nor mine has yet seceded, sir. And I don't think Virginia will.

—Oh, you do not? Even after Sumter? Trezevant looked surprised.

—No sir. According to the last reports I heard, there's still considerable unionist sentiment in the convention.

The captain said loftily, —Unto, unto, sir; all that will change in very short order, perhaps has done so already, while we were at sea. Let me be frank, Claiborne. We have seen action together, after all. You have proven yourself an exceptionally competent officer. Moreover, you are a gentleman of good family. I believe the government which tendered me a commission could be persuaded to do the same for you.

He straightened. The moment had come; he could no longer purposely misunderstand or evade what the man who had taught him so much was asking of him, was offering him. He said, as gravely as the other had, —I appreciate your interest, Captain. And thank you for your compliments. But I cannot accompany you South. I have made my decision, and will stay where I am.

They stood facing each other now, and suddenly he felt as if someone he loved were dying. He put out his hand, impulsively, and felt it gripped hard in return. He looked into the sunken eyes as the captain said softly, —I understand, my boy. I respect your decision, and hope it brings you fortune.

—I wish you the same, sir, with all my heart.

They were both looking shoreward again when the pilot joined them. —'Scuse me for busting in, gentlemen, but we're making up on Mount Vernon. It's traditional for—

—For naval ships to salute the father of our country, Trezevant finished. Ker could not tell if his tone held irony or not. —Exec, make it so; lower the ensign, and toll the bell. Toll it slowly, sir, slowly. For these are not the happiest of times.

The unfinished monument was a white stump beyond the open Mall and the low line of the Long Bridge. Through the glass he made out the pillars of Arlington, the stately home of the Lees. The White House was not visible from downriver, but the Capitol rose in lofty splendor, crowned with scaffolding and the spindly counterbalance of a crane. As they turned into the Anacostia a tug cast off and made for them, puffing a tumultuous column of smoke. It set itself against their bow and plodded along in company.

At the navy yard a swath of green firing range stretched down to the riverfront. Several smaller vessels lay moored in the stream. As soon as the sloop was alongside, Trezevant went below. Ker supervised making up the lines, making sure she'd ride safely whatever the river did. As his men set rat guards, Duycker touched his cap. —He give you any idea what he wants to do with the crew?

—Hold everyone aboard until I return from calling on the yard commander. Don't make any promises about liberty.

He jogged down the gangway, then staggered as his boots touched dressed stone. The movementless land rolled ponderously beneath him. He waited for it to steady, then walked the sloop's length, checking the lines, running an eye over the hull. Aboard once more, he wrote *Moored alongside Washington Navy Yard* in the log, signed it, and called Eaker to set the in-port watch.

He was pulling on a fresh shirt in his cabin when someone tapped at the door. It was Jerrett. The captain desired all officers in the wardroom.

Trezevant looked so changed in a brown sack suit and slouch hat that Ker doubted he'd have recognized him on the street. His carpetbag and leather sword case waited by the door. A black overcoat with velvet-covered buttons was draped over them. Ker heard Ahasuerus rattling about in the pantry. He wondered if the Kroom would go with the captain.

—Claiborne. Join us.

He took his place next to Eaker. Glanced at Steele and Schuyler, Glass and Duycker, and the few other officers and midshipmen left. He remembered the merry times they'd dined and sung together, and the party seemed small and the little room far too large for the few who were left.

Ahasuerus lurched from the pantry. Shippy tagged behind, looking solemn. The servants set out wine and glasses and withdrew.

The captain cleared his throat. —Gentlemen, I can no longer maintain my place among you. But I thought we might share a drink before I leave, as we have been through so many pompey-doodles together.

The gurgle of the wine was the only sound as the cruet circulated. Ker recognized it before he tasted it. They'd given H.M.S. *Medusa* a "dash" of throat-scorching U.S. Navy whiskey when the two ships lay together in Kabenda Bay, and been gifted with a cask of Royal Navy Madeira in return. *Owanee* had had the advantage of that exchange. The junior officers fingered their glasses. At formal dinners, when guests were present, it was customary to make the first toast to the president of the United States. Perhaps Trezevant was thinking this too as he paused, pursing his lips.

—To our time together, he said at last.

They lifted, and Ker tasted, in the dark savor of grapes and sun, West Africa in all its loveliness and squalor.

Schuyler said, —Recharge your glasses, gentlemen. To our absent friends.

—To wives and sweethearts.

—May they never meet.

—Thank you, Dr. Steele, for the requisite note of levity. Trezevant looked around as if memorizing their faces against his return. —Gentlemen, no one regrets this parting more than I. I pray next time we meet it will still be in friendship.

No one spoke. Eaker seemed about to, but then seemed to think better of it. Ker looked around at the others' bemused expressions. Then he picked up the cruet and served round again.

—To our captain.

—Our captain, they echoed. Trezevant did not touch his own glass, as was proper. Simply inclined his head, and blinked.

He left a few minutes later, followed a pace behind by the old African. Ker watched them go from the quarterdeck, and it was as if a piece of himself walked away from him. The part he had always thought best. The exemplar of courage, and honor, and rectitude. That was what Trezevant had been for him, from the day he'd stepped aboard.

Damn it, he thought. Damn them, damn this damned time, this damned war or revolution or whatever it would be; whatever you called a whole country rushing toward the brink, splitting and hammering itself apart like a frozen river going over a waterfall. One by one they were walking away, and he had no power to change or stay them.

The captain turned, looking back at the sloop, most likely, a last glance as he left her; and their eyes met one last time. He raised a gloved hand. Ker straightened, and brought his own up in salute.

A few more steps, to a carriage waiting at the head of the pier; and then he couldn't see them anymore.

———

Straight as a gun rammer, hook beaked and fierce eyed as an aging osprey, Captain Franklin Buchanan was known the fleet through as "Old Buck." Now Ker stood in the commandant's office as the old man studied his card with keen azure eyes. The legendary salt's grip was still firm, but he'd gained weight and lost hair since the last time they'd shaken hands.

—Sir, I had the honor of dining with you four years ago at the home of your kinsman William Goldsborough, in Annapolis.

—I recall you, sir. Good dancer. Good swordsman. A high-toned young officer.

—You flatter me, sir.

—Perhaps. To what do I owe the pleasure of this visit?

—I'm *Owanee*'s exec, Commodore. I'm here to report our arrival.

He was thinking that the awe he'd felt at meeting Buchanan as a mid was still there. The man before him had carried aggressiveness, impulsiveness, and personal bravery to the point of myth. He'd entered the navy as a fourteen-year-old midshipman during the War of 1812. He'd not only commanded the *Germantown* at the battle of Tuxpan, he'd led his landing force ashore through heavy Mexican fire and personally taken the battery at La Pena. He'd been Commodore Perry's flag captain during the 1853 expedition to Japan. Now the corners of his mouth tugged down as he peered behind Ker. —Is my old friend Cy Trezevant not well?

—Sir, he sends his respects, and asks me to inform you he's on his way to Main Navy to tender his resignation.

—I see. Buchanan's hair was gone in front, but he passed a hand over silvering wings above either ear. —Yes, I see. All too well. Well, sir; will you take tea? As you may recall, I do not consume spiritous liquors.

—I should be grateful for tea, sir.

Over a cup of Darjeeling Buchanan asked about Charleston. Ker recounted their rather disappointing performance off the bar of that rebellious city. —I don't want to cast aspersions on anyone, sir. That's not my intent, but I ascribe our impotence to the divided state of command. To *Powhatan's* absence, too, but I think we might have made an effort.

—You would have, had I been there. Or if Cy'd been unquestionably in command.

He thought Trezevant had seemed less eager to take the lead than Buchanan assumed, until it was almost too late; but he sipped tea instead of saying so. —At any rate, here we are as ordered, though our engines badly need attention. I hope we can call on your boilermakers.

—I shall have my superintendent report to you for direction.

—Has Sumter's fall had much effect?

Buchanan's brows went up. —Had much effect? Of course, you have just stepped ashore. Mr. Lincoln has called out the militia, to the tune of seventy-five thousand troops.

Ker sat stunned. Through the numbness he noticed he couldn't feel his hands, they had no more sensation than if his fingers were whittled of wood. Just like when they'd sat him down and told him they'd found the boat drifting overturned off Cape Charles, that his mother and father were gone and would never return. He let the teacup down very slowly. —So he intends to invade.

—No doubt in my mind. His aim's to subjugate the South, and all because of this rascally Northern quidnuncing with the institution of servitude.

—What's happening here in the capital?

Buchanan made a disgusted moue. —An amazing amount of vacuous blather, as usual. An attack is rumored preparing against Fort Washington, which would bottle us up here in the Potomac. There are also rumors the B&O will be cut in Baltimore. This city is quite defenseless. Certainly if Maryland goes out of the Union, it will be untenable.

Ker studied the old man, his jolly sparkling eyes, the restless energy that made his boot bounce restlessly even as he affected a careless pose. Remembering what this very man had written to Trezevant, that one could be "absolved" of one's oath. He said, —And you, sir, are a Marylander.

—I certainly am, my boy. Certainly am. And I own colored servants, sir, whom I have always treated with the utmost consideration. Your own view, sir?

—I'm divided. I won't disguise from you that the harsher aspects of the peculiar institution revolt me.

—But are you prepared to go where the abolitionists are pushing us? We in the South must resign ourselves to the loss of our way of life, if our dusky workers are colonized elsewhere. Or else, if they stay, accept the inevitable result of social equality: a mulattoized and utterly degraded race. Stowe and the rest of those pious liars won't have to live among them. We will.

Ker contemplated this. —It seems to me we could have argued that case within the confines of the Union.

—No gentleman stays in a house where he's insulted. Why should we? If we desire to free ourselves from Yankeeism, establish a country of our own, that is our right. Is it not?

—I suppose so. But I note that you, sir, are still wearing the uniform of the United States.

Buchanan shrugged, and poured himself more tea. Ker refused with a shake of his head. —I believe my state will follow yours out of the Union. When that event occurs, I will follow my immediate government, and offer my services to her.

—And in the meanwhile, sir?

The shaggy brows leapt upward. —In the meanwhile? Why, by the Lord God! In the meanwhile I'll defend this post to the death. If necessary I shall touch off the magazine, and take anyone still inside the walls with me.

Ker nearly smiled at the dramatic tone, but caught himself in time; the old sea dog was perfectly serious. —Did you intend us to participate in that defense, sir?

—I have received no orders in respect of *Owanee.* I shall refer you to Mr. Welles for that, sir, as you seem to have succeeded to command.

He nodded, thinking such would be brief if what Trezevant said about the new secretary's dislike of Southerners was accurate. He glanced around for his cap. —Thank you for the hospitality, sir. If you will send your engineer superintendent down to see my Mr. Hubbard, we shall begin repairs.

—Do you require ammunition? Stores?

—We never fired a round off Carolina, sir. I'll have my purser look into the matter of necessaries. He rose and bowed. —Your servant, sir.

The old warrior returned his bow with one even more courtly. —*Your* servant, Lieutenant. I am glad we were able to renew our acquaintance, and may God advise you, and us all, in these parlous times.

He asked directions of Buchanan's writer, and shortly after boarded the trolley for the seat of government, four miles away. The horses clopped along stolidly, noses to the pavement like bloodhounds. The rail carriage rumbled and clacked past ramshackle wooden houses. Most of the streets were the same yellow mud as the river, just less diluted. A drunken woman annoyed him on the car, but he turned his head away and she moved on.

The Navy Department was on the east side of Seventeenth, a small brick town house opposite the intersection with F Street. The interior smelled of mildew and the gas jets flickered and smoked. The creaking floor was covered with a worn ingrain carpet, patterned rosettes and anthemia like the one in the parlor at home in Eastville when he was little.

He remembered it with wistful surprise, because he didn't remember much else about the big house. Even before that last doomed trip his parents had not been doing well. There'd been Claibornes in Northampton County since 1640, but the tobacco-drained land had yielded less and less as the years went by and finally they'd had to move to the little house outside town. He frowned; why was he remembering all this just now, all these memories of times long past? This was not the occasion for it. He climbed to the second floor, announced himself to a yeoman, and took a chair in the hallway with several other men, most in civilian suits. All were smoking, and after a few minutes he lit a cheroot himself.

Half an hour later he was ushered in. An old boy with a white beard and an incongruous head of long chestnut hair that Ker realized after a startled moment was a cheap wig was scratching away at a desk, glasses clamped to his nose. The new Secretary of the Navy looked like a harassed, overaged Father Christmas.

—Lieutenant Ker Claiborne, executive officer of U.S.S. *Owanee*, sir.

—Be seated, Lieutenant. Welles waved fussily toward a worn chair. It creaked like a poorly fished spar as Claiborne set himself cautiously into it.

At last Welles wiped his pen on a felt scrap. He unhooked his glasses one earpiece at a time, and goggled at Ker suddenly with bulging eyes and opened mouth. He looked senile, or else demented. Ker started when the old man shouted, evidently to someone in the outer room, —Ask Captain Paulding to step in.

Hiram Paulding was small and hard looking, with a mouth like the first axe cut into a beech tree. Ker got to his feet again and introduced himself. The chief of personnel did not offer his hand. He said, New England nasal in his speech, —We had the doubtful pleashah of an interview with your commanding officer this morning. You're heah to follow him South, I presume.

—No sir. I'm here to report our presence at Anacostia as ordered.

Paulding's mouth turned down even more. —Are you aware he's resigned?

—Captain Trezevant shared that intention with me before he left the ship.

—I've noticed that treason's communicable.

He halted the hot words that first occurred to him. Welles was sitting back, playing with his pince-nez, glancing from one to the other. Maybe this wasn't the time to insist too closely on his honor. Not with these two ancient Yankees. Paulding was most likely trying to bait him into some incautious statement. He said as evenly as he could, —Are we to lay by for some time, sir? I should like to undertake repairs to our boilers and engine frames.

—You want to put your engines out of order? Paulding said, suspicion sparking like a cut diamond in his eyes. —Weren't you just overhauled in New York?

—We were pulled out of Brooklyn before they laid a wrench to her. The boilers are leaking and the shaft's out of true. We had several breakdowns on the way up the bay.

Welles had been combing his beard with his fingers. Now he said, —Lieutenant, would you leave us for a moment? I shall call you back presently.

Back in the anteroom, the other callers shifted their feet, smoked, and spat. A fat horsefly droned around the room, then headed out the open window. From outside, from the direction of the president's house, came the sleepy slow clopping of a one-horse carriage. He relaxed in the chair, waiting for the guillotine to fall. The room seemed very warm. He caught his head nodding and hitched himself upright, then went to the window and looked down at the street. It was deserted except for an old black man who wandered slowly down the gutter, apparently searching for placer gold.

—Lieutenant Claiborne.

The door closed once more. This time Paulding said grudgingly, —Are you trying to tell me you're staying with the government? Despite birth, family, and your house in Norfolk?

—Virginia hasn't seceded, sir. As to personal loyalty, I hope my service to date speaks for my future conduct.

—You don't want to apply for California service?

—I considered it, sir. But I took my pay and my commission when the government offered it. I think I owe it my support when it's threatened.

Welles squinted, looking not senile now but canny as a country lawyer. After a moment he nodded. He drew a half sheet of foolscap from his desk, and his pen scratched again.

—I'm appointing you to temporary command of *Owanee*, Lieutenant. Dispose your officers as seems best. Advance masters and midshipmen to fill vacant positions. Advise Captain Paulding if you need more crew.

He stood, rather taken aback. —Aye aye, sir.

—Replenish coal, wood, and provisions, then anchor in the stream. You may undertake minor repairs, but don't disable your engine. I want you ready to steam at two hours' notice. Should we have to skedaddle out of here, you'll take the president and as much of the government as possible north. Also, prepare a strong room with a stout door and reinforce the floor to take a heavy weight. These orders to be kept most strictly confidential.

—I understand, sir.

Paulding burst out, —Sir, I must protest. You can't trust him. Not with this.

Welles said mildly, —I have observed, if I rely on a fellow, he most often turns out trustworthy. The lieutenant is correct. His state has not yet withdrawn its allegiance, nor has he. We don't have enough sea officers left that we can dismiss them out of hand just because they were born on the wrong side of the Mason-Dixon. The secretary shuffled through his desk, then handed over a bundle of letters tied with red ribbon. —Your official correspondence, Captain Claiborne. Oh, and you'll find an order in there temporarily detaching your chief engineer. Mr. Lenthall requires him for some special duty.

—You're taking Mr. Hubbard, sir? I'll have a hard time steaming without him.

—We're shorthanded all round, Lieutenant. You will simply have to make do as best you can.

A moment of silence stretched out in the bare office. Paulding glared, hostile as a winter wind. Ker cleared his throat, addressing the old man. —Aye aye, sir. Should you require our services, consider *Owanee* at your complete disposal.

—Oh, we shall. We shall indeed; but thank you for the offer.

Welles returned to his scribbling. Paulding sat with arms folded, still scowling. Taking that as dismissal, Ker got up, made a very deep, perhaps an unnecessarily deep, bow to them both, and took his leave.

17

---◆---

New York City,
April 13th, 1861.

Dear Cousin and Friend,

I take pen in hand to tell you spring has at last reached our stony island. I had a pleasant ride through the Park this morning. It elevated my spirits, which have been cast down of late. El Cid is glad of spring's return too, and was most eager when I suggested a canter.

Barlow, Parkinson, Maire, Mrs. Kerigan, and the others wish to be remembered to you.

I *most earnestly* hope your health is good and that the chest weakness of which you told me is relieved by the sea air. If there is any medicine lacking or any provision you should like, let me know and I will send it at once.

This morning the papers carried news of the opening of the bombardment against Sumter. The surprise was immense as the last dispatches said Davis had directed Beauregard to let supplies pass, and that the possibility of hostilities had passed.

For once I was not disappointed in the common people of the street. They were one and all indignant for revenge and vowing they would not allow the Flag to be covered in the spittle of traitors. They forced that loathsome reptile Bennett to put the Stars and Stripes out his window so that his shop of lies should not be burnt. The *Times,* and the other *respectable* newspapers are full of wonderment at such uncalled for attack.

Yet all may yet be for the best. I have had a note from Mr. Phelps, who tells me this must be a short conflict. He assured me the so-styled Confederate states cannot muster a tenth the money necessary to carry forward a war. Once the matter is settled I hope we can settle the Slavery issue as well. We have extended a pacific hand and it has been rebuffed with a curse; let us renounce forever the idea of compromise with the leaders of this evil conspiracy.

My previous letter, which must be to your hand by this time, told how I felt when I saw you off at South Street. Did you spy me waving my handkerchief? It gives me endless pride to think one so close in a family tie is defending the starry Flag. If only a young woman could find a way to put her hand to the plow.

I have been seeing a good deal of Mrs. Lispenard. I believe you have not met Harriet yet. She has been upon the stage, and now teaches Elocution. She is rather older than I but a good companion for someone so isolated in the midst of the great city as myself.

Now I must tell you of my interview with Uncle, the subject being the Van Velsor investments. I entered upon the meeting with hope, which in the event was *dashed utterly.*

Whatever happens between us, Eli, you must know that I do not intend to permit anyone else to manage my portion for me. Perhaps I am one of those "unnatural" women we are warned not to become; but I do believe it would be best both for my future husband and myself if this were clearly understood before we entered into that sacred union whose name is Matrimony.

At any rate, I scheduled the interview using Mrs. Lispenard's name. You will forgive me the subterfuge as you know he would not give me the "time of day" in a business way otherwise. Throwing off my veil, I made a polite and well reasoned plea to your father for an account of his management of my mother's money.

He would tell me only that its value fluctuated, and the market being down with the uncertainty, the value was necessarily somewhat reduced. When I insisted on more details he at last admitted that the *funds had been commingled*—I believe that is the term—with those of the Firm, and that no separate accounting was kept.

Eli, I may be inexperienced in the financial world, *as in so much else,* but I am not so much of a fool as not to realize he means me to have *no say and no control* over what Mother left me, even when I should come of age. This is a *most bitter realization* and one I have not yet searched the bottom of, added to the list of your father's injustices and tyrannies over us.

I have never expressed a wish to live independently. Such is not my intent, nor my desire. Yet I have seen how difficult it is in this world for a woman who does not marry; and I do not know at present if marriage is my destiny. I say to you now as directly as I would say it to a friend of my own sex: *I do not wish to live at the behest of others,* no matter how closely related or loved.

Being treated as a child cannot do otherwise than try my patience. If you were here I would propose we kneel together and ask for guidance. But you are not and I must deal with your Father alone. And this is right, for I am asking for *what is my own,* and should depend on no one else to do this for me.

Eli, I feel that I am changing. Perhaps you are changing as well, facing the "Grim Visage" of war. I fear I cannot continue in your Father's house. But can I leave it? Would I be able to make my way in the great world, or fall and become dust beneath the feet of the hurrying multitude?

I must tell you an honest thing. Though I love you it may

never be more than the way one loves a brother. You do not deserve to be burdened with one who feels toward you as I do; and you have a holy mission to abolish slavery from the face of the earth. I have told your Father this. Let the consequences be what they may, I only wish I might suffer them for both of us.

Yours most affectionately,
Araminta

P.S. Mary has just brought the astonishing news of the surrender of Sumter. She had gone out to deliver a note and was at the telegraph office when it was posted upon the chalkboard. I confess myself astounded. Had not the contest only begun? I thought certainly your expedition would hold the position. But I gathered my thoughts and recalled the brave Anderson had only seventy men under his command, while ringed by thousands of the enemy. Then it seemed less of a surprise, but still a grievous disappointment.

I know if there had been the slightest chance of success, you and our brave navy would have thrust into the fray, but evidently such was not to be, though there seems no clear explanation yet why not. Never mind, these *rebels* as they are calling them here will yet feel the displeasure of the aroused people of the North. If they demand war to prolong their tyranny over their helpless victims, then *war* they shall have and the *trying hour* cometh.—

A.E.V.V.

18

C AL Hanks lingered on deck after the line parties had been dismissed. He shaded his eyes, looking toward the Virginia
shore, then toward the distant city.

—Forget it, big-un, said Billy Ripley. What I heard, we gonna
coal, then ol' Girnie wants to paint the sides. They ain't goin' to let
none of us ashore.

He didn't answer and after a moment the boy sniffed and drifted
away. Cal lingered about the gun, stooping occasionally to make it
look like he was attending to the shifting-trucks. But actually he was
watching Babcock as the warrant gunner stood talking with Archbold and Yardley.

They stopped talking as he came up, all three staring coldly at
him. He touched his cap to the chief. —Gunner.

Babcock didn't even look at him, left it to Archbold to say, —
What do *you* want?

—Wanted to see, I could get ashore tonight.

Archbold laughed. —It ain't Sunday, boy. What, you want liberty
on a workday? Ain't you still on the *black*list, anyway?

When they were done chuckling at that one, Babcock said, idly slapping the colt against his leg, —Mr. Eaker hasn't given us no word on liberty yet, Hanks. My guess is, ship's company'll be held aboard while we're here. However long that's going to be. And I figure we're due to coal this afternoon.

—I'd sure like to get just a couple hours, see some folks I knows.

Archbold shook his head wonderingly. —You tellin' me you got family in Washington?

—Put him to work, Del, Babcock said. —If you got nothing I'll send him to the bo's'n, he can help chip down the chain cable.

—You 'eard the gunner, Archbold said, returning his blue gaze to Hanks. —Get to work.

He didn't answer, just nodded and looked to the side and then walked away. As he did he heard Yardley, —You can smell the black on that son of a bitch upwind. Don't you ever hold a scrub-down party on him?

Two of the other seamen, New York b'hoys, were talking as he went down the forward companionway. He caught a word or two: — She had a bush just like two handfuls of horsehair out of a mattress. And a face like a surveyed snatch block. But you can bet your pile she can French. One caught sight of Hanks. —Hey there, chummy. You talk to old Tar Breeches? What'd he say?

—Said no liberty all the time we here.

They cursed. One looked warily about, then spat on the deck. The tobacco left a mahogany stain on the clean straw mat.

—You hear what that Goddamn Rooshian Finn said? The one in Maintop Division? Said this was a Jonah voyage on a Jonah ship. Said we wouldn't never get back to Brooklyn.

—That old squarehead's got bugs in the attic. He's been talkin' hex an' bad luck since he came aboard. You there, Snowflake! You believe this ship's cursed? Maybe it is, for you, huh?

He didn't answer, just touched the juju surreptitiously under his blouse. He didn't like talk about Jonahs and curses.

When the b'hoys ambled off he went the other way. He went all the way forward and came out on the berthing deck.

At night it was close packed as a bat cave, resounding with snores and mutters and the soft speech of hammock mates. Now it was bare and dark, the hammocks made up and struck topside along the bulwarks, and empty save for a stench of bilge water and man farts and a few of the boys who'd trickled back down now that the lines were set. Several sat on the deck playing all fours. One of the coal heavers was stripping off his overalls. They were crusted with black grease and coal dust, and only a crease of white skin showed around his eyes. He stared at Cal as he went by, gaze belligerent. Cal didn't return the look. He reached down the dipper and got a drink of water out of the scuttlebutt. Then rubbed the back of his hand over his mouth, considering.

Eight bells rang out at measured intervals, four beats of two; the end of the forenoon watch. A moment later the boatswain's pipe shrilled. As soon as its high note dropped away a drum began to beat. The men laughed and straightened instantly from their lounging attitudes. The cardplayers jumped up and crowded to the companionway.

Topside the sky was darker. He wondered if it'd rain. They'd coal in the rain, but they couldn't paint.

As the drum continued to roll, a small procession emerged from the next deck down and wound its way slowly topside. The mate of the spirit room, the captain of the hold, Mr. Glass's steward, and the jack o' the dust. A marine escorted them, bayonet fixed to his long rifle musket. The mate walked just behind an oval tub of wood bound in bright brass. It was full, and heavy, to judge by the strained faces of the two men carrying it. The captain of the hold carried the tot cups, the tinware rattling on its marline loop. Cal fell in at the tail of the column. Reaching the open deck, its members ranged themselves in a solemn semicircle on the port quarterdeck. The master-at-arms fastened a line between the fife rail and the pinrail, and Hanks joined the crewmen gathering behind it.

With the pomp of a bishop celebrating high mass, the mate swept off the lid of the firkin. Under it a semicircular shelf was bored through with eight holes. Beneath that rippled the dark raw liquor. The captain of the hold unstrung the cups. He rattled them into the holes as the steward unfolded the grog list. The officers stood on the starboard side, talking in low voices. The whole ship seemed subdued, the usual clatter of mauls and work aloft stilled as if God Himself were about to speak.

—Abbott, the paymaster called. A scarred landsman ducked under the line as the mate dipped a tin, then brimmed all the tots at once with one sweeping pour.

—Balston. The next man took his tot, tossed it back, smacked his lips, and went forward to his mess. One by one the others followed, the master-at-arms keeping an eye out for doublers or men on the sick list.

—Hanks. He ducked under the line and went forward, and took his tot in the wooden cup that hung, carefully separated from the rest, by the side of the cask. Wiped his mouth and threw the cup into the firkin and went forward, dragging his sleeve over the burning of the raw liquor. Behind him the others complained and shouted; the damn nigger had thrown his cup into their whiskey. He did not look back.

The colored mess squatted cross-legged on the stoned planks around the mess cloth. The boiled salt pork and dog's-body seemed skimpy and bland without jam and soft-tack and the rest of the pogey bait Ahasuerus had prigged out of the wardroom stores. They talked and joked, free among themselves for a few brief minutes out of the long workday. When one bell sounded Cal wiped and rolled the tarpaulin and stowed it in its place in the overhead. The messcook carried the tin dishes off to wash, and the other men pulled out pipes and cigarritos. He sat glumly silent, rubbing at his neck. He didn't smoke. He'd been saving every cent of his pay for Mr. Ira Fort.

Now the lawyer was dead, and he had all the bastard's money. But he had no idea what to do next.

At two bells the pipes broke out again, first faintly up on deck, then taken up by the boatswain's mates all about the ship. The men got up reluctantly, knocking out pipes in the sand buckets. They'd expected to coal, but instead the call was "All hands" first, then "Sweepers." When they were done with the sweep-down the word came down for washday. He stood in line for fresh water, scrubbed his off jumper and button-front trow, but didn't touch his neckerchief. Once rolled it stayed rolled, till they laid you on a plank, covered you with a flag, and slid you over the side. Every seaman knew that. They wouldn't think anything of it, that it was rolled tight and that he slept with it tucked under him in his hammock.

As soon as the clean laundry was hung out, it started to rain.

Midafternoon a flat came alongside, and they carried split wood for the cookstove and provisions and casked water aboard in the cold rain. After it was empty the tug came up the river and took it away. By then it was nearly time for supper, and another tot.

As dusk came down, Hanks stood on the forecastle, wondering if he should start smoking again. He'd counted the money from Fort's strongbox. It was nearly a thousand dollars, a sum he found it hard even to imagine, let alone believe he owned. He could have tobacco or new duds or a new knife, just go down and buy them from the slop chest. He could have rum, as much as he liked; the spirit-room mate was known to pass a tickler on the side, if such were suitably rewarded.

But that wasn't what he wanted. The rain fell slowly, as if it always had and always would, making everything look dreary and gray. He looked across the riverfront past the curved stone of the quay, over the jumbled banks of timber and pyramids of cannonballs, to the city beyond, the dusk falling so that the white bulk of the Capitol shone like a white ship gone aground in the midst of hundreds of twinkling lights.

He sang softly, lips barely moving.

> *Go way, Old Man.*
> *Go way, Old Man.*
> *Where you been all day?*

227

If you treat me good
I'll stay till the Judgment Day.
But if you treat me bad,
I'll sure to run away.

No liberty?

All right then, he'd just have to fadge for himself.

The skiff lay a few yards off, rocking gently. The dilapidated patriarch who captained it had rowed out from Poplar Point that afternoon, flung a rock-and-rope anchor overboard, and wedged a cane pole into the thwarts and a battered pipe into his toothless mouth. Then he'd lain back with his hat over his eyes and bare feet dangling in the ocher flood. Cal had watched him all the time they were tramping back and forth loading stores, and for all those hours he hadn't stirred. Not even when it started raining. Maybe he was asleep. Maybe he was dead.

At last he went below and got a potato off one of the messboys. He waited till no one else was in the heads, then ducked down so he was out of sight from the deck and whipped the tater high into the air.

The old man shuddered when the spud plopped into the water. He pushed his ragged hat back and turned his head from side to side. He even squinted up at the ragged clouds before his slow gaze wheeled around and snagged at last on Cal's beckoning hand.

Grandpop feathered his oars under the bowsprit. This close his face was a withered scuppernong. He blinked up with the dull clouded orbs of an ancient turtle. —What you want, sailor boy?

—Doin' any good, Uncle?

—Nary a bite. You a navy man, nigger? Sure 'nough?

—Uniform and all. You sees it.

—I 'spect so. What you wants wif me?

—Wants you to row me 'shore, Uncle.

The boatman examined the ship, followed the gangplank landward. —All you gots to do is walk.

—They watchin' to cotch me that way. Two bits in it, you rows me round the wall there.

—How you gone get back? I ain't gone wait on ye, no suh.

—I figure that out later.

He coaxed the old fellow closer, holding out the bright coin as if tempting a raven, and at last the rickety boat sidled the last few feet in. He swung himself down the shit-slippery fore-chains, over the yellow-brown water. Hung from the bobstay, then let go. He dropped onto one of the thwarts, rolled off, and tumbled into the bottom of the boat, striking his shin so hard his leg instantly went numb. He crouched down at once and the old man threw a fishy-smelling blanket over his head.

With a steady creaking of the thole pins they rowed into the falling dark.

The old man landed him not at a wharf but at a decaying wooden bulkhead that leaned out over the tide-marsh edge like rotting teeth. A dog raged beyond a backyard fence as he stepped up on the skiff's bow, gauged his distance, then levered himself over. Clamshells grated under his brogans. Pain skewered his injured leg, but it held. He peered around into the unlit darkness. Cold fear washed over him like a rising tide, and sweat prickled up along his shoulders.

They caught him here, he'd go back to Georgia. That or be sold downriver, die chained in some steaming Deep South rice swamp. Either way, he'd never see them again.

He took a deep breath and asked the boatman where he could find a darky cathouse.

The old fellow cackled. Told him, and added, —You watch out for they curfew walkers, now, my man. You don't want to get carried to they nigger jail. Don't go well for no colored folk there.

The two blocks felt like an hour's walk, exposed in the blue uniform for what he was: frencher, runaway slave, murderer, thief. He pulled that cold sweat off his forehead. Felt like the brand of Cain was burning on his brow. Only the dark comforted him. He suspected not many went out after nightfall, this side of town.

The house was unlit as he approached but for a faint glow deep in a first-story window. He went around back, found the jamb by feel, and scratched. A stout colored woman answered, barely cracking the rickety door.

—Evenin' ma'am. This here Miss Ruth's house?

—Who you seekin, sailor?

—Man tol' me I find some comfort here.

She ran a look up and down him, then opened up a smidgeon more. Just enough to admit him. The glow came from a single lamp, lard lamp by the smell of it, somewhere deeper in the house. He made as if to go toward it, but the woman took hold of his blouse and pressed her hips in close. —You be took care of right here. My name Calisha.

—I needs me some other clothes, Calisha.

She didn't act surprised. —You makin' sticks?

—Naw, needs to see some people in town. Can't go round the streets in these skins. You got patrollers?

—We gots po-lice. They near 'bout as bad.

He pulled out a roll, fifty dollars he'd extracted from his necker-chief hoard. —I pay you good.

Her eyes lingered hungrily on it. —You wants clothes, huh? Want a drink first?

—No, don't got much time. Got some shirt and pants I can wear?

—I might could fine some.

In a dark closet that smelled as if a mule had died in it she pulled rags from a heap on the floor. —Take those, they ought to fit you. But I ain't got no boots for feet that big.

—I wear these just fine.

—Who you goin to see?

—Can't tell you that, honey. Best you never saw me. Got a hat in that slop pile?

He hesitated just inside the door a few minutes later, dirtied by the feel of the rough cotton osnaburg. Whoever had owned it had made a living killing things. One shirt arm was stiff with a dark stain he was certain sure was blood. The black coat was too tight, but he'd improved that with a jerk on the back seam that left it split hanging over his ass. The trowsers were ragged too. None of the hats came anywhere near fitting him. He hated to go hatless but didn't have a choice. He started out, then turned back. He pulled two things he needed out of his blues, the roll of shin plasters and the folded-up paper that told his enlistment. Then rolled the uniform neatly and left it on top of the chifforobe.

—What you got there? That paper?

—Enlistment paper. Says I in the navy. Don't like to be walking nowhere without no paper.

—You smarter den you looks. Gone be back tonight?

—Be back two-three hours. Don't sell them things I left, now. Be fi' dollar more for you.

—I keep 'em right here for you. Then you gone stay awhile? Kick up yo' heels wid Calisha?

—Sho. Why not? He pushed his hand between her legs, felt the hump of her sex thrusting back against his hard fingers. For a moment he considered pushing her down there in the stinking room but then remembered that the night was wasting and he did not know how far he had to go.

—We have us some fun then, girl, he murmured, and pushed past her and out the door.

He'd never been in this city before. It felt familiar, though, because as he got to the gas lamps and taverns he saw more and more colored, despite the curfew. It was a city of his own kind, but he moved through it wary, cocked, making himself into a shambling shadow that stuck to the dark of the street.

He'd never been here before, but he knew where he was going. He knew by word passed at campfires and slave hearths, from mouth to ear at the risk of flogging or death. Those who told it had been forbidden books and writing, so they used memory and poems and songs and games and the folk cunning of Anansi the Spider and Brother Rabbit. The word passed in whispers and code, so, even overheard or gasped in extremity of pain or fever, it struck white ears as raving or superstition. Guided by it he walked for miles north and then west, till the air sickened with a gut-rotting stench and cobblestone sank into knee-deep mudholes and the gaslight vanished again to leave only torches guttering before low gin dens. At last, not far from Murder Bay and the city dump at the bottom of Seventeenth, his eye searched the lintels of the passing houses. Unable to make out the sign he sought, he at last stopped someone as ragged as himself. A pointing arm directed him behind a darkened house. As he slid past a jumble of broken wagons and ancient carriages he sucked his lips to get juice started in his dry mouth and began crooning, low and soft.

> *Down to the water I be baptized, for my Savior die*
> *Down to the water, the river of Jordan,*
> *Where my Savior baptized.*

His voice trailed off and he waited, heart thudding so hard he saw fireflies flitting at the circle edges of sight.

—Who out there? came at last. Woman's voice.

—Pilgrim from Egypt.

—Pilgrim be wandering a mighty long time, came the whisper. Get you on in here.

He found himself in a kitchen annex, or maybe a little woodhouse room, being inspected by three well-dressed mulatto women. They examined him by the light of the tallow candle the youngest was holding. He kept his mouth shut till the oldest said, —You is a big old boy.

—I is about full growed.

The youngest didn't laugh, but the eldest did. —What you want here, son? You begging?

—Need to find me Mammy Gree-oh.

—Ain't never heard of no such a one. Who you be? Where you come from? We ain't had nobody sing that song round here long time coming.

—What you mean? Ain't no railroad no more?

—Roads done seal up. Too many white mans patrolling 'em. Too many white sojers. Bad time a coming, uh huh. Things gone get a lot worse 'fore they gets better.

—Cain't get no worse for us.

The oldest sister, if they were sisters, her broad cheeks pitted with smallpox scars like a claybank blasted with buckshot, shook her head sadly like he didn't know nothing. She took the candle and brought the black-smoking flame slowly so close to his face he felt the heat. Then lowered it to his coat, lingered on the stain on the arm. Lowered farther, his feet.

—Where you get them govermint boots?

—Got 'em off a sojer laying drunk. Just slipped them right off. Pinch a little bit.

—I seen you limp. What you doing here? You gone get us all in trouble.

—Followed the drinkin' gourd couple of years past. Now you tell me where I find the Mammy.

—What you want him for?

—You just tell me where, girl. Then I be on my way.

They fell silent. He grinned at the younger woman, wondering if she fancied him, but she dropped her look to the dirt. At last the scarred woman said to the middle one, —Is that Matthew here?

—I think. In the basement.

—You wait here, she told him. Don't you move nohow.

The boy she came back with was ten years old, with alert bright eyes and the look of a mischievous old man. That was all Cal saw before the sack cut off all vision. A used croker sack, dusty inside with what smelled like millet chaff; it made him sneeze when the women pulled it over his head. Then everything was dark and he was stumbling after the child, whose small hand was warm and nearly lost in Cal's big hard sailor's mitt.

He could tell at one point they were in an alley; the slippery slick squish of mud under his boot soles told him that. Then he felt hard angular shapes through the leather—bricks, or old-style cobbles. He blundered into a fence and it gave with a rusty shriek of old nails. Then more soft ground, and dry grass swishing past. The boy told him to bend down and slip under, and he folded obediently. Then after that a long walk blind, lifting his feet one after the other, wondering what they'd set on next.

Till at last the whisper came again, —You can take it off now, and he pulled it off and found himself under the same black sky but somewhere else, a walled garden of shadowed big old boxwoods rank with the smell of cat piss and the heavy perfume of rotting camellia blossoms, noiseless, soft, underfoot. And in the midst of it a leaning darkness shot through with a fiery yellow flicker.

—He in there, the boy whispered. You go on. I wait out here.

—Where the hell we at?

—Cain't tell you dat. You ask for him, I done took you here. So go on. Just remember, you cain't never tell what you see in there. What you hear. An' you cain't never come back, never. The bad man, he strike you daid if'n you do.

The boy retreated. He took a step toward the flicker, then another. The smell of damp earth and human urine, decaying flowers and wood smoke and something else, some root stink or herb fetor that got thicker as he went on. He saw now it was a little house, no, just a shack, crazy and leaning; here could be anywhere, maybe one of the back lots that trailed the wide avenues. Just a shack no bigger than a two-hole outhouse, with the orange light glimmering through the chinks that outlined what, now he was almost to it, could reach to it, he saw was a sagging door held by rope hinges.

He pushed it open, and stepped through, and jerked it shut behind him. Blinking in the fire heat, the firelight. For a second he couldn't see, just squinted as the heat and light hit him like a fist blow, the close, sealed-in hot of a yellow-pine blaze in a mud-and-stick fireplace like the ones he'd grown up shivering beside, in the north Georgia winter. No chairs, nothing but the bare dirt floor and a heap of rags like the one the woman at the whorehouse had pulled the stinking crusted shirt from.

Then the pile moved, and he stumbled back, till his shoulder-blades struck the wall and the flimsy house shook and moss and mud and crawling things fell soft-tumbling from the darkness overhead.

The woman blinking up at him in the fluttering light was shrunken like the mummied squirrel he'd found once in the rafters of the smokehouse. Killed and dried and preserved by the smoke, a hollow hard fragile shell of which the only squirrelness left was the silver-tipped brush of tail. She wore a checked gingham head wrap, from which tufts of white wool escaped at the side, and her tight dark dress seemed to ripple with some pattern he couldn't make out in the writhing shadows. The rags were wrapped around her, she emerging from them like some ancient locust hatchling creeping out from its root bed after a hundred long years gone.

No sound in the room but the crackle and spit of the fire, and his harsh hurried breathing.

—Yal gone see it cut de feather, she said. Her voice was a goosegabble, palateless, without tooth or cut into the smooth flow of sound. He really did not make out a word of it until some seconds had passed, till he could figure and sort through what she might have said.

—What you say, Auntie?

—Yal gone see it cut de feather.

—I don't understand. What is it gone cut this feather?

—Yal done seen a sword into the sky. That great fire sword, pointin' down to the Southland. What you think that mean? So strong, stronger'n red oak lye. What the Lord aimin' to tell us, sendin' a sword like that?

He groped for some meaning in the strange babble. He wasn't sure that was what she'd actually said. —Uh, might could mean some times coming.

—Mean it gone fetch fire behind it. That what it mean. You boy. What for you here? What you want wif ol' Aunt Sally?

—You no Aunt Sally. You is the Mammy Gree-oh.

To his surprise the rags quivered. —You not believin' that old story. How that Maman Griot s'posed to be the great mam'bo, know everythin', 'member everythin'. Take a look at me. What you see?

—See a wise woman, gon help her chilluns anyway she can.

—You got the honey tongue on you, boy. But you don' know nothin'.

—I knows somebody knows. I think it you.

—You 'muse me powerful, boy. Tell me what you thinks I know.

—You knows what I need to know, do what I need to do.

—S'pose you say what that be. An' why I be moved to tell you, s'posing I does.

—My name Caesar Verity, he said. He took out the money and laid it on the bare ground between them. The nestled coil of bills uncoiled like a serpent. The old woman's eyes caressed it, then looked up again, slitted and sly.

—De Emperor of Truth. That a powerful name for a big dumb nigger. Tell me where you borned, an' who be your marster and missus.

—You mean when I borned? It was in Screven County, up on the big river. Old Marster Gerries had him a heap o' niggers. My mama named Suritah. She and Andrew and James and me, we was bid off when I can just remember. Tanny and Sarepta, they come coffee-an'-cream but slaves just the same. Then Aeleen and Little Jake, he born after James die of the hoopy cough.

—Who you sold to then?

—Man name Mister Lucas Tretwaite Verity. He live downcounty, toward Scarboro. That's who name me Caesar Augustus. He read it out of a book, he said. Name me that 'cause my mammy name me Luke when I borned and he don't like me having the same name as him. His missus, Missus Helena Scarborough Verity, she didn't like it atall.

—So what you want from me, boy.

—I wants to know what about my fambly. About Suritah and them others. He pushed the coil of bills across the dirt. —I knows you know it.

The old woman rocked back and forth. —Suritah, she still there. Andrew, he done gone.

—Gone? Where to? You mean he cut sticks like me?

—No. Andrew, he gone where ain't nobody can follow.

He couldn't help it, he was shivering. He felt evil gradually unwinding in the still room, seeping out from the mess of tatters and the cracked whispery voice old as the dark. He wanted to run, to jump up and make his heels fly. Instead his fingers found the juju pouch around his neck. —What about the others? How I gone get to them?

—It don't make no never mind.

—What you mean? Got to get 'em. Get 'em out to freedom. He took a step forward, a few inches nearer to her, almost in reaching distance now, and pushed the coil of money forward again. —There it is. You takes it. And tells me what to do.

She looked on the bills silently, and there was no sound in the room but for the fire.

Then her hands moved, drawing her skirts aside. As the hem rose it revealed something beneath the ragged cloth. It was the size of a spirit-cask, rounded, like the swelling root of a swamp cypress, but with a soft-looking, mottled brown surface stretched smooth and shiny over its bulk.

He stared, and then couldn't breathe. The swollen thing was her foot. Rotting skin hung in loose folds over toes swollen fat as summer sausages. He swallowed back the sick spit that suddenly flooded his mouth. The heat made his head swim.

Above the grotesque foot her leg was as large as a rum keg, blown up into a parody of an African elephant's. Her calf and thigh were as thick as his waist. Then she parted her skirts even more, and he clapped his hands to his mouth as a rotten-sweet stench welled out, choking him.

—How bad you wants to know, boy?

He took a breath and said, pretending anger and outrage, but dismayed at the shaking of his voice, —No. I give you the money. That's enough. Now tell me how to get my fambly.

The skirts closed slowly, hiding the horribly malformed limbs. The old woman leered. —Your family? You not gone to see your family before long passage over de river. The sword I tole you about is comin' down.

—But what sword is dat?

—You don't been listenin' to me, boy. Now pay 'tention. You seen dat great fire sword burnin' in de sky. The handle is to de North, and the point toward de South. You sees? De North gone take that sword and cut de South's head off wif it. But if Abraham make dat sacrifice, he gone lose his head too. Everything be cut in two. Freedom on one side. Death on the other. Even the loas not know which way to go. Who you gone trust in, Caesar Augustus? The old gods? Jehovah? Jesu Christi, Mary 'Maculate?

—Trust in the Lord.

—Who you call on, Emperor of the Sword?

—Calls on my Lord, calls on my Lord! He jerked suddenly out of the horror and jumped to his feet. —Come to find the railroad, but this here is devil stuff. You nothing but some old conjure woman.

—Yes sah, yes *sah,* see, thass what ole Mammy been tellin' you right along.

He looked into the black eyes and realized for the first time, seeing close, they weren't the eyes of an old woman. He didn't know when they'd changed, but they weren't the same ones she'd looked up with from her stare into the fire. Now they weren't human eyes at all. They were the unblinking, feelingless stare of some other kind of creature, not hot and pulsing like a creature born of breath and earth, but a scaly cold thing whose blood oozed veinless and sluggish.

As that realization ran over him, chill as a piece of wet ice run up his spine, he felt someone else in the room. A second later he jerked his eyes back to the fire. He hadn't been looking at it. He'd only suspicioned something with the cut-corner of his eyes. When he looked right at the writhing flames and the hot wavering red embers, it wan't there no more. But just for that one second, *something had been looking at him out of the fire.*

—I knows you, Calpurnius Hanks. Knows you and the murder secret you carries, too. No, you can't tell Maman Griot who you is. You ain't even know yet who you is.

He couldn't speak. Simply stared at the fire, spelled by what he couldn't see.

—You the true emperor, the cracked voice went on. —You is the one sent bringin' the fiery jubilee. Descended of the kings of Ifé, royal blood of the city of ancient time. The Hanged Man still a-walkin', spat out de mouth of Death. No tellin' which ogou you serve. Bacossou or Legba or ancient Israel Father Yahweh. But they given you the power. The land will be devastated by fire, by water, by iron, and by lead, by poison, and by famine, and by war. I see all the sons and daughters of Africa layin' dead in this land. I see them singin' with voices raised hosanna in freedom. How comes I sees two? Like there be two times ahead, two roads to Time, and confusion waverin' between.

—You don't see that, you old root woman! You don't see nothin'!

—Oh, you seen me there. You seen me in the fire.

She began to laugh. It started cracked and whispery, like dried branches dragged to sweep out the footsteps of a runaway. Then mounted like hounds yelping in the bayous, echoing from moss-draped trees.

—Go on out of here, Lucas Caesar Calpurnius Augustus Hanks Verity. You got the legion of names, but you is the split twig. Yal gone see it cut de feather, burn stronger'n red oak lye.

Her laughter keening in his ears, he stumbled out of the shed. To find himself suddenly and without knowing how not in the back garden, with no small boy waiting, but out on the stinking beach of the slimy river, its black surface like a flat road stretching ahead with whispering ripples, and overhead the bright stars pointing him out with glittering light, overtaken even as he watched by a sliding cloak of cloud stealing silently out of the north.

19

Crossing the Long Bridge ♦ A Mission to Norfolk ♦ Parading of the
Richmond Light Infantry Blues ♦ Bearded by an Agent ♦ The Brotherhood
of Engineers ♦ An Early-Morning Arrival

THE Long Bridge was deserted this early morning, its plank
causeway carrying nothing save dank-smelling wind. The
river below, braided like dirty yellow hair, was empty too.
Theo Hubbard met no one on the walk across, until a bearded stal-
wart in homespun overtook him driving a buckboard. They examined each other, the driver apparently thinking about offering a ride.
But finally he did not, simply spat, flipped his reins, and rumbled
past, revealing a pair of buck Negroes sitting knees cocked, chained
in the bed of the buckboard. They barely glanced his way before returning to their gloomy contemplation of the Potomac sliding by.

Theo returned his own gaze to the heavy trusswork, the iron-
bolted oaken beams that supported the road surface between stone
piers. He swung the carpetbag, glad it was light. It held a change of
linen, a razor, the plan sheets of a two-cylinder, seventy-two-inch engine, and two books: volume one of *Engineering Precedents for Steam
Machinery,* and Pope's *Manual of Electric Telegraphy,* which he intended to read on the train.

At the Virginia end of the bridge two howitzers were set commanding the approach. A squad of blue-coated soldiers sat near them

on kitchen chairs fetched out of the bridge keeper's house. One straightened and motioned Hubbard over. —Where to, Mac?

—Norfolk.

—Business?

—I'm a naval engineer, traveling on orders. I have a pass from the bureau.

The corporal glanced over it. —I'd of thought you'd be going by steamboat.

—I tried, but they aren't running. No one seems to know why.

The soldier reached out a hand as he started away. Theo halted. —You gonna keep that with you? That pass?

—Trouble?

—The dominion ain't decided which side they're on yet, but the local shoulder hitters already made up their minds. Tear it up. Put it in the fire bucket there. Where you headed? Train station?

—Right. Down to Alexandria.

—Hire yourself a cart by the tavern.

—I've been at sea awhile; don't mind traveling shank's mare.

He cast a longing glance back over the river, to where the Capitol floated like a distant mountain. No, not a mountain; its truncated whiteness resembled more closely an extinct volcano covered with snow. It seemed blurred from here, as if by fog or rain, though none threatened. Perhaps it was the miasma rising from the stinking marshes that lined the city's water edge. He looked down at the pass again, then ripped it into bits.

He'd been given the paper, signed by John Lenthall, chief of the Bureau of Construction, Equipment, and Repairs, when he'd reported to Main Navy at first light. He'd wondered if six was too early, but officers had been bustling in and out. The naval constructor welcomed him in a businesslike tone. Lenthall was courteous and elderly, with tobacco crumbs on his paunch and old-fashioned throat whiskers that left his chin and mouth clean. He said, —I'm glad to see you're in civilian clothes.

—I think I know why you want me, sir.

—Oh, you do?

—You need me in Norfolk.

—Mr. Isherwood said you were one of his bright young men. I am pleased to see he was right. Oh, there you are, Lenthall said to a clerk who thrust his head in. —Pull me a copy of number 1325 for Mr. Hubbard.

To Theo he said, —I have ordered Mr. Isherwood to the navy yard at Norfolk. Mr. Welles has directed me to move as many serviceable vessels as possible to a place of safety. I am stretched very thin for engineers. We have only two hundred, and half are deployed. Can you proceed to his assistance?

He started to say *Owanee* needed him, but realized Lenthall wouldn't have asked if the situation wasn't dire. Refusing orders wasn't the way to advancement, if advancement there might be. —I suppose so, sir. If you need me to.

—I do. Get to Norfolk by the swiftest route available. I will write you out a pass and a draft for fifty dollars. I don't think you'll be in any danger, but I should advise you not to draw attention to yourself en route.

—Very good, sir. He rose with the constructor, then hesitated. —Sir, I've been developing some ideas as to mechanical improvements needed aboard ship. I don't wish to add to your concerns just now, but if I might send you a note about them, one of these days. . . .

Lenthall grimaced. —I doubt we shall have time for novelties anytime soon, Mr. Hubbard. I should give ten years of my life just now for four good dependable side-wheelers.

The corporal said now, interrupting his thoughts, —Well, walk if you like, but there's a bunch of wild boys at the inn may give you trouble. Got a Deringer in that bag?

He was beginning to wish there was, but told the corporal, —I'm not armed.

—Well, good luck.

Theo said thanks and walked on. As soon as he stepped off the bridge approach, the road turned to black mud. He slurped along for several paces, sinking in to his ankles, then waded to the verge. Once on grass he made better progress. A quarter mile on he passed the buckboard, reins wrapped over a hitching post in front of the tavern, the Negroes lying back with burlap sacking over their faces. Despite the soldier's warning, no one was about.

Two hours later, after a pleasant walk during which the sun rose high in an oyster-colored sky, he reached Alexandria. The town began all at once, mud turning to cobbles, close-set brick homes springing abruptly as mushrooms from loam-turned fields. Life seemed to be going on as usual, though he noted a strange flag displayed in the window of the Marshall House. At first glance the eye told you it was different, but not how. A second look with hand shading his brow gave him three broad stripes, the central one white, and a circlet of stars on a blue jack.

With something of a shock, he realized it was the flag of the Montgomery secessionist government, the self-styled Confederacy.

When he stopped to get his boots cleaned the shine boy directed him to the station of the Orange and Alexandria line. At that beautiful pile of bright pink brick the ticket agent told him there was no direct train to Richmond. The best he could do was route him via Manassas west to Gordonsville, thence southeastward to Richmond on the Virginia Central. He could change at the state capital to the Norfolk & Petersburg. His through ticket would cost eight dollars and thirty-three cents, four and a half cents a mile on the first railway but only three cents a mile on the latter. The agent examined the New York banknote he tendered, but said nothing other than that trains were running late; he should not expect the ten-fifteen for at least an hour yet. He shoved through ticket and change and snapped the wicket closed.

The waiting room was nearly deserted, but the bar was full, judging by the shouting. Hungry and thirsty after his walk, he hesitated at the swinging doors, then pushed his way through.

About twenty men were playing cards and talking and drinking at the long bar. Smoke hung in sheets like the layers of a French pastry. The board floor was slippery with sawdust, old newspapers, and the remnants of a considerable quantity of expectorated tobacco. His entrance didn't turn a head. He propped his bag on the footrail and ordered a dish of lager. While the barkeep, a stolid fat man with a walrus mustache, drew it, he gazed at broadsheets and circulars, auction announcements and notices of lawsuits pasted up behind the bar. The oldest were gone so coffee-dark no scrap of print could be discerned on their surface. The most recent urged the election of John C. Breckinridge and the Southern Democratic Party.

Standing there, he worried first about the ship. *Owanee*'s engines needed continual coddling, and the boilers were long past safe service. MacNail was willing, but he wasn't much more than a jumped-up oiler with a strong back. Well, perhaps the yard mechanics could do something, if she lay alongside for a few weeks.

The next item of discontent was that to return the decommissioned ships at the Gosport yard to steaming status meant someone was thinking about abandoning Norfolk. He knew that town. It would be hard to find a navy man who didn't. The navy yard wasn't actually in Norfolk, but across the Elizabeth River, near Portsmouth. It had been a shipyard since colonial times. The Royal Navy had called it Gosport, had repaired British frigates and sloops there before the Revolution. Taken over and enlarged over the years by the U.S. Navy, now it held huge repair shops, sail lofts, warehouses of stores, gun parks, ship houses, and the sole and only dry dock south of Boston. Abandoning it would mean losing the best repair and ship-building facility in the country.

He was musing on this when a youth with a scarred face thrust himself up next to him. —Buy me a smile, friend.

—I believe I'll decline.

—"I believe I'll decline." Who the hell you think you talkin' to?

Theo looked him over. The boy couldn't be over sixteen. His face was cratered with pimples and his breath fruity with alcohol. His hand rested on a sheath knife.

He didn't mind a scrap. Bare-knuckle skirmishes in engine houses and mills had taught him how to impress his will on men who resented his being placed over them. However, fighting just here, just now, did not seem the better part of wisdom, given Lenthall's admonition not to draw attention. So he returned a soft answer. —I'm talking to you.

—Damn right you are. Where you from, shrimp?

—From the District.

—Headed where?

—Richmond.

—What you doing in Richmond?

—That's no concern of yours.

—I don't like the way you talk, mister.

—It permits me to be understood.

— Sound like you from Massachusetts.

—Actually I am from Hartford, Connecticut.

—Close enough. The boy raised his voice, directing it at a group of men who sat together, while Theo's glance lingered on the scatterguns propped by their boots. —We got us a sure-'nough Yankee here, boys, and the little rooster's darin' me to lick him. Watch this.

—Lay off him, Jamis. Get over here, boy.

—No I ain't. Just havin' a little fun.

—I said *git* your sorry ass over here. Leave the gentleman alone.

The barkeeper stood back against the mirror, watching them stolidly. —I vant you listen your oncle, sohn, he said.

The kid flared up instantly. —Go to hell, you fuckin' Dutchman.

—Give it up, Jamis, said the man from the table again. He sounded weary. —Tell you what: if they was three of him, I'd let you lick him. It ain't odds otherwise. Anyways it's time to muster. He stood, drained his mug, came over, and seized the youth by the shirt. He said to Theo, —He's a good boy, just snapt on corn likker and some excited. We're all excited, I reckon. My apologies, sir. Hope you have a good trip.

—Much obliged.

The tap of a drum sounded outside. He picked up his lager and went to the window.

Men were falling in where the streets crossed, streaming down alleys, swinging off horses or mules, taking their places in ranks. Some wore blue uniforms without caps. Others, civilian clothes. He saw printers in aprons, a butcher, draymen, clerks in shirtsleeves and cuff protectors. Only one was armed, a graybeard who toted a flintlock musket. The older men took their places solemnly, the younger ones skylarking under the eyes of the girls who'd gathered around the square. A trio of officers stood patiently.

A smaller group had gathered outside the tavern, these latter in uniform like the officers, and now they took out fifes and trumpets. They marked time with the drum for a moment, then plunged into a whirling tune unlike anything he'd ever heard before. It danced along the street, bright and gay and devil-may-care, making his boot toe tap on the worn sill. A tune once heard no one could forget. A melody without solemnity, but somehow not needing it to seize the heart. A dose of musical nitrous oxide, lifting whoever heard from the muddy gumbo of the street into a madcap glory.

—You know what that is? he asked the Dutchman, who'd come over to watch with him.

—Dot's the militia. They been mustering hefery day, and hefery day more boys join up.

—I meant the music.

—Dot there is vat they call "Dixie." You not know it?

—I've been away.

—Ya, ya, dot is "Dixie." Dey plays it all de time.

—You aren't mustering?

—Not me. I Union man. Maybe go back to Pennsylvania if they keeps oop dis foolishness. I like dot music but not enough to be soldier. Dat vy I leaf Chermany, too much soldier.

—Say, they got any sandwiches for sale? There in the station?

—Nebber mind dot *scheisse*. I make you nice pumpernickel und sausage.

The train clicked slowly through the afternoon, swaying so he found it difficult to nap. Pitch-pine smoke hung behind the engine, turning the air in the coaches blue. He watched the countryside pass.

Rolling piedmont valleys, here and there a team plowing, interspersed with dense stretches of forest. The tracks vaulted creeks on timber trestles: the Occoquan, the Rappahannock, the Rapidan, the North Anna. Occasionally swamp slid past, slowly waving marsh grass green as a wheat field, footed in muck that looked soft as damp black velvet.

At Manassas Junction, not even a town but just a frame station house amid orchards and fields, a young lady settled an alligator-skin satchel in the seat in front of him. She wore a traveling dress and a black straw hat not unlike a sailor's.

He watched her bright hair for several miles, contemplating tipping his hat and introducing himself. He was on the point of getting up when another passenger, a natty individual in a rust-colored frock coat, did exactly that. He bent over her for a few moments. She shook her head abruptly. The fellow persisted, and Theo began to imagine himself as rescuer, protector, knight-errant. But then the girl rose. She straightened her hat and picked up her satchel and went forward through toward the next car. The drummer returned to his seat, shrugging and smiling as he passed Hubbard. Theo met his eye coldly.

He thought about her as the miles clicked by. Could not rid himself of the image of her neck, so white and exposed. A curl of hair had freed itself beneath her hat, blowing against that smooth skin as the wind came through the opened window, freighted now and again with the smoke that made every surface inside the car damp-gritty and left smudges on one's gloves and anything they touched.

He'd had a heart interest once, in Hartford. Miss Walker had filed in the drafting office, rather a curiosity, as one saw few women at Pease & Morikin or indeed at any industrial concern aside from the textile mills. They'd scarcely exchanged six words at a time, but he'd begun to look forward to getting plans there, then fabricated a difficulty with a double slider-crank chain he'd been designing to make repeated visits. Mustering his courage, he'd finally asked her to walk out with him. They'd gone to a tearoom and then to a lyceum to hear a phrenologist. But then things had gone smash in the Panic and he'd been so concerned to find the position in Washington that before he found his feet he got the letter about her marriage.

He wasn't a monk. He'd had carnal passages in the years since, at Cyprian establishments, as much from curiosity as from the male need. But his affections had not yet been engaged.

Now he remembered the girl he'd dreamed of in Africa. The dream had started in a café in Paris, which was queer as he'd never been to France. He'd been acting rowdy, throwing bread. He wished he had some now; there was nothing to eat on the train, and although a belch returned the gaseous essence of German sausage, his stomach was empty again. In the middle of the dream the girl had appeared next to him, slim as a willow and with dark brown hair tumbling to her shoulders, and had said gravely, —You can't throw bread here. And he'd said, —Yes I can, and she'd taken his hand to prevent him. In the dream he'd felt softness and warmth, and wakened to find he'd had an untoward occurrence, there in his lonely bunk.

Since then he'd tried to dream of her again. But she'd never come back.

He opened *Engineering Precedents* but found it difficult to concentrate on Isherwood's discussion of running a smithery engine with and without steam cut-offs. Reclining his head against the rough horsehair seat, he closed the book and his eyes, wishing she would come again.

He reached Richmond at five that afternoon. The ticket agent there told him that contrary to what the one in Alexandria had said, there was no train to Norfolk from Richmond. He'd either have to take a stage to Hampton, and the ferry from there, or else take the Richmond & Petersburg to Petersburg and transfer there for Portsmouth on the Norfolk & Petersburg. Due to a legal suit pending between the roads, his through ticket would not be honored. He had to purchase a new one. This was not all the unfortunate news, however. He'd just missed the stage, and the next would not leave until the following day. —Trains south are all delayed, the agent said, accompanying this information with a dropping of the lids and a narrowing of the eyes, meant, Theo assumed, to convey that he knew far more than he was at liberty to say.

He pushed ten cents over. —Should I wait?

—Why thank you, sir. There's no point waiting here. The Richmond & Petersburg station is crosstown on Byrd Street. You'd need to take a hack over and make your arrangements with them.

—Are you telling me I have to Jehu from one station to another to switch train lines?

—We have five railroads serving the city, sir, but as yet none interconnect. You would do as well to stay over and proceed in the morning. The Columbian is a high-class hostelry, convenient to that station.

He didn't want to wait that long. The smells of pickles and beer from the station bar reminded him he was hungry, though. Lenthall couldn't grudge him stopping for one meal on the way. He hadn't cashed his draft yet, but it was too late now to find a bank open. He picked up his bag and then put it down again and asked the agent, — Could you cash a draft for me?

—How much?

—Fifty dollars.

—That's a lot of money.

—It's a U.S. government draft.

The fellow's head came up, he grew suddenly interested. —The United States are no longer in business, friend. At least not at this location.

He was sorry now he'd opened his mouth. Muttering, —Aw, never mind, he picked up his bag again and decamped across the waiting room. When he glanced back the agent was still watching him. He felt like a turtle bereft of his shell.

But he made it to the door, and walked rapidly at random off down a side street. Dusk was falling. A mulatto lamplighter made his way down the avenue, head thrust through his ladder. Behind him rows of small flames danced, prisoned each in its glass cage. The next thing he noticed was the sweet dusty smell of cured tobacco. It was in the air, in the street, bales of brown weed stacked on the carts that rumbled past.

He stepped aside to let a carriage pass, and came out at the head of a broad avenue that ran down to the James. Down there in the failing light he made out a Y of bridges, a scatter of forested islands broken by pale foamy rapids. The land sloped down to it and then rose again on the far side of the river. Graceful homes stood amid patches of forest against the hills. Along a flat by the river a foundry glowed and smoked pillars of black smoke up towering into the evening air. It was a scene of surprising beauty, a small city set precisely as a gem in this peaceful valley, not yet overwhelmed as New York was with its commercial establishments and mills.

At the crest of the hill the avenue circled an Ionic temple. He stopped, surrounded by a hubbub and ferment that surely this graceful space did not see every day. Schoolchildren ran about. Knots of top-hatted men stood talking and hammering the grass with canes. Someone asked if he'd heard. He shook his head, suddenly unwilling to voice plain Connecticut speech. They said the convention had voted eighty-eight to fifty-five. Virginia was out of the Union!

He nodded a rictus of a smile. With that unwelcome news, the secession of the only state in the South with any real manufacturing capacity, the nascent Confederacy had probably doubled its military strength.

A florid man mounted the temple steps and began orating. —The enemy is at our door! But we shall meet the accursed usurper and his seventy-five thousand paid cutthroats with the reception they deserve. Though our pathway be through storms of fire, we shall not turn aside! Your full-blood Yankee will never stand in the presence of cold steel!

The crowd roared its approval. Theo ducked his head and went on, watching the lights flicker on down along the streets, candles and lamps set in the windows till they glowed from cellar to attic as if afire. The few homes not illuminated were set apart by their drawn shades. He was wondering if this denoted loyalists when someone grabbed his arm from behind. He turned to find the ticket agent holding his elbow, the one he'd asked about cashing a draft.

—Unmitten me, sir.

—I will not. Spy! Spy! Help!

—You're cracked. Let go my arm or I'll punch your nose.

The grip relaxed, but still held against his pulling away. —Then what are you?

—A naval engineer. I'm supposed to help evacuate Norfolk.

—Norfolk's being evacuated?

—That seems to be the import of my orders.

He felt guilty the moment he'd said it, as if a cock should crow. He didn't mean to disavow the flag, but it seemed that matters were moving more swiftly than Mr. Lenthall had anticipated. The word "spy" wasn't encouraging. The penalty was traditional and drastic: death by hanging. He'd never have believed a whole people could turn so quickly away from their allegiance. It made him think of mass delusions, like the Dutch tulip manias, or the South Sea Bubble. But a whole state, a whole section of the country didn't go mad overnight.

They really thought themselves separate, a nation apart. And they probably had for a long time now.

The agent said, renewing his grip, —I'm turning you in to the authorities.

—Who'll send me on my way. Look. You're a sovereign nation now? You'd better treat us foreigners with more courtesy. No war's been declared between us.

—Lincoln declared war.

—That's ridiculous, Theo told him. —Now you're just talking nonsense. Let me go.

A drum throbbed in the distance. He realized he'd been hearing it for some time, far off, but growing steadily nearer. The same sound he'd heard at the militia muster at Alexandria, but deeper, more regular, from many more instruments.

By now the two of them had drawn a circle of interested faces. He saw the lamplighter looking down at them from the ladder. He might be next up that lamppost, only with a hemp collar pinching his cervical vertebrae.

A copper, thank God. —This fellow giving you trouble, Mr. King?

—Says he's on his way to Norfolk. He tried to cash a federal draft.

—I never denied it. I'm here on business.

—What business is that, my man?

—Navy business, connected with the Gosport yard.

—Have you any official identification?

He didn't, and began to suspect from the expressions around him that the guard at the Long Bridge had done him a disservice in advising him to tear up the pass.

—I didn't think a man needed it. Not in a free country.

—It's free, all right, but not for Yankees.

—I'm traveling from Washington to a federal installation.

—Sumter was a federal installation.

—This is different, this is a naval yard. Even if the North and South separate, we should keep the navy together. Why spend double the money for two?

The faces around him hung suspended. It was obvious they'd never considered the question. It had occurred to him on the spur of the moment, but it did not sound prima facie untenable.

The drums came louder now, and suddenly officers on horseback trotted round the corner. They were in epaulettes, sashes, sabers, and as they came on the citizens ran for the sidewalks and began huzzaing as behind them ranks of marching men swung into view, dressed, aligned, in step. Bayonets caught the streetlight flickering in a moving sparkle. Flags dipped and swayed, advancing in a steady pace. These were no untrained militia. This was a crack unit, drilled and well equipped, and they kept coming, company after company, till the whole avenue was filled. The troops wore sloped caps and bright green scarlet-lined capes with gold buttons big as twenty-dollar pieces. The horses' hooves blazed sparks from the cobblestones with an iron ringing. The men holding him stood rooted as they came on.

An officer glared down from his charger, waving them from his path with a drawn saber. Theo took a step back.

Then he was jerked nearly off his feet, pulled forward as the others fell back before the clattering hooves. A whirling stumble, a flurry of angry faces; he was being towed through the crowd behind a large, powerfully bearded man in threadworn Levi's, who shouted back, —Looked like you wanted a hand out of there, friend.

—Thank you. Thanks. He suddenly felt his knees go weak. He'd really thought they were going to hang him. Like the mobs in Carlyle, *On the French Revolution.*

—What's in the grip, friend?

—Just some books.

—That fella said something about a draft. Where is it? Quick, let's see it.

He saw now why he'd been rescued. He gave the bearded man all he had left on him, the draft and three dollars in notes, and his benefactor disappeared without a backward glance. He turned instantly and shoved downhill through the crowd, keeping the thick of it, and the compact passing files of troops, between him and the ones who'd grabbed him. He'd lost sight of the agent and hoped the reverse was true. He went down side streets until he felt safe, till the cheers and shuffle-thud of marching boots were distant again. More Richmonders pushed past, cheeks flaming and eyes alight. For a few seconds he breathed easier, though his knees still shook. Then he realized just not being hung wasn't enough. He was hungry, surrounded by an insurrection, and now he didn't have a red cent in his pocket.

A crash and thunder, the "Marseillaise" this time; another band, another regiment, these in blue uniforms. Women trailed after the troops, carrying torches. They were singing "I Want to Be an Angel." He tilted his cap over his eyes and went on, down the cobbled street toward the river.

He sat on a bench, hiding behind a *Dispatch* he found discarded in a coal chute, till it was quite dark and the cheering and marching had died down. In the course of the night three women asked him if he was joining up. He muttered that he was thinking about it, trying to drawl out his words. He didn't go near the Richmond & Petersburg depot till midnight. Even then he didn't go into the station. Instead he jumped down onto the tracks, and followed them past the platform.

The locomotive stood panting like a hard-used dray horse. Behind an immense prow of riveted strap iron were four swivel-truck drivers and then four big driving wheels painted scarlet and gold. Above it rose a huge balloon stack. The fireman was reaching up into the light box. It flared up as Theo neared, the big curved mirror focusing spermaceti flame into the gathering dark of the river valley.

Three workingmen stood by, watching the lady passengers and the soldiers, a good many of whom were boarding the train. He went boldly up to them and touched his hat. —Good evening. May I ask which of you is the engineman?

A tired-looking, mustached fellow hitched up his coveralls. —What you need, mister?

—I hope you will pardon the intrusion, but I noticed you have one of our first-class Amoskeag locomotives here. And she looks very well cared for, too. Are you quite satisfied with her?

—Yeah, this here's a pretty good engine. One of yours, y'say? What, you work for Amoskeag?

—I have the honor to be an engine designer. How are your cylinder valves? They often present difficulties in heavy service.

—Them D-valves seem to hold out all right, but these links here get loose all the time.

—That's the Stevenson variety of linkage in this model, is it not? If you'll let me listen to them in operation, I can show you a better way to set them.

—You from up North, ain't ya?

—You mean the unrest up in town? I imagine you'll still need locomotives whatever happens. And we'll still be making them for you.

—Well, I'm from Schenectady way myself. You're right, they're still going to need both of us. You got a pass or anything?

—No, but you can telegraph your directors—perhaps Mr. Robinson. He'll vouch for me.

—I don't have time to hang around waiting for no telegraph. We're going to Petersburg, to the shops there. You want I can put you on a freight coming back.

He said that would work. Down the platform, the conductor stepped out and waved. The engineer lifted an arm in acknowledgment. —Toss your truck in the tender, mister, and let's get 'er rolling.

In the close hot-smelling cab the engineer perched himself at the window. He jerked back the throttle slightly and glanced ahead along the rails. The Negro fireman clanged the firebox open and started heaving heavy yellow chunks of split pine at the flames that streamed away from the powerful blast of incoming air. To a clanging jangle and the hiss and throb of steam, the locomotive eased forward, lurching, then steadying as it gathered speed down the grade, across the long trestle, and out and on into the Virginia night.

He rode with them to Petersburg, then examined the links and had an interesting discussion of the relative expansion rates of two pieces of heated metal, of the same alloy but with different diameters. After which, at the trainmen's invitation, he accompanied the off-duty crew to the roundhouse for boiled coffee and cold sliced beef. He napped at the stove for two hours, then went outside and hauled himself up into an empty house car bound east.

He swung down before dawn in Portsmouth, walked seven blocks down High Street in a fine rain, and crossed the Gosport bridge as the sun first showed itself. The masts of many ships rose ahead. More lay alongside a riverfront wharf, and three rode at anchor in the stream. The top-hampers of still others reached skyward from amid huge wooden ship houses, powerhouses, cranes, rope walks.

A thick column of coal smoke pumped steadily up from a large ship bow on to him in the river. Its masts were stumps. Its deck had been roofed over. The thump of engines came over the water. As it angled in toward a wharf he saw the smoke came not from its own funnel but from the stack of a tug snugged alongside.

Workers with lunch pails were congregating at the gate. Other men stood about arguing with the ones passing into the yard. Two were shouting in each other's faces, close to blows. Once inside the gate the workmen dispersed down alleys and into sheds and shops. He walked toward the wharf and the rising smoke. The brow came sliding down as he came up, and he loped up it and dropped his grip, looking at last around the greasy, iron-littered deck of the steam frigate U.S.S. *Merrimack*.

20

Mrs. Catherine Wythe Claiborne to Lieutenant Ker Claiborne

16 Freemason Street,
Norfolk, Virginia,
April 16, 1861.

Dearest Ker,

I received yours of the eighth today, sent on to me from New York by the paymaster of the *Pocahontas*—is that correct? I have been following *Owanee*'s travels in the newspapers, where we have notice of ship movements as soon as they occur. How different from hearing of you only twice or thrice a year, a great batch of letters arriving all together, as when you were in Africa. But now I am told the next Baltimore steamer may be the last one North for some time. Only having your letter in my hands for a few hours, then, I urge forward my reply. So that this missive will take a roundabout way to reach you and it may be we shall even see each other again before it does. The which will not cause me any trouble at all! If it means you are with us sooner, perhaps to stay.

Little Rob is much better now. He recovered within a few days after your leaving, and is now quite his old self again. He bears close watching as he has become fascinated with fire. On cold mornings he lies in front of the hearth and at mealtimes he is always at Betsey to open the oven and show him the flames. He hangs back from it, though, since what happened when you were here. You recall, you said "hot" to him and pointed at the stove. He happily repeated "hot, hot" and went up and laid his palm flat against it. But though he understands the word now through the cruel medium of experience, the memory of pain does not diminish the fascination of the flames.

I am very sorry for our differences over him, you know to what I refer, and will endeavor to exert more mastery over my emotions. I can only plead that we are said to be the weaker vessel and sometimes I certainly feel it is so.

Enough of all that. It was very disquieting to hear of the political differences among your fellow officers. I fear the more danger lies ahead rather than behind us. There is much violent speech here about what will happen should Mr. Lincoln send down troops. The ladies talk of what we shall do if the scenes of the Revolution are repeated, when the British bombarded and burned the city. Some of the older ladies have quite frightening tales to tell so it seemed wise to lay in a little extra store of flour and meal and so on, I have done so to the extent of five dollars.

I ordered the new Silver at last and know you will be glad to stop eating out of these worn spoons you often complained of. It came to seventeen dollars and fifty cents but they are good quality and should last us out our lives.

With the men you mentioned and others leaving the service, may there not be at last some room for promotion? I know such would please you if it could be obtained. As for myself I can only say I am proud to be your wife whatever letters you put before (or after) your name.

I see by the telegraphic reports that *Owanee* was one of the ships off Charleston during the firing. I apprehend from the newspaper that you were not in any great danger, except from the stormy weather, but I know that keeping at sea is never safe entirely as you recall you said to me when that man went overboard. I prayed for the safety of the garrison, the men with you, and of course for my loved one. I prayed also for those in the forts about Sumter, for they are defending their rights and families too.

Your letter shewed how clear is your own conviction on the evil of dividing the country. As for myself I cannot quite see how it is that the Northerners who have the government now can feel Union can be preserved by force. Either we wish to be one or we do not, and how can one reconcile liberty with armed repression? We are citizens, not subjects, and to keep a union by force is not possible. One Section can be Conquered with the sword but it could never be kept with the same. If it is the colored at stake, they have always been well treated in my family. Do those who censure us treat their laborers as well? Old Turney was with us quite useless but kept comfortable many years until he died at eighty-one.

I received the likeness from the daguerrean artist that you had taken when you were here, and it is now quite prominent in the parlor. When you return I very much desire to have one taken of the three of us, or perhaps it wd be best to wait a little. I will address that in a moment.

Mother sends her best and she hopes you are not working too hard as she knows the fever still plagues you at times.

I have to say recent events have everyone very upset here in Norfolk. The Farraguts are leaving. As you know Capt. F. is ashore on leave and he goes down to Birnham's every day. He expressed the opinion that Mr. Lincoln would be justified in calling out troops to protect the Federal property in those states which have decided to part. Susan told me a man called him a "croker" and they nearly came to a disagreement. It is most unfortunate for Susan for she is a Marchant and all her family is here.

The ladies in the circle have been most delicate with me, but many of them have husbands and sons who have joined the volunteers and hard things are said against those who do not join. If I had to shift for myself I would take Rob and Betsey and go to my Father and Mother in Richmond, but then there is the question of how you would visit us. I do not know the answer to this quandary.

You mentioned the possibility of asking for duty on the California coast, is it possible? I have heard considerable about the city of San Francisco. There is no doubt that State will become quite prosperous and the report I read in *Harper's* of its beauty was most enticing. If you think this the best means of proceeding I will of course follow in whatever course you deem best. All I should like is to have a few of the tender years together before we are old.

If on the other hand you feel it is best to leave the navy it may be that you can find a place here in Hampton Roads as a pilot; or with one of the shipping companies. There are many on Water Street and once past these troubles trade must rebound. I know you love the Sea and I think you could be quite happy as captain of a merchant vessel. We would see you more often and perhaps might even go to sea with you, I know Captain Sterrett took his wife and family to London not long ago. He has a half Interest in his ship and does quite well out of it.

I shall close with the information I have been longing to impart all this time, but was loath to put to paper so long as there was the slightest chance to inform you in person. If not, then here it is: not without trepidation as you recall how difficult the passage was with Rob. I cannot say my heart is without fear at the prospect of repeating such. But then I look at our son as he plays and I would be willing to go through any ordeal for him so it may be my misgivings are only weaknesses which I shall pray God to replace with perfect Faith and Confidence. I think it is certain enough to tell you now that we may be expecting an addition to our family, which event would occur in September next.

Truly Thine,
C.W.C.

21

LI coughed into his fist, then pulled the ribbon off the heavy
scroll Claiborne had just handed him. *Owanee* lay anchored
off the navy yard now, yawing slowly to her hook beneath a
bright morning sky.

—Your volunteer commission? said the Virginian.

—Appears to be, he murmured, trying to decipher the ornate cal-
ligraphy. The president of the United States reposed special trust and
confidence in him. He was officially commissioned as a master's mate
in the United States Volunteer Navy, backdated to April 1. There was
the Rail-Splitter's signature, sure enough, hasty looking but perfectly
legible.

He read it a second time, feeling suddenly as if someone had kindled a lamp in his breast. It was the first thing he'd ever owned his father hadn't bought for him.

He looked up to find the others offering their hands. Schuyler
said, —Congratulations, Eli. Maybe now Judah'll pay you.

—It is a most handsome emolument, Glass said deadpan. —Forty dollars a month. If you should require assistance in disbursing such a princely sum, I'll try to help.

—We'll swear you in at quarters, when everyone's assembled, said Claiborne. To them all he said, —There'll be other changes as well. We'll receive a draft of landsmen today, and I have determined to advance Mr. Duycker into the position of executive officer, effective immediately.

Claiborne handed Duycker an envelope. —There appears to be some activity downriver which bears looking into. Please look these orders over and make ready to get under way. Mr. Eaker, make ready the guns. Advise Hubbard . . . I mean, advise MacNail as well.

Eli was left holding his commission as the others went off. He reread it, pressing his left hand on his chest, then rolled it up and slipped the red tape on again.

The pleasure passed more quickly than it would have if he hadn't felt so wretched. Shortly after falling asleep he'd been jerked away by a sinking, hollow sensation at the pit of his stomach. He'd lain awake for hours in his cramped cabin, staring up into the shadows. Sweat running down his face. Coughing so hard that when light finally came he'd barely been able to crawl out of his bunk and force down the strong coffee the steward had boiling in the wardroom. That and a bite of breakfast had improved him, but he still felt unsteady.

—Congratulations, sir, Babcock said reluctantly.

—Thank you. He returned the gunner's salute, and took as deep a breath of morning air as the obstruction in his chest would permit. —See to our readiness, if you please. We'll be getting under way shortly.

—Without the men the yard requisitioned? They told me we'd get 'em back directly.

The night before, a draft of twenty men had gone off to load grapeshot and powder on wagons, to take boat howitzers and a marine battery to Georgetown. He told the gunner to make do with what he had for now, and to draw and reload the guns.

———

266

At six bells the boatswain piped quarters for muster. When the men were assembled Claiborne read out the orders appointing him to command. They responded heartily enough when old Girnsolver proposed a cheer, but Eli caught doubtful looks. Their new captain did not remark on this, simply continued, —I have appointed Master Duycker as my exec, effective at once. We also have an official addition to our ranks, though he's been with us for some little time now. Mr. Elisha Eaker, front and center.

He paced forward, conscious of his awkwardness in front of the Academy-trained officers; came to a halt before the captain. —Raise your right hand, Claiborne said.

As he repeated the words of the oath he looked down the deck, at the rows of men and of guns. The flag snapped overhead. He looked back into the captain's eyes, blue as the heart of a gas flame.

—So help me God, he finished.

Claiborne shook his hand. —Welcome to the club, he murmured. Eli saluted, made a clumsy about-face, nearly falling, and went back to stand in front of his men.

The new commander paused, letting the lap of the water, the distant whistle of a train punctuate the momentary silence; then resumed.

—Now to the orders of the day. The department has a report that militia forces are erecting batteries to close the Potomac. That is at Aquia Creek, about thirty-eight miles downriver. We shall take a little excursion to look into it, as the river is the only avenue to and from the capital now that Baltimore has cut off rail communication north. Make your preparations accordingly. Mr. Duycker, they're yours.

The men stayed in ranks, the officers and petty officers took over, assigning posts and duties for the morning, then dismissing their men in turn. Eli was going over the ready service numbers with Babcock, making sure what ammunition would be ready to hand, when the new captain came strolling forward. —I trust we shall be prepared for action?

—We'll pull and reload in the stream, sir.

—I should like the howitzer put into the cutter. With twenty rounds of canister, if you please.

—Are we sending a party ashore, sir?

—It might be necessary. Claiborne leaned against the bulwark, looking toward Virginia. Where the land opened to admit the river, low green hills and farmhouses and darker copses of forest dotted the far shore. Eli watched the commander's face for any sign of how he felt, but saw nothing. The pale eyes were unclouded, the jaunty mustache and small pointed beard perfectly trimmed.

—Did you go ashore last night, Mr. Eaker?

He coughed into his hand. —I did, sir, for a few minutes. To the telegraph office.

He'd walked up to M Street to send a message to New York. Standing in line at the window to hand in his filled-out blank, he'd listened to the talk around him. Listened to rumor swirling up out of the Southland, crossing to the Southern city around him. Three thousand troops were camped at Mount Vernon. Trainfuls of men from Alabama had arrived at Harpers Ferry. Ten thousand troops were on their way from Richmond.

—Anything of interest?

The lieutenant looked almost too relaxed, too studiedly unconcerned. His forearm rested casually on his sword hilt. Girnsolver flashed a warning glance at Eli behind his back.

—No sir. Just idle chatter, he said at last.

—It may be a bit more difficult going down than it was coming up. All of our pilots seem to have vanished.

—How about the fellow who brought us up? Smallwood?

—No one's available just now. We shall simply have to go the lead and keep a close eye on the chart.

He looked at the muddy, narrow stream, at the broad rippling river shining like brass in the brightening sunlight beyond. The only road out now. Placing *Owanee* and her soft-spoken captain in a most particular position. He did not reply and after a moment Claiborne called out to the new exec, —Quarters for getting under way, Mr. Duycker, if you please.

———

—All hands weigh anchor. Girnsolver put his whistle to his lips. The boatswain's mates took up the call. The norman was jerked out of the drumhead. The heavy ash capstan bars slammed in one by one, and the gang shook their shoulders out around it. One of the marines brought his fife on deck, squatted on a bitt, and set to work. The great spindle began turning to a swinging stamp, the clank of the pawls, and the sprightly air of "Heave Away Cheerily."

> *The wind is free, and we're bound for sea,*
> *Heave away cheerily, oh!*
> *The lassies are waving to you and to me*
> *As off to southward we go.*
> *Sing my lads cheerily, heave, my lads, cheerily,*
> *Heave away cheerily, oh!*
> *For gold that we prize, and sunnier skies,*
> *Away to the southward we go.*

Eli stood by one of the thirty-twos, feeling a changeable breeze play against his cheek. Claiborne had set the outer jib and the spanker. Dirty smoke chuffed from the stack. A hand pump thudded belowdecks. Seamen leaned out at the cathead, spraying mud off the chain as link by slimy link it emerged from the stream, fed around through the windlass, and crept sullenly below like a rebuked python. Duycker stalked the deck like a hunting heron, gray long hair lapping over the collar of his greasy worn coat.

A shout from forward: —Short stay. Up and down.

—Very well. Avast heaving.

The new exec stalked aft. Claiborne returned his salute gravely, then bent to shout down the speaking tube. The engine room's answer must have been satisfactory, for Duycker went forward again and the clanking resumed.

—Anchor's aweigh, sir.

—One bell, if you please, Mr. Eddowes. Commence heaving the lead.

Ding . . . ding. A stirring in the hull, gradually accelerating to a steady bump and slam, the quivering beat of the warped shaft going around. The river boiled gently. The navy yard bridge and the dough-faced homes of Uniontown dropped aft. On the bow Girnsolver was supervising the making off of the anchor. The leadsman cried twain and a half.

The bowsprit came slowly left and Eli remembered the arsenal at the point, but the gunner was foreprepared. The white smoke of their salute jarred out suddenly, then slowed and floated out over the flat water as the report traveled on, clap-echoing off the distant walls of the unfinished Capitol.

The wide river showed only a single moving speck far down-stream, a ferry, perhaps, crossing to Alexandria. The engine order bell clanged again and the screw increased its beat as they moved out into the saffron current, the sprit swinging smoothly round to point south as it began hurrying them along.

Leaning to look down, coughing, Eli watched thick ocher water writhe like battling snakes along their waterline. Interesting, that no pilot could be obtained. Maybe they were better off without. A traitor could run them on a shoal so firmly they'd never get off. With *Owanee* burned or captured, Washington would be isolated. If the rumors were true, the massing rebels could brush the bridge pickets aside, take the capital, capture the administration. The war would have to be fought from Philadelphia or New York City. And by some-one other than Lincoln and Scott and Seward.

—By the mark, three, the leadsman's cry came clear and high and thin as that of the gulls that wheeled in the bright air.

—Seen the *Star?* Schuyler thrust a smeared and refolded broad-sheet at him. Eli flattened it on the hatch coaming, ran eyes down the blurry mismatched columns of hastily set type.

The same astonished disbelief gripped him as whenever he picked up a newspaper these days. The governors of the several states were responding to Lincoln's call for militia by telegram. Maryland and Delaware's governors had answered loyally, though their legislatures were divided. Kentucky had refused her quota. North Carolina had responded courteously, but in the negative. Jeff Davis had read the message out in cabinet, to the accompaniment of laughter. Massachusetts had doubled her quota. The Democratic candidate for governor, a man named Butler, would command her brigade. Governor Sprague of Rhode Island would general his state's forces. Eli had met Sprague, found him a nearsighted, self-absorbed little bantam. The great question was still what Virginia would do. He looked again to where their new captain stood, staring out at the passing river coast.

Hard to conceive, that those greening hills, the white homes each with pier jutting into the clouded stream, might soon be land of a declared enemy. That hostile eyes might even now be following their progress. He ran his gaze over the pivot gun. He felt more comfortable with the weapons now, between watching Babcock and studying the books. He'd fired them several times during the cruise up through the Chesapeake. But only in drill, never yet in anger. He rubbed his throat, staring vacantly over the bulwark at a high bluff slipping past. He caught Duycker standing near the captain, both with glasses leveled at the bluff. A chill ran over his arms as he realized what they were looking for. He stepped up behind them as the leadsman cried,

—By the mark, five!

—Captain.

Claiborne did not lower his telescope. —Mr. Eaker?

—Should we not have the men at the guns, sir? In case we encounter a hidden battery?

—I think we'll have time to beat to, Eli. Should the eventuality occur. What do you think, Nick? Should we put the t'gallants to work, and perhaps the tops?

—They might pay their way.

Back at number one he caught a glance from Hanks. The master-at-arms had apprehended the big Negro sneaking back aboard the night before. Eli had remanded him from the brig after they got under way. They were too short of hands to leave a skilled gunner in irons. But he'd have to come to some understanding with Duycker about him. Discipline had to be preserved, but Eli didn't want to witness another hanging. He turned his eyes from the black's, only to meet Claiborne's look from farther aft. He turned from that considering gaze as well, pacing back and forth along the waiting guns. Then the coughing came on again, and he began to sweat. At last, seeing no immediate necessity for his services, he felt his way carefully down the companionway to his cabin.

The sloop thumped steadily on all morning, the only change the endlessly passing countryside. The land was greening fair under the high shining sky, the lofty silver clouds. Plantation houses and waterfront hamlets passed by. Eli spent most of the forenoon below, bent over Matthew Fontaine Maury. But he wasn't really interested in the feeding patterns of whales. He was wondering again about Araminta. Since Charleston he had thought of her more and more often. He put his hand in his pocket and flattened out his handwritten copy the clerk at the telegraph office had thrust back at him.

DEAR HEART IN WASHINGTON NOW HAVE NOT FORGOTTEN OUR ENCOUNTER ON STAIRS STOP HOPE YOU AND FATHER ARE WELL STOP FEEL A BIT HOMESICK LETTERS APPRECIATED STOP ELI

His door slammed open, cracking against the bulkhead like a pistol shot. It was Duycker. The master yelled, —Fire quarters, Eaker, didn't you hear the pipe? Stir some goddamned sticks! A commission don't mean the rest of us do your fucking work!

—Sorry, sir. He started guiltily up, felt Duycker's reddened eyes on him like a petty officer's colt as he scooted up the companionway.

Claiborne exercised them at fire drills for an hour, dragging pumps about the deck, manhandling hoses, identifying which lines to cut to let burning rigging go by the board. He clewed up and furled the t'gallants, tops, and jib, leaving neatly made up canvas aloft. Then secured drill, and ordered the cutter overside.

This was the second time Eli had seen this evolution carried out. He studied it carefully now as Girnsolver piped orders.

The cutter was *Owanee*'s largest and heaviest boat. Usually riding in a gallows frame forward of the mainmast, it had to be lifted, swung outboard, and lowered to the water. The first step was to square the main yards. While the braces were being worked other seamen were making up the purchases, guys, topping lift, and slings on the boom as it lay on deck.

Meanwhile Girnsolver was securing a gantline to the maintop. The old boatswain sent a running block up in a bight, then rigged an upper fairlead. The fairleads gantline went to a snatch block at the base of the mainmast, leading the gantline to a portable capstan in the waist of the ship. Then the topping lift went up, hoisted hand over hand till it came in reach of the topmen, who leaned over far in the sky to shackle it to the mainmast while the deck gang made up the purchase to a threefold through fairleads at the base of the mast.

At this point Eli lost track. Not till Girnsolver stepped back and the boom soared suddenly aloft, horsed skyward by twenty hoary palms, did his eye comprehend the sudden functionality assembled in midair from the tangle of wood and cordage and iron. The butt of the boom swung mastward, following its guiding vang. Pinned to the mainsail yard truss, pivoted at the mast, that left its outer end suspended over the starboard bulwark by the topping lift.

Meanwhile the guy parties had braced boots and bare feet against the deck. The boatswain flicked out a finger left, left, right, till the head of the boom centered over the cutter. The men on the downhaul topped the boom a few more feet. Then the topmen, swinging down like apes on the ratlines, belayed it to the mainmast.

No audible command, not a word passed; the gray-bearded boatswain simply nodded at one man after another, or at most lifted hollow silver for a peremptory pipe. Two seamen rose from within the cutter holding a sling. The main purchase dipped to meet their hands, and pins darted in, With a cupping motion of his hand Girnsolver moved brawny backs off the topping lift and put them against the main purchase.

A slow rotation of his index finger in the air, a thumb's jerk upward. The seamen on the threefold bent to the line, the line captain shouting "Heave" and the men grunting "Ho" as they put backs and legs and arms into the jerking purchase; and the whole massive weight of the cutter rose slowly and smoothly up off the deck. The boatswain slacked one guy and sweated the other till the tapered massive shape pivoted outward, rocked snubbing lines taut with a manila squeal, then went smoothly down to keel-kiss the passing river. The sea painter came taut and the boat rocked and pushed in against the hull like a young manatee nuzzling its mother. The boom swung inboard again, plucked the boat howitzer off the deck with all the delicacy and very nearly the rapidity of a lady lifting a teacup, wheeled it across, and dropped it into the bow.

—Cutter's in the water, Cap'n.

—Very well, Bo's'n. Overhaul the boom, if you please.

When the hoisting gear was rigged in, the marines began beating the tattoo. The shrill notes of "Smoking lamp" whistled down the passageways. Ripley and Jerrett and the other monkeys' feet pattered as they ran the powder charges up in their copper buckets.

During all this time the river had opened gradually, exposing a wide flat sheet of faintly rippled bronze to their view. Looking out, Eli saw the stream narrowing again ahead in a great sweeping loop eastward. Toward the end of the cutter work he'd noted a column of smoke climbing in the distance. Now he saw it came from behind a point on their right hand. The land spit covered what looked to be a creek, an estuary creeping back into the country. Another pale gap in the green opened a mile or so beyond it.

This, then, must be Aquia. The bluffs from beyond which smoke billowed were the site of the rumored rebel battery. The river here was two miles wide, the slowly moving water punctuated only by the leaning stakes of fish traps and trotlines far on the opposite shore. *Owanee* lay in midriver, somewhat closer to the Maryland side than otherwise, her guns pointed toward the smoke, as the captain and the exec bent over the chart.

—It's shallow as hell in there, said Duycker loudly.

Claiborne said, —Well, let's just feel our way over. There was a range mark hereabouts, was there not? I seem to recall markers in that direction, leading in toward the steamboat landing.

—There were. Some secesh bastard took 'em down.

—Well, we'll go on in and see what happens. Mr. Eaker, stand by.

Eli snapped back an "Aye aye" and went up beside the forward pivot. The huge gun, five tons of black cast iron, looked eager to snarl. The crew looked steadily off to starboard. Archbold bent to range his eye along the gun tube. Babcock stood beside Eli, slapping his colt against his thigh as he stared at the approaching bluffs.

Archbold turned his head. —Shall I insert the primer, sir?

Eli muttered, —Gunner?

—I'd tell him to do so, sir. Our shell should be on its way before his arrives.

—Very well, Archbold. The gun captain nodded. He plucked one of the shiny copper tubes from a compartmented box filled with them. Held it aloft, examining it, then set the box aside. He pushed the primer into the touchhole, set the hammer, and stepped back, paying out the lanyard. Then all was stillness again and the heat of the sun coming up off the melted bronze. Eli passed his handkerchief over his face.

—By the mark, three!

Three fathoms; that was eighteen feet. The sloop drew a fraction over twelve fully loaded and ready for sea.

The eddying column of smoke towered up as they angled toward it. The clouds sailed overhead like passing schooners. No one spoke on deck. He swallowed, expecting at any moment the flash of a discharge, the howl of a shot. —Lay as soon as you see gun smoke, he told Archbold in a low voice. —But don't fire until you hear the command.

—Aye sir.

—By the mark, two and a half, shoaling.

—Engine stop, said Claiborne. Eddowes stepped to the bell. The beat of massive pistons slowed, then ceased. The sloop carried forward silently, moving with the ghost of momentum through the uneasy roil. Eli saw shallows ahead, greasy-looking, raddled, dangerous-looking water.

—Stand by the bower anchor, Bo's'n. Port your helm, Mr. Eddowes. One bell ahead . . . Steady.

—North northwest.

—Keep her so; nothing to the west. We will stand off here. Mr. Duycker, man the cutter.

The exec yelled, —Lay in the boat. Smartly, people! Hold on to that lifeline!

Eli leaned over the side to watch the landing party clamber down and drop one by one into the cutter, which rocked crazily in the muddy flow. To his relief, considering how low he felt, he hadn't been told off for boat duty this time. One of the passed midshipmen took the tiller, glancing anxiously at the shore, then up at the ship as if sorry to leave her oaken walls.

—Away the landing party, away. Cast off the sea painter.

Claiborne stepped to the lee, cupping his hands. —Handsomely, Mr. Thurston. Remember, do not engage. Return at the first sign of pickets or hostile activity.

The midshipman raised his cap. The cutter sheered away, turned short round, the starboard oarsmen pulling while the others backed water, and passed under their stern. It grew slowly smaller toward the first point Eli had noted, and at last disappeared around it. Then the river lay empty, though all was in motion, the brazen golden water, the moving clouds, and the smoke still ascending lazily into the shining sky. And after a time came the rattling clatter of the anchor running out.

The *clop, clop* of caulking hammers came from aft, where a party was overhauling the leak he'd reported above his cabin. Eli sat gazing blankly out over the river. The crew was busy about the decks, the sailmaker's mates with a main stays'l stretched out to restitch the cringles, others blacking down the standing rigging or picking rope into baggywrinkle. Then a shout from the masthead snapped heads up. He shaded his eyes to make out a many-legged water bug creeping its way across the flood.

As it crossed the last few yards between them Thurston handed the tiller to the coxswain. The midshipman stood in the stern sheets as the boat came in, gauging its approach, then grasped the Jacob's ladder and scampered up. The cutter sheered out and stood off, oars vertical as a dozen lightning rods. Thurston saluted Claiborne. —Sir, reporting the cutter. No activity ashore, sir.

—No activity? What was that smoke?

—Burning farmhouse, sir. No one about.

—A burning house and no one about. Recently occupied? Or an abandoned dwelling?

—Recently occupied, sir. Dead horse in the barn. Barn on fire too.

—You are most admirably terse in your reporting, Mr. Thurston, but let me beg of you slightly more detail. No sign of military activity?

—No sir. We went a mile up the creek, landed, circled back up the top of that hill there till we could see the ship. Nobody around. Sort of spooky.

Claiborne nodded slowly. —Very well. Mr. Duycker! Bring the cutter alongside and weigh anchor. Ask MacNail for as much steam as he can safely make. I shall run us under Brent Point, as the chart here calls it. If no one shows himself, we'll make as much distance back toward Washington as we have light for.

Not fifteen minutes later they struck ground. The screw had barely begun to revolve, the prow to part the muddy river, when the gradual cessation of movement, rather than any sound or motion, save perhaps for the faintest possible frisson, signaled she had taken a shoal. The leadsman sang back, voice carefully bland, —By the mark, twain.

Duycker went to a gunport, stared down at the water. —We seem to be aground, Captain.

Eli looked landward again, with considerably sharper interest than he'd felt when it had seemed they were departing. Claiborne had brought her quite close in to the shore. Here the greening woods marched right down to the riverbank, clothing the land in an eye-baffling cloak that the advancing afternoon only darkened.

The bell jangled aback. The engines thumped for several minutes, sending a murky clay-colored current swirling along the hull, but without other visible effect. Claiborne stood looking over the side, where the bulwarks hinged down to give the nine-inch a clear field of fire. When it was obvious she wasn't stirring he glanced aloft, then to the opposite shore.

Eli noticed he'd never once looked toward the near shore, and the disquiet he'd half nursed and half denied lifted its head again. Perhaps this grounding was not as accidental as it seemed. He glanced at Babcock, at Duycker. At Bob Schuyler, who'd come up on deck and stood by the pinrail. The marine looked piratical with cutlass and pistol thrust under his pipe-clayed belt.

When he touched his hat to the captain Claiborne looked back calmly. —I wish I'd hoisted the cutter in, Mr. Eaker. Putting her over again would lighten us considerably.

—Indeed, sir. Shall I get the guns ready to go overside?

—Once again, Mr. Eaker, you are anticipating commands. We shall make shift to get her off before we have to go to those lengths. Claiborne raised his voice. —Boatswain! All hands aft, if you please.

Moving the weight of a hundred and eighty men to the stern did not seem to make much difference. Nor did setting the topsails aback. Eli saw that once aground, the sloop's shallow draft worked against her. A deep-keel hull could be sallied, running the men from side to side to wedge out a channel. Or inclined, by swaying a dismounted gun out on a cargo boom. Not so with *Owanee*'s hard-turned bilges, her nearly flat bottom. Tilting her only dug her deeper. Claiborne had to know that. Why had he taken her in so close? If they were to escape she had to be lightened, and fast, as the tide was running out.

He glanced at the red-stained sky to the east, the shadowing forest looming all too close. Whoever was burning houses and barns, he didn't want to be trapped here with them when it got dark.

—On deck. Boat putting out from the creek, port quarter.

Claiborne turned quickly and put the long glass to his eye. He held motionless for several seconds, then slapped the scope closed. — Mr. Schuyler: marines to arms, and into the maintop. Mr. Eaker, cover her with a gun as she approaches. Lookouts! Keep a sharp eye on the riverbank.

Eli passed the order to the number two gun, reminding them to aim low. Meanwhile the captain, the exec, and the boatswain were discussing lightening ship. Their quickly reached conclusion was to dump drinking water first. Men ran below to start butts while others manned the pumps. The water would flow into the bilges, then be pumped out, a more expeditious means of getting it overside than slinging up heavy barrels.

—Shot'll go next, Mr. Eaker. In fact you might begin bringing it up and stacking it along the pinrails.

—Aye sir. He passed that to Babcock and paced back and forth on the deck. Should he mention his misgivings to Duycker? First the captain had run them ashore. Now they were disarming. The men seemed rooted at their battle stations, looking across the narrow strip of water. Each individual tree could be made out from its fellows. He could tell maples from oaks, and a stand of pines was set off a little way up the hill.

—I said, keep a gun trained on that boat, Mr. Eaker.

Eli started to say, —Yes sir, but it caught in his throat. He nodded instead, coughing, hurrying toward the port side.

The gunners were shifting tackle. The craft, a rowboat, had emerged from the creek now and was paralleling the shore between *Owanee* and the bluff edge. He could make out several heads, more than three but less than a dozen. They seemed low in the boat, as if lying down on the ceiling boards.

—Aloft! D'ye see, are they armed?

—No arms, sir. Six souls in it. Some might be women.

Just then one stood, nearly upsetting what Eli saw now was a small and possibly waterlogged skiff. The figure was in earth-colored clothes, and glanced back fearfully over its shoulder as it raised and lowered its arms to hail the ship. Then it dropped back below the gunwales again.

Babcock growled, —Why in the devil's name are they lying down like that?

—They may be trying to make up on us, said the exec.

—Then why'd he just jump up and wave?

Eli couldn't follow the discussion after that. He was bent over, coughing hard. Something seemed to be caught deep in his chest. At last the spasm or cramp passed and he straightened, drawing his cuff across his mouth, trying not to gasp for air.

—I think they want to come alongside.

Claiborne's voice rang across the deck. —Boatswain: the Jacob's ladder, if you please, to port. Let us find out exactly what these people are about.

Their movements were like those of burdened beasts: slow and tentative, as if directed not by reason but by instinct. Their hands were swollen, oversized, as if they'd put on extra gloves of thick tanned leather. Their slow gazes stayed nailed to the deck. They were barefoot, with the splayed toes of folk who had gone so all their lives. Four women and a man, the women in bulky, shapeless dresses, flat faces pulled tight over bucked teeth. They clutched bundles desperately tight. They watched with shy astonishment as a seaman went by lugging a heavy shot, let it drop over the side, and headed below again.

Duycker said angrily, —What do you people want aboard here?

The man answered, but in speech so liquid soft Eli couldn't grasp a word. Nor did Duycker or Claiborne, apparently, for they stared as blankly as he.

—Suh, I can tell you what they says. If you wants.

They turned in surprise as Hanks stepped from behind the pivot. Claiborne pursed his lips, then nodded. The big gunner went up to them, put his hand on their shoulders. They leaned together as the women spoke, glancing fearfully at the ring of white faces.

—Sir, they hear Massa Lincoln gone free 'em, and is we the ship he sent for 'em. They see us out here, think we waitin' for 'em to come on out.

Several crewmen burst out laughing. Duycker's glare stopped

them. Claiborne stood stroking his mustache. —They're runaway slaves? he said at last.

—Thass right, cap'n sir. They sure enough runaways.

The gunner looked back at the refugees with a troubled expression. Eli wondered if it was true, if Hanks was a fugitive too.

Claiborne said, —Well, our duty under the Fugitive Slaves Act is quite clear.

Hanks looked at his boots, then at the little party at the head of the ladder. He said in a low voice, —Sir, their master finds out they run away, they gone be whipped an inch of their lives. Maybe get their feets broken, so they not run again.

Duycker said sardonically, —Maybe that's what we should do with you, Hanks. Keep you from taking French leave out every time we touch port.

Eli took another step closer. He was fascinated by their dumb lowered looks. One saw blacks up north, but these seemed to belong to an earlier order of humanity, barely emerged from the mists of antediluvial time.

Claiborne said, as if to himself, —Mr. Lincoln has made it quite clear that the federal government will not interfere with the domestic institutions of the states. The law is clear; they must return to their masters.

—Sir, I is not gone to tell them that. They seen our flag—

—Which does not shelter theft of property. Tell them, Hanks. Tell them now.

The women began wailing. The man stood blinking, shoulders slumped. Claiborne lifted his voice. —You, there. What's your name?

—Dinkins, sir. Name Lyrus Dinkins.

—Lyrus, return to your home now, before your master misses you. And tell the other servants not to believe foolish rumors. Put them into their boat, Lance Corporal.

The marine came forward, but before he had his rifle well unslung the fugitives were bowing, muttering hasty words, backing toward the ladder.

Just then the sudden flat crack of a pistol exploded. The marine whirled, leveling his musket. —Who was that? Duycker shouted. —Master-at-arms! Who fired a—?

A flash and another crack beside the wheel, a whiff of gray percussion smoke. Jerrett ran yelling across the deck, hands over his ears. The Negroes sank to the deck, eyes blown wide in terror. Eli stared around, at a total loss for what was happening.

Then a tiny dark object fell through the air, and another flash and whip crack near the mainmast left torn copper spinning at his feet.

Billy Ripley pointed into the rigging. —There! There! he screamed.

Far aloft, a tiny capering shape leaned out from the maintop. Its paw flashed out, and something fell glittering through the air.

—Auguste! Claiborne shouted.

—Cover the powder! Babcock shouted, and wheeled and threw himself over a copper bucket, gripping it with both hands, shielding it from any stray spark with his own body.

Eli bent and picked up the expended cannon primer, looking aloft to where the monkey flung down a glittering handful, followed it with the empty box, then swung out and around the t'gallant halyard and scuttled straight up the topmast. The men on deck covered their heads as a flurry of fulminate cracks and bangs like a Chinese New Year's raced among them, among the powder charges and shells laid out ready to the guns. He tensed as he waited for the explosion. But when the smoke cleared the ship was still there, and the beast was chattering indignantly high above as the cursing topmen pursued it out onto the forestay.

Claiborne put his cap back on, locked his fingers behind his back, and walked away without a word. The Negroes looked from one face to another, then picked themselves slowly off the deck. They clambered overside and cast off. The man searched their faces a last time from the boat, then bent and took the oars.

Eli said in an undertone to Babcock, —That was rather a brave act, Gunner.

—What's that, sir?

—Covering the powder bucket like that.

Babcock eyed him as if he'd said something insulting. —A sailor takes care of his shipmates, sir. He turned away, deliberately giving him his back, and began shouting at the men to get the spent primers policed up and turned in for salvage.

The skiff was halfway back to the shore when Girnsolver said suddenly, —Sor, I believe we're free.

Simultaneously Eli realized it was true. They were moving downstream, the bowsprit swinging deliberately around toward the Maryland side. Duycker shouted orders. The beat of the screw resumed. *Owanee* picked up the motion of the river, nodding her way back toward the channel. Eli looked back, watching the skiff as it dropped astern, then merged with the shore. He felt something in his throat again. His chest ached. He strolled to the bulwark and coughed into his fist as discreetly as he could.

The cough grew deeper, turned into a deep hollow roar. It seemed to be squeezing up from inside him. He bent double over it, closing his eyes. Again. Again.

This time something came up, and he felt an instant of relief.

Then he tasted it.

He held it in his mouth for a moment more, knowing from that taste and feel what it was. After a moment he groped for his handkerchief. Turned aside, and opened the crumpled square of cambric.

The blood was fresh and bright, frothy stripes in yellowish mucus. As he stared at it the unquellable pressure began once more. He doubled the cloth and hacked again and again, bringing up what felt like a full mouthful of blood. He swallowed it, nauseated, dizzy. He opened his eyes to find himself against the bulwark, looking down through a freeing port onto the uneasy river.

—Mr. Eaker?

He turned away instinctively, fending off whoever was behind him with a waving arm. He could not speak. Unattached voices floated past his ears.

—He's not been well today.

—Take him down to Dr. Steele, if you please.

—Sir, can you walk? This way. Companionway down, mind your head.

He submitted thoughtlessly, mind still filled by the image of that bright blood. Red as blowing poppies. Red as the stripes in the flag, with the sun shining through them. Bright life's blood, draining away. He let them lead him, placing his boots carefully on the treads down and away from the light.

Dr. Steele received him in his cabin, little larger than Eli's own. The ship's surgeon stood aside as Schuyler and Thurston helped him to a chair, then lowered his own considerable bulk down very slowly onto a rumpled bunk. The stateroom smelled of drugs, which Eli only gradually noticed hanging in bunches from the overhead and ranged in glass bottles on shelves. Plaited marling held them against the motion of the ship. The doctor himself smelled of his wonted brandy.

When the others shut the door Steele heaved himself up, bustled around the cabin, then let himself down on the bunk again. He rubbed his jowls. —Feeling a bit under the weather?

—Better now, thanks.

—How about last night? I passed by your door at about four bells of the midwatch. An old man's bladder, you know. Steele searched around, found a glass, and tilted more brandy into it. Held up the black bottle. —You would benefit from a stimulant, my dear. *De vino nil nisi bonum.*

—I do not partake.

—As you will. Perhaps I can find a more acceptable elixir. You will take an infusion of camphor?

—I have no objection.

Steele studied him as he choked down the strong liquid. When he set aside the glass the surgeon said quietly, —I think you would do well to take your shirt off for me, Eli.

He complied reluctantly, recalling that other, much larger office, the muttonchops and green spectacles of one of the finest diagnosticians of Park Avenue. When he got his flannels off Steele became businesslike. He examined the blister scars, then leaned his ear close and began tapping. He auscultated for some time, ear pressed lover-close to Eli's chest.

—Do you experience fever?

—Occasionally.

—Lift your arms, please. Breathe deeply as you can. Again. Do you sweat at night?

—Last night was very bad.

—Describe it to me.

He did so. He felt as if he ought to protest, but he was too weak. He was also frightened. Steele motioned to him to resume his flannels, then took his wrist and pulled out a large silver watch. Eli looked past him at the little deadlight, at the miniature watercolor of afternoon river it framed. A sudden prickle of tears burned his sight. He wiped his eyes surreptitiously with his fingers.

—I have noticed your color, young Eaker. And listened to your cough night after night, as closely as we are thrown together in this vessel. What was your occupation before you joined us? Have I heard that you were a student?

—That's right.

—A sufficiently effeminating occupation. Have you consulted a physician?

—I have.

—Who?

—Dr. Wetmore, my childhood doctor. He called it a passing affection.

Steele pinched the back of his hand and watched as the skin resumed its shape. —What was his treatment?

—Blistering and Peruvian bark.

—But the fever did not respond to quinine.

—That was when he recommended I see Dr. Janeway.

—I've heard of Edward Janeway. What did he say?

—He advised I had weak lungs.

—Did he administer treatment?

—Emetic tartar.

—Surely he did not stop there?

Eli said unwillingly, —He advised me to withdraw from my studies and abandon all indoor labor, if I wished to recover. He said I should seek change of air, change of location, change of scene. I should live in the open air, with plain food and abundant sleep.

—And where are these *summa bona* to be found?

—He advised me to either go west, or to sea.

—To which we owe your presence among us?

—It was part of my impulse toward the navy. Have you completed your examination?

Steele opened the lid of an instrument case. Within were rows of strangely shaped knives, saws, and forceps. He fingered several, but finally closed the lid again and set its hook. —I believe I have.

—Your conclusions?

—We have anemia and daily hectic fever, associated with sweating over the upper but not the lower body. Tussis, purulent expectorations, and now haemophthisis. Cachexia is not observed, but an active process is auscultated in the upper right lung. My conclusion is that you are in an early stage of lung disease, my dear.

—"Lung disease"? Or consumption?

Steele said gravely, looking directly and not unkindly on him, — To use the proper term, consumption; yes. I'm sorry.

Eli closed his eyes. The dread word had fallen, like the knell over a grave. His mother had died of it. Now the seeds in the blood were blossoming.

—I'll die, then.

—As will we all, my young friend. But your rendezvous with dread Azrael may be deferred for some considerable time. I've seen consumptives weather a crisis and live on for years. Occasionally it even seems to vanish. This is a most erratic and unpredictable disease. Did Dr. Janeway discuss it with you?

—He didn't say I had it.

—Then I assume he did not. Are you interested in learning about your affliction? Perhaps hear some cautionary advice? Or are you simply resigned to the will of the Deity?

—I should be grateful for whatever you can tell me.

Steele leaned back, considered a moment.

—The disease we know as consumption was described by Hippocrates. He called it phthisis. The ancient Hebrews knew it as *schanhepheth.*

A knock at the door. Jerrold, sent to enquire after Eli. Dr. Steele sent him back on deck with a reassurance. He reached Eli's glass and added another tablespoon of camphor.

—I could adduce references from Leviticus and Deuteronomy; but you may be more interested in our modern views on the subject. You are familiar with the theory of Brunonian excitability?

—I have heard it mentioned.

—Dr. Brown taught that pain, inflammation, and fever are due to an imbalance between exciting and calming stimuli. We may divide all diseases into four classes: those caused by bad air, such as malaria, yellow fever, and plague; communicable or infectious diseases, such as smallpox; the sthenic diseases, due to overexcitement of the organism; and the asthenic diseases, which follow from a decline in the vital actions. Obviously consumption is to be classed with the sthenic order, until the latter stages, when the patient enters into a putrid state.

—We then ask, from whence does it arise? Richard Morton believed phthisis to be carried in damp, smoky air, and also due to a hereditary disposition from the parents. Franciscus Sylvius also considered consumption hereditary. I should say most medical authority would agree; asthenic stature, effeminizing employment, and hereditary influences predispose to consumption; smoke or damp air hasten its progress. Have any of your close relatives suffered with lung disease?

He said hoarsely, —My mother died of it.

Steele nodded. —That would accord with the theory of blood predisposition. But there is also another view.

—Which is?

—Frascatorius believed disease was communicated by something he called fomites, invisible disease seeds, which supposedly cling to clothing and bedding. We know smallpox is spread in some such way. Why not others? As you know, I've practiced in the Spanish-speaking countries. Unlike us Anglo-Saxons, they regard consumption as infectious.

Eli drew his sweating hands across his trowsers. —And your opinion?

Steele shrugged. —My dear, who can say for certain? The great Laennec confessed himself puzzled by consumption. Before it killed him. The hereditary connexion is most convincing. Yet early transmission by proximity, not showing itself till the young adult years, might look like hereditary influence. If I were you, I should take certain precautions. Cover your mouth with a clean handkerchief when coughing. Do not share your bed or eating utensils. Perhaps the Spanish are wrong, but it would show a due regard for others.

He took a deep breath. He felt better, as if the simple objective discussion of his condition had lifted the weight a little.

—I take your meaning, Doctor. How long would you say I have?

—Oh, my dear fellow! Anyone who claims to know that is a humbug, pure and simple. I see you wear flannel underclothing. That is excellent. I will prepare a balsamic draught to ease your cough. There is also an instrument that will relieve your lungs, if you determine to try it.

—Whatever I can do, I will.

—Whatever its root cause, consumption is at base a mechanical disease. Inflammation breaks down the lung. But we know the tubercles, the characteristic ulcers, can heal. Laennec showed by dissection that once-active lesions could close and a patient live on for many years.

Steele pulled a book down and showed him a pipelike tube invented by a Dr. Ramadge in London ten years previous. The inhaling tube restricted the passage of air out of the lungs, requiring the patient to expel it by force. The effect was, first, to break up active ulcers and expel their contents. This uncomfortable process completed, continued use of the tube closed up the cavities where the inflammation resided. Also, he should bathe daily from the waist upward in the coldest water he could stand, avail himself of fresh fruit and vegetables, stay in the open air as much as duty would permit, and above all, not succumb to despair.

—As much as you can, free your mind of worry, young man. Hope is the greatest antagonist of disease. And you have real grounds for hope.

—Thank you, sir. You have eased my mind.

He began to rise, but halted at a peremptory motion.

—Let me add one more caution. The surgeon peered over his glasses. —I said you might live a long time. But I've also seen deterioration proceed very rapidly indeed. If you have anything you wish to do with your life, my advice is to be about it now.

Eli stood for a moment, feeling there had to be something more to say. Something else to ask. But he couldn't think what it might be. The moment of relief, of near acceptance, was fading. Maybe it had been Steele's words about hope. Meant to cheer him, no doubt, but their actual effect was to mock everything else he'd said about survival, about cure.

—Yes? said Steele.

But he only nodded and let himself out and went down the passageway to his cabin.

He lay looking up at the overhead, listening to the thump and rumble of the screw, the whish of river passing his ear, and let the oncoming shadow close softly and silently as black funereal drapes drawn between those without and those who, like him, looked forward only to death.

22

YOURS OF SIXTEENTH TO HAND STOP ELISHA YOU MUST HELP ME STOP MICAH LEAVING FOR WASHINGTON THIS MORNING STAYING WILLARDS STOP AM LEAVING HIS HOUSE WHEN HE DEPARTS STOP HAVE GOOD REASON DO NOT OWE HIM DUTY OF WARD AND NIECE STOP DO NOT INFORM HIM WHERE I AM STOP YOU HAVE A GREAT CAUSE TO SERVE UN-FAIR TO BURDEN YOU STOP BUT YOU MUST SUPPORT ME IN RIGHT TO MY OWN INHERITANCE STOP ALTERNATIVE IS STEP I FEAR TO TAKE STOP YOU MAY CONTACT ME HOME OF LYDIA MARIA CHILD STOP YOUR LOVING COUSIN ARAMINTA

23

The Navy Yard Redux ♦ Unpleasant News from the Convention ♦
Obtaining an Inhaling Tube ♦ Meeting with Mr. Paffholter ♦ The Parlor at
Willard's ♦ Reaction of Micah Eaker to Araminta's Defiance ♦ Unorthodox
Disposition of a Commission in the United States Army

A S Eli came on deck the next morning Claiborne turned to watch him cross the quarterdeck. —Mr. Eaker. Feeling restored this fine morning, I hope?

Eli touched his cap. —Much, quite. Thank you, sir.

—Old Pills take you in hand? Everything all right now?

He nodded instead of answering, turning away from the captain's inquiring glance and looking across wrinkled water to the approach of land. Clouds leaned close above the church spires, but the rain had stopped and patches of blue showed gay as colored lining through a Shakespearean actor's doublet. The floodwaters had receded, drawn back like contemptuous lips to show black gums of marsh, the skeletal jut of duck blinds, abandoned rotting boats. The city itself seemed unchanged and unchangeable, but the beams and shadows playing over it, first highlighting, then throwing into obscurity the unfinished marble whiteness that crowned the hill, seemed to mirror the ever-altering nature of all human passions and all human afflictions.

Like his own. He'd had one more episode that night, but that expectoration had been rusty and clotted rather than arterial bright. Steele had sent Jerrett to Eli's cabin with the draught he'd promised. He hadn't coughed as much after that. He'd slept, though with disquieting dreams, until waking to find the sloop standing in for the Eastern Branch.

Duycker, coming up behind him: —Eaker. You fit for duty today?

—I'm feeling better. Sorry I couldn't stand my watch last night.

The elderly master examined him doubtfully. —Sure you're fit?

—I will take the deck now if you want me to.

By eight bells they were moored. A marine stood waiting with a dispatch pouch as they came alongside the quay wall. He came aboard as soon as the gangway was over.

Watching him speak to the captain, Eli saw Claiborne's face go still, saw him waver on his feet as the import of whatever he said hit home. Then he braced himself, regaining his poise through what looked like an effort of will. He nodded, took the pouch, and looked aloft. Told Duycker to see to the lines. Then spun on his heel and went down the companionway.

He intercepted the leatherneck at the brow. —Bad news?

—Bad enough, sir. V'ginia's out of the Union.

The sergeant waited, but when he didn't respond went on, —Got the news yesterday. Cap'n Buchanan wanted your skipper to know soon as he got in.

—I see. Eli remembered the burning, abandoned homestead Midshipman Thurston had reported, the ominous stillness along the river. Suddenly he wished *Owanee* were not the only warship lying along the quay. —Have any more troops arrived? Any word from the North?

—Haven't heard of any, sir. Unless there's something about it in the dispatches there.

He returned the man's salute, and stood looking after him as the marine descended the gangway, crossed the muddy ground, and disappeared amid a jumble of sheds and stores.

———

Claiborne came back up some minutes later and stood looking off into the distance. Eli debated approaching him. Something in the set of the lieutenant's back discouraged it. But at last he did. —Sir, permission to go ashore, for a medical reason. I will return within four hours, no more.

—Ah. Mr. Eaker. The Southerner found an envelope about his person and extended it. —From this morning's bag.

He opened the telegram rapidly. Read it, stopping at the line about her leaving the house, then again at the sentence about a step she feared to take. He glanced up, but the captain's gaze had returned to the far pillars of Arlington. He felt frantic, both at the distance between them and his impotence. But perhaps he was not impotent. Perhaps there *was* something he could do. If his father was here, in Washington. . . .

—Sir, this telegram makes it even more essential that I get ashore.

—I see. Your destination?

—My father is in town, staying at his usual hostelry. It's a family matter, I'm afraid.

—It all resolves to family, doesn't it? In the end? Claiborne smiled wearily. —I suppose we can spare you for a few hours, if Mr. Duycker concurs. And if you feel you're strong enough.

—I apologize for my weakness last night.

—We all must fall out occasionally. I suffer from the Guinea fever myself from time to time.

Duycker concurred with his departure, albeit grudgingly. Eli went below and got a topcoat and boots. He passed through the yard barely seeing it.

The streets weren't well peopled, but a few pedestrians were out. His cab ride was interrupted by an army officer who ran out of an oyster shop, seized the bridle, and by main strength dragged horse, driver, and equipage to a plunging halt on the muddy cobblestones of Pennsylvania Avenue. He shied back when Eli leaned out in uniform. —Beg pardon, he said. —Didn't see it was hired.

—What's the trouble?

—Dispatch for General Scott.

—In that case, you're welcome to it. I'm almost where I'm going.

In truth he welcomed a few more minutes to prepare himself. As he saw Willard's ahead, four stories of red brick screened by noble elms greened by rain and the advance of the season, his pace gradually slowed. Then he noticed another place he needed to call. With a sense of relief at postponing the meeting with his father, even for a few minutes, he turned aside into the apothecary's.

The shop smelled of pennyroyal and bitter quinine. Behind the counter a younker in shirtsleeves and cuff protectors listened to his description, then called to someone in back. An old pill roller, the owner, apparently, came out wiping his hands on a towel. When Eli explained what he wanted the latter nodded. —I do indeed know of such an implement. Had some in stock last year, but they were of such an inferior quality of india rubber I sent them back when the drummer came round again. A Ramadge tube's what you want.

—I think we're talking about the same thing. It's a specific for . . . consumption. The first time he'd said the word in public.

It didn't seem to shock them. The apothecary said, —I know a gentleman who can make up the genuine article for you, in silver, gold, or Spanish platina. I don't recommend the wooden models. In my view they contract impure matter from the air, and might well poison the entire system.

—Silver will answer. I'd like it as short as possible. A traveling model. And a fitted case.

—We can accommodate you, sir. Shall I send it round? Or will you call?

Eli said he'd call, and as he was a trifle short of the ready, would a note of hand be sufficient? At this the proprietor's friendliness flagged; he was sorry, but he could extend credit only to his most regular custom. Eli started to say, —On second thought, charge it to my father. Then remembered Micah's parting words in New York. Damn the old man; he'd not give him the satisfaction of refusing his note.

They compromised on sixteen dollars on account. When he finished counting out the bills, his pocketbook was nearly empty.

Outside he stood on the curb, not looking toward the hotel. The sun bathed his face. Despite the shadow of the white plague, it felt good to be alive. Maybe he felt it even more keenly, appreciated it more deeply, than when he'd taken health and youth for granted, and life had stretched out like a broad highway without ever an end. He wanted to keep walking, enjoy the shopwindows and the scent of daffodils nodding brightly from window boxes.

But today was not to be enjoyed. He was here on a matter of obligation.

He finally forced himself through the entrance at the corner of Fourteenth and Pennsylvania, up to the desk, where he said through gritted teeth, —I should like to send my card up to Mr. Micah Eaker, please.

The Eaker and Callowell office was in a Georgetown town house two blocks uphill of the Chesapeake & Ohio canal. That was where the hotel clerk had directed him, saying Mr. Eaker was not at present in his rooms. Eli paid the hack driver with his last coins. He would have walked, but recalling how fragile his lungs probably still were, felt it prudent not to presume on the recuperative powers of nature.

The ground-floor office was open and quite empty. He remembered how grand it had seemed to him as a child. Now it was just a dusty, rather shabby counting room, smelling of gaslight and the nearby canal. The oak floor was dark-ringed where spittoons had served generation on generation of the nearsighted and careless. He lifted the leaf on the counter and announced himself at the foot of the stairs. After a moment a gruff accustomed voice echoed down. It was not the one he'd expected, but no doubt his father was up there as well.

The second floor was open and rather sunny, when the clouds permitted. A shellacked maple banister ran around the central portion of the office. Josef Paffholter sat with two other men his age, all three substantial both in their persons and in their clothing and thus presumably their financial positions. Paffholter's face was the color of a freshly washed earthworm. Eli bowed to his father's Georgetown agent. —Mr. P., good morning.

—What a delightful surprise. Gentlemen, may I present Elisha Eaker, son of my principal, Micah Adolphus Eaker, Esquire.

—Pleased to meet you.

—I didn't know you were in the naval service, Eli. You look very well in uniform.

—Thanks, Mr. P. I took the oath only yesterday.

The strangers shook hands gravely, rising with some difficulty, then reseating themselves. —Spurred by the insults offered so recently to our flag? one said.

—Something like that, sir.

Paffholter pushed a bottle toward him. —Will you take a tonic, Eli?

—I'd hoped for a word with my father. He looked round. —I have only a brief leave from my vessel. Is he here?

—You missed him by a quarter hour. He's very busy just now. Been closeted with Mr. Chase already this morning.

—Mr. Chase?

All three regarded him gravely. —Mr. Salmon P. Chase, said Paffholter. —Of the Treasury.

—Oh, that Mr. Chase. Did Father say where he was bound?

—I believe he was returning to Willard's to meet with a party there.

He was turning to go when he recalled how generous the family's Washington representative, a confirmed bachelor, had always been with him as a child; the sweets and toys. And turned back. —Sir, I confess myself embarrassed as to funds. My naval pay has not yet commenced. If you could see me through the next week or two—

—Say no more, my boy. Paffholter drew out a sizeable billfold, extracted several large notes of an unfamiliar pattern. —Will five dollars see you through?

—I am indebted. That should be more than enough. He examined the bills, saw that they were on a Philadelphia bank. —He's back at Willard's then?

—I believe that was where he said his next engagement was. Wait, wait, my boy. You're not leaving already.

—I am afraid I must. My time is limited. He winced inside at the unfortunate sound of that; then took old Paffholter's large soft hand, lifted his cap gravely to the others, and withdrew through the deserted room below, back out into the sunlight and the open air.

This time the clerk, a tall pasty Englishman in a too-tight frock coat, deigned to condescend to him. Perhaps it was the dollar Eli was able to pass across the counter now. —Has Mr. Eaker returned?

—I believe so, sir. Bell captain! Another gentleman to see Mr. Eaker.

He followed the red-capped boy up the carpeted staircase to the second floor.

Willard's was the best hotel in the capital, though neither as large nor as luxurious as the finest New York establishments. It catered to the Northern political element, as the National traditionally had to the Southern. Lincoln had stayed here before the inauguration, playing the game of cabinets. Now Eli passed majors and lieutenant colonels, looking concerned and self-important; passed politicos in black frock coats and wide-brimmed hats. Waiters threaded among them, bearing decanters and covered trays.

The parlors consisted of a sitting room and inner chambers. Four men glanced up as he entered. The door to the sanctum was closed. He didn't speak to them, just crossed and tapped at it.

—He's engaged, one of the sitters said. —You will have to wait your turn.

Instead of replying he tapped again. The door displayed a two-inch slice of an annoyed-looking Reeves. His expression didn't alter when he recognized Eli. He muttered, —Your father's very busy. Very important matters.

—I should like to see him for a few minutes nonetheless.

—Take a seat. I'll tell him you're here.

The door closed. The other gentlemen looked vindicated. There were no more chairs, so he leaned against the doorjamb. It opened again and two more frock coats came in, looked at those already waiting. One said, —Leather, Mr. Newsome?

—Indigo, Mr. Fanshaw.

—If he's unwilling I can secure you a buyer who believes this is the time to plunge. I'm at the Saint Charles.

He would have expected casual conversation, but no one else spoke at all. Instead they smoked until his eyes began to tear; then he began to cough. He took out the vial Steele had given him and sipped the bitter compound. The tickle went away presently, soothed.

Half an hour later another frock coat arrived, went through the anteroom without looking at those who waited. The fellow beside Eli identified him as Representative Henry Winter Davis of Maryland. Instantly admitted, he did not stay long, but hurried out, again without looking at anyone.

Reeves, at the door. —Your father will see you now, Eli.

The large room within was brightly lighted by the large windows, which faced the grim Doric frontage of the Treasury, just across Pennsylvania; by the gaslights, which were all on; and by the gemlike brilliance of several spermaceti candles as well, which permeated the air with their delicate and unmistakable fragrance. Micah stood at a sideboard, helping himself from a collation of cut apples, pears, and cheeses. He said through a full mouth, —Reeves, a moment alone. Eli, what're you doing here?

—My ship's at the navy yard. How are you, Father?

The elder Eaker grunted. He gestured vaguely at the buffet. Eli examined his white hair, the familiar knobbed nose. It struck him for the first time that his father was growing old.

—But how did you get here, sir? I heard the railroads were closed past Baltimore.

Micah poured himself a quarter glass of wine. —A business associate there provided a carriage. It wasn't a pleasant trip, though. Baltimore is close to revolt, to judge by the street mobs.

—Did you see any troops headed our way?

—More rumors than troops, but a body of Pennsylvania militia was close behind us. The Seventh New York should be here shortly as well. I've heard nothing of the Massachusetts men. I do not doubt there will be trouble when they try to pass through Maryland. He napkined his face and sat. Looked through several pieces of paper, then seemed to recall his son was still there. —Still in your sailor suit, I see.

—Yes sir. We went down the river yesterday to investigate reports of a battery being set up. He reached out boldly for the wine. Micah lifted his eyebrows. Eli drank a tumbler off and shuddered. It was supposed to lend one courage, after all.

—Sir, I wish to speak to you concerning myself and Araminta, specifically in relation to her funds invested with us.

—What? That matter's settled. Been settled for years.

—I don't believe it is, Father.

He'd tried to order his thoughts in the sitting room. Somehow he had to persuade his father to give Ara what was due her. He also had to deal with the closely related question of their engagement. The marriage had not been broken off, only postponed. What made it even more awkward was that he was the one who had first suggested delay. She hadn't said a word against it before that. He could argue for putting it off by telling Micah about his disease. But he didn't want to do that. Admitting himself an invalid would remove whatever independence of action he'd gained. His father would take over instantly, pack him off to some high-Alps sanatorium like a sick eight-year-old.

Complicating it all now was that more and more, since facing hostile guns in the Charleston night, now he wanted what he hadn't before. More and more, he realized he'd made a mistake in asking Araminta to put off their plans for a future together. That, in fact, he loved her. But now he sensed she was moving away from him, away from both of them, and he would have to win her back. But cousin or intended, she had pleaded with him to sue on her behalf; so he went on doggedly, —Sir, she has shared with me what passed between you in regard to her legacy. I believe we owe her a separate accounting of her mother's funds. We should even offer to place them in her hands, when she comes of age.

—And why do "we" owe her that, sirrah? Micah's lips turned downward; he frowned and looked back at the sideboard.

He took a deep breath, trying to conquer his fear. He was too big to cane, after all, and his father had already cut him off financially. What else could he do? Aloud he said, —Well, she's got a bee in her bonnet about being independent. But most of all, because it really is hers. It's elemental fairness.

His father smiled in astonished disbelief. —Elemental *fairness,* he repeated heavily. —You amaze me, Elisha. As to fairness, here is my view of the matter: I would sooner give Ming porcelain to an infant as entrust either of you gas-headed half-wits with money. You would be eaten alive in the market. You don't need fairness. You need *protection.* The matter is very simple. The two of you will marry, and her assets will stay under my management within the firm, until such time as I judge you fit to take over my interests.

—Sir, let me be frank. She won't treat on those terms. I think she will still marry me, given a bit of time to think it over. But she wants to think herself independent.

—Oh, does she? She can do without me? Why, then, I'll sell that damned black horse of hers. See how she likes that.

He thought of Araminta's plan to run away. Perhaps by now she already had. —She's a strong-willed girl, Father. She may attempt something . . . drastic. Or unsuitable.

—What? Micah shook his head slowly, cheeks darkening with a lace of blood. —Are you threatening me, boy? Or is *she?* Let her do her damnedest, I will not give in. She can die a whore on the streets, for all I care. She knows that.

—Those are not fatherly words.

—I'm not her father! On the other hand, I *am* yours. Her inheritance is more substantial than I've told her. Just now we can double it—maybe triple it, if this war bubble continues to grow.

Eli started to speak, but Micah interrupted, searching angrily through papers on a table. —That's all, Elisha. I can't blather with you any longer, even if you could understand what I'm talking about. Those fools up in the city are sitting on their gold, waiting for the smoke to clear. As soon as I heard the news from Sumter, I liquidated all our fixed instruments. At a decided loss; but this is the time to look ahead. Leather. Guano, for saltpeter. Lead. Cotton. And most particularly, to lease as much shipping as one can lay hands on. I have plans for you too, son.

—Sir, this is not the time for me to engage in business.

Micah snorted contemptuously. —Oh, I'm perfectly aware of your distaste for vulgar trade, Elisha. So I've made other arrangements for you. He found the paper he was looking for and pushed it across the table. It skated across the polished wood and wafted to the carpet. —A commission in the Seventh New York Volunteer Regiment. It is currently entraining for this city. You'll join it as it arrives.

—Sir, I appreciate your efforts, but I hold a naval commission already.

—I have to give you that, boy. You thought ahead. But not far enough. This war will be fought on land. When it's over, an army record will be the key to a future in politics. The Seventh is a prestigious regiment. Several young men you know are in it.

—I don't want to go into politics.

—You'll think differently in a few years. His father's iron visage hardened. —Take it.

He eyed the document, hating it, hating the man who stood watching; then bent slowly and did as he was told. His father sighed. —Thank you. If a parent should say thanks, for the obviously reluctant obedience of a child.

—I'm sorry I've caused you trouble, Father.

—Well, let us declare the breach healed. Shall we? I apologize too, for putting you on the tapis. Stay with me till your regiment arrives. We'll enjoy ourselves tonight.

He murmured something, unable to meet his father's eyes. To his rage and shame the commission trembled in his hands. He made one last effort. —To return to the matter of Ara's accounting—

—I have important things to discuss now, Elisha. You must excuse me. Reeves! Show the indigo factor in.

Standing outside, coughing, he had to admit he was a coward. He'd never been able to face his father outright. Micah was too intimidating. And the threat of being cut off was sobering to a man who'd never earned a dollar on his own.

He stopped suddenly in the carpeted hall. But he *had.* He *was.* Forty dollars a month, Glass had said. The salary of a master's mate, U.S. Volunteer Navy.

He unrolled the commission. It was briefer than his naval document, less flowery, more hastily produced.

An hour later, he sold it to a well-dressed man standing in line outside a recruiting office. He smiled at the thought there were now two Elisha Eakers. He sealed the money up at the post office and addressed it in care of Mr. David Child. Then went down the street, heart lighter than it had been in some days, and caught a horsecar back to the ship.

Part IV

Hampton Roads, April 17–21, 1861.

24

———◆———

THEO took shallow breaths, nearly gagging. The shadowy air stank of years of old grease, smoke, shit, and vomit, all drained together to the bilges and left to fester and rot into the hull oak. Stripped to the waist, as black-smeared and greasy in the lantern dim as the other images of Satan around him, he put his weight against the downhaul. A rattle of chain links, a clack of gear pawls, and a looming blackness eclipsed the oblong sky.

—Two more feet this time, called a stocky, tousle-haired man, handsome as a Booth, though here in the depths of the engine room he was stripped like the rest to blue trowsers shiny with beef tallow and bilge scum. Theo set his boots against a crossbeam and took a fresh grip, staring upward at the immense iron casting that hovered above them, held up only by the thin web of manila and blocks and bull's-eyes. If they slipped, if any one of those web strands broke, it would come crashing down on them; and there was nowhere to run, not down here.

He had been working without a bath, a hot meal, or a change of clothes since he came through the shipyard gate.

The moment he stepped aboard *Merrimack* a stocky bullheaded fellow in dirty pants and an even dirtier singlet had seized him around the shoulders. He wasn't that much older than Theo. Beneath the grime his curly hair was glossy dark. His clean-shaven chin thrust out like that of one who has never doubted his mission in the world. Yet despite his youth and the condition of his clothes Theo recognized Benjamin Franklin Isherwood, the first chief engineer to be promoted from within the naval service itself.

Speaking rapidly over a handshake that left Theo's palm blacked, Isherwood told him that not only were the steam frigate's masts unshipped and all her rigging sent ashore for repairs, her machinery had been torn out down to the foundation braces. Most had gone straight to the scrap yard. Salvageable components lay scattered through the yard's foundries, machine shops, and smitheries. Ordered by Secretary Welles to get her under way for Philadelphia, the yard commander, Commodore Charles McCauley, had telegraphed back it would take a month to put the ship back in steaming order. Isherwood had reached Gosport three days ago, made a quick inspection, and thought they could get it reassembled and ready to move at least a few miles under power in less than a week.

Looking over onto the silent quay, the deserted yard, Theo had asked how.

—You're right, everyone seems to have gone home, don't they? Last payday there were five hundred men on the rolls. They've caught this secesh grippe. Most of the naval officers have resigned, but a couple of the yard engineers are still helping out. I went out in town with the foreman and got about fifty machinists and boilermakers to come in. We've got the engine room gang off the *Cumberland* down there, and the marines' tail on a line when we need 'em. We're working three eight-hour shifts. I want you to take over the second.

—I'm at your disposal, Theo said.

—I've left aside the question of whether she's worth it, of course.

Isherwood took five steps aft and stopped, looking down through the ripped-apart deck at the engine space. —Of the Wabashes, this was the worst-engined of the lot. A ton and a half of coal an hour.

The engines race in heavy seas. So much friction the propeller binds up. Isherwood had shaken his head slowly. —When we grope in the dark, we fail more often than we succeed. But those are our orders; and carry them out we will, Mr. Hubbard, carry them out we most definitely will.

—Lower away. An inch at a time, and be ready to check her, Isherwood shouted now.

With a grating screech the huge iron mass of the steam chest started down, dragging against a hatch edge. Theo put his weight on the downhaul but the immense upward force pried him relentlessly out of his boots. Someone muttered through clenched teeth, —Better get more hands on this line. The complaint of dragging iron grew into a scream.

One of the straining figures suddenly slipped. His boots kicked in the slippery bilge and found no footing. Theo staggered as he slammed into him. He managed not to knock down the next man, but the line jerked out of his hands. He grabbed but it was running now, slipping through his desperately clutching fingers, the rough hemp burning the skin off his palms.

Above them the screeching became a shriek, interspersed with great hollow booms. The rattle quickened as the mass of iron gathered momentum. —Jam it! someone shouted through the din. Tinkling and clanging, some small metal thing came falling down through black space. Shouts chased it from above. Then a sodden splash somewhere in the black nastiness at their feet.

Ducking, reaching out at the same time with his other arm to the downhaul, the stocky man plunged his hand again and again into the briny darkness, seeking amid strakes and stringers the key to hold back the thunder. As his eye sword-crossed Theo's, strong ivory teeth flashed in a confident grin.

——————

But since then he'd been working not eight but more like eighteen hours a day, snatching a few minutes' rest when he grew dizzy in one of the stripped and comfortless cabins aft. He and a yardie named Paddy Cummiskey had combed the yard for link gears, valve sleeves, journal bearings, saddle blocks, and eccentric rods, checking off each part on the constructor's drawing of *Merrimack*'s engines he had brought from Washington. The lighter components they snatched off scrap heaps or out of vises and hand-toted aboard. The heavy castings, like the huge, seventy-two-inch-diameter pistons, had to be inspected, hauled to the proper shop, and hastily rough-trued with files and hammers. Working parties lifted them again onto railcars, hand-trundled them across the yard, and carefully lowered each down to the reaching arms of the installation crews in the engine and fire rooms.

Isherwood didn't sleep at all. "The Chief," as the yard engineers called him, worked the clock round, obsessive in detail, relentless in oversight, fertile in resource when a part had to be jury-rigged. Theo saw him brazing fittings, tinning bearings, winding pump packing. When it came time to hoist a casting into position for bolting, Isherwood's powerful shoulders were always beneath the heaviest metal.

During their brief breaks for bread, cheese, and warm beer a boy carried into the yard in buckets, he'd subjected Theo to a relentless quizzing. Isherwood approved of his apprenticeship at mills and machine works. He cross-examined him on his understanding of engine construction and operation, then went on to probe his readings of Rankine and the other theoreticians of the heat engine.

Theo gazed enviously on the engineer in chief's treelike arms and muscled chest, revealed in all its hairy glory. Yet the quick alert blinking of intelligent brown eyes, the graceful flight of his hands in conversation meant the coal heaver's frame was inhabited by a mind of no common quality.

—What about cutoffs? Isherwood had asked.

—I read your report on the Michigan experiments.

—Doesn't mean you agree with it.

—I can find fault, if you want me to.

—Go right ahead. I'm after the truth, Hubbard, nothing more and nothing less. You can never offend me by seeking it too.

—Well. First, then; you were attempting to find out experimentally the most useful point to cut off steam flow into a piston, so that the expansive power remaining in the steam would all be extracted in the interest of motive power. Yet none of your cylinders were insulated; your steam pressure was very low; you didn't superheat the steam—

—I wasn't in a laboratory. I was trying to find out the most efficient way to run a fifteen-year-old paddle wheeler.

—But why look backward, instead of forward? She was outdated years ago.

Isherwood hunched forward. His heavy brows bunched in a scowl. —But how can we design new engines, when no one understands the old ones? Mariotte and Joule base their theories on assumptions no one ever saw in an engine room. Perfect conductors! Perfect insulators! Perfectly elastic gases! They live in a cloud-cuckooland. While the engine designers work by rule of thumb, ignorant of theory and proper operation alike. We must learn what *is,* and what we can make it do for us, rather than speculate on what can never be.

—We also need the inventor; do we not? The man who can bring new ideas into existence.

—Oh, certainly; all glory to him! But have we not the germ already of every machine we really need? We must measure, and observe, and reason painfully to the truth. Till then we are apes sketching in the dark, and the engines we contrive monstrous abortions.

—You would not class your own designs among them?

Isherwood had laughed, throwing back his tousle-curled bull head. —Hell, yeah, I would! They're too heavy. They're overbuilt. Inefficient. But they run! What's more, I can take a mason or a printer off the streets of Albany, give him three days' training, and he can *keep* them running. That's what the navy's going to need. Steamships, with engines that run.

—You mean in case of war.

—In *case?* It started six months ago, Hubbard. Have you heard about the privateers?

—Privateers?

—Davis has offered letters of marque and reprisal against the U.S. flag.

—He's arming privateers against us?

—Same strategy we used against the British in 1812. That means we'll have to blockade. Close the whole Atlantic and Gulf coasts, without a single harbor of refuge in case of storms. What's that suggest to you?

—That we'll need more ships. A lot more ships.

—I came to that same conclusion in February. We've contracted for four new gunboats since then. Letters have gone out for nineteen more. This war will be driven by steam, Hubbard. God help the Union if you and I can't deliver it.

Theo said cautiously, —Have you ever considered burning a liquid fuel? Such as petroleum?

Isherwood didn't dismiss it as Lenthall had. They talked about it on and off as they put the three-dimensional jigsaw puzzle of *Merrimack*'s engine room back together. The chief had his doubts, but grasped at once the most significant advantage of the scheme: the enormous saving in manpower in stokers and shovelers, as well as the ability to respond within seconds to changing demands for power.

Isherwood emerged from the sump with the pin in his hand, his shoulder still braced against the downhaul. Meanwhile the man who'd slipped had caught the line burning through Theo's fists and taken a round turn on a stanchion. When it braked to a halt Isherwood blew out noisily and let go. He ran lightly up the ladder, and soon a second hoist took the strain off. The steam chest lurched, inched the last few feet downward, and settled into place with a sullen clang as if disappointed in its goal of crushing someone. The hoists rattled slack and the fitters swarmed up over it, clapping bolts into place.

—That's the last major assembly, Isherwood said. —We can steam without the condenser for a few hours, just fill the water tanks and exhaust to atmosphere. Four or five hours at three knots, and we can anchor under the guns of Fort Monroe. What coal we have left in the bunkers should do very well. Hubbard, check the main steam connections, then prepare to light off. He surveyed his greasy forearms. —I'll clean up, then tell McCauley we're ready to get under way.

Theo made sure the fitters knew what they had to do, then climbed to the deck and went ashore.

In the cavernous machine shop, Cummiskey and two of *Cumberland*'s gang were finishing a makeshift reversing link. Their search had failed to yield the original, an arc-curved iron casting twelve feet long. All the molders at the foundry had disappeared the day Virginia seceded. So casting a new link was out of the question. At last he'd set them sawing and filing on stock brass. They'd reproduced the requisite curves six times, inner and outer, in half-inch-thick sheet, then drilled and bolted the leaves together into a rough lamination. He examined it as they stood around. He figured the link might hold through several reversals before deforming into uselessness. They could replace it later with steel, once the frigate was safe from capture.

—Take it aboard, he said. —Then help the fitters with the steam chest, and we'll light off.

They were laying the fires when Isherwood returned and told them to hold off, but to continue their preparations otherwise. Commodore McCauley wanted *Merrimack* and *Cumberland* to leave together, but not until the next morning.

Theo went forward and fell into a bunk. He did not move again until a fireman shook him awake at six the next day.

By nine o'clock they had fires lit, steam up, and had tested the engines at the pier, all except the reversing gear, which he didn't want to stress before they had to. The sky was clear today, the rain had passed, the river lay open and inviting before them. A party of Cumberlands detailed to help in the move cleared away the awnings and helped secure for sea, then singled up the lines to get under way. The little yard tug came around from the basin and made up to their outboard side, then clung there, chuffing away contentedly as they finished their final preparations.

At half past nine a note arrived from McCauley. The shipyard commander hadn't made up his mind yet as to when they could get under way, but said he'd let them know shortly.

They lay to the pier with steam up, smoke and soot jetting up in black solid-looking pillars whenever he let off steam. The mechanics and seamen stood about on deck watching the Norfolk waterfront. Several small boats moved about over there, then went off downriver out of sight. At noon, still without word from McCauley, the coal heavers, firemen, and engineers reported for cold mutton sandwiches and hot strong tea with honey in the unaccustomed luxury of the wardroom. At two o'clock Isherwood went ashore again to try to locate the delay, and also to locate Commander Alden, the line officer who was to take her out.

He looked grim when he came back aboard. —Extinguish the fires, he said, and kicked a piece of scrap iron into the scuppers.

—What? Theo frowned at him. —I don't understand. We aren't getting under way?

—The commodore refuses to release us.

—You mean, he wants her left here for the secessionists. He's in with the rest of the yard officers, the ones who resigned.

Isherwood threw back his massive head, ran black-nailed fingers through his curls. —I don't think so. He's a Pennsylvanian, and I don't doubt he's *loyal* enough. I really am not sure what is going on over there. I speak to the man, I reason, I even shout; he agrees with everything I say, but he *will not* let us cast off.

—What possible objection can he have?

The chief engineer looked across the river. —Well, that varies. Just now he's afraid these rebels will take her over on the way up the river; he's heard somewhere they're arming ships to close the Elizabeth; or that she'll go aground, and they'll capture her that way.

—But if we leave her here, we'll lose her most certainly.

Isherwood sighed. —Well, not for the moment, at least. *Cumberland*'s guns command the yard and the town. Unless the locals practice some trick, we can hold this position until reinforcements arrive. I hope. The nub of the matter is, McCauley has been fifty-two years in the service. Perhaps he was well enough once, but he's a confused and timid old man now, in over his head and frightened to death of doing the wrong thing. So he does nothing. Unfortunately Commander Alden doesn't have the ballocks—pardon my bluntness—to disobey him. He won't take us out unless McCauley gives his permission.

Theo lowered his voice. —If he won't, we have firemen and coal heavers. We've got a lead line. It's only eighteen or twenty miles! You and I can steer her to Fort Monroe, surely.

The chief engineer looked sorely tempted. He began to speak, but ceased and shook his head. His lips tightened. Finally he said, —I'd do it if it were just my career, Hubbard. By God, I'd do it in a heartbeat! But I can't, and neither can you. I've just been appointed to this post. The line officers would never let Lenthall keep me on if I defied one of them. Worse, their suspicions about us would be confirmed. This isn't the time to split the service between line and engineers. I'd rather lose ten steam frigates than do that.

Isherwood kicked another piece of scrap, sending it caroming off the bulwark, then stalked aft. Theo followed him. In his cabin Isherwood began throwing clothes into a worn carpetbag. —Where are you going? he said from the doorway.

—Back to Washington.

—I'm coming with you.

—Not this time. McCauley showed me the telegram. You're off *Owanee,* aren't you? She's on her way here with troops.

—I hope she makes it. Her engines aren't in much better shape than *Merrimack*'s.

—As for going with me. Isherwood reached out suddenly with both hands, pinioning his arms in a grip of steel. —I shall need young engineers. Trained, reliable men. In the bureau and in the field. Rest assured, Hubbard, I'll call on you. When I do, be warned. I'm not an easy master. You'll work harder than you ever have in your life.

Theo straightened and cleared his throat. He said he was the chief's to command.

Topside the stocky engineer looked out over the great yard; at the towering ship houses sheltering the grand old battleships; at mast houses and timber sheds, spar houses and provision houses; at *Germantown* and *Dolphin* and the others lying deserted alongside and in the basin, at the unsmoking chimneys and silent workshops and vacant walkways. —I feel like Lot's wife, he said.

—It can't be that bad.

—It's worse, Hubbard. That which we dreaded above all has come, and yet we are still dead asleep. I'll try to sound the tocsin in the capital. Try to save as much as you can here.

Theo watched him walk away. Then turned to Cummiskey, and in a voice that sounded strained even to his own ears, told the mechanic to draw the fires and dismiss the men.

25

A Delicate Cargo ♦ Under Way for the Lower Bay ♦ A Second Interview
with Captain Paulding

KER had expected new orders, as quickly as events were moving now. But he'd never expected these. Feet propped on what had formerly been Trezevant's writing desk, he conned the letter again in the privacy of the captain's cabin. They were to head south again. Not as far as before, but to a locale of the greatest importance.

It was signed by Gideon Welles. A hasty endorsement at the bottom brought the unwelcome news he'd have not one but two senior officers embarked, and would operate under the command of none other than Commodore Hiram Paulding.

He folded the paper and thought for a few minutes, holding it over his eyes. Then he rang.

Jerrett, looking apprehensive, one of Ker's dress boots in his polish-stained hands. —They're almost done, sir, just let me buff them down.

—Very good, I shall need them shortly, if you please. Have you seen Auguste, Jerry?

—Sir, he was in the mizzen rigging not long ago.

—Coax him down with a handful of pinders and lock him in the gun room. But first carry my respects to Mr. Duycker, and ask him to step down.

317

The elderly master listened stone-faced to his orders. Make all preparations for leaving harbor. Ensure the water tanks were topped off. Range both bower cables and pay special attention to the cathead stoppers and shank painters of both bower anchors. Sway aboard and secure the special cargo, which would be arriving shortly aboard *Anacostia.*

—Fortunately we still have empty cabins, he said. —I'll vacate this one in favor of Commodore Paulding. He and Captain Wilkes are to be in charge of the expedition.

—Wilkes *and* Paulding? Duycker whistled. —Don't they know every four-striper they add, that's half the chance of getting anything done?

—That's enough, Nick. Expect them momentarily; we're to be under way before noon.

—The men'll think getting under way on a Friday is a Jonah, sir.

—This is a man-o'-war, Nick, not a haven for superstitious old women. Turn them to, and give her a clean sweep-down and brushing-up fore and aft. Tell Girnsolver to flemish all the lines and set a crew to scrubbing down the port stripe. I want everything ataunto when Paulding steps aboard. Oh; and what did your investigation of the leak turn up?

Since they had touched ground at Aquia, a slow leak around the shaft had begun to flow considerably faster. Duycker said he saw no way to repair it out of dry dock, but the steam pumps were keeping ahead so far.

The exec touched his cap and withdrew. Ker opened the orders again, but couldn't concentrate. His polished boots stood just inside the door. He pulled them on, lit a segarrillo at the betty lamp, then walked back and forth, puffing anxiously.

Virginia had declared her independence. What he'd feared for so many weeks, had tried to persuade himself would never happen, had come to pass.

The post would be going soon. He had to get a letter to Catherine. She and Rob would have to leave Norfolk. But whence? Washington? It would be under siege before long. Baltimore? All indications were

Maryland would go out within the week. Farther north? Catherine had family in Philadelphia. Not Wythes but her mother's people, the Fraziers. With this news, the Farraguts would have to leave Norfolk too. Perhaps she could travel with them.

A jolt ran through the hull, and through water and oak came the rapid heartbeat of a small steam engine close alongside. He sat quickly, and the steel pen-scratch whispered as from above came shouted commands and the rumble of running feet.

When Ker went on deck again, formal in full dress and gold-laced cocked hat, he found the sky gray as wet ashes and the crew falling in to load stores. The steam tender lay alongside, booms rigged out for transfer. Girnsolver stood on the stern, directing the lashing down of the metal tanks as each came slowly down to touch the deck. Eaker was on the pier, supervising the loading of the extra powder.

Billy Ripley ran by and Ker collared him on the fly and gave him his letter to Catherine. As the boy ran down the brow Ker paused by the bulwark, checking his watch and then looking toward headquarters, wondering if he had time for a call on Captain Buchanan. But what would they say to each other? Their ways were parting, perhaps forever. Instead he penned a quick note of farewell and gave it to Mr. Glass to deliver on his way to the yard paymaster's.

A tank lifted from the tender's deck. Rotating in the sky, it swung across and descended into the upreached guiding hands of the after-deck party. He eyed its fellows, manhandled into position and now being rose-lashed down along the quarter bulwarks. The tanks were filled with spirits of turpentine. They were taking aboard twelve of them and twenty barrels of gunpowder, twelve barrels of cotton waste, and a hundred and eighty flares.

His orders did not specify what or where, but plainly their mission was to destroy something.

Paulding came aboard at five bells, 10:30 A.M, from a private carriage on the quay. Ker drew his sword and held it at the salute as the pipes wailed their lugubrious greeting. When they cut off he sheathed his blade and stepped forward, extending his hand. The commodore affected not to see it, hands locked under his coat, squinting aloft to where his swallow-tailed pendant snapped in the breeze. Paulding was in undress uniform, rumpled and not entirely clean. He looked dyspeptic, as if he had just tasted something rotten. —Are you ready to get under way, Lieutenant?

—I am, sir, with the exception of my engines.

—What's wrong now? Brusque and suspicious; the little Yankee was nothing if not predictable.

—As you recall, sir, I reported them in poor condition when I arrived. You denied permission to repair them, and sent my chief engineer to Gosport. Now my assistant engineer says he doubts they'll turn over.

—We will proceed, sir, under sail if necessary. An order is to be obeyed, not winked at.

He said that was very well, and asked Midshipman Eddowes to show the commodore to his stern cabin. But the commodore wasn't ready to go below yet. He kept looking toward the capital. Ker asked him, —Will the city be safe, sir, without our guns to cover the river?

—That's not your concern, Lieutenant. But I will tell you five hundred Pennsylvania troops arrived yesterday. They're quartered in the Capitol. Imagine it, Kansas volunteers in the East Room of the White House. We expect five hundred New Yorkers today. The Baltimoreans stoned them as they passed through the city, several men were hurt. He threw a quick cold glance, as if the stoning were Ker's personal offense.

—But do they have artillery? A movable battery such as we are could take the bridges under fire, or prevent movement down to them—

—That will be enough elementary strategy, Lieutenant. I'm expecting Captain Wilkes shortly. Leave me.

Ker felt his face heat. He turned on his heel and stalked aft. He had met Northerners before who acted like Paulding, as if senior rank gave them license to treat juniors with contempt. Unfortunately it was futile to expect satisfaction. Dueling had been outlawed in the navy for decades.

He sent a boy below with his sword, tugged his collar open a bit, and set his service cap at a slightly more comfortable angle. Glass came back from headquarters with more unwelcome news. Not only were no river pilots available, so many crewmen had vanished neither of the yard's tugs could get under way. While he digested this a sweating MacNail climbed out of the engine room companionway. He was in his singlet, smeared with coal dust and grease, and his great hands were black. He saluted, or rather waved, in the general direction of his shaggy hair, and said, —Cap'n, about them boilers.

—I hope your report's better than last night's.

—Sorry, sir. 'Tain't. We're not holdin' off the steam. I can get up to seven, maybe nine pounds, and then she drops off, like something in her opens up. T'other boiler's even wuss.

—What speed can we make?

—Sir, I misdoubt if we can give ye more than one bell. And we've still got that leak along the shaft piercing. That will take steam too, to run the bilge pump.

He glanced aloft again, then shoreward, at the plumes of smoke from District breakfast-fires. They trailed southward, making the wind northerly, perhaps north by northeast. It wasn't strong, but it was a fair wind for the Chesapeake. He told MacNail to do the best he could, he would assist the screw with the sails and the tide. Also, to wear a shirt and cap of some sort the next time he came on deck; with a flag officer breaking his pendant aboard, they had to mind the proprieties now.

—Another four-striper in the offing, sor.

—Thank you, Bo's'n. That will be Captain Wilkes. Honors, if you please.

For a second time the pipes cleaved the morning air. Duycker stood at attention behind the double line of side boys. A tall forbidding figure climbed the brow, paused at the top, sending a gaze over the waiting men, the ranked guns.

Though they'd never met, he knew Charles Wilkes by his service reputation, the anecdotes and tales that made a man's character in the near-incestuous circle of the peacetime navy. Wilkes was a New Yorker, a self-trained mathematician and surveyor. Probably the most notable event of his forty years of service had been his expedition to Antarctica, making him the only U.S. naval officer who could claim discovery of a new continent. Since then quarrels with other senior officers had kept him on the beach. Wilkes resembled the portraits of Wellington he'd seen, the same Roman nose and lofty carriage, the magisterial gaze, the full, confidently set lips.

The imperious eye fell on him and he stepped forward, touching his cap. —Captain Wilkes? I am Ker Claiborne, commanding *Owanee.*

—Pleased to make your acquaintance, Lieutenant. I see Commodore Paulding is already aboard.

—Yes sir, he just broke his flag. Would you care to join him below?

—I should like to look about your sloop first, if that is all right with you.

—Most honored, sir. I'd accompany you, but I still have preparations to make before we cast off. Mr. Thurston! Show Captain Wilkes wherever he wants to go.

Both senior officers disposed of for the moment, he made sure Girnsolver was getting the deck stores griped down and that the t'-gallants, tops, spanker, and foresails were ready to be loosed. *Owanee* was moored bow upriver on an ebb tide. A tug would have made short work of swapping her end for end, but without one the East Branch was a tight corner indeed, with mudflats waiting on the south side. It would be a nice test of his ability to handle her under sail.

The exec, hand to his cap: —Ready to get under way, sir.

He returned the salute gravely. —Very well, Nick. Stand to forward and aft and brace the head yards round. I will cast her off on the port tack with spanker, jib, and fore-t'gallant; boxhaul about, and make the rest of the t'gallants and tops when we are headed fair. Have a stream anchor made off in the event we cock up.

—Leave the stern line fast to the quay?

—I think with this wind she'll spin fast enough not to need it. Very well, all hands to stations, and brace around the fore.

The men were already lingering at their posts; less than a minute after the piping ended Duycker was back reporting ready to get under way. Ker started to say, "Very well," then remembered he was no longer the senior officer aboard. He sent Mr. Eaker below to Paulding. He returned with the commodore's permission, but no evidence of his person.

—Very well, then. Mr. Duycker: make spanker, jib, and fore-t'gallant; on second thought, make the foretop as well.

The men went up the ratlings without a word; Girnsolver passed the commands by the silent pantomime of the old sailor. As the lines came in the bow fell off before the wind, and the sloop began to walk ahead in what he found gratifying silence, free alike of shouting and confusion and the intrusive noise of steam machinery. Ker smiled faintly, strolling back and forth across the quarterdeck as the steering ropes creaked. She stepped away from the quay as the t'gallants and tops filled. He picked out a waterfront house on Poplar Point to gauge his distance by. The bottom shallowed in a hundred yards, yards *Owanee*'s squared-off, shoal-sucking keel was ticking off quickly in her downwind drift.

Eaker was watching from the forecastle, his face a study in puzzled absorption. Ker gave the New Yorker a broad wink, and was amused at his look of surprise. At last he smiled wanly back.

Speaking in a low voice to the boatswain, Ker braced round the t'gallant and sheeted in the spanker. The sloop picked up speed, pushing her cutwater through the frowsy river at the pace of a trotting horse. He watched the t'gallant carefully; the lift of its leading edge was the first clue you were teasing the wind. Checked his distance from the quay, then rapped out: —Helm astarboard, Mr. Duycker! Fore-topsail aback by the port braces. Fore-t'gallant aback; make all t'gallants and tops.

Owanee responded with a quick lightness that joyed his heart, rounding up into the wind, then braking as the steadier breeze aloft took the upper sails aback. He leaned over the side, watching patches of foam and trash slide past and gradually slow. A moment before their motion ceased entirely he told the helmsmen in a quiet voice, —Hard down.

—Hard down, sir. Helm hard aleeward.

—Very well.

Dead in irons, the sloop hesitated for long seconds, the tide carrying her with noiseless steadiness westward still, so that the blocks of the quay wall were ticked off one by one by the yawing sprit. Then she began to gather way astern. The white house grew larger. Duycker looked toward it, then at Ker. He kept his expression nonchalant, fingers spliced together only a little more tightly than usual behind him; but no one could see that. The bow was swinging to port rapidly now, stern coming rapidly up into the wind.

—Helm amidships! Main and mizzen by the wind. T'gallant and tops by the wind. Make all courses by the wind, heave around briskly. Steady as she goes!

—Steady west-southwest, sir.

—Very well, keep her so.

Sagging only a few more yards to leeward, her now forward-set sails adding their impetus to the tide, the sloop straightened and began running for the open Potomac. Ker glanced at the line of sticks off the point that marked shoals for oyster boats, made sure she would clear, then looked aloft again. —Mr. Duycker, all remaining sails. Center of the river and mind the lead. Set the underway watch.

He took off the heavy cocked hat, letting the wind cool the sweat that had crept into his hair. Then he went below to see to his guests.

In what had been Trezevant's cabin, then so briefly his own, Paulding and Wilkes were sitting around an anker from his Africa stores. They did not rise; after a moment the New Englander reluctantly gestured to a chair against the sideboard. He brought it to the table. Shippy brought out another glass. Ker helped himself to the decanter; the senior officers already had.

—Sir, we are under way and headed fair downriver.

Paulding did not answer, unless an annoyed jerk of eyebrows was a response. Wilkes said, holding up his glass, —You keep a good cellar, Lieutenant. Malaga, if I am not mistaken.

—Exactly so, sir. You've sailed those waters?

—In the *Fairfield*, under Foxhall Parker. You remember Parker, do you not, Hiram?

The commodore grunted. Wilkes eyed him for a moment, then said, —Do you recall old Pons, who used to be pilot at Port Mahon?

Paulding did not answer that either. Ker, uncertain whether Wilkes had intended the question for him or Paulding, said at last, —I'm afraid that was before my time, sir, though I've heard the name.

—And Berry, who kept the hotel? Many joyous hours there. Unfortunate he resorted to that trick, sewing the heads of the woodcocks to the bodies of the pigeons.

—If I may proceed? said Paulding grimly.

—I'm sorry, Hiram. You have the floor.

Paulding said, —The department learned yesterday that even before Virginia passed the ordinance of secession, Governor Letcher began moving against federal installations on her property. Specifically, against the armory and rifle manufactory at Harpers Ferry, and against the Norfolk navy yard. He spared Ker a poisonous glance. — The president is taking vigorous action in response. Today he'll proclaim a blockade of all Southern ports.

—Blockade, or closure?

—I said blockade, Captain Wilkes. The distinction between closing and blockading is moot now. At any rate, the paralysis at the seat of government seems to be yielding to action. Secretary Welles has ordered me to proceed at once to Norfolk. Five ships of the line lie there, two sailing frigates, two sloops. And the steam frigate *Merrimack*, the most modern and powerful. Of which I would like you, Captain Wilkes, to take command.

Wilkes nodded. —Very well, sir; a position rather junior for my rank, but I am glad to step in if needed.

—As for myself, Mr. Welles has directed me to take over the Norfolk yard at Gosport. The current superintendent there is either a traitor or suffers from a defect of will. I am to hold Norfolk, repelling force by force. Or if we must withdraw, to sortie all movable vessels and destroy the yard, leaving nothing behind which may be of use to the insurgents.

Wilkes lifted his fingers in astonishment. —*Destroy* it, sir? That's the only dry dock south of Boston. If we're going to blockade, we must have Gosport, and have it with its facilities undamaged.

Paulding smiled unwillingly. —I intend to hold it if at all possible, Captain. But your point is well taken. The yard contains everything necessary to construct and maintain a modern fleet. Therefore, if we cannot hold it, better to destroy it than to leave it to the so-called Confederacy.

—We're not sent on this alone, surely? said the explorer, pouring himself another glass of Madeira.

—*Cumberland*'s already there, fully manned. *Germantown, Plymouth,* and *Dolphin* are provisioned but lack crews. And then of course there's *Merrimack.* We've assembled men in Brooklyn, but they can't arrive until the twenty-first. The receiving ship at Baltimore is dispatching recruits by commercial steamer. We have chartered a steamer in Philadelphia, to take more marines to Norfolk, but it seems to have broken down.

—Is there a crew for *Merrimack*? Wilkes asked.

—Those are the men en route from Brooklyn. Though they may not be trained.

—I can't believe we have so few men in reserve. Did we learn nothing from the war with Mexico?

Paulding said dryly, —Congress never sees the point of a navy in peacetime. But they'll feel perfectly free to reproach us for being unready. At any rate, we must make all speed down the bay. Letcher's trying to take Harpers Ferry by a coup de main. We can expect the same in Hampton Roads, and we must be prepared when he makes his move. He helped himself to more wine, then stared challengingly across the table. —Lieutenant Claiborne.

—Sir?

—When last we spoke you pointed out your state had not seceded. Well, now she has. Are you still as devoted to our flag as you were two days ago? Or will you be leaving us in Norfolk?

—I've made my decision, sir. I've written to my wife to remove our household to Philadelphia.

Wilkes smiled loftily and lifted his glass, as if to toast him. —I see, said Paulding, but he still looked unconvinced. —Very well, then, our duty is clear. Proceed as expeditiously as possible to Fort Monroe, embark the troops waiting for us there, then proceed to Norfolk and prepare our defense. I have no more to say at present.

At that brusque dismissal, Ker swallowed what remained in his glass and rose. He bowed to his seniors, tapped at the pantry door for Shippy, and took a thoughtful leave.

26

A Meeting at the Hotel de Dion ♦ Incendiary Address Interrupted by the Metropolitans ♦ Consignment to the Tombs ♦ Micah Demands the Return of the Fugitives ♦ The Fourth Position

ARAMINTA hesitated in front of the Hotel de Dion, drawing her wool cape a little tighter against the wind that whistled down Church Street. Surely this could not be it.

The society's meetings were seldom in the best parts of town. This one had been originally scheduled at a church, but the vestry had voided the invitation as soon as it saw the speakers' list. At the last moment it had been moved to the West Side. But no respectable hotel would host the New York Anti-Slavery Society, many of whose members were not permitted into a public hostelry, unless by the servants' entrance.

Maire stood beside her. —This can't be it, miss, the maid said.

—I'm afraid it is. She was peering into the window again when a dandified young fellow in a striped shirt, rings glittering, stepped up, lifted his top hat, and with great aplomb asked her if she would like to accompany him to bed.

—I beg your pardon, sir.

—Oh! I beg yours, miss. A thousand pardons, I mistook you for someone else.

—You didn't mistake her for nothing, you creeping worm. Maire's hand shot out, and the macque's eyes bulged as she yanked his necktie tight. She shook him till his hat fell off, and sent him staggering into the street, where he was nearly run over by a hansom. —Get to hell an' out o' here or I'll call my brothers on ye, she shouted.

Araminta smiled. —Thank you, my dear. I think.

—Ye let me deal with these sons of Satan. A lady like you! Don't ye even speak to 'em.

Ara looked at the door again, then went quickly in, before her misgivings overcame her.

The lobby was as decrepit and littered as she'd guessed from the building's seedy and peeling frontage. A drummer gaped at them from a worn armchair, cigar poised in midair. The room stank of old tobacco. This did not seem a hopeful inauguration to her new life. Her carpetbag sank to the floor. So little one could carry. A carpetbag, and the dun velvet day dress she had on her back; and the spoon bonnet with rose trim; and the dagger-pointed letter opener she had secreted inside her undersleeve.

For this was her flight from Egypt, and she could not resist glancing back into the street for the hosts of Pharaoh. But no chariots came storming after her. Only the evening-coming bustle of a New York street, with the "Broadway statue" who'd accosted her standing across the street now, whistling at an unaccompanied lady climbing into a carriage.

She looked away from the drummer's leer and and gestured Maire to take up her bag. —The antislavery meeting? she asked the whiskey-redolent old picaroon at the desk.

—Straight through that door, miss. Sure you want to go in there?

—Why should I not? My friends are there.

—You're not that desperate for friends, are you? Sure and lots of fellows'd be friendly to the likes of you.

—Get to *hell* out and mind your tongue, she said sharply, and was rewarded by an amused smile from Maire.

———

The meeting room was crowded with white, African, and mulatto men and women. A baby wailed while its mother unbuttoned her bodice. Manhattan was no hotbed of abolition, and none of the meetings she'd attended before had mustered a tenth this many people. Crowded together, their smell nearly turned her stomach. She pasted on a smile and plunged in. She didn't recognize anyone. Then a petite lady waved from the far wall, dark-eyed, jet hair streaking with gray, and Ara wedged her way between two well-dressed black men toward her.

Lydia Maria Child pressed her hand, then kissed her cheek with a hearty smack and stood back to shake her. —My dear, so glad you found us. I feared you would not, given that we had to change venue so quickly.

—Thank you for taking me in, Mrs. Child. I couldn't stay with my uncle another day.

A smile transfigured the plain features of the celebrated author of *Philothea* and *Appeal in Favor of That Class of Americans Called Africans.* —I am committed to the freedom of Woman no less than to that of the slave. *Every* shackle on *every* human soul binds me as well. And you are one of my adopted daughters, dearest Araminta! How I regret that in my youth I did not take my freedom with both hands, as you are doing!

—What do you mean? You're the freest of us all.

—Would that it were so! Child laughed, and extracted a folded slip from her reticule. —Go thou, and do otherwise than I have done. And take this, from Eli to you through the mails this morning.

She stared at the bank draft, then snatched at the note folded around it. She laughed out loud. —My uncle bought him an army commission. He sold it. Now I really am free!

Child said dryly, —Yes; for a thing without price, it is remarkable how necessary cash is to truly enjoy liberty.

A gavel rapped and the room quieted. Ara smoothed the draft out, noting which bank it was on as Mr. Reid rose and called the meeting to order.

—Tonight we must welcome our brethren from outside this city, who have come together to take counsel, he began. —Events in Charleston have brought the hour of decision upon us. Tonight we are graced with the presence of Mrs. Lydia Child; Mrs. Lucretia Mott; Miss Mary Ann Shadd Cary; Miss Anna Dickinson; Mr. Frederick Douglass; and Mr. William Lloyd Garrison, our inspiration for lo these many years. I welcome you all and *pace* the ladies, will make bold to invite Mr. Garrison to first take the floor.

The publisher of the *Liberator,* lean and tall and bald and spectacled, spoke for some time, without notes, on the irony of Southern secession. For many years, Garrison said, he himself had advocated "coming out" from a corrupt government by refusing to obey its laws or support its institutions. For years he had soldiered under the motto "No Union with Slaveholders." Six years before he had publicly burned a copy of the Constitution, and later convened a secessionist convention in Worcester. He had always maintained that separation was not only legal, but the only moral choice.

But now, he said, in a strange twist of fate the very divorce he had advocated had been initiated by the slaveholders themselves. What, then, should be the society's position? Some voices called for war against the South. Yet war was as great an evil as slavery; and bloodshed to preserve a Union with slaveholders would be an outrage as great as slavery itself. The new United States of the North would be geographically smaller but morally greater. Purged of the bloody sin of racialist slavery, it would lead the world into a new dawn of freedom.

Garrison drew applause, but not as wholehearted as Araminta had expected. The Negroes clapped dutifully, but she caught whispers. Douglass, who sat just behind the publisher on the platform, was even shaking his head.

Mrs. Child, who spoke next, was just as fiery. Araminta hardly breathed as the old lady said, —One way or another, Sumter marks the end of the slave power. Say they succeed in disunion. What then? Slaves can escape north without being remanded by federal judges. Slaveholders will face insurrections without the aid of federal troops. And the North will give the world the example of a true republic.

The authoress stepped down to rather heartier applause. Reid introduced Mrs. Mott next. Araminta folded and refolded the bank draft, wishing she were closer to the door. But to leave she'd have to step over several men sitting on the floor.

Suddenly it dawned on her why this was no ordinary meeting. The people who were being introduced weren't from New York. They were from the hotbeds of abolitionism, Boston and Philadelphia. They were discussing a national strategy. Some spoke against war. Others, as much as they regretted the prospect, seemed to welcome it. And sitting behind them, brow growing steadily more thunderous, glowered Douglass, a black Jupiter contemplating a lightning-bolt.

But she was only half listening. She'd planned to go back to Massachusetts with Mrs. Child. Beyond that she had not thought, so eager had she been to shake the dust of 372 Fifth from her sandals. But with two hundred dollars, she could go anywhere. Even Europe. Even . . . Paris.

At the thought of the City of Light she had to put her hand to her throat. Really, what would she do buried alive in Wayland, Massachusetts, with the Childs and the Grimké sisters? Perhaps she could find a situation in France. Be a governess, like Jane Eyre. Jane too had been orphaned. Had had to struggle for her bread. She'd read that novel so many times when she was thirteen that the pages had turned transparent.

Whatever happened, she would never, never depend on a man again.

A stir in the audience; a clearing of throats, a shuffling of gaiters. Douglass had risen from his seat. The baby began to cry, and its mother cradled and crooned to it.

Douglass spoke slowly, with only an occasional gesture of his large-knuckled hands. His immense head, crowned with a center-parted storm cloud of hair, turned from one side of the room to the other. But he too seemed unsure, as if Sumter and war had left him as bewildered as the rest. Then he halted.

Then, suddenly, the thunder burst forth. —Who has brought us this war? he demanded. —Is it Lincoln, who has assured the slaveholder over and over again he will not touch their human property?

—No, someone yelled from the floor. Mr. Reid frowned, made a shushing gesture.

Douglass did not even look at him. —Is it the black man, the black woman who has brought this war on us? Have we offered to slay our masters in their beds, as they have so often alleged?

—No, no! It wasn't us!

Douglass suddenly straightened, seeming to stand twice as tall as he had before. His hair stood straight out from his head, his great chest swelled as he shouted, —No one has brought us this war but *God!* If Jehovah the avenger of the weak has brought us war, should we not welcome it as His almighty decree? If those who resist His will snatch up the sword of war, must we abandon our brothers and sisters to their bloody mercy while we mewl and prate, "Peace, peace"? I say we must march—we must march—we must *fight!*

Garrison and the others on the platform sat frozen as the Africans, the freedmen and slaves in the assembly, surged to their feet shaking their fists and screaming "Amen" and "Speak it, brother," as he called for making the war for the Union a war for liberation.

Suddenly the door resounded with blows. Douglass stopped in midword, midgesture. All heads turned, as if simultaneously magnetized. She saw the handle turn.

Then it slammed open, and a stream of husky roughs with oaken nightsticks kicked their way in. One of the freedmen shoved back and was smashed down with a club in the face. A roundhouse punch knocked a woman's glasses flying. Behind the muscle came a mustachioed man in a sack suit, shooting his cuffs calmly as he gazed around at the pandemonium.

Garrison shouted, —Who are you, sir? By what right do you interrupt a public meeting?

The intruder held up an eight-pointed copper badge. —Inspector Callahan. Metropolitan Police. This meeting is closed by order of the mayor. Disperse immediately or be taken in.

—By Fernando Wood? Does the Constitution not apply to Tammany Hall?

—It don't apply to disorderly houses, which is what you got here.

Douglass shouted, —We will not disperse. We will not close this meeting! We will be heard!

—Suits me. See how you feel after a night with the bummers. — Chain 'em up, boys, said Callahan, and the roughs began snapping irons on the men. The women were simply shoved out the door.

—Miss Van Velsor! Holy Mother, let her go, ye blacklegs!

Her head snapped back as two men grabbed her. She fought but got a knee in the stomach that doubled her over. She tried to scream but couldn't get her breath. They carried her to the door and shoved her down the stairs. She slammed into the banister, nearly fell over it. Too late, she remembered her carpetbag. But there was no going back; the coppers were throwing the others down behind her in a tumult of screaming, blows, police whistles, and the thuds of boots into bodies.

In the street the Black Maria was surrounded by hooting, tattered denizens. A shout went up as they carried Douglass out. Ara saw one bystander lunge forward and plant his fist in the shackled orator's bloody face. —Coward, she cried, but her voice was lost in the din. Then came Garrison, spindly wrists bound with iron. He howled, — Liberty for all! Man above all institutions! The supremacy of God over the whole earth! Then four detectives kicked him up into the closed carriage.

The mob howled and danced in a mad shambling jig. A bottle flew overhead and burst on the cobblestones. She realized more people were running toward them. A riot was starting. A flaming, grinning Irish face thrust itself close to hers, and rough hands rammed beneath her crinoline. She kneed him away, but he kept tearing at her skirt.

She gathered her strength and punched the man so hard in the face she felt her thumb break. It didn't hurt. He shook his head, and she hit him again, howling and screaming at him soundlessly in the maelstrom of the mob.

The bummers' cell was a single enormous space that stank beyond all the bad things she'd ever smelled in her life stewed together and left in the dark to rot. No lamps were permitted at the Halls of Justice. The only light came from narrow slots high up on the stone walls. That watered milk of daylight fell across two hundred drunks, harlots, vagrants, pickpockets, and assorted cutthroats and shoulder hitters, across stone pavements stained black, across walls blotted an ugly brown to the height of a man. The stone sucked up all warmth and light, and focused all sound back into the ears of its huddled and benumbed captives. There were no privies or chamber pots. Drunks urinated against the walls or squatted in the corners. Abandoned children wandered through the throng, weeping in terror. The society members found a free square of vomit-stained pavement and huddled together, the gentlemen spreading their coats for the ladies to sit on.

She shivered, cradling her right hand. It was swollen now, and throbbed ferociously. Punching people was not as easy as it looked. And this place . . . how often Barlow had driven her past the frowning granite portals at Centre Street, with what blind equanimity she had admired the lofty Egyptian pillars of the Tombs. She'd had no idea what horrors lay in its belly, in the lowest sewer of the great city.

But worst of all was that her money was gone. Disappeared in the scuffle, gone, not only the two hundred Eli had sent but the fifty-two of her own she'd saved so laboriously from the household accounts, a penny or a nickel at a time.

A tear tickled its way down her cheek. She smeared it off roughly, turning her head from the others.

Maire yelled over the din, —How are ye bearin' up, miss?

—I'm cold.

—It'll get colder tonight. We'll just have to stand it.

—Tonight? She looked around vaguely. —Surely we're not staying here all night.

—This is where they hold ye, waitin' of the judge. We'll be here till six tomorrow.

—They're taking us to trial? she murmured. Somehow it seemed that *she* should not be kept here. *She* was not a criminal like these others. She kept feeling for the money, and feeling sick to her stomach all over again each time her fingers missed it. The noise was deafening, overwhelming, so loud it drowned any rational voice in her head.

—Not a trial. Just police court, said Garrison, overhearing. —I believe they'll let us go, once I set forth our case. Unfortunately they will listen to no entreaties until then. Try to rest, miss. Mr. Douglass and I will keep the lookout. With his stout arm, I believe we will be safe.

—You can stand a night of it, miss, Douglass said. He did not look unkind, only very determined. —Let us remember, in our discomfort, those who are entombed with no hope of escape.

She sat down at last, clapping her hands over her ears. The din was tremendous, it seemed like it could not continue, but it never ended or even slackened. Howls and wails, profanity and obscenity she could barely recognize as human speech. A child was screaming off in the deepening darkness. Mrs. Child got up and plunged after it, shrugging off Mr. Reid's cautioning arm. She thought of following, then realized, shamed, that she was too frightened. Beneath her cape she slid a hand into her sleeve. She undid the ties of her engageant. Then, gripping the handle of the letter opener, stared blankly into the din.

Maire tugged at her sleeve sometime later. —Miss? They're calling for you.

She flinched. Then struggled up, realizing she'd dozed off. Incredibly, the pandemonium was even greater, the crowd press closer, and now the great room was dark, the slits far above black with starless night. It was easy to believe in Hades, in the Tombs. She murmured weakly, —I beg your pardon?

The stentorian shout echoed again beneath the lofty ceiling. — Van Velsor; Miss Araminta Van Velsor. Come out.

Her uncle waited at the entrance with two uniformed officers of the law. A bull's-eye lantern swung in fitful flashes. Behind them opened a vast and gloomy corridor. Micah looked her up and down. He nodded briefly, then turned to the policemen. —I will take her on my recognizance.

She caught her breath, first in relief, then in horrified self-disgust. How easily she surrendered. The policemen were staring at her curiously.

—What is it, my dear?

She took a step back, into the darkness, but could not speak.

—Why, what is it, daughter? He reached out to take her arm, and she jerked back as if to avoid defilement.

—I won't go with you.

—Oh, you'll do as we says, my girl, said one of the coppers. —If we says stay, you stay, and if we says go with yer daddy, you'll go with him. Make nae mistake about that.

Micah took out a billfold and passed a note to the turnkey, who had stood watching stolidly. —For your services.

—Thank ye, sir. Much obliged. Go with the gentleman now, girl, and be thankful you've got family that cares for ye.

Instead she backed away, back into the stinking darkness. Her heart seemed to be the center of a storm, as if so many voices were shouting in an echoing room no single one could be heard. Hardly believing what she was saying, she screamed, —I won't go with you. Maire! Mr. Douglass! Mrs. Child! Maire!

Micah shook his head, looking sad. He said to the men, —I will reason with her. She is a very willful child. If you don't mind.

The cops moved away, but kept a wary eye on them. As soon as they were out of earshot Micah snatched her hand, making her gasp with pain, and said in an angry voice directly into her ear, —Now listen closely. You are making a fool of yourself and of me. You are a disobedient and evil girl. You stole money. You stole clothes. You will come home immediately.

—You can't force me to come.

—Oh, I am well within my rights. Shall I tell you what will happen if you do not come quietly? Stop *pouting*! If you do not come

with me, I will prefer charges against your friend Mrs. Child of running a house of assignation.

—You wouldn't dare. No one would believe that.

—There are very many who would. Do you think anyone would
buy her books after that sort of publicity?

—I will accept that risk, said Child from behind her. She was
holding a little boy about six years old by the hand. He looked up at
her wonderingly. —You do wrong to stand in this young woman's
way, Mr. Eaker.

—I need no advice from you.

Araminta said, —Thank you, ma'am, but it is not your place to
stand between me and my *loving uncle*. To Micah: —You may force
me to leave here, but I will not go home with you.

—That you will, girl. Home is where you belong. Talking to a
doctor. Or an alienist, if you persist in this madness.

—You stole my inheritance. Now you think you'll steal my freedom.

—You're making scenes again. He said to the policemen: —She
wants to be an actress.

—Pretty enough to be one, governor, said the younger cop. Then
begged his pardon, and as an afterthought, hers. Araminta saw his
eyes on her bosom and out of nowhere, from some detached part of
her mind, panted a little and threw her head back.

His eyes widened, and he took a step forward.

And somehow the tiny drama gave her back possession of herself.
The terror and anger drained away. She felt like a rider suddenly discovering she could master a terrified horse, turning its wild strength
to her own purpose.

She inclined her head slightly as if in submission. —Very well; as
you say. But Mary accompanied me. If I leave she must come too.

Micah grunted, —Fetch the O'Houlihan girl.

—And the charge of theft?

—Forget it, forget it. I'll deal with her myself.

Araminta took the fourth position: left foot obliquely forward,
placing her weight on the ball and turning slightly to the right, she

raised her right heel slightly. Extended her hands in the simple affirmative, arms curved like the willow twig. —You may take me back, Uncle, though it is against my wishes. Your will be done!

—Speak sense, girl. Come back to where you're safe.

—I will go with you. But I shall not stay, Father; in the presence of God I swear; these gentlemen will bear witness to what I say; I would rather die than stay.

She arched backward, feeling all their eyes on her, laid an arm across her face, and slowly and deliberately fainted into the young policeman's arms.

27

Repassing Aquia Creek ♦ A Therapeutic Trial ♦ "Annie Laurie"
in the Wardroom ♦ A Dangerous Accident ♦ Explanations to
the Commodore ♦ Advice Tendered by Moonlight

AQUIA Creek again, the same stretch of river *Owanee* had inspected two days before. Smoke no longer towered from inland. They had not seen a boat on the stream or a human being on the shore since they'd cast off from Washington.

Eli stood by the bulwark, watching the passing water as the irregular knocking of the engines and full t'gallants and tops bore him rapidly along on the yellow-leather belt of the Potomac.

He was contemplating his sudden inability to pray.

That morning he'd taken the new inhaling tube from its padded case and settled himself on his bunk. A valve was soldered at one end, like the bowl of a long silver pipe. It opened to admit his indrawn breath. But when he exhaled it snapped shut with a click, reducing the aperture to the diameter of a pin. He struggled, then set his chest muscles and bore down.

Something tore deep in his chest. It was quite painless. Like stitches ripping out of soft leather, or maybe out of cheese. A pulling sensation. It went away as he inhaled. At the second breath it happened again. A slow warmth under his breastbone. This isn't too difficult, he thought. This doesn't feel too bad.

A moment later he doubled in a paroxysm worse than anything so far. The pipe clattered to the deck. He gagged, staring at nothing, then fell to the cabin floor as if wrestling with an invisible opponent. He coughed blood and pus onto the scrubbed pine boards. He groped for his basin under the closet, pulled it close to his face, spilling the night's urine, and vomited helplessly into the stench.

When the attack ebbed he lay there panting for some time. Shaking and sweating. At last he dragged himself up. He felt about in the deck beams and found the vial Steele had given him. The bitter draught burned as it went down. He stared at himself in the mirror nailed over the washbasin. His eyes looked like two hot coals glowing in a high wind.

Now, standing at the bulwark, he drew crumpled cambric from his pocket and tossed it overboard. The handkerchief dropped away into the bow wave, bobbed, then sucked under as the river creamed over it. He stared after it, no longer caring about the hostile shores they passed. Then gradually forgetting his sickness too, forgetting everything as he stared mesmerized down into the ever-changing play of light on water.

—Eaker. If you don't have any work to do, why don't you take the deck?

It was Duycker, of course. He said,—Aye aye, sir, and the elderly master turned over the watch glass and disappeared down the companionway. He moved back by the wheel and conned the passing banks with the telescope. Virginia seemed empty as it had when John Smith had arrived. No, emptier. For there were no Indians now.

They were gliding along off Point Lookout that evening, on a port tack with the main, fore-topgallant, fore-staysail, and a fore-trysail aloft in a strong cool northeasterly breeze, when the boiler exploded. Eli was in the wardroom, attempting to participate in the singing after partaking of a rather tough chicken Shippy had boiled. Glass had persuaded him to join in on "The Minstrel's Returned from the War" and then "Annie Laurie." They'd reached the line about "the dew on the Gowan Lion" when an abrupt report jarred the bulkheads. Shippy fell to his knees, dropping the port decanter to shatter on the deck. The dark liquid soaked instantly into the rug. The overhead lamp jostled in its chains, the flame flickering.

—A gun?

—That was no gun.

—Please God, Steele breathed, —not the boilers. He cradled the brandy bottle, which he'd snatched from the serving boy as he went down.

Eli followed the others out into the passageway, hesitated, then went toward the fire room.

The hatch was open. A Niagara roar came through it, so loud no voice could be heard. Frightened-faced Irish in sweaty, ragged duck were pushing through for the open air. He hesitated, smelling steam and hot smoke like the breath of hell. Then reflected grimly how little he had to lose, and stepped in.

The air within was murky as a London fog. It smelled of hot iron and fine gritty ash. He groped his way in, burned his hand on a steam line, and then heard shouting.

Claiborne was listening intently to Pappy MacNail, who was shouting into his face. Eli couldn't make out a word above the hubbub of men, the clang of shovels, above all the triumphant malevolent howl of suddenly freed steam flaring off above their heads. The stokers were clawing burning coal out of the furnaces, raking flame into hand barrows and tin buckets with long iron hoes. The air was choking hot. He coughed as the floating ash caught in his throat. Then the steam blast lessened and words emerged through the din.

—Not intirely sure yit, sir, MacNail was shouting. —Somethin' let go inside the boiler. Just lucky as hell the shell held, we'd all be scalded dead. I vented the main and we're drawin' fires.

The captain acknowledged Eli with a curt nod. He asked the assistant engineer, —Can we steam at all?

—B boiler won't hold a teaspoonful. I could kick through it like a wet newspaper.

—Can we make Norfolk?

—I don't know, sir. Is it downwind from here?

—I mean, how much longer can you give me steam?

—That's just it, sir. We can't make you steam. Least till I get boiler A opened up and find out what just busted. Ruptured tube, most like. But it's got to cool awhile before I can put a man in there. You best put some men at the hand pumps, meanwhile. No steam, I can't run the steam pump, and that shaft's leakin' a little more every day.

Eli looked at the captain's face, realizing Claiborne would have to report this to Paulding. What he'd seen of that grim and withdrawn little Yankee, shriveled and hard as pork smoked on a stick, made him pity the Virginian. On impulse he said, —Sir, if you'd like me to inform the commodore, I'll do so.

—Thanks, but I fear that pleasant duty belongs to me.

—It's a mechanical failure. They can't blame you for it.

Claiborne curved his lips upward, but the bleak smile didn't lighten his face. He told MacNail, —Open her up as soon as you can. See me when you know what is wrong.

He cast a last glance at the sweating stokers and left. Eli lingered, then saw that the laboring men had no need of him either, and followed the captain out.

Ker paused outside the door. He could hear their voices inside the cabin. He didn't want to go in. So he forced himself to knock quickly, and turned the handle.

They looked up from the table, in almost the same positions he'd left them in that morning. Cards and small stacks of silver lay on the green felt. The advantage was to Wilkes, from the glance he had before Paulding leaned back and said coldly, forestalling his greeting, —I do not recall asking you to join us for dinner.

—I'm not here for dinner, sir, but to report a casualty.

Wilkes turned over a card. —What sort of casualty, Lieutenant?

—Something's burst inside the boiler. Fortunately no one was hurt. Unfortunately, our other boiler will not hold steam.

—How convenient, Paulding murmured.

—I beg your pardon, sir?

—To the seceshers in Norfolk, I mean. We are hurrying reinforcements to forestall their occupation of the yard. And now we are unable to do so.

He took the flag officer's meaning, would have taken it even without the ironical look Paulding sent across the table to Wilkes. He took a deep breath to keep his anger from showing.

—Sir, I'm continuing under sail. I have a fresh wind. We can make the fort tomorrow without engine power.

—I should certainly think so. Are your stuns'ls set?

—It is a bit fresh for studding sails, sir.

—If the wind is as you describe, you will benefit from them.

—I do not like to send the crew aloft at night unless it is particularly necessary. She will make seven knots good under courses and t'gallants.

Paulding said, —I hope she will, Lieutenant Claiborne; I most certainly hope that she will. I will not disguise from you that I disagreed with the secretary when he retained you in command of this ship.

—I was there when you registered your displeasure, sir.

—No, you were not. Not unless you had your ear pressed to the door.

—I am not in the habit of eavesdropping. Nor am I in the habit of suffering imputations.

—Yes, yes; we know how jealous you cavaliers are of your honor. No matter what villainy and sedition you are actually engaged in.

He and Paulding regarded each other with frank hatred. Then Wilkes cleared his throat. —Hiram? We should perhaps leave the captain to the managing of his vessel.

Paulding harrumphed and examined his cards again. —I expect to see Old Point Comfort in the offing before the meridian tomorrow.

—If this wind holds, you'll see it by eight.

—You're dismissed, Lieutenant. Wake me at dawn.

He closed the door behind him and stood trying to overcome his anger. It was growing increasingly difficult. Even when there was a

difference in rank, gentlemen addressed social equals with the presumption the other was both honest and honorable. But men like
Paulding seemed to expect others to cheat him and lie to him. He'd
met Paulding's brand of Yankee before. He didn't like their air of se-
cretive cunning, and he found their obsession with the dollar con-
temptible, but most arrogant of all was their self-righteousness in
proclaiming how others should live their lives. As if their own heart-
less and mercenary order were some model of virtue.

Girnsolver came out of the storeroom, a brush and a length of rat-
tan under his arm. The boatswain flattened himself against the bulkhead as his commander, unseeing, went by.

Night fell. Thurston had the deck now. Eli would stand from eight to
midnight. He paced back and forth before the port binnacle, watching the card reel about in its tiny sealed home as *Owanee* dipped and
rose to a following sea. They were still headed south, canvasing down
the great highway of the Chesapeake. Point Lookout light shone
steady astern. The deck surged and rolled beneath his boots.

The night sky had cleared, only scattered clouds eclipsing brilliant
stars. The moon glowed like a Drummond light ahead of their dipping bowsprit, paving the black bay with a coruscating road so bright
he could see the ranged guns, the boats lowered at the quarter, the
on-watch sitting about the deck. The men talked in low voices. From
aloft came the twang of a Jew's harp.

A red coal glowed near the companionway. He took a step in that
direction and called, —The smoking lamp is out on deck.

—Mr. Eaker. Surely you'd not begrudge a devotee of the leaf an
evening segar.

It was Dr. Steele, his nightgowned shoulders and tasseled nightcap
silvered with moonlight. Eli said, —It's not that I begrudge it, sir.
You know the regulations better than I.

A great sigh; then a small comet arched over the bulwark. Steele
said, —I tell you, I don't relish thinking about what lies ahead. And
now we haven't any engines, I understand.

—Perhaps we can obtain repairs at Fort Monroe.

The melancholy chant of the leadsman told them six fathoms lay beneath the keel. Steele said, —Monroe's an army fort. We won't get any repairs there, although there's a fine hotel on Point Comfort.

Eli leaned on a gun carriage and examined the moon. It shone with a steady cold light, blotched and pustuled like the face of a smallpoxed child. —Let me sound your opinion on something, he murmured. —Do you think the captain's loyal?

Steele started to laugh, then cut the sound short. His tasseled silhouette reared back, then turned, searching into the shadows around them, and a smell came on the wind and Eli realized the doctor was deep in the arms of Bacchus. —Who among us is completely faithful, my dear? And to what?

—Where do you call home, Doctor?

—I am from Delaware myself, but that was many years gone. And does geography truly shape our constancy? Or is it a question of family? Or perhaps just of where one's bread is best buttered? Steele rolled a chuckle deep in his throat, then spat it over the side. Drunk, he seemed to relish grandiloquence of language.

—You don't sound attached to either section.

—Must I be? Men's bodies, their health, will need attention, no matter what flag they sail under. If you prick them, do they not bleed? If you tickle them, do they not laugh? If you poison them, do they not die? And if you wrong them, shall they not revenge?

—You think we wrong them? These rebels? These "Confederates?"

—I was trying for a somewhat more subtle point; but let it go. Can I take Old Abe's shilling, and stay nonpartisan in this affair? I shall try.

A silence stayed between them for a time. Eli watched a darkness, an eclipsing of the northern constellations that might be a squall. He was about to go below again, rest for an hour before going on watch, when he remembered what he'd meant to ask. —I ordered one of the inhalation tubes you recommended. In Washington.

—I'm glad to hear it. Are you using it?

—I tried it out this morning. It wasn't pleasant.

—I warned you it wouldn't be. But you must continue, my dear. You are preventing the primary material from disseminating, forcing a regression to a fibrous apical focus. If you do not, the process will penetrate the adjacent tissues, producing secondary foci. These latter grow and coalesce, producing what we term exudative phthisis—the so-called galloping consumption. You are bathing daily in cold water, as I advised?

Eli wiped his forehead. Was that the clammy moisture of fever? He said hoarsely, —Do you remember what you said to me about hope, when I had my attack? That I must not lose hope.

—I recall giving you that advice, my boy.

—I wondered if it was because you had no real help to give. If all this is merely to palliate, or to keep me occupied.

—Oh no, my dear. Not at all. It is not to be trifled with, but I believe you have a good chance of a favorable outcome.

—But you cautioned me to look to my life, or words to that effect.

—I don't recall my precise comments *verbatim ac literatim.* I hope I advised you to see to the welfare of your soul, and to the desire of your heart. But not because of your disease.

—Then why?

—Because none of us know when the end will come. I cautioned you to bear that in mind, no more and no less than I caution myself each morning.

Eli stared at his face in the moonlight. The moon and Dr. Steele's face were not unalike. Round and time-ravaged, and both with a side that could not be seen but only guessed at.

He murmured, —I was betrothed. But I did not think I loved her, and used my illness as a pretext to put off our marriage. Now I regret having done so.

—In other words you are human; and now you want me to assume the mantle of Mentor. Well, I have very little advice for you. *Iatre, therapeuson seauton,* as Luke says.

—Physician, heal thyself.

348

—Exactly. Which in my life I have not been able to; for no man goes to sea who has anything better left to him on land; and yet you consult my sagacity. Well, my advice is, don't press any suits just now. Let the course of events reveal your way. The old man pressed Eli's hand as it lay beside him on the bulwark. —You had best get some rest, my dear. Do not call too heavily on your strength.

He thanked Steele quietly, and went below. But paused in the companionway, looking back up at the moon-gilded deck, at the quiet forms that lingered there, under the stars that slowly swayed beyond the yards and sails.

He did not know what the truth was. He did not know what awaited them in Norfolk. He did not know if the doctor was humoring him behind his learned bombast. But for the first time since he'd seen his own bright blood, a sweet gladness simply at being alive quivered pure as a plucked viol string, deep within his heart.

28

THE wind held fair through the night, but dropped toward
morning. Slowed by the dying airs, and delayed by the tide
after passing Back River, *Owanee* let go her anchor off
Fortress Monroe, at the entrance to Hampton Roads, at a little after
eleven the next morning.

Beneath a blue sky and fleecy clouds the great enclosed bay was
dotted here and there with small sail. Oyster dredgers in their rakish
bugeyes, small craft of all sorts plying busily to and fro. Closer to, a
civilian steamer lay alongside the fort with fires banked. Paulding had
the cutter lowered and went ashore to consult with the commandant.

In the afternoon they upped anchor and warped alongside the
engineers' wharf, where the Third Massachusetts Regiment left the
steamer and filed aboard the sloop with field gear and rifles. By four
o'clock three hundred and fifty of the lanky, awkward-striding mili-
tiamen packed the berthing deck so closely not an inch of scoured
pine was visible. They crowded into the wardroom and lay about so
salt-cod tight topside the watch trod on their limbs as they went
about setting sail.

When the commodore returned they got under way again, headed this time up the Elizabeth River. The full moon came up ripe and red as a blood orange, sporadically visible between gray rags of squall cloud that careered across an inky sky. Her courses drawing full and bye, *Owanee* plowed with a nodding lean across the foam patches glowing in the moon gleams, and very slowly the amber light of the fortress fell astern.

Eli didn't miss the engines. Instead of their endless thumping he heard the whine of the rigging aloft and the hiss of three-foot seas. Instead of coal smoke he smelled the surrounding land, a fecund marshy odor that accompanied the sloop like the gulls that whirled down to her wake and up again, crying like lost children. That, and a piny, resinous spiciness, pleasant enough if one did not think about its source: the huge square tanks lashed along the counter, the highly flammable spirits of turpentine swayed aboard in Washington.

He stood at the starboard bulwark, leaning on the selvagee straps of a thirty-two-pounder and staring into the western darkness. The junior officers had been evicted from their cabin-holes by the staff officers. He'd tried to doze in the wardroom, but failed. Too many sleepless men playing euchre and drinking whiskey. Now he stared blearily into the night, wrestling with the angels of fear and regret.

ALTERNATIVE IS STEP I FEAR TO TAKE. What had Ara meant? What could she do more daring than fleeing to the Childs? He'd left a telegram for her at the fort, but the signals officer had advised him personal messages might not be sent for some time, given the volume of official traffic during this crisis in the life of the nation.

And what lay ahead, closer with every mile of southing? When he thought of it his vitals seemed to shrivel. But he'd been afraid off Charleston, too. He was not as apprehensive now; as if experience, and the cauterizing acknowledgment of his mortal disease, had burnt away a bit of whatever bump in the brain produced the faculty of fear. Far off to the westward a single light, some plantation house, perhaps, gleamed now and again. Ahead, a saffron radiance. Norfolk, not yet in view, but still casting ahead of it the sky glow by which one saw a city for hours before she rose over the curve of earth and sea.

—Got the mournfuls, friend?

A fellow shadow; one of the troops, by his accent. Eli said no, he just couldn't sleep.

—Same here. Got 'n'ythin' chew on ye?

He said briefly that he had not. When the soldier drifted away, he popped a locofoco with his thumbnail to check his watch. He snapped it closed, flicked the match overboard, and stepped over snoring bodies toward the kerosene gleam of the binnacle.

The buttery lamplight, cupped close above the compass card, ever swaying, ever the same, lit up the helmsmen's sinewy wrists. Gradually Eli made out a shape near the mizzenmast. —Captain? he murmured.

Owanee's commander cleared his throat in the darkness. —Eaker?

—Yes sir.

—Was it you who lit a lucifer a moment ago? Pray do not repeat it. We must show no lights as we close the shore; and you were perilously close to the turpentine.

He reflected that might have been better, to end his life in flame and explosion, a brief lurid bonfire on black water, rather than what most likely lay ahead: cadaverous decline, invalidism and the racking cough that was all he remembered of his mother. But aloud he merely murmured an apology, and asked where they were. Claiborne searched the blackness, turning his head to inspect each quarter. Then led down the companionway, to where a gimbaled watch lamp reeled above a chart table.

The inland bay of Hampton Roads was shaped like a great gulping fish. Its open mouth faced the Chesapeake, with Willoughby's Point defining the lower lip. Its upraised tail was the James River. Its rear fins pointed into the Nansemond; its front fins, into the Elizabeth. At their tip, past Norfolk on the eastern bank and Portsmouth City to the west, lay the party's destination, the great United States Navy Yard at Gosport, Virginia, with all its ships and stores and guns.

Owanee's commander ran a finger down a penciled line. —It wants but fourteen miles from Fortress Monroe to Gosport. I judge our speed at six knots, but the land shadow will pare this wind as the river narrows. We'll double the lookout as we pass Fort Norfolk. The rebels are reported to be sinking condemned vessels in the channel.

Eli studied the labyrinthine windings of the Elizabeth, in places no more than a couple of hundred yards wide, hemmed in by wharves and piers. Not overmuch water at best, and the chart showed rapid shallowing either side of the center of the channel. He said slowly, —So we'll be running until we reach Wise's Point here; then a broad reach, gradually shortening to abeam as we pass this projection of land.

—That's the old naval hospital.

—And then we shall fall off again. But if we run foul of one of the wrecks, or have to turn back?

Claiborne said, —No question, it's a foul wind for a quick escape.

—And we have no engine power. How will we claw off? We can't tack in a channel that narrow.

—We shall simply have to rely on MacNail to get one of those boilers back on the line.

Eli pursed his lips, remembering the muted but terrifying detonation on the way down. If the abused, salt-rotted boilers let go again they might not be so lucky. A full-scale explosion would scythe iron shards through the crowded berthing decks, ripping the sloop apart like a paper packet savaged by a mastiff.

And he couldn't help remembering going aground in Aquia Creek. Claiborne had failed then, if his purpose was to cripple the ship. But now, tonight . . . the captain was a Virginian, after all . . . He resolved to muster all his vigilance.

An hour crept by, with no more speech or sound than an occasional murmur of "Meet her" or "Starboard your helm" to the helmsman, that and the long-drawn-out reports of the leadsman in the chains. At five bells Claiborne sent him forward to rouse the on-deck watch, trimming sail as the sloop bore around to eastward. A little later he went forward again to reef the foresail, to give the lookouts a clear view ahead. The sky brightened slowly, rose and saffron mounting to challenge the flickering moon.

Claiborne murmured, —Ask the commodore if he will step up, please.

Paulding was reading in his cabin, bald head and white side-whiskers glowing in the light of a taper. He rose when Eli tapped, pulled on a reefer jacket, and followed him on deck.

After the candle glare the night was black as a coalhole again. As Paulding and Claiborne discussed the channel, Eli asked the quartermaster, —Have you been up this river before?

—To Gosport, sir? Maybe a score of times.

—Is it always this dark?

—Oh no, sir. Rapp explained lights usually burned on each point.

—Somebody's put 'em out. To make it rough for us to get in. That's all shoal off to starboard there, and damn little water to port either.

—You'd not obey an order that might put us aground, would you?

—You pullin' my leg, Mr. Eaker? I kissed the wooden lady enough to know, an officer gives me an order, that's what I do.

—Belay that chatter, came Paulding's voice. —Helm hard aport.

—Hard aport, aye sir.

—Steady as she goes. Lieutenant, let us shorten sail.

Sheet-blocks and fairleads rattled, and the jibboom eased to leeward. The sloop lost way, the rush of water along her hull dying away. Then he saw what they'd just avoided. Spiky shadows walked the larboard side. A sunken ship's top-hamper sticking up atilt from the dark sea. Yards and spreaders set like boarding pikes to pierce an unwary hull, rigging to tangle and hold. He wondered darkly if they'd have avoided it if Paulding had stayed below; whether Claiborne would have simply sailed them on into the obstructions, crippled or damaged the ship. Fortunately there didn't seem to be any boats out as pickets. They ghosted past silent and so far, it seemed, unobserved from the shores that pinched in closer and closer now on either hand.

Back by the wheel, Ker stared as intently to starboard, trying to jigsaw and guess black masses and occasional pricks of light into the scoops and juts of land on the chart. Paulding had gone back below, with orders to call him as soon as Gosport yard was in sight.

He couldn't shake off a guilty disquiet. He felt like a son returning to burgle his father's house.

Another shadow mounted the companionway to the quarterdeck. From its height, Ker greeted him quietly as Captain Wilkes. Along with being the discoverer of the southern terra incognita, Wilkes had a reputation as an "old bruin," a case-hardened sundowner. At the moment, though, he seemed pacific. He stood looking silently forward, as Ker's thoughts returned to Virginia.

For all his voyaging, this was his native land. He knew the line of her seacoasts like the parting of his hair. He'd hunted the broadleafed fields of the Tidewater, and sailed the southern Chesapeake from Smith Point to Fishermans Island, gunkholing the creeks and bays; had reefed through many a squall in his grandfather Ker's old sailing skiff. His mother was a Custis of the Eastern Shore, his father a Claiborne of Richmond. He carried their pride and their blood close as the beat of his heart.

Now that fair land had turned against the Union she'd led for so long, the republic her sons Washington and Jefferson and Patrick Henry had set above all others as a refuge of democracy, a hope for the future.

He'd sworn an oath to the Flag, and fought beneath its folds. How could a gentleman break his word? He could not. But as Buchanan had asked: could he fight against his kin and kind?

But Farragut would turn that argument about. Could he refrain from fighting, when his brothers raised their hand against their country?

His unquiet mind could not forget that his wife and son were sleeping somewhere off in the darkness at his left hand. If he was ordered to shell the city, they'd be in range of his guns.

He remembered the action at Kisembo. The Portuguese and the natives murdering each other ashore, looting and burning held in check only by the guns of the English and American squadrons moored along the waterfront. That had been hard enough, to see men kill one another, to send the murderous breeze of grape and canister to lay them out in windrows, even if they were strangers to him. But this time . . . The house on Freemason Street was frame, with pine clapboard siding. He'd just paid thirteen dollars to have it painted.

Was it possible that there *was* no honorable course? And in that case, if honor gave no guide in this the most agonizing choice of one's life, then of what use was it? Was all a fancy, an illusion, a myth? But his mind recoiled at the idea of a world without it. Without honor, no man could trust another, just as without chastity, no man could trust a woman. Society could not exist without it.

Suddenly a drum began beating to quarters in the darkness ahead. Beside him Wilkes lifted his head like an old war-horse sniffing battle.

—I believe we should run out, sir, Ker murmured.

The captain sounded surprised at being consulted. —You are in command, sir; but I would say that is the action manifestly indicated.

He looked around for the gunnery officer. At that moment the New Yorker loomed up. Ker snapped, —Mr. Eaker: cast loose the starboard guns, in silence. Run out and provide for close firing. Mr. Thurston! Below at once, and notify the commodore.

Owanee's deck stitched with running shapes. He heard the scuff of boot leather, the swiftly hushed protests of wakened troops, the muted clank of slings and relieving tackles. Touchholes were hastily uncovered, port lids triced up, tompions jerked free, guns run rumbling out to whispered commands.

Meanwhile the sloop, gradually borne ahead by the dropping zephyr, neared a black mass that lay steady in the gloom. Rubbing an icy trickle off his brow, he couldn't decide where he was. If they were making four knots, he'd passed Gosport town and was abreast of the navy yard. If three and a half, then that flatness might be the bridge across Gosport Creek, which would make the steadily closing mass an island. He suspected not, though. He'd sailed the Roads enough to know any land thereabouts would lie low to the water, given what he was nosing; fish guts and crab shells, the dead stink of coon-tracked mudflats.

He suspected it could only be another warship.

A cry against the wind, but so faint he could not cull meaning from its trailed-off moan. He cupped his ear, but caught only the muted ripple of the bow wave, a creak and flutter aloft like settling wings as a bereft sail luffed in the dark.

Eaker, in a tense murmur: —Batteries manned and ready. Charges and shell on deck for close firing.

—Stand by to fire in succession from forward, Mr. Eaker. Remind your gun captains to aim low.

The shadow loomed closer. He could almost decipher its shape. A wedge of sable presence, and . . . the moon slipped free of her shift of cloud, Diana's naked form shining out just for a moment. Long enough to limn the upperworks of a large ship not a hundred yards off. Not a gleam from her, no riding lights, so either hostile or abandoned. A fire ship? Or loaded with powder, a floating bomb?

He murmured to Wilkes, —Shall I hail her? Or commence fire?

A stentorian voice hailed from downriver. —Don't fire. It's *Owanee*.

—That there's the *Pennsylvania*'s bo's'n, sir, said Rapp, not turning his gaze from its mesmeric preoccupation with the compass card. The quartermaster eased the wheel a spoke. —The guardo ship. Sitting on the bottom, she is, been there so long she's gone ashoal on beef bones and coffee grounds.

—Ahoy, the *Owanee*.

Eli leaped into the ratlings. Cupping his hands, he shouted so loudly it felt as if he was ripping the lining out of his throat: —Ahoy! What ship?

—United States ship, the *Cumberland*.

From the dark came a sudden roar of male voices: three hearty cheers. Dark lanterns snapped open. Standing by the number three thirty-two-pounder, he felt his knees come close to giving way. A moment more and the two men-of-war would have swept each other with grape and shell. He felt as if he'd inhaled some intoxicating fluid that made his brain float and dance like Dr. Morton's anæsthetic ether.

When he heard the hail from ahead, Cal Hanks slowly unwound the lanyard from his fist, then let it drop.

He'd been at the forward pivot, ready to fire. *Eager* to. Prepared and more, to let flame and shell belch forth.

Shrouded in the night, he rubbed his mouth, glancing from side to side at the pale oval blurs that were his shipmates' faces. Most were Yankees, from the flinty shores of Maine to the sandy Delaware beaches. A few were Westerners. Others spoke seagoing English with an Irish brogue or a Dutcher thickness.

But no matter where they came from, they didn't know where they were. To them the darkened shores that pressed around them as *Owanee* felt her way into the heart of the land were at most enemy territory. Or even home; he'd heard one of the midshipmen say Lieutenant Claiborne, Captain Claiborne now, was from near here. That he had family in Norfolk.

Mother, brothers, sisters . . . he'd had them once too. Then they'd been taken, torn away, till all he had left was his own empty hands.

He knew this land for what it was. A hell where the press of his foot on the shore would strip him of freedom and even maybe life. One step on the marshes he could smell on the wind would make him not man but hunted beast. The pinpricks of light that slowly passed reminded him that below their glow human beings slept on corn-husk pallets or floors, hungry and beaten and afraid.

Covered by the dark, he reached out again and took the lanyard. Caressed it, rubbing the coarse knotted linen with thumb and forefinger.

He was creeping at last back into the land of Pharaoh; and beneath his barely stayed hand lay the plague of fire.

As they passed close aboard *Cumberland* Ker saw she was moored fore and aft in the tidal flow off the shipyard. He knew her, twenty-four guns, one of the last sailing sloops built. She had no engine power. If she was going to leave against this wind, someone would have to tow her. Beyond her, as *Owanee* glided on, two vast apexes of darkness, like shadowed cathedrals, gradually took shape against the sky. Gas

lamps glimmered along the river edge, but save for them the yard
seemed deserted. As they closed he ran his glass along the verge. The
gas flares leapt closer, and below them the glimmer of water beneath
planks and dolphin heads.

—The wharf, sir, a point to starboard. Just beyond the ship
houses.

—Very well. He aligned his mind with the wind and began snapping orders. In normal times a steam tug would nudge alongside, a
yard pilot conn them in. But he saw no sign of either in this uncanny
stillness. Going alongside under sail was a delicate evolution at best.
Tonight the wind, the current, and the dark added enough complica-
tion that *Owanee* rocked as she hit, scraping her sheer strake along
the oaken pilings with a spine-shivering screech. The heavy bower
anchor to starboard, catted out ready to drop, caught several project-
ing planks and twisted them up, shrieking and cracking as their
spikes pulled, before she eased to a stop.

Men stepped out from the dark. Girnsolver shouted from the
forecastle, lines clapped down on the wharf, and before many minutes had passed they were moored fore, aft, and springs. One of the
line handlers called up in a hoarse voice that they were too late. The
yard workers, Democrats to a man, had downed tools and left at
noon. The commander of the yard had ordered the ships scuttled.
They were sinking now.

—He *scuttled* them? Paulding shouted down. —What do you
mean, man? Which ships?

—All of 'em's what I heard. Better talk to McCauley y'self, you
want the straight of it.

The commodore didn't wait for the gangway; he swung himself
stiffly over the side and went down the boat ladder. Wilkes and the
staff officers followed, disappearing into an alley that led off amid
lofts and storehouses.

Eaker, at Ker's elbow as he leaned down to inspect the damage to
the sloop's side: —Captain. Shall I run the guns in? Or at least put on
the lock covers? The night is growing damp.

—I should prefer you to remain in the utmost state of readiness,

Mr. Eaker. Post a sharp lookout toward the channel. If anyone should descend on us, I suspect they will come from that direction.

Duycker. The exec said, —Sir, the bower anchor: the stock is carried away and will need repair. Also the army major wants to put his men ashore.

—He may place them on the wharf, but no further, until the commodore returns.

A score of grunting seamen ran the gangway out. The line handlers caught the pier end and guided it the last few feet to ground with a rattling thud. The troops, who had been standing by with rifle muskets and cartridge boxes, began loping down. Chevied and yelled at by corporals and sergeants, they formed up facing the eerie darkness.

A slight figure gradually emerged from the recesses of the yard. Ker thought it looked familiar. He went to the brow to meet him. Then the light fell on his face, and he gripped his hand in welcome as he stepped aboard. —Hubbard. I am very glad to see you again.

—Not as happy as I am to see you. I'm afraid everything's gone to smash here. Paulding's at Quarters A with McCauley. He wants you to muster a demolition party and report there as soon as possible.

Ker raised his eyebrows. —I beg your pardon. My impression from the commodore was that we were to hold the yard. Not destroy it.

—Those might be your orders, sir, but Commodore McCauley commenced destruction at noon. *Germantown* and *Merrimack* are sinking at their moorings.

—Sinking. *Sinking?* But I understood they were ready for sea.

—They were. The engineer sounded bitter. —But you'll see 'em heading for the bottom if you walk a hundred paces and look around that stone shed.

He peered into the dark, wondering if it could be true. Navy ships sinking at their moorings! He didn't think it had ever happened before. *Bonhomme Richard* had sunk in battle. *Chesapeake* had been captured in battle. Even Decatur's valiant burning of the captured *Philadelphia* had been undertaken under hostile fire. Of which he had seen no evidence yet here at all, unless one counted a few overaged ships sunken more or less in the channel. But to the little engineer he said only, —Very well, what's he want of us? A demolition party, you said?

—Marines and sailors, as many as you can spare, and well armed.

—All right, I'll take care of that. Now listen: we are just now completely without engine power. Our last boiler let go on the way down the bay. The wind was fair to get us here, but if you ask me how we're to escape, if escape we must, I must say that just now I don't know. MacNail seems willing enough, but I think—well, would you do me the favor of looking below, and getting us enough steam to make way?

—I'll give it a try, sir.

As the engineer went below Ker turned to the problem of who to send ashore. He heard no firing yet, only silence and distant shouts. His first thought was himself and Duycker. Then he realized that if they had to get under way in a hurry, they'd need the first lieutenant and the boatswain. Perhaps with luck they could kedge downriver, though that was killing work in a contrary wind. Gunner Babcock would serve to lead a shore party. With Eaker in nominal charge, to blood the volunteer.

He called Eaker to him and gave rapid orders. He finished, — Take them ashore and report yourself to Quarters A for orders from Commodore Paulding. I will follow in a few minutes, as soon as I have a word with Mr. Duycker. Now, there seems to be some confusion ashore. Do not take unnecessary risks. Keep your head. Understand me, Mr. Eaker?

The New Yorker saluted. —Keep our heads, he said. —I understand you, sir. Aye aye. Port battery, stand fast! Starboard battery, draw small arms and boarding axes, and fall in to follow me ashore.

Cal didn't want to leave the gun. He'd wanted to fire it all the way upriver, all that night; he'd wanted to fire when the challenge had rung out of the dark. He damn near had, even without the order. But the word had never come, and now he felt cheated and angry.

And now here they were in Virginia, and the dark silent shipyard inland looked spooky and threatening. He wasn't afraid of any man, but he felt the juju inside his blouse and said a half prayer, half invocation, who to, he could not quite tell. He only asked to be protected, and shown what to do.

When Babcock passed the word for the landing party he went below and joined the line where carbines and cutlasses were handed over the armorer's counter. The men were excited, talking and swearing. But the gun captain was in front of him, and ordered him out of line with an oath. —Get along topside, nigger, and get you a boarding axe. We ain't giving the likes of you no guns.

He felt his fist crimp close of itself, felt the muscle desire to smash through that pasty grin and those malevolent blue eyes like a topmaul. But then he remembered what had happened the last time he did that, and his throat seemed to close as with tightened hemp and his hand dropped reluctantly back to his side. He growled, —You think these rebels gone to fight, Archbold? I wishes they would.

—It ain't no business of yours what any white man does. You just go get that boarding axe.

He got it and carried it out on deck, and stood ready to muster, looking toward the shore. It was dark over there, but he could see lights out in the town.

Yal gone see it cut de feather, burn stronger'n red oak lye.

What fool talk that old woman had give him. Fool conjure talk about split twigs and voodoo kings and burning swords in the sky. He'd figured that one out later, thinking about it on deck at night. She meant the comet, the one that had lit up the night the year before. But it hadn't looked like no sword, and it hadn't pointed south, either. Just to confuse him and make him leave his money. Fool and his money, soon parted. His still wrapped tight in his neckerchief. She didn't know nothing about his family, either. He just been fooling himself, going to ask her what to do. Anything a man did in this world he had to do on his own. He'd get to his family somehow. Didn't know how just yet, but he'd get to them, get them out somehow and free. There wasn't nothing else that mattered. He could take

Archbold's hazing for now. Just swallow it for now, like he swallowed so much.

He hefted the axe, wanting to smash it into the mast, wanting to smash it into a blue-eyed face. He grinned to himself, behind his blank slow slave-learned mask.

Maybe he'd get to do just that tonight.

While the men were drawing weapons, Eli went below to his stateroom. He pulled the shallow pallet off his bunk, uncovering the box stuffed into the unused inches at its foot. Took out the revolver Ara had given him on a rainy night in Brooklyn and loaded it, smearing each chamber mouth with tallow after ramming the ball home so fire could not flash from charge to charge.

He found Quarters A a pistol shot inland, a tall narrow house in Flemish-bond brick. A ten-foot wall separated it from the street, on the far side of which several quite impressive homes were a stone's toss away. From their lit upper windows civilians in frock coats and evening dresses looked down as he led his party through a tasteful garden square with sand pathways. He halted them before the central entry. The anxious dark faces of servant women peered out from an iron grate near ground level. He hesitated, then told Babcock to have the men ground arms and stand easy until he returned.

Two gracefully curving flights of granite steps mounted to the front-level door. It stood open. From within came a blaze of light and the shouts of angry men. He loosened the revolver in his belt, went cautiously down an entrance hall, and found himself in a drawing room.

His entry made no impression on the excited, sweating officers who surrounded a small, confused-looking personage seated at a polished desk beneath a dozen candles burning in a cut-glass chandelier. The seated officer wore full dress and a commodore's epaulettes. Two huge box-lock boarding pistols, elaborately chased and engraved, lay cocked on the desk. Another was thrust into his sword belt. Open bottles and glasses stood on a walnut sideboard. This had to be Mc-Cauley, the shipyard commander, and from his glowing face, slurred speech, and unsteady seat, Eli saw he'd been at the liquid courage for some time.

—They've all left me, McCauley moaned, clapping his hands to his face. —My executive officer, all the foremen, all the superintendents. I can do nothing, do you hear? Nothing. Leave me, gentlemen, leave me in my misery.

—You have committed a colossal blunder, said Paulding harshly. —Do you understand, sir? There was no necessity for this. But now that you have started it, I must carry it through. I relieve you, by order of Secretary Welles. We have just enough men to destroy everything, if we commence instantly.

—I disagree, Hiram, Captain Wilkes broke in. —We can hold this station. We can stop the scuttling, and hold the walls with our troops and marines, and the waterfront with *Owanee*'s and *Cumberland*'s guns.

McCauley tossed off a whiskey, shuddered, and refilled his glass. —I had no choice. All alone. Fifty thousand militia mustering at the railroad yard.

—Nonsense, sir. Be quiet, you are beside yourself, Paulding said contemptuously.

—Be quiet? Be *quiet*? I've been sitting here listening to the trains come in all day! Thousands of rebels! We must leave instantly or they'll hang us all!

Paulding's glare fastened on Eaker like a grappling hook. —You. You're from *Owanee*, are you not?

—That's right, sir. The party you requested.

—Do you know the yard? Proceed to the ordnance building. Draw twenty barrels of powder and take them down to the dry dock. Understand?

—Uh, not entirely, Commodore, Eli said. —What shall I do once I reach it?

—You will so emplace the explosive as to destroy it, sir, Paulding told him. —This . . . *officer* has scuttled all the ships we came down to secure. He has destroyed at one stroke a quarter of the fleet! Without them we can neither defend the yard nor remove the heavy ordnance. All that remains is to destroy as much as we can, as completely as we can, before the rebels seize it.

Eli stood uncertain. —Sir, I'm not sure I would know how to do that. Blow up a dry dock—

Wilkes interrupted him. The explorer spoke slowly, deliberately, as if addressing a congenital idiot strapped to a bed. —Hiram, I must object. Take thought for a moment. No one is threatening this yard. There is not an enemy in sight! Let us place sentinels, and examine the situation at first light.

Paulding glared back, just as determined. —I hear your objections, Charles. But the rebels have only to sink a few more blockships and we'll be snared here. We *must* get under way before dawn. You— Eaker—if you don't feel up to the dry dock, take charge of burning the ship houses and other buildings. Rope yards and storehouses, everything that will burn. You can set fire to things, at least, can you not? Prepare everything, but do not set your matches before I signal with a rocket.

Wilkes still didn't agree. He kept arguing. The raised voices around McCauley grew hysterical. One officer gestured so violently his brass-mounted scabbard chipped a corner of the marble fireplace. Eli about-faced smartly and left.

He stood on the landing, looking over the wall into the town. In the lighted windows the townspeople pointed at him. What he'd just heard rattled in his head.

Babcock saluted grimly as Eli and Claiborne walked up, both simultaneously, Eli from the yard commandant's quarters, the captain from the waterfront. The black gunner, Hanks, was a step behind Claiborne, who looked angrier than Eli had ever seen him. —Eaker. Is it true? the captain said. —They're destroying everything?

He tried to gather his thoughts. It was difficult; they scampered about like frightened rabbits. —It seems so, sir. The yard is to be burned. All scuttled ships to be set afire. The dry dock must be loaded with powder from the ordnance shed and blown up.

—Burned? Babcock said wonderingly. —You sure you heard him right? There ain't no misunderstanding?

Claiborne blinked, and his jaw opened and closed. —That's impossible. I've got to hear those orders myself.

—Go right on in, sir. You will hear it all.

As Claiborne went up the steps Wilkes came down, the explorer drawing on a glove coolly as Eli was trying to decide where to start. —You there, said Wilkes, spotting him. —Are these your men?

—Yes sir. This is Gunner Babcock, from *Owanee,* and I am Volunteer Master's Mate Eaker.

—I regret to make your acquaintance under such circumstances, sir. Well! We must burn the largest federal installation in the South. So be it! But first we will rescue my command, at least, from this shameful catastrophe. Take half your men here and follow me.

—Sir, Commodore Paulding ordered me to destroy the ship houses.

—And I have just ordered you to follow me, and save a United States ship from abandonment and destruction. Which of us do you prefer to obey?

—You, sir. The way Wilkes spoke, as much as what he said, made the answer obvious, but Eli yielded his little authority with positive gratitude; he had no stomach for commencing his naval career by burning government property. —Where are we going, sir?

Wilkes said regally, pulling on his other glove and adjusting his sword and then, noticing the watching ladies, turning to doff his cap gallantly across the wall to them, —Where? Why, to salvage U.S.S. *Merrimack,* of course.

Stripped to the waist in the fire room heat, Theo Hubbard knotted the bandanna tight around his head, raging at the recalcitrance of machinery and the imbecility of braiders. He'd sent MacNail aft to check on the Worthington. All his and Isherwood's work gone for nothing, and meanwhile *Owanee*'s plant had gone to Hades in a hand basket. One boiler that held barely four pounds of steam. The other with what seemed to be a tube rupture. One pump left working, and he could use it either to drain the rapidly filling bilges or to supply water to the boilers.

Goddamn the line officers. What did they use for brains? They'd stuck everyone's heads into a noose, and unless he got very lucky in the next couple of hours, they'd still be in it when the trap let go under their feet.

As soon as he came down, he'd drawn fires and started draining feedwater overboard from both boilers. Boiler A was already cool, of course. MacNail had secured it after the explosion. But you couldn't work inside one while there was steam in the other. If the isolation valve leaked, whoever was inside would get scalded to death. He'd seen a stoker die on the *Susquehanna,* when a gauge glass broke and sprayed boiling water and steam across the boiler front. The surgeon had tried to sew his face back on, but it had sloughed off like a mask made of boiled pork, showing white bone beneath. Even stuffed with opium, the stoker had screamed until the captain ordered him gagged. It had been an inglorious, long, and exquisitely painful death, one he had no desire to emulate.

While B was cooling he went aft and looked at the leak in the shaft alley. It was rising fast now that the pump had stopped. He went back to the boiler front and watched the pressure gauge falling, jigging from foot to foot with impatience. When it was down to less than an inch he jerked the cover off A and crawled in, holding a lantern ahead of him in order to see.

The iron had blown out where the tubes joined the upper steam dome. Metal was exploded out all around the rupture, and cracks ran up the side of the boiler. Looking up at it, he shivered. They'd come within an ace of being blown to kingdom come. He twisted himself out and stood on the fire room flat, looking at it. Useless.

He turned around and looked at B.

This was the boiler MacNail had kept a banked fire under to run the pump. The fact it would still hold a little steam meant it wasn't completely useless yet. If he could get it up to ten pounds, or even eight, he could turn the engines. He checked the water glass. They'd drained it, but it was still hot. As he crouched before it the radiated heat baked the moisture from his eyeballs till his lids dragged over them. It would be like the sweatbox in there, the steam-heated punishment that awaited recalcitrant sailors.

He pulled his shirt back on, buttoned the sleeves, buttoned the neck. He tied another rag around his neck and pulled on heavy leather gloves. Then set the wrench and began yanking nuts off the manhole cover.

MacNail came back as his boots kicked outside the manhole, then disappeared after the rest of him. —By the sufferin' Christ, Mr. Hubbard. What are you doing?

—You're right, we can't patch A. So we've got to figure out some way to hold more pressure in this one.

—You shall roast in there like a darling little piglet, said the assistant engineer. —At least let me lash a line around ye, so I can draw ye out when ye're done all the way through.

—Send Hart for water, he said, feeling sweat pop and prickle along his back as he hauled himself in. He held out a hand, and MacNail put the bail of the lantern in it.

Inside the boiler the residual caloric radiated from every inch of the rapidly drying iron. A moist, scorching, cupric smell sawed at his throat. He couldn't take this for long. He was probably a fool for trying. He thrust out his arm again anyway, and MacNail handed in the mallet and cat's-claw and cold chisel. He squirmed around, wincing as the scorching metal burned through the thin cloth at his elbows, and began wriggling back along the length of the boiler, between the bracing rods that led from top to bottom and side to side and flue to flue, in toward where in the dim flicker of his lamp the fire tubes bristled like a forest of iron saplings.

Twenty feet in, rust scale and salt scale gritty under his pushing belly, the rotten patch came into view, or as much as it ever would in the darkness. He inspected it, lying on his back. The lamp showed him an old patch, one he remembered installing last year. Only a year, and boiling salt water had corroded it to a russet lacework. Unfortunately it was on a curved section of the steam drum. It was also in a very awkward place to reach. Well, the first order of business was to get it off. Breathing shallowly, he positioned the chisel above his squinted eyes. Four mallet blows knocked off the rivet-heads, but the patch itself clung tight, welded by rust to the boiler metal.

He gasped, tried to fling sweat and grit out of his eyes, and hammered grimly at it until he had to retreat to the access. —Water, he grunted, and MacNail threw a pail of it over him, so shocking cold that for a moment he couldn't breathe at all, just gasped like a landed trout.

—I'm gonna need a shell patch, he said when he could talk again. —About a foot square, and bend it to a curve before you hand it in. Get the biggest octopus you can find.

The octopus, so called for its shape, was the outer section of the shell patch. Thrust through a hole, it provided the anchorage against which an iron plate could be drawn tight along a threaded rod. He hoped that once it was in place, steam pressure in the relit boiler would press it so firmly against the interior of the drum that rivets would be superfluous. Thus, a temporary repair.

But if he couldn't get the old patch off, no smooth surface would present itself; and the steam would bleed off through the gaps.

MacNail yelled at Hart, sent him after the patch. Then peered in, face twisted with concern. Theo shook his head angrily, squirmed around, and crawled back in again.

Against the fire face once more, his body hooked like a warp amid the woof of the fire tubes. This time the blind despairing ferocity with which he mauled the rusty metal bent one edge free. He worked the cat's-claw under it and pried, but the aftermost fire tube was in the way and he could gain no leverage in the cramped space, so coffin-narrow his chest pressed cooking-hot iron each time he sucked in the scorching air.

Cursing, blind from the stinging sweat and rust scale gritting under his eyelids, he grappled in the darkness with recalcitrant metal. Without steam, the ship was doomed. But even if he succeeded, it might not be enough to both turn her shaft and run her pump. Even if this patch held, other sections might give way, perforating and finally rupturing under the terrible force of steam.

If they were lucky. If they weren't, a seam would split, releasing all its power in an explosion more violent than a mortar shell.

Another douse of icy water. His heart stalled like a centered piston; quivered in his breast for two or three rapid, disquieting, vibrating beats; only then resumed its duty. He found himself back at the manhole, not knowing how he'd gotten there.

MacNail peered in anxiously. —You got to get out of there, *caraid*. Ye're after bein' parboiled alive, like them lobsters at Delmonico's.

—Ain't nobody else small enough to do this, he grated through clenched teeth. Somehow he'd burned his face, in the moments he had lain unconscious. It felt numb, dead as cooked meat. Wriggling an arm around, he thrust his hand out. He could think of only one way to get that stubborn metal free.

—Hand me in a musket, he said. —And tell the boys to stand clear.

Ker came slowly back down the curved steps, fitting his gloves to his fingers. His ears rang with the shouting. He could not believe what he'd just heard, could not encompass what he'd just been ordered to do. The most fully equipped naval installation in the country had apparently been neglected at the highest levels, ungarrisoned, left to an incapable and panic-stricken commander; and now, in extremis, it was to be destroyed. In the drawing room above, the most senior officers in the service were shouting at and threatening one another, drunken, abusive, weeping, incompetent. Displaying behavior that would never be tolerated in the rawest plebe at Annapolis.

He couldn't believe the United States had come to this. He shook his head slowly, standing before McCauley's house.

—Lieutenant. Lieutenant!

He started, and glanced into the darkness. Iron bars gated the wall, but beyond it was simply a town street, cobblestoned and gaslit, with homes opposite. All their windows were lighted. He went a step or two toward the gate and saw the man. Several men, actually. He loosened his sword in its scabbard.

—Someone called me?

—We did.

Now he saw there were three of them, gentlemen merchants, perhaps, by their frock coats and stovepipe hats. One took off his hat and thrust his hand through the bars. —Let me introduce myself. I am Mr. William Peters, of this city. This is Captain Samuel Watts, and this is Captain James Murdaugh.

He took the extended palm reluctantly. —What can I do for you, gentlemen? I am afraid I am rather pressed at the moment.

—I understand, I understand, the first speaker said hastily. —Well sir, we are a committee, you might say, of the citizens of the town. Sir, we have heard that the authorities are preparing to burn the shipyard. And we thought we might come and ask Commodore McCauley if that were true. May we come in?

—I'm sorry. These gates are closed.

—Is it true? Is he planning to burn the yard?

—Excuse me, gentlemen. He started to turn away, but one of the men reached through the bars and caught his arm.

He turned back instantly, throwing the hand off and drawing his sword. The fellow let go instantly and stepped back from the bars, holding out both palms. —I am unarmed, sir. Unarmed. Sir, you are no Yankee. We can hear that in your voice. We are pleading for the citizens of Portsmouth. Look at the wind. If you burn the yard, the entire town is doomed.

—I can't help you. I am leaving now.

—Will you take a letter in to Commodore McCauley?

—He's been relieved, gentlemen, and I can tell you now it would be a waste of time for you to beg anything of Hiram Paulding. I cannot discuss his intentions with you, but my advice to you is to go home and start wetting down your roofs.

But though his tone was hard, he could not help sympathizing with them. Cheek by jowl as the yard was, firing it would most likely set fire to the town as well. He shook it off, and simply said again, — I am sorry, gentlemen, I can neither admit you nor plead your case. This is a military matter.

They called out to him, raised their voices, at last cursing and threatening him; but he did not reply. Simply touched his hat to them, turned his back, and joined the marines and bluejackets who stood silent and waiting in the garden. Said to Schuyler, —Have your men charged their muskets, Lieutenant? Very well, then. Port your arms, and follow me at the double time.

Merrimack was going down, Eli thought. No doubt about that. He looked across at the glossy black sides, filled with horror at the waste and the shame. Her gunports were only inches above the motionless black water.

—She's only four years old, said Babcock, and the old gunner's tone was as horrified as his own. —Forty Dahlgren shell guns behind them ports. Not a ship in Europe she can't batter to pieces.

—Maybe we can save her, Gunner.

—She's powerful low in the water, sir. But I guess we can try.

—Come on, Wilkes yelled, waving them aboard, and the party stumbled across the brow, *Owanee*'s men staggering beneath the burdens they'd carried and rolled down the waterfront.

—Eaker, was that your name? You and the warrant, get below. Find the sea cocks. Close them, or plug them if they've been broken off. I'll look into the moorings.

Telling Babcock to follow, Eli pounded across the quarterdeck and plunged down the companionway, pausing only to touch a lucifer to a lantern he found hanging from a hook. The ladders led into deepening darkness. Spar deck, gun deck, berth deck. He reached the orlop to find a Styx-dark lake shimmering at his boots. The lantern light played across its black oily surface, from which poked silent shafts and piston headers. The hull groaned around him.

Staring into that blackness, he said, turning his head, —Gunner, where would the sea cocks be under this? Can I find them underwater?

—Not a chance, sir, not in the dark. You'll never come up again.

—Do you know at least approximately where they might be?

Babcock hitched up his pants. —If I knew, I wouldn't tell you.

Eli was abruptly angry. —That is not a proper response. I must confess, Babcock, your attitude toward me falls short of the proper respect more often than otherwise.

The old gunner spat into the black water. He said scornfully, —Sorry, sir, but I've been in this man's navy for thirty years. How long you been wearin' the blue? Go ahead, dive in if you want. Anyway, the pumps are underwater too. She's on her way to her long home.

Eli considered saying more but decided this was neither the time nor the place to have it out. Still fuming, he climbed the ladder and reported to Wilkes. The captain nodded grimly. —I suspected as much, but we had to try.

—Leave her, sir?

—No. Burn her.

Eli watched him turn on his heel, and leave the ship he'd been ordered here to command.

—The combustibles have been placed, sir, if ya want to inspect, Babcock reported a few minutes later.

He'd arranged the turpentine tanks in a V leading forward from the mainmast, stove them in with axes, and wedged wads of cotton waste among them. The men had piled on ladders, gratings, hawser ends, anything that could nourish fire. Two barrels of pine spirits had been broached and their contents dumped down the companionway.

He hesitated. Paulding had said to wait for a rocket. But considering the confusion, cowardice, and incompetence he'd witnessed so far tonight, he doubted it would be sent up, or that anyone would be back to touch the match if it was.

He knelt, uncapped his lantern, and held it to the powder trail.

The blaze moved faster than a man could run. It climbed the rigging as quickly as it burrowed down into the ship. In seconds the gunports and aft cabin windows glared a harsh, vibrating yellow-gold.

From the pier, he watched the great ship wrap herself in flame. The waste and horror of it wrenched at his heart.

At least, he thought, *Merrimack* would be no use to the Confederates.

———

Running at the double time, Ker and Schuyler led *Owanee*'s sailors and marines down the long straight street that led through the center of the yard. Huge brick storehouses loomed up and slowly fell past.

Ker knew exactly where the powder magazines were. He'd loaded stores here many times for the old *Mississippi*. A string of handcars stood on a siding. He told Schuyler to appropriate a couple. A narrow-gauge rail line led from there down to the wharf, with a spur southward, toward the dry dock. The cars' wheels rolled hollow thunder down the stone-paved lane.

The copper-sheathed doors were locked, but he put Hanks to them with his boarding axe. A few minutes' work and the leathernecks swarmed in, pointing their rifles into the shadows. Schuyler shouted to them to get back out, not to touch their triggers or they'd blow every man there to hell. But at last a safety lamp was lit inside its heavy glass porting, and they stacked their Springfields and began carrying the hundred-pound casks out to the hand car. When one car was piled full Ker ordered the next rolled up. He called a halt when they had two tons of gunpowder loaded.

When they came out into the way again the popping of distant muskets bounced down from the sky. The clouds glowed a faint warm red, like hot iron-wool. The sailors set shoulders to the cars, and with a clack and a rumble set them in motion. The marines jogged alongside the rails, pointing their bayonets down each side alley.

Four hundred yards on they emerged from the huddle of buildings. An irregular shape to their left turned out to be a disorderly jumble of keelblocks and braces. Beyond was an oblong blackness Ker approached cautiously, feeling a chill of muck and stone and dank water like a ghost's breath in his face.

Emptiness opened below his boots, reminding him of the caldera of an extinct volcano he'd inspected in the Azores. Massive blocks of granite made a giant's staircase all the way to the bottom. The growing light glinted off pools of water far below.

—Where you want this powder, Cap'n?

He jerked his head up, to meet the gunner's bloodshot gaze. Hanks stared back, directly into his eyes, like a white man. He pointed to the lock end, toward the blackness of river beyond. —The lock gate's the vulnerable point. Should be a culvert down there, where the pumps are installed. If we destroy that, it'll take years to put this dock back into service.

The Negro took a long look downward. —You sure you wants to blow it up?

—Those are your orders. Just carry them out, if you please.

—Yessah. Just want to make sure. He got his arms around the first cask, rolled it off the car, and swung it in one easy motion up onto his back. —All right, you sojers there, start toting them casks. Rest of you, grab some dry boards off that there pile and follow me.

It took Cal some considerable time to get to the bottom of the dock. Behind him the others descended cautiously, picking their way like cats down a tree.

It felt like he was being swallowed by some great beast. That was what he felt like, Jonah man being swallowed by Leviathan. The wet-darkened stone rose gradually into the sky as he worked his way down, bent under the weight of the cask, setting his boots carefully on the slippery granite ledges. Behind him, two on a barrel, the marines cursed as their feet slipped. He tensed, held his breath. Bounce one of them kegs of powder sixty feet down off rock and you'd have yourself a taste of Hellfire right here on earth.

Behind him Captain Claiborne said something anxiously to one of the white sailors. Cal didn't turn his head. Find the lock gates, the captain had said, and a culvert. That's your orders. Just carry them out.

Aye aye, cap'm sir.

At the bottom of the dry dock huge granite blocks interlocked to form the floor. Chunks of adzed wood lay about, looking like hacked-apart bodies in the red half-light. Cal walked across the openness, boots splashing through puddles of rainwater. The great wicket gates rose ahead. He thought of the river they held back, how fast it would crush the human fleas crawling down here.

He wondered what Pharaoh's charioteers had thought, the moment before the sea crashed in on them.

A black gap opened gradually ahead. A hole, a tunnel, drilled back under the stone mountain that gripped the gate. He hung back. He didn't like being closed in. Then he grunted in disgust at himself and put down the cask on a dry spot and scrambled up and in.

Bent over, hunched forward, darkness closed on his open eyes as he groped in, fingers crab-searching over rough stone. Till his turtled head banged into solid oak, and push as he might gave no way past or through.

He scuttled back toward open air, relieved, and jumped down to the wet floor of the dock. The captain called from above, —Is there room for this much powder?

—B'lieve we can pack it all in there, sir. He heard a grinding and jerked his head around and yelled, —No, you fool! Roll that cask, you'll send us all up the spout. Get two jacks inside and we'll hand 'em in. Stove in one of 'em. Careful, now. Use the butt end of one of them keelblocks, don't want no sparks. Switzer, bring those boards over here.

The men moved fast loading the powder. Maybe it was that now and then they heard a shot echo down, reverberating between the stone walls. Or maybe from knowing the ship would leave at dawn, and the sky was growing light. It was a funny light, though, brighter and with more flicker to it than the dawn.

—That's the last, 'ceptin' for the one you got there, said the sergeant, dusting his hands and backing away. —Goin' to take my boys up out of here now. All right?

Cal nodded absently and laid hands on the breached barrel. Plunged a hand down into the dense, gritty grains, as he thought about how to do it.

Water killed gunpowder. So he couldn't lay the train on the wet stone.

The planks were the answer. He lay one from the culvert down to the ground, then another cocked up to the first level of stone wall. Taking a double handful of black grains, large as corn kernels but heavier, denser, he rubbed them out between his palms, gradually stretching a black rope down the middle of the plank.

A foot splash, and he glanced up to see Claiborne and Schuyler coming toward him through the puddles. —How long'll this train burn? the captain asked.

—Going to use a slow match with her, suh. Give us about an hour. You don't need to stay for the lighting, Cap'n.

He took the coil of slow match out of his blouse and stretched it, working his fingers along its length. Splices or kinks would stop the crawling fire. He took out his knife and sawed the end off square, then thrust it into the powder train.

He glanced up again, to find the officers still there. —It is my duty to see all is done properly, the captain said.

—Nothing left but to strike fire. I was you, sir, I'd both of you head up top out'n the way. Case of a stray spark or such as that. No point riskin' more souls than we got to.

—You may be right at that. Claiborne bent for one last examination; then seemed to make up his mind. —Let's clear out, Lieutenant. Gunner Hanks here will close the ball.

The scuff of shoe leather faded as they retreated. He glanced up to see them outlined against a pale rose sky.

All right now, Mr. Negro who ain't good enough to captain a gun. They have finally found something you good enough to do for them. Oh, yes.

Holding the fuze clear of the powder train, he scratched a lucifer on the side of the cask. It took with a hiss and sputter like a threatened cat.

The question is, you going to do what they wants? Is you going to blow up this yere dry dock like they say?

Holding the burning match cupped in his hand, he sat back on his heels and thought about it.

So let us say you do. And that them rebels can't do nothing without it, can't fix they ships or build ary new ones; and so two–three months from now the navy sails back, carrying army with them, and brings these men who believe they are above the law of God and even the minky justice of the white government back to the fold. Yeah, back they come to the starry flag, just like ever it was, and them still holding death-tight to their plantations and their womens and the grinding heat and sun of the fields, stretching on and on to ever more thousands of black folks' backs bent in everlasting pain.

That what the comet meant, pointed like a sword toward cursed Egypt? Or did the Lord who deliver those Israelites, all them years ago, have in mind something else?

Did he have in mind that the Union come back, yet all else go on like always?

Or did he want war and plague, on and on to ruin; the wrath of the destroying angel poured out on all the firstborn?

You tell me what, Lord. You give me the word, like you did ole Moses. Want me to blow her up? Or want me to let her go, let her help these rebellers out till it comes on war, real war, war that'll make the white Yankees look around for some reason they shedding their blood like water? And what reason could that be?

Only and ever freedom for every living soul under that cut and bleeding flag.

The fuze whispered to him in stuttering crackles. He held it between the massive pads of thumb and forefinger, head cocked, till it sizzled into his flesh. Then held it still, till fire seared every nerve and he came close to crying out.

—Gone cut de feather, he whispered. —Stronger'n red oak lye.

But it wasn't no loa talking to him, or any spirit, least as far as he could tell. It was just seeing sudden and clear how it had to be. How there was no other way it *could* be. Like as if always in his life before he was trying to pilot through sea fog, so thick you couldn't see the end of the bowsprit. But now just for a second or two it was somehow given to him to see plain and clear, like from the foretop on a blue day way out ahead to the far-off horizon of how things would be.

And maybe he thought then, tranced and his hand shaking, shaking, as the fire gnawed toward the bone, maybe it *was* some spirit or angel taking him; because just for a moment he could see them, the two ways stretching out ahead of him. And on the one, the starry flag again, and quick peace, and the thousands of bent black backs. And on the other, more thousands.

Only these, dead.

Only these, thousands of bodies, white and black alike, lying dead on the ground, floating in the sea, in the river, scattered through woods and forest. The dirty smoke of cannons. A grim smile came to his face as he looked out over it. To where, sure as hell out there, through the shifting haze of future time, there were the two ways his people could go in this land; all to be free, or all to die; 'cause there was no other way. They couldn't be slaves no longer. The time for that was over.

And right here, right now, held in his shaking fingers, was the split twig in time that led down them two different ways to two so different ends.

With a sudden sweep of his arm, he dashed it into a gap between two massive stones. The fuse spat and jumped in the water like a dying rattler.

Then it went out.

He kicked the board over, dumping the powder train into the churned-up muck at the bottom of the dock. Sat a moment more panting, head down. Then sprang up and ran with mock-frantic haste, waving his arms in warning, toward the officers who waited above.

The steam gauge read a fraction under ten pounds. Standing in front of the boiler front, Theo stared at it, gnawing at a fat blister on his under lip. Ten pounds per square inch was barely enough to turn the engines at dead slow, and then only if the condenser was giving him a hard vacuum. On the other hand, the pressure had held more or less constant for some minutes now.

With a rattle and a scrape and a Gaelic curse, grimy biceps and square-bladed coal shovels shot another charge of fuel onto the grates. He drew a sweat-and-ash-streaked arm across his face. The temperature in the engine spaces was a hundred and climbing. The pump clattered and vibrated. A leak hissed. He studied the glass a few seconds more, then crossed the boiler room and spun a valve wheel free. A blast of live steam tornadoed out, deafening him, filling the compartment with whirling ghostvapor and a stink like scorched wool. He let it bleed off for three seconds, then cranked the line closed and checked the gauge again.

—Quarterdeck, he yelled into the speaking tube.

—Aye.

—It's Hubbard. Captain up there?

—Captain went ashore. Mr. Duycker's left in charge.

—Tell him B boiler's holding ten pounds. No promises how long. I can give him one bell. Maybe close to two, for a little while.

—Quarterdeck aye. A rattle as the plug went in, and he reinserted his. The firemen glanced up at him, sweating rivers as they dug their shovels once more into the bunkers that opened to either side, seagoing mines into which they tunneled. He wiped his face with his bandanna, and returned his fascinated attention to the shimmering, perking, trembling, and delicate line of silver mercury trapped and shivering in the glass.

The ship houses were burning. Millions of board feet of dry old pine kindled such prodigious torches that as Eli led the scuttling party back toward the wharf he could see every cobblestone beneath his boots. Beyond the great arched structures, back among what Babcock told him were timber sheds, boathouses, rope walks, warehouses of ship's stores and food, the flames were rising too. The other parties, the army troops and *Cumberland* men, had been at work. Great writhing palls drifted off to the southward. Leading the column at double time onto a causeway over a fitting-out dock, he saw *Owanee* lit up ahead, every detail of gunline and top rigging glowing in the ruddy light as if on stage at Niblo's Garden. But beyond her the river swallowed all in blackness, so she wavered in the firelight as if illuminated before a bombazine curtain.

To his surprise he'd only coughed a little all night long, and he didn't feel tired at all. Just now he felt like he could run forever. Maybe he was feverish. Or maybe this was the furor of battle he'd read about. Where every minute seemed like a year, where destruction became sublime, where fear vanished and a man became a hero despite himself.

His chest swelled. Leading his men, he knew he would never die.

An iron clangor jerked his head around. In the firelight hundreds of troops and marines and sailors labored over recumbent forms that after a moment he recognized as heavy guns. As the hammers fell a mournful tolling rose like a city full of leaden bells. Others carried armfuls of rifles and pistols down to the water. Men raced about, some carrying torches, others rifles, still others fizzing flares that they tossed into buildings, the fusees wheeling through the air blazing off circular veils of sparks and the gay blue smoke smell of Fourth of July fireworks.

Yet still he saw no sign of an enemy.

As they trotted back toward the ship a rifle crack pulled his attention toward the buildings that had not yet begun to burn. A soldier yelled a warning about sharpshooters. He wondered then how much longer they'd stay. Fiery timbers were rumbling down inside the burning ship houses, knocking up great geysers of embers that rained slowly down among the moored-out ships. He remembered the leaking turpentine aboard *Owanee*.

Suddenly his fervor a moment before seemed childish. If anything happened to the ship, they were stranded. He didn't relish the thought of being here when day came, in a hornet's nest of enraged rebels. He searched anxiously ahead for the sloop. There she was, still alongside, though smoke was jetting from her funnel and he could see crewmen on the pier singling up her lines.

So that when a party of men clambered up onto the wharf, his squad was almost on them before the two groups noticed each other.

At the same moment a steam whistle screamed out over the river. *Owanee* was calling her scattered children back.

—Hey, who's these boys now? said Babcock angrily. Eli held up a hand, and the party jogged to a confused halt close behind him.

The men ahead straightened, having tied off their boat to a piling. They wore dark blue uniforms, but without belt buckles or caps. They carried pistols and rifles.

—You there. Identify yourselves, he shouted in as martial a voice as he could manage, sweat-soaked, smeared with tar and dirt, surrounded by fire and destruction.

—Hallo, one of them called. —We are the Portsmouth Rifles, of the Third Virginia Volunteer Regiment. Governor Letcher has ordered us to take possession of this yard. You are our prisoners.

—The devil we are, he yelled, thinking: So here they were. The secessionists, face-to-face at last. But they did not lift their arms to aim; nor did the sailors behind him. His hand dropped to his revolver butt, but stopped there. They wore his own uniform, spoke his own speech, a little softer, that was all. —Disperse, gentlemen. Get in your boat and leave. I don't want blood shed here.

And they must have felt the same uncertainty, the same disconcertion as to enemy or countryman, because for a long moment no one moved or spoke, there on the wharf. They simply looked at each other, sweaty faces flickering in the fiery light.

Babcock stepped up next to him. The old gunner called, —You fellers heard what Mr. Eaker here said. Go home, get out of here peaceful.

—This here is Virginia property.

—Oh, like hell it is, Babcock shouted back. This here's *navy* property.

—You won't surrender? God damn you, then. One of the Portsmouth men whipped his pistol up, and to Eli's horror he saw that it was aimed directly at him.

A flash, a report, and he heard the ball thud home. Not into his own body, though, but into a stocky frame that had stepped to the left, throwing out its arms, directly in front of him.

The sailors jerked their carbines up and returned a ragged volley.

He pulled his Colt free and cocked and triggered madly. The flashes seared his eyes. The noise seemed to dent in his eardrums with huge blunt points. Thick white smoke, glowing saffron orange in the firelight, drifted off behind them. Then the hammer clicked on a dead cap, and he drew his saber and ran forward, yelling until his throat ripped raw and he stumbled to his knees, coughing helplessly in the sulphurous cloud.

When the smoke blew clear the wharf planks lay empty once again. The militia, or whatever they were, had jumped down into their boat, cast off, and were pulling for the darkness. The firelight rendered them still visible, though, and his sailors, who had dropped to their knees and reloaded with much swearing and clanging of ramrods, rose again and blazed after them with their Maynards till the straining oarsmen blended back into the night.

He stood fumbling with his revolver, attempting to reload the cylinder, but he kept dropping the ball. His fingers jerked and trembled and would not obey. Finally he thrust it back into his belt uncapped.

—Sir, the gunner's down, one of the men yelled.

—Oh Christ. He bent over Babcock. —Thomas, are you right?

—Only a scratch, sir. Took a lot worse than this in Panama.

But pulling up the warrant gunner's blouse, he saw that blood covered the tattooed chest, pumping forth body-hot beneath his hand, gleaming black as tar in the ruddy light. He sat back, striking his fists on his knees. Why had he waited? He should have fired first. Instead he'd gaped at the intruders like a mooncalf.

—You took that ball for me, he said.

Babcock barely opened his eyes. —You ain't much, he muttered. —But I take care o' my officers.

—We can't leave him 'ere, sir, said Archbold.

—Of course not. We'll get him back to Dr. Steele. Take him up. Gently, now.

They found the gig standing by opposite where *Pennsylvania* was burning, and tumbled in, sliding Babcock carefully onto the bilge-boards. As they pulled past the receiving ship the heat lit their exposed skin, so near and scorching he had to shield his cheek with one hand. The other gripped the gunner's, who blinked up calmly into the flickering sky as the men rowed. Great white-hot flames were pouring up out of the old three-decker's gunports.

A shot boomed out, scattering sparks, and he realized the guns aboard the deserted battleship were still loaded. They were pointed directly over the gig. He was glad when the floating furnace finally fell astern.

When they bumped alongside, Captain Wilkes's craggy visage peered down. —Get aboard at once, Wilkes called. —We are getting under way to tow *Cumberland* out. Send that boat back for Commodore McCauley.

As Eli scrambled up the boarding ladder he saw old Girnsolver staring out to landward. So were the troops. They lined the rail with expressions of awed rapture. As he reached the sheer strake he turned, intending to bear a hand with Babcock, but froze, transfixed like the others.

The shore was a surging storm of flame, the ship houses pyres so bright he could no more look steadily at them than at the sun. Behind those enormous cones of white fire, storehouses pulsed red within sooty columns of smoke. To the south *Germantown, Merrimack,* and the older ships along Rotten Row were patches of concentrated flame. Closer at hand, fire streamed out from the gunports and open companions of the *Pennsylvania.*

—It is utter destruction, he breathed.

He realized he'd spoken it aloud only when Wilkes, beside him at the bulwark, answered, —I am very much afraid that we have brought this on ourselves. All those years of promoting seniority, rather than fighting men and daring mariners.

He turned his head, and was astonished to see tears glittering on the explorer's face. He stammered, —At least we've left nothing of use.

Wilkes laughed sardonically. —Nothing of use? There are two thousand guns in the ordnance sheds. We knocked the trunnions off six of the older ones, but the Dahlgrens and Parrotts are unmarked.

That's enough modern artillery to arm every fort in the South. We may just have lost this war tonight, my lad.

—I cannot believe that, sir. We'll be back in a week with more troops, and recapture all.

—I am glad you are so sanguine. I confess, I am not.

—All hands, stations to get under way, Duycker shouted. Eli turned away, and saw Shippy drawing a blanket over a motionless body. Dr. Steele knelt nearby, thrusting cruel-looking tools back into a canvas bag.

Eli knelt. He took Babcock's rough hand, with some confused idea of saying he was sorry, with some confused idea of saying thanks. To his surprise, for he had never really thought he cared for the man, a tear fell on the tattooed image of a straddle-thighed whore. But the old gunner's callused fingers, hard and unyielding as oak, were already cold.

29

A LATE Saturday afternoon, and Broadway was thronged with home-goers and the first of the night's revelers. Ara sat waiting on one of the chairs one rented in City Hall Park for a penny an hour. She wore a plain brown overdress with black riding cape and gloves. The seats were filthy, and some of the other women called invitations to men walking by. She sat erect, spine six inches from the back of the chair, gripping her fingers in her lap. The air was warm, but she was glad of the muff. It hid her shaking hands, at any rate.

—These seats are rather common, she said.

—I certainly agree, said Mrs. Lispenard, beside her. —But they are better than strolling back and forth in public.

One of the passersby, bedraggled, tieless, in scuffed brogans, halted to inspect the merchandise. She looked past him, toward the red-and-white striped awnings of the shops. Mrs. Lispenard dealt with the situation differently. She motioned sharply with a gloved hand, a sign that after a moment Ara recognized as a variant of Repulsion. He grunted, spat beside their gaiters, and moved on.

The Third Avenue car rumbled by, drawn by mismatched chestnuts who labored with their heads dropped. She thought guiltily of El Cid. She'd not ridden him since her return from the Tombs. The stable would exercise him, but she still felt as if she was neglecting the massive black.

But he'd never really been hers, had he? Not even the clothes she wore were her own. She clenched her fists inside the muff as a shoal of black-haired children ran past shrieking in some foreign language, followed by a trotting crone with shawl drawn about a face like a dried apple. She watched them leap about, screaming and chasing one another. Her uncle hated immigrants. He said they threatened the Republic and spread disease. She found it hard to imagine these shabby, docile people threatening anything. As for disease, the children looked healthy as little foxes, though their shoes were falling off their feet.

She remembered the frozen child again, the one they'd found on their doorstep. How glad the poor must be that spring had come!

—My dear Miss Van Velsor.

She looked up to see Mr. Phelps raising his hat, smiling in the sunlight. An opal-and-silver stickpin glinted in his lapel. He wore not a stodgy bowler, like the clerks lined up for the cars, but a slouch hat. He smiled under her inspection, and she lowered her eyes. Should she blush?

—Mrs. Lispenard, may I present Mr. Ellery Phelps, a close friend of my uncle's. Mr. Phelps has interests in Albany.

—Mrs. Lispenard. I believe I may know your family.

—I sincerely hope you do not.

The political man laughed. He stirred the grass between the ladies' boots with the tip of his cane. —Indeed?

—Lispenard is my *nom de théâtre*, Mr. Phelps. As I am certain Phelps is not your real name.

—It is sobering to find my incognito so easily penetrated.

Ara saw that though Harriet was past thirty, she'd deftly gained center stage in Phelps's interest. She wasn't jealous. Harriet was on her side, and they'd planned the evening as carefully as Caesar ever a campaign. But she admired how effortlessly the older woman had done it. Truly, she had much to learn.

She cleared her throat and Phelps turned back to her. —Miss Van Velsor, you look particularly lovely today, out in the open air.

—Is it not delightful? Such a change from our miserable weather just past.

He dropped her hand as he straightened from his bow. Past him a cabriolet was waiting at the curb. The leather hood was up despite the warmth, and a sprightly, intelligent-looking roan stared straight at her. Its driver, reading the *Police Gazette* with muddy boots propped on the apron, did not look nearly as clever or as interested in the world about him.

—Your conveyance, sir?

—I must confess it is not. My wife has taken our carriage to Arcadia for the weekend. This rig belongs to a gentleman connected to the New York Stock Exchange. In fact he is the vice treasurer.

—Arcadia, as Longfellow's?

—Arcadia, as in north of town. She has a lady friend with a cottage in Vandewater Heights.

—I had not meant for you to deprive yourself of your wife's company for mine.

Phelps raised his eyebrows. He straightened, looked right and left, stroking his mustache. Then lifted his hat. —I don't think of it as a sacrifice. Will you ladies accompany me on a ride to the Central Park?

Mrs. Lispenard smiled steadily but did not reply. Ara took a breath, not quite able to meet his eyes. She said, still looking down, —I had another destination in mind, if you are open to an adventure.

She directed him uptown, and the roan left Broadway at Forty-second and clop-clopped toward the North River. The rumble of traffic stilled behind them as they moved into a quiet, narrow street.

The house bore no sign or indication it was anything other than a private residence. Mrs. Lispenard leaned forward and tapped the driver with her fan, and he lifted the reins and the horse trotted them to the curb. Phelps leaned out, looking up at the brownstone.

—Our mysterious destination?

—The same. You might tell your man we could be here for some time.

—Sean, I see a tavern at the end of the street. Here is a trifle for your trouble. I will expect you to be master of yourself when we send for you.

—Yes sir, Mr. Phelps. Touching his cap with his whip, taking the money.

Phelps shook his head, smiling faintly, and helped the two ladies down. He very nearly lifted her, he was quite strong. She felt the added pressure of his hand, but kept her eyes lowered and did not return it.

Mrs. Lispenard rang the bell. The door opened a few inches, showing darkness within. She held whispered converse with someone inside, and it yielded a bit more.

The vestibule was dark. A window above the door admitted a soft ray of blue light through deep cobalt glass, but it was immediately absorbed by the heavy folds of tapestries hung from brass rods. The thick weaving gave the room a hushed feel. It smelled of patchouli and, beneath that, of some lingering, resinous scent, not quite pine and not quite incense, but akin to both.

It took some time in the dimness for her to discern the little man bowing before them. He was elderly, shrunken nearly to the size of a child. A vapory beard curled against his robe. His mandarin cap had an onyx button at the crest. His upper body hunched forward, as if he'd been snapped in two and carelessly reglued. He said nothing, but accepted Mrs. Lispenard's overdress and hat and took them into an alcove. Then returned for Ara's outer garments and, last, for Phelps's. He gestured to a row of list slippers on the floor.

—I say, Phelps whispered. —Precisely what sort of place is this?

Mrs. Lispenard murmured, —One complies with the customs of the house, Mr. Phelps. Or one does not enjoy its perquisites.

Ara took the brocaded robe the attendant held out to her. Her heart was beating rapidly. She did not trust herself to speak. Glimpsed in an ormolu mirror, her dim image was startlingly pale.

When they were robed and shod, the Celestial gestured them toward a staircase of black mahogany, with curious carvings in the Japanese manner. At first glance they appeared to be of intertwined vines, interspersed with fruits. But at a closer inspection, animals and birds lurked amid the foliage, and the leaves themselves were peculiarly individuated, one wilted, another etiolated, a third showing fine pinholes where a borer had gnawed. As they ascended the carpeted steps music seeped from the walls, the strains so muffled and indistinct as to be indistinguishable almost from silence.

Mrs. Lispenard paused at a double door. —You may be startled by what you see, Mr. Phelps. I confess I was, when I was introduced to this . . . chamber, and its occupants. Yet those whose hearts are pure need fear nothing on earth or beneath the earth.

—I submit to your direction, fair Beatrice.

The door opened, and suddenly the obscurity that had followed them from the vestibule to the upper landing was replaced by light.

The interior was one enormous space. A marble fountain bubbled in its center. The footing was Persian carpets so thick and soft their entering steps were noiseless. Braids of incense smoke streamed up in the corners, freighting the sultry air with an enervating perfume. The light came from candles, flickering within globes of ruby glass. Wheeled shades were suspended above them in a cunning fashion, and Ara saw that the upyielding air turned dangling mirrors, sending a thousand scintillating flecks moving and searching about like fireflies. Chinese silks depended from the ceiling, housing them beneath a vast and opulent tent. Luxurious divans were set along the walls. Some were occupied, others invitingly empty. Most of their occupants were ladies. Many wore dominoes. Above them mirrors leaned out, reflecting the searching light, the patterned hangings, the vermilion candle globes, giving back a hundred rooms, a thousand reclining occupants, universe upon universe opening out endlessly in an ever-moving kaleidoscope. She could hear the music now, though its source was still hidden, a soft play of harp and some Oriental instrument endlessly interwoven in a bewildering pattern that both puzzled and charmed the ear.

Phelps said, —A scene from some exotic painting, surely. Perhaps a Delacroix—

—Exactly so: *The Death of Sardanapalus,* is it not? You are acquainted with Mr. Delacroix's scandalous work, Mr. Phelps?

—I am a scandalous man, Mrs. Lispenard. Yet I confess you have shown me a new thing under the sun. I had heard such venues existed in our city. But one needs a personal introduction, it appears.

Ara had to speak. The byplay with Harriet was becoming too close. She moved closer to Phelps. —I've seen that painting too. Or a print of it.

—Indeed?

—I must confess my curiosity was aroused.

When he looked intrigued she took his hand and drew him, not toward the divans but to an alcove a few steps off. It contained a comfortable-looking scatter of brocade-worked cushions, more rugs, and a small ebony table upon which a scarlet candle burned with an elongated, smoking flame. As they sank into the cushions, she heard Mrs. Lispenard murmuring to a mulatto boy in a Turkish fez.

Phelps lowered his gaze from a caged nightingale. —Your friend's an interesting woman.

—Let us speak no more of her. We are alone together. As you requested, in your note.

—As you wish. I was most . . . intrigued by our correspondence. You are a puzzle to me, Miss Van Velsor.

She took off her glove, hovered her palm over the candle. —We've progressed to "Araminta" and "Ellery" in our correspondence. Why not in person?

He was leaning against the cushions, arms locked behind his head, staring at her frankly now. She took a breath and went on, trying to keep her voice from shaking. —I must confess, I find you intriguing. You are handsome. You are powerful, as the world counts power. I will not deny I am quite young. Nor that it was difficult to fashion a situation in which we could be alone together. You run a risk being here, I imagine.

—Not nearly so great as the one you undertake, Miss . . . Araminta. It is not customary for respectable young ladies to frequent such locales as this.

—You disapprove?

—I did not say that. Certainly one must accept risk, at times, to obtain what one desires. His eyes ran down her robe, lingered where her slippers emerged.

She nearly tucked them back under her, then remembered what she was here for. She leaned back, stretching like a cat. —I have thought of you often since you came to our home.

He moved closer to her on the cushions, and she lifted her head. Mrs. Lispenard had told her how lovely her neck was. The alcove seemed curiously hot. He seemed about to speak when the boy entered, silently placing a tray between them. Enameled in the Arab manner, it bore minuscule cups of an aromatic tea that steamed in the heavy air, adding its spicy fragrance to the drifting smoke. A silver dish held several waxy-looking lozenges. He eyed them, then her again.

—More and more astonishing. Are you an habitué of this house?

—I've been here only once before. It's not easy to slip away from my . . . dull and cloistered life, as the ward of the great financier.

—Your friend's not joining us?

—She'll be in another room.

—Indeed. And what are these?

—They're made from the hemp resin, with cocoa, honey, opium, and a small quantity of henbane. She plucked one up and held it to his lips. With an inclination of his head and a faint smile, he opened his mouth and she popped it in.

—You do not indulge?

She selected a pale yellow tablet. Harriet had advised her they contained the least potent tincture of the drug. While those of deeper hue, like old amber, contained the most powerful narcotic.

They lay back for several minutes, not speaking.

Gradually the room dissolved into separate shapes, each so significant and meaningful in itself that it would repay years of study. The candle flame was a living being, a messenger sent to tell her of transcendental existence. Fortunately she had decades, she had centuries in which to lend them her fascinated attention. In the midst of it she found his eyes, locked with hers across a million miles of space. The objects around her vibrated with consciousness, and wisdom, and more than earthly meaning, but his eyes held none. It was the strangest thing. There was nothing behind his eyes at all.

She came back from innumerable millennia of reverie to feel Phelps's hands passing slowly over her body. She felt their pressure, warmth, through the thin fabric, but no sensation beyond. She'd felt nothing since the night she'd discovered she could lock her bedroom door and her uncle might knock, he might call in to her, but if she did not open he could not come in ever again, never again.

She blinked slowly up at the reeling color, at the milling coruscating vibration of which all that had being was made. Through all shapes, all hues, flowed the same golden light, refracted and split apart, recombined into a million forms and actions, but beneath and supporting all that seemed so solid in waking time. It only took different forms. Some were ugly, squalid, or tragic, but only to those who did not see the singing oneness beneath. She was made of it. Phelps was made out of it, although he didn't know. The old Chinaman. Down to the most humble thing on earth.

A great pink blob came between her and the light. It took several seconds before she realized it was Phelps. His cheeks and forehead were rosy. The ends of his mustache hung down.

When he lifted his lips from hers he whispered, —Is it possible that we may become more than friends?

She searched her mind for what she'd meant to say. It seemed unimportant now. What did it matter where she went, or what she tried to do? The pure light shone through all, eternal and reassuring. But at last she remembered. She could see the words emerging from her lips, like colored bubbles. —I have the greatest respect for you, Ellery. You are a man of power. A man of affairs. I find that very exciting.

—I'm not sure what you want, Araminta. Whether you are proposing what I think.

—I may be a maiden, Ellery, but I cannot remain one forever.

—You know that I am married. We should have to be discreet.

—Is this not discreet? I know you are what is called a man of the world. That such beings as women are not unknown to you.

—Yes, I know women. I know all humanity. *Humani nil a me alienum puto.* Terence. And I know that for every boon there is a price. What do you want of me, Araminta? What cost, to possess such beauty?

She didn't answer. He bent, and again she endured the unpleasant taste of his mouth, the greasy scratch of his mustache. It smelled of stale wax and dead cigars. But she held the kiss, wondering through the hashish enchantment at her own coolness.

She knew women did not enter into lovemaking as the male did. They yielded from importunity, from necessity, from duty in the bonds of marriage. Perhaps that was why she felt so cloven from herself. Split into the body that reclined, offering up a white softness that he gradually uncovered, laying apart the folds of the robe, then manipulating her buttons, her stays. And on the other hand the spectator, observing, detached, as if the one who watched through her eyes were not herself but another person, far away, and much older.

He raised his face from her breast. To her astonishment tears sparkled in his eyes. —You're so beautiful. A young goddess. An angel. Is it possible you should return my devotion?

Past him she saw the emotionless visage of the mulatto boy peering in. She whispered, —If you desire privacy here, the portiere may be drawn.

He looked down at her, and for that moment she was afraid.

Afraid he'd seen something she had not meant him to see. But he didn't seem to. Or if he did, accepted it, accepted that the price he had mentioned would someday fall due. As he rose his slipper entangled itself in one of the tasseled cushions. He shook it free impatiently and swept the heavy curtain across. The fountain, the lounging ladies, the splendor vanished, and they lay alone together in a fragrant darkness.

30

WHEN Ker got back to the ship Nick Duycker was on the forecastle supervising the men, taking aboard a heavy hawser from the *Cumberland*. The exec said Commodore Paulding had sent a runner ordering them to prepare to take the flagship in tow.

He stood rooted, wondering why they were rescuing *Cumberland* and not *Merrimack*, before he remembered McCauley had scuttled the steamer. Then another difficulty occurred to him. —We can't tow anyone, First. We still don't have steam.

—Hubbard's patched things up. Says he can give us slow ahead, at least for a while.

Captain Wilkes came striding down the deck, hair flying. He saw Ker and snapped, —Lieutenant Claiborne. You were assigned the dry dock, were you not? You will warrant it is settled for?

—It is, sir. Two tons of powder. He fumbled for his watch. — About thirty minutes yet until it goes off.

—Very well, you had better be clear by then. I'm going back ashore.

—You're not leaving with us, sir?

397

—Don't worry about me. As soon as you complete preparations to tow, take in your lines and get under way. And keep a sharp lookout, it smells like fog out there.

Ker saluted and followed him to the gangway. Then stood looking at the flames.

The nearest ship house was barely eighty yards away, just across the wharf and a short patch of worn earth from the sloop's side. Its heat seared his cheeks. Sparks floated in a long veil above it. Each time the wind dropped they fell like burning snow through her rigging to *Owanee*'s deck. Men stamped them out, those who were shod; others carried sand buckets and doused the glowing embers where they lay.

He reached out and felt the mizzen staysail sheet. Its pine-tar dressing was softening, hot to the touch on the side facing the flames.

It was a sublime sight, but it was madness, it was all madness, this wanton destruction the work of Bedlamites. Part of him still seemed to be back at the gate, listening to men who spoke with the timbre and accent of his own voice. Reasonable men who pleaded for moderation and for safety, for people's homes and families and the safety of property.

The exec cleared his throat, and Ker recalled his wandering thoughts. —All right, then, Mr. Duycker. All hands back to quarters.

The rumble of the drum brought those below topside. At the same time, as if called by the tattoo, the marines came marching down out of the yard. As they came they broke ranks to throw torches into those buildings as yet unignited. They fell in on the wharf under the rain of embers, amid the massive roar of the flames.

Schuyler stumbled up the brow, coughing. The marine's face was smeared with soot. He drew himself up stiffly. —Sir! Reporting back aboard. My men are mustering on the pier.

—Very well. Have you seen Commodore Paulding?

—He's still at Quarters A. McCauley's making some difficulty about coming with us.

—Difficulty? What difficulty?

—He won't leave. Keeps saying he wants to die at his post. He's quite drunk, of course. If I may say so.

—Well, the other senior officers will have to deal with him. My orders are to stand out into the stream. Get your men aboard as soon as your muster's complete. Put them below, please; I will need the decks clear to handle the tow cables and the guns.

Hubbard trotted across the quarterdeck. A red bandanna was wound around his head. Ker ignored the unorthodox uniform. He said rapidly, —Hubbard, you can give us steam?

—Give me five more minutes and I can answer two bells on one boiler.

—No chance of more power? I've been ordered to tow *Cumberland* clear as well.

—We're lucky to have that. Boiler A's played out. I jury-rigged a patch on B, but I can't tell you how long it'll hold.

Ker said grimly, —Very well. Go below and stand by for bells.

He recalled himself to the job at hand, and eyed the angle between the sailing sloop, out in the stream, and *Owanee*'s stern. Duycker had laid the hawser out along the wharf. The end made fast to their towing post was fended out on a spar to keep it from fouling the screw. He'd need to pivot outboard, pass astern of the anchored sailing sloop, and speak her to cut her cables as he went past. They'd pass close alongside the burning *Philadelphia*, from which an occasional shot still boomed across the flickering water. Then make a wide, low-speed turn, minimizing the strain on the cable and bringing the heads of both *Owanee* and her massive tow north again.

He wasn't thinking about the other thing. He couldn't, not now. His first obligation was to his ship.

Duycker saluted stiffly, gray hair sticking up from beneath his cap, and reported ready to get under way. Ker turned to nose the wind one last time, noticing a dank mist that smelled familiar . . . a morning fog brewing up. Wilkes was right. Well, it might serve their purpose, if they hoped to slip out of this snare with their pelts intact. He looked aloft, checking flying jib, staysails and spanker, the fore and aft sails that would do the most good close-hauled. He crossed to the bulwark, stepped up on the horse block, and swept his glance the length of the ship. The wind would glue her to the wharf; they'd do some damage getting under way, but that could not be helped. The heat was growing by the minute. —Port bower ready to let go, Nick?

—Bo's'ns standing by the pelican hook, sir.

—Very well, take in fore and aft. Ahead slow. Starboard your helm, and steer for the gap between *Cumberland* and *Pennsylvania.*

But instead of moving ahead, *Owanee* drifted astern when the last line came in, driven back by the river current.

She scraped to a stop directly opposite the burning ship house. The heat grew so intense men dropped on deck, curling beneath the bulwarks for shelter like scorched ants. He threw up his arm, feeling the radiated flame sear his flesh beneath the scorching wool of his uniform. A thin ghostly smoke began rising from the whole starboard side, from the rigging aloft, the sheets and halyards on the pinrail.

He looked up imploringly. The sails were shivering. Black smoke billowed from the stack. It barely rose before curving over and streaming landward, following the immense upward lift of flame-heated air building over the still-growing inferno of the yard. The artificial wind was pulling her slowly but inexorably backward, sucking her back into the flames.

—By God, we can't stay here, Duycker said.

Ker said dryly, —You are perfectly right in that observation, Exec. Hard astarboard your helm, and see if four bells makes any difference.

It seemed to, or perhaps Hubbard had been letting power build up gradually. The sloop lay motionless for thirty seconds, a minute, the forward push of the screw just balancing the backward ebb of the river. Then she began to inch ahead. The wharf slid past, slowly, but board by board the sloop gathered way through the moving tide-run. And as she advanced, the immense pyre finally fell astern, foot by foot, yard by yard.

As it drew away, the wind lessened, the mind-deadening roar retreated. He leaned on the pinrail, easing out a relieved breath. If those smoking sails had caught . . . but now Duycker was threading the needle between the moored-out warships. They passed under the lee of the burning guardo, but far enough away only a faint heat stroked his cheek. Then came about, pirouetting slowly in the firelit Elizabeth, and churned downriver, skipping the towline over the black water in a great seinelike loop.

—Engines stop, Duycker shouted. —Stand by the port anchor.

When she'd drifted to a stop and the anchor bottomed at short stay, he went to the side again, rubbing his scorched prickling face. The firelight reached across the river, lighting slowly thickening tendrils of mist rising from the black surface, lighting the shore opposite. He focused his sight wearily. Was that movement, over there? Or only the play of fire-shadows?

Then he remembered what those buildings were, not four hundred yards off across this narrow neck.

—Mr. Duycker: be so kind as to place your glass on the St. Helena gun range there. Do you detect any activity?

The point opposite was the gun depot and testing range, where new Dahlgrens and Parrotts from Pittsburgh foundries were fired across river and marsh to the southeast. There were most likely heavy weapons there now, complete with carriages, powder, shot, everything necessary to make things very hot indeed for a stationary vessel silhouetted against a mass of flame. Duycker lowered his glass, saying the leaping shadows made the eye imagine movement where there might not be any. Ker considered sending a spiking party across, but decided it was too late in the game. If *Owanee* came under fire from there, he'd simply have to sweep them with shell.

He realized another thing then, with a queer detached clarity: that any of those shells that went long would land in Norfolk.

He swung round and conned the Gosport waterfront. All afire now, from the ship houses all the way to the rope walks inland. Showers of sparks whirled into the air. Fortunately the wind was carrying most of them south, away from the town. He took out his watch. Ten more minutes. He didn't want to be here when the dry dock exploded. Two tons of powder would send stone and jagged iron flying for hundreds of yards.

He looked aft, to where boats and gigs and rowing tenders were still coming off, making their way across the fire-shining water like agitated water bugs. To his surprise, they were making for *Cumberland*. Then he understood; the sailing sloop was McCauley's flagship; Paulding, taking over command, was transferring his flag there.

As if to confirm it, signals fluttered up. Firelight lit them as distinctly as day. Blue, red, blue, and red-and-white. Eddowes read off from the signal book, —"Under way, to get: having regard to mutual convenience and safety."

Ker lifted his voice, —Very well; acknowledge. Mr. Duycker, one blast on the whistle. Boatswain! Bring in the anchor, handsomely, and hold at the cathead. Hands aft, stand clear the towing gear. Mr. Thurston! Into the quarter boat with our best leadsman. I shall want you to precede us, two hundred yards ahead. Mr. Schuyler, your best marksmen into the rigging to cover him.

The sloop's decks emptied as those who had so far occupied themselves with watching the fire scattered to their stations. Girnsolver reported the anchor aweigh. The engine began thumping. Sparks shot from the stack, drawing hot wires across the night. The hawser came up out of the water like a curious sea serpent. Ker was watching it when a rocket whished off the flagship's deck. It cometed upward, vanished, then, seconds later, exploded high above the river.

The ship quivered beneath his feet. A gentle quarter-wave drew itself out on the river. *Cumberland*'s bowsprit yawed around, responding to the steady pull. He asked the helmsman, —Have you way enough to steer?

—Think so, sir.

—Follow in the wake of the quarter boat. Mr. Eaker! Draw your shell on the forward pivot and recharge with grape.

He wanted grapeshot ready in case they were waylaid by small craft near the obstructions. Eaker requested permission to clear the bores by discharging the gun. Ker told him permission denied, to clear by hand. Shell could ricochet across water and flatland for miles. Portsmouth lay to their port hand, and on their starboard, as

Owanee churned her laborious way forward, the mist-cloaked lights of Norfolk were slowly emerging from behind the withdrawing land.

And like that gradual emergence, the realization he'd come to at the yard gate slowly became a fixed purpose. But he could not yet act on it. His ship and his men were not yet safe.

The firelight reached far out ahead, throwing their shadow black and threatening on the steadily thickening fog. The towering torches of the ship houses, behind them as they thumped onward slowly, so slowly, illuminated the merchant wharves and the vessels crouched alongside them, lit the town.

His hand trembled on the bulwark as the city drew nearer. For a moment he didn't understand why.

Then he did, because he'd read a story about what he suddenly felt. Poe, that adopted Virginian, had written it. He had met Poe's stepbrother once, a well-to-do Goochland County planter. A hearty, prosperous fellow, as different from the brooding, doomed tale weaver as a human being could well be.

It was the Imp of the Perverse who capered and grimaced by his side, who breathed into his ear as the helpless city passed slowly under his guns. The malignant spirit that urged one on to the unthinkable, in defiance of reason, of reflection, even of the deepest love.

For it *was* unthinkable, was it not? That one word from him would send a broadside of Hell into defenseless homes? Those lighted windows would be filled with people watching the immolation across the river, waked by the hollow roar of destruction. His own wife, his own child perhaps, watching him pass as a shadow in the night. He should not think such a thought. Even to conceive such a wish was the product of a disordered mind. But still the demon whispered! And the command trembled in his throat! Till he remembered the mournful writer's advice—*prostrate oneself backward from the abyss*— and swallowed hard and jerked his eyes away and rasped, —Helm astarboard now, Mr. Duycker! Sheet in all sails.

With the deliberate grace he'd always loved her for, and would miss so much, *Owanee* swung slowly to leeward, aligning herself with wind and channel to glide forward under suddenly filling sails. She leaned as the wind took her, like a woman lying back in the arms of a lover, and the ripple of water along her stem became a hiss.

Minutes ticked by. He suddenly remembered the dry dock, and jerked the watch from his pocket. By the light of the binnacle lamp its hands reached ten minutes past where the explosion should have come. Could the match be slow? Or had something gone wrong? He fingered the watch uneasily, then thrust it back into his coat as ahead the tilted masts and spars of the scuttled obstructions took shape again out of the darkness, out of the thickening fog.

—Is that a light, Cap'n?

He peered. —I believe it is, Bo's'n. Mr. Duycker. Let us steer to starboard of the easternmost blockship, the one leaning out of the water. That seems to be where Midshipman Thurston is pointing us to go. —Jerrett!

The boy whirled from his station by the mainmast. —Captain?

—Lay to my cabin. Bring back my writing box and some paper. My pistol box as well; it is in the overhead rack with the navigation books.

While the boy was gone he glassed the river. They were nearing its narrowest point, where the commercial wharves thrusting out from the foot of Main Street nearly met the wooded spit of Hospital Point opposite. The insurgents had sunk their obstructions here, derelict lightboats and rotten schooners. Now a swaying dark-lantern marked Thurston's surmise as to the way through. He hoped the boy was right. If his tow went foul, dawn would discover them still in the harbor.

But the shadowy masses of rigging slipped down their port side without even a scrape of wood against wood. *Cumberland* glided quietly along behind, docile as a sheep on a lead, her own helmsman pointing her into *Owanee*'s faintly rocking, foam-flecked wake.

At last he breathed out, took off his cap, ran a hand over his wet hair. Only one test remained. The guns of old Fort Norfolk, the 1812-era citadel that still guarded the city's inner harbor. One thing in their favor, the fog was growing steadily thicker the wider the river opened.

—Sir? Ink and paper, and your pistols.

—Thank you, Jerry. Put the box down there. Oh, and I should be grateful if you would secure Auguste for me. In a stout croker sack, if you please.

The boy left again and Ker opened the writing kit. Pinned a half sheet against the folding writing leaf, dipped the pen, and began. The words came as if he'd rehearsed them for weeks. He wondered if perhaps his heart had been doing just that, while his mind had all this time denied, denied.

A gentleman could not live without honor. But there were other things a man could not live without as well.

When he was done he folded a rough envelope and tucked it inside his coat. He adjusted his sword. It was his own, bought with his pay. He couldn't think of anything else aboard that was his. His correspondence, the sextant, everything else was the navy's, though he'd had use of it for a time.

Just as he'd had *Owanee*. For a time.

The black mass of the point drew closer. He felt the men's eyes on him. Eaker was standing behind the starboard battery. When the gunnery officer looked his way, he motioned him over.

—We are about to pass Fort Norfolk, Mr. Eaker.

—Yes sir. It's on the far side of this point, isn't it?

—That is correct. It is most likely in the insurgents' hands by now. They may have overlooked us coming in, but with the commotion we've caused tonight, I doubt they'll mislay us going out. They've had plenty of time to heat hot shot and make other preparations. If they open fire on us, you will deliver an immediate and heavy bombardment with all guns.

—Aye aye, sir. At what range do you intend to pass?

The volunteer seemed unaffected as ever. Really, Ker thought approvingly, the fellow was a cool customer. He had done well off Charleston, and had kept his head tonight. But aloud he said only, —

Not more than five hundred yards. Remember that the wind's off our bow. Be ready to fire in sequence from aft.

The point grew, became a compact darkness on their starboard hand, its earthen embankments eclipsing the weird foggy glow of the receding city. The men ready on deck, the marines with rifles in the tops watched silent and intent, as the minutes passed by slow as damp sand from a watch glass. But gradually it fell in its turn aft as well. A few small balls of fuzzy light, perhaps fires, perhaps simply candles, glowed from where he judged the fort to be. But the two ships floated past without an alert rocket, without a shout, without a shot.

He felt his legs sag again, this time less in relief than in something like disappointment. Surely someone should have tried to stop them. But no one had. *Owanee* and her trailing charge were clear now. His mission was complete, his duty done.

He was free to go. He raised his voice for the last time. His last order rang clearly across the deck. —Engines stop. Port your helm, Mr. Duycker. Bring her to the wind and let her luff.

Duycker passed the order. The helmsmen answered. Other than that, no one spoke. No one asked what he was doing. They had that much trust in him. He put his hand to his eyes, grateful for the darkness. Grateful for that trust and that faith, and sorry beyond anything he'd ever felt that he could not be all things to all who deserved well of him.

The thud and clank of the engine slowed, and stopped, and into the interstices of silence came a liquid slap, their wake-waves catching up and lapping the hull. He heard the clap and rustle of slacked sail far above as the sloop lost way, floating to a halt on the dark seaward current. He murmured, —Lower the dinghy, Nick.

He could make out the startled blur of the first's face, and realized the first light of dawn was filtering through the cotton fog around them. —The dinghy, sir? You mean the cutter?

—No, the dinghy. Are you satisfied we're in the channel and headed fair? Clear of all the obstructions, clear of the fort?

—Yes sir, we seem to be clear. Far's I can see.

—You are confident as to the route back to Fortress Monroe, and so forth? Don't look so puzzled, First. All will be plain in a moment. The captain's ledger and other papers for the ship are in my desk, in the after cabin. I have something I would be most obliged if you would do for me.

Duycker said he would be happy to render any service, and Ker took the letter from his coat. —This is a personal note for Secretary Welles. A note of thanks for his trust, and an explanation of how I found it impossible to continue to act in accordance with it. Therefore I am resigning my commission, but not before accomplishing the mission he set me and seeing the ship on its way safely.

The exec understood then. His jaw set. He didn't say a word, just took the letter.

—You'll deliver it, Nick? If you don't, a different interpretation could be placed on my departure. I should not like that misapprehension to occur.

—I'll deliver it.

—Your word on it?

Reluctantly, —All right; I give you my word. But—wait—

He reached out, gripped Duycker's arm. —No, no more. Just give it to him. It will explain. She's yours now, Nick. Take good care of her. Don't forget your after-action report to the secretary. There are several men who might be mentioned for promotion. Oh, and remember, you still have Mr. Thurston out ahead of you in the quarter boat.

He extended his hand, but Duycker didn't take it. Nor did he answer. The master just looked after him as he went to the bulwark and straddled the oaken rail. He leaned down and dropped the pistol box into the dinghy, which was rocking and bumping in the half-light, and then motioned to Jerrett, who stood waiting, looking apprehensive.

The burlap jerked like a bag of kittens. An outraged chattering came from within. He tucked it under his arm, looked around the deck once more, the officers staring at him, the enlisted men looking away; then went down the boat ladder quickly, hand over hand, and stepped in and cast off the painter.

Alone. The black mass of the sloop's stern receded slowly into the mist as he arranged his baggage in the ceiling boards. He set the oars in the locks, placed his boots, and took a first pull.

Light to the east, the direction of land. A second long pull, his shoulders cracking as they loosened out. The open curving sea-darkness of the Roads to his west. He heard a low rushing hiss like dumped sand, Hubbard bleeding steam off; then the slow creak and thud of the sloop's engines churning into motion again, sounding hollow and distant through the fog, and through the hull planks of the dinghy the submarine throb of the screw, like a strange heart beating away under the sea, moving steadily away into the half-light dawn.

He looked after her for some time after she disappeared. It felt strange to hear her walking away without him.

When *Cumberland* too had passed clear, so close he could hear men talking on the deck, he bent to the oars again and glanced over his shoulder and started pulling. The wind was against him but it had dropped, and he made way easily over a slight chop. The marling-worked oar-hafts were rough against his hands. Should have brought gloves, he thought. But the rhythmic effort, the bending and straightening, felt refreshing, as if he were rowing into a new life.

The familiar coast emerged gradually through a dawn mist of rose and opal. Forest and field sloped down to the river. Fog hovered in the treetops. A feeling compounded of both loss and discovery battled in his breast. He put thinking aside and compressed his lips and pulled, putting back and legs into long powerful strokes. The oars dipped and rose, flinging drops and now and then a little spray away in the cold morning light. The bundle jerked and mewled at his feet.

When a glance back showed him the shore close ahead he gave a last long haul and shipped oars. He pushed himself to his feet, turned, and stood upright, riding with the sway of the boat, letting her carry the last few yards in, till the bow lifted and with a grating whisper grounded a few feet off the marsh grass that lined the verge.

A group of men stood on the beach. They were dressed like farmers. Two carried shotguns, the others stout sticks. He did not greet them yet. He bent for the bowline, gauged his footing, then paused.

He bent again and pulled his boots off, then levered himself over the gunwale to plant his feet in inches of cold water and beneath that the soft clinging mud and sand.

And suddenly he remembered that feeling; the gritty squish of black mud around his toes, and cold salt water; the smell of early morning on the bay. It was how he'd grown up, a boy in a skiff on the Eastern Shore, and he blinked rapidly at the memory of his father's hand on his back, smelling again somehow, in that redolence of marsh and salt wrack and sand, his father's smell, pipe tobacco and sweat, taking him out sailing for the first time.

They moved back warily as he approached them. Both scatter-guns were aimed at him, so he walked slow and kept his hand away from his sword.

—Where you comin' from in that skiff, mister?

—From that ship out there.

—Them's Yankee men-of-war, ain't they? The ones just burned the navy yard. And that there's a navy uniform. What you doing here?

And Ker Claiborne said simply, there in the Virginia dawn, —I am come home, gentlemen. I am come home.

31

E LI stared aft, disbelieving as the others who stood rooted and
incredulous around him, as the dinghy faded into the graying
light. Then a swelling murmur ran about the deck. Men began leaving their guns, walking aft to see. He spoke sharply, and they
checked in midstride.

Girnsolver said in a low voice, —Mr. Eaker, who was that in the
dink?

—I'm afraid it was the captain, Boats.

—Where's he going? *Cumberland?*

—I don't think so.

The bearded boatswain discharged his cheek into the lee channel.
Then said, still in an undertone, —He's abandoning us? Take him
off, sor. That's the best thing.

—Take him off? he said, not comprehending.

Girnsolver said deliberately, —A charge of grape, sor. Like you
got in the forward pivot right now.

Eli looked at him in horror, finally grasping what he meant. —
What are you saying, man? I thought you respected Lieutenant Claiborne.

—Aye, that I do, sor, an' always hiv. He's a good seaman, and a damn good officer. That's what I meant. We should bag him now, when it's easy. The next time we see him, he'll be able to shoot back.

Rather than dignifying this with a reply, he went to the bulwark and peered over it into the fog. Minute by minute it was gathering a faint dull light into itself. Claiborne had shoved off only a few minutes ago, and already he was cloaked. The dinghy was gone. So was the flagship. The only reality was the vague cool mist that surrounded them.

Duycker spun suddenly from where he stood looking over the stern. He held one hand to his breast, as if, Eli thought, he felt the captain's departure there. The exec snapped, —Back to your posts! We're still at quarters. I am assuming command of this vessel. Rapp, where d'you hold us?

—Just abreast of Wise's Point to port, sir. The leadsman reports by the deep six, but the channel's narrow here.

—Mr. Eaker, Mr. Eddowes, Mr. Schuyler. To me, Duycker said.

When they were assembled on the weather quarterdeck the master said rapidly, —I never trusted him. I expected him to betray us. And now he has.

Eli ventured, —Sir, he made certain we were out of danger.

—D'ye think we're out of danger now, Mr. Eaker? Do you fancy he left us here for no reason? Duycker sneered, and didn't wait for an answer. —Eddowes, take the deck. Eaker, look to the charging of the guns; make sure he didn't play any tricks before he slunk off. Robert, keep your men alert in the tops.

Eli saluted and went forward through the sifting mist. He stopped at each gun to check the priming. At the forward pivot he warned Archbold to stay alert, then stepped around a big shadow he recognized as Hanks and went up into the eyes of the ship. Stood beside the lookout, trying to penetrate the confusing light. The tarnished silver of dawn and the lead of darkness alloyed, amalgamate, distorted by river fog driven slowly past by a dropping wind.

Gradually he became aware of an interruption in the stilling surface of the river. He couldn't say it was an outline, exactly. Rather an absence, a darker hole in the weirding quarter-light. He said to the leadsman, who was boloing the heavy lead around his head preparatory to slinging it out, —Do you see something out there to port?

—Cathead lookout thought he heard something a couple minutes ago, sir.

—Then report it! Eli snapped.

—Object in the water to port, sir, the lookout called back.

At that instant flame split the fog, a livid lightning low to the sea. The flash outlined a craft of some sort lying low to the water. Then it was gone, swallowed in the mist, and a ball or shell rushed overhead, howling like a Hell-bound soul. He ducked, then realized the gun crews were watching. He straightened, feeling blood rush to his face. I must never do that again, he told himself.

Hanks was shouting at the men on the training tackles. They bent and hauled, and the whole huge mass of iron skated smoothly around, the little wheels spinning on their greased rails. —I gots it, sir, he shouted.

Archbold was shouting too, telling the crew not to obey him, the damned black was not the gun captain. Eli left them to sort it out, running aft till he met Duycker coming forward. The master yelled, —What is it?

—A little two-poster, a pinky or a cat schooner. The forward pivot's laid on it.

—They're firing solid shot from some kind of popgun. Duycker said to the men at the wheel, —Starboard your helm, come to west-sou'west. Bo's'n, brace up aloft.

Rapp said, —Sir, we don't have much room to port here.

Duycker told him with an ugly oath to shut his trap. Eli said, —Shall I take it with a broadside, sir?

—Just stand by, Mr. Eaker. Everybody just keep his damned hole shut and his opinion to himself! I'll tell you what to do and when to do it.

The sloop leaned as the t'gallants took the last of the wind, and she picked up a little speed.

The starboard lookout: —Sail ahead, another sail! Coming up the river on our starboard hand!

A second flash, a second tearing roar. Lower this time, and accompanied by a solid crack as something connected with a spar.

Eli understood suddenly even as he yelled, —Point, point! to the gun captains to train on. *Owanee* was silhouetted against the growing dawn. The pinky, or whatever it was, could make her out, while from the deck where he stood only inky night still lay to the west. So small a craft didn't seem like a threat, not to a sloop of war. But now there were two, and perhaps more lurking in that deadly mist. A river bushwhacking? He said again to Duycker, by the binnacle, —Let me give her a broadside back, sir.

—Eaker, I told you to close your trap. I have to see her first.

—I tell you, I did. I saw her by her gun-flash.

—She show a flag? She may be on her way to the yard to assist.

—No flag I could see. They're firing on us. We must defend ourselves.

Duycker said reluctantly, —Very well. At her next round, correct your train and fire into her.

—Ship to starboard passing close aboard, sir.

Duycker told the lookout very well, and stepped over to look.

The other ship appeared suddenly out of the roseate mist and growing light, materializing not eighty yards off. A schooner, gaff rig veered out, sliding downwind at a tremendous speed. The silver mist curling up off the water cloaked her hull. He saw men in civilian clothes, hatless, looking across from her as they closed. He made her as a merchant coaster returning from sea, wondering no doubt what the firing was about, what the strange flicker was in the sky.

Then as she rushed nearer the mist thinned, the hull emerged, and he saw the open mouths of the run-out guns. Saw their black open lips, the bells of the old-fashioned muzzles swelling, for an endless incredulous moment before a yellow-orange flash and a huge burst of powder smoke obliterated them from view.

A storm of iron hail clattered across the deck. An invisible but deadly fist punched a hole through the foot-thick oaken bulwark next to him, and a deadly whir sped past his head. Men flew backward from one of the thirty-two-pounders, which flipped absurdly, then jammed pointing upward, tangled in the train ropes. Dimly through the storm of shouts, screams, and pounding feet he heard himself yelling the order to fire. The men nearest to him must have heard it, because Hanks set his feet and pulled the lanyard.

Owanee's broadside exploded in a rippling thunderclap that somehow sounded not as loud as the one they'd just received. But the schooner had swept on. One shell erupted in spray and smoke in her wake. The rest howled away into the fog and sent back nothing but an echo, booming back eerily from the fog-hidden shore.

When he dropped his gaze inboard again the crews were in furious motion, a human machine triggered into desperate activity. Swabs flew. Powder cartridges rammed home. The shell men ran the projectiles in sabot-first till the pointed ogive was fair with the muzzle, then jerked their rammers out as the number three man snatched off the fuze cap and passed it to the gun captain. Meanwhile the tackle men were slewing their guns around, but their target was rapidly drawing astern. Duycker shouted, and the aftermost gun exploded, but Eli saw Yardley had laid it too low and the shell clapped straight into the water, boring an instantaneously visible hole in the gray sea before it disappeared in a burst of foam.

The schooner, still flying before the wind, had suddenly jammed her helm over. She was wearing around, fast, angling across the wind and across *Owanee*'s wake.

A moment later he saw why.

Cumberland loomed out of the fog, still coming ahead on her tow cable.

The schooner was still turning, still wearing around till she must be near losing the wind. A fore-and-aft rig pointed better than any square-rigger, but no craft made could defy the wind entirely. There: he could hear her courses shivering, like a distant audience clapping, as they lost their grip.

He leaned forward, understanding at last. She was cutting between the two Union ships. It was a brilliant move, the more so in that her captain must have decided to do so in the split second the flagship loomed up out of the fog ahead of him. Passing between them, she could fire both broadsides at once, and rake them both. Her solid shot would rip through her opponents from end to end, mowing oak splinters through the crews and taking minimal fire in return.

But even as he was marveling at the audacity of the maneuver, he realized what the schooner's skipper didn't know. What he hadn't seen, and couldn't have anticipated.

Just ahead of her rapidly advancing stem, slithering through the low gray-green waves like a water snake, was the six-inch-thick towing hawser that still connected the two Union warships.

The grating of gun trucks and roller handspikes on the sanded deck snapped his head back around. —Prime, he shouted, the yell scraping the inside of his throat as it went out.

—Aim!

For *Owanee* too was still carrying around as Duycker held the helm to starboard and the rudder to port. She was turning fast, and as she spun the portside guns came onto bearing. He watched for the lifted arms from each gun position that meant they were laid on. He crouched to the sight line of number four to be sure any ricocheting shells wouldn't continue on into the *Cumberland*. As the schooner's stem reached where he judged the hawser to be, he shouted, —In succession, commencing from aft, ready, fire!

Boom. Boom. Boom. Gun after gun recoiled, blasting flame and smoke out over the river. With each detonation he saw a visible wave in the air itself travel away through the fog. Spouts of white foam leaped up just aft of the schooner. But she slipped onward with easy grace, as if spurning the white hounds nipping at her heels.

—No, he yelled, and clutched his head in sheer frustration.

Not only had they missed again, the schooner had sailed unimpeded and unslowed directly on over the hawser. Duycker's hard turn must have slacked the towline, letting the shallower-draft ship run right over it.

The two ships were still turning, a whirlpool, each attempting to gain the advantage of a raking fire and avoid the broadside of the other. But they had closed, the schooner slowing as she came into the invisible shadow *Owanee* cast in the fitful, mist-laden wind. Slowing, her bowsprit dipping as she pitched to the remains of the sloop's wake, she was downwind of them now, less than a hundred yards away.

Eli looked across the water, through the pale, fog-whitened air, to see her gun crews working furiously. They looked raw compared to his own well-drilled men, and suddenly he knew that the result was foreordained and unalterable. Neither zeal nor bravery would avail these brave men. Whatever militia depot or courthouse lawn the other ship had gotten her old-fashioned pieces from, they were no match for heavy shell guns, worked by experienced crews and moved by the power of steam. Bird-graceful as she was, the schooner was doomed. As soon as he could bring a broadside fairly to bear, she would die like an albatross with spikes through her wings.

But then the flame burst out along her length again and the shot came howling and ripping along the deck, throwing men down like ninepins. Girnsolver suddenly dropped on one knee, and Eli blinked puzzled before he saw blood pumping out over the sand and burnt powder grains and splinters that littered the deck. The old man clutched his shattered limb but made not a sound, though elsewhere along the deck others shouted for the surgeon, or lifted unworded screams of terror and pain.

Just then, with a slight lift of her bow, *Owanee* gently but remorselessly took the ground. She went onto the shoal all standing, still with steam-way on, and the shock leaned the masts into the stays and the spars clanged and jostled with a long, drawn-out lament as if the ship herself were groaning in pain and dismay. It wasn't a sudden jolt, like hitting rock; it was gentler and went on and on, but men still staggered and fell against the guns. The helmsmen lost their grip, the wheel roared into a blur of spokes, one of the binnacles tilted and crashed over.

Duycker stared around the deck, face gone pale as foolscap. He screamed at the helmsmen, —I told you to steady north!

—Sir, you had us hold her hard over.

—God damn you, you'll hang for this. You've put her aground. You put her Goddamned aground under fire.

The exec stared around at them, at Eli, at the midshipman, at Girnsolver, who lay motionless in a stain of his own blood. The boatswain had twisted a piece of small stuff into a makeshift tourniquet. He said, in not too loud a voice, —Sor, them boys on the wheel done just what you told them to. I'll lay to that, if nobody else will.

Duycker closed his mouth and fixed the boatswain with a threatening look. Then shouted to Rapp, —Make a hoist to *Cumberland:* "I am aground."

Midshipman Eddowes, touching his cap: —Sir, perhaps we can work our way off. Sheet in the spanker, get a bit of sideways twist on her.

Eli said, —Yes, but what about the schooner?

—What about her? Where did she go? The exec scowled anxiously around, as if the other craft were a disobedient boy to be collared and caned.

Eli stepped up onto the horse block and peered out over the ball-splintered bulwark into the inchoate glow into which the rebel ship had disappeared. Shoal water over there, but she drew less than *Owanee.* Passing over the hawser had proven that. Most likely her captain had counted on that, making his turn under her stern—that once past he could carry on toward Craney Island, shoal though it was; the deeper ships could not follow him there.

Duycker said, —Well, if she comes back, we'll sink her. There's nothing they can bring against us out here we need worry about. He seized the bell rope and gave several jangling strokes. —Let's see if we can back off. Girnsolver, I want all forward sail clewed up. At once, do you hear? Handsomely, handsomely!

—Just a moment, sor, said the boatswain. He was looking forward from where he lay on deck.

Eli glanced that way too, but didn't see anything. Just that the fog was starting to burn off. It rose from the river surface in curling tendrils. They twisted about themselves and slowly vanished, like uneasy spirits touched by the rising sun. He could see the sun, too, or at least make out a brighter patch to the southeast.

He looked back at the old warrant. —Bo's'n, shouldn't we get you below, where Dr. Steele can work on you?

—No hurry on that, sor. It don't hurt, and she needs me on deck. Girnsolver paused, head lifted. —D'ye smell that?

—Smell what?

—I just smells something, sor. Like a smoked-out pipe, it smells.

Just then Eli whiffed it too. It made him think of winter and campfires and home. —Maybe it's the navy yard we're smelling, he said, then realized it couldn't be; Portsmouth was far downwind. He blushed at the inanity.

Rapp, coming up the companionway with the chart: —It might be a woods fire, on Sewells Point.

—Fire . . . to . . . starboard, the aloft lookout called down.

He flinched, and ran to the starboard side.

A yellow glow flickered through the mist, but he found his mind blank of any idea what it might be. He spurred it into reasoning. Fire didn't burn in the middle of a river. Something had to be out there. Some kind of craft.

—It's a fire ship, sor, Girnsolver said, and his voice was flat. — They're sendin' a fire ship down on us. That was the first craft you saw, sor. Remember? The schooner, she ran past to stand in our light while the crew, they torched 'er and shoved off. Now she's comin' down on us with the wind.

The engines began to thud, coming up to speed in reverse. The stern shook. Clouds of yellow mud churned up, as if subaqueous monsters battled below the surface. But *Owanee* didn't move.

When Eli looked back at Duycker, the master was rubbing his mouth. He said in a low rapid voice, —We've got to work her off. Gunner! Stand by the battery in case the schooner comes back. Where is the gunner? Where's Babcock?

Eli felt strange. He said, —Sir, you remember, in the yard—he was shot—

—You, Minter, that's who I meant. Stand by the battery. I will go forward and fend off the fire ship. Bo's'n! "Fire quarters," right now.

—Gun captains, stand fast! Eli shouted through the keen of the pipes. He stepped on a gun carriage, then up on the trunnion, and from there to the bulwark, where he took to the ratlings and went up into the main. He reached the top and swung around it, feeling himself weakening with the height, but keeping on grimly after a pause for breath up the topmast shrouds, hands clamped tight to the rough tarred line, boots digging into the sagging ratlings.

As he climbed the surface fog thinned, till he was looking out across what seemed like a flat, vast snowfield. *Cumberland*'s upperworks were the first thing he saw, towering stationary above the fog. And there were the schooner's topsails, magically unconnected to any visible hull, moving slowly across the field of white. She was on a starboard tack perhaps a mile away, beating to windward. The Dahlgrens could reach that far at extreme range, but it was useless trying till the gunners could see. The fog was still thinning, though. It might not be long before he could essay a shot.

Twisting around in the ratlings, he looked off to starboard, and his hands tightened in near panic.

The fire ship was very close. The flames, nearly transparent in the growing light, shot up through the fog. At their edges, as at the verge of a volcano, mist-wisps streamed upward before vanishing in the heated air. Licks of flame wrapped the mast. There was very little smoke. No sails were set, just the bare poles, but the wind was driving it down slowly but inexorably on them as they lay stranded.

Clinging there, he cast desperately around for some way to stop it. He could fire on it, but it was unmanned; its motive power was the wind; unless he could sink it instantly, and he doubted shot or shell could do that no matter how well directed, he couldn't see how shell or ball would help. They could put a boat in the water, try to get a line aboard and tow it off, but at the rate it was coming on it would be alongside before they could have even a quarter boat underway.

He ended up where Duycker apparently had: their only chance was to try to fend it off when it struck, and fight any fires it started aboard *Owanee*. The only alternative was abandoning ship. They might be aground, but twelve feet of muddy water was enough to drown in. He could swim, but he knew most of the seamen couldn't.

A clot of smoke burst from the stack and dropped rapidly downwind, doubly dark against the writhing surface of the mist. Then raising his eyes he saw beyond it, as if reflecting that shadow, a massive towering reef of blackness, an iron wedge splitting the light-filled sky.

Smoke over Portsmouth, the aftermath of their night's work.

The beat of the engines increased. Hubbard was still down there trying. He wondered if the engineer knew about the approaching fire ship.

A dull deep thud from astern. *Cumberland,* firing a gun to call their attention to signals. Rapp shouted, —Flagship's backing her sails.

Eli suddenly realized he was the only officer left aft, and swiftly plucked his way back down to stand on the bulwark, one arm twisted in the shrouds for balance. Duycker and Eddowes were forward with the fire party, and Thurston . . . my God, he thought, Thurston is still drifting out there somewhere ahead of us. —Very good, he said, and called down to Girnsolver, —Boatswain! Flagship is backing her sails.

The old boatswain had crawled over to the pinrail and was lying propped up against it. At Eli's words he lifted a hand wearily. He looked aft, then aloft. Placed his pipe to his lips, and gave a fading call.

As the upper yards came around Eli turned his head left and right, sniffing out the wind as it came breathing out of the lifting fog. He could make out land to the east, a dark suspicion of it. He could feel a very faint motion underfoot, too, which meant *Owanee* wasn't as hard aground as she might be. The combination of the backing screw and the wind on her spanker was gradually twisting her stern upriver.

So she might come off, slide her bow off the mudbank of the channel edge, if only they could put more force on her, exert more leverage somehow.

But now the fire glare cut through the vanishing mist. The hulk was in full view now, a length of low bulwarks built high with flames. It was close enough now to reach with a heaving line. A knot of *Owanee* men stood ready on the starboard bow, holding boathooks and buckets. Others maneuvered a spare spar forward, like ants carrying a dead centipede. The hose party was hastily rolling out the coils of canvas tubing across the deck.

Jerrett, saluting quickly, Adam's apple bobbing before he got words out: —Mr. Duycker wants to know, where away the schooner, sir?

Recalled to his task, Eli looked out over the boiling, slowly dispersing fog. Their enemy had hauled around to starboard, apparently crossing the wind, and was headed back toward and somewhat upwind of where they lay. He called that down to the boy, then looked toward the boatswain. But Girnsolver wasn't there, only a bloody patch on deck where he'd lain. He'd passed out at last, no doubt, and had been dragged below to Steele's surgeon's cockpit.

He felt suddenly frightened, more so than when the militia had fired on him, more even than when iron had cracked and whistled through the air like a dozen drovers' whips. It was another kind of apprehension; like a child facing a grown-up's task, while one by one those on whom he'd depended to lead and advise, Trezevant and then Claiborne, Babcock and then Girnsolver, were swept away by the time and the tide that wait for no man.

At least he still had the master. Duycker might be old, he might be petty and vindictive and a self-important son of a bitch, but he knew the ship.

Another thud, by its note one of *Cumberland*'s thirty-two-pounders. He wondered what they were firing at. Maybe Paulding was just keeping the schooner at bay.

Suddenly the bulwark trembled beneath him. Spars and rigging clanged as iron sheaves and clews and parrels jarred. A tearing crunch succeeded as the fire ship drifted into them, driving the burning spears of its spars in amongst *Owanee*'s top-hamper. The whole length of the steam sloop was crawling with men now, running to space themselves out along the hose, others hauling around on braces to clear the rigging, still others hastily fitting bars to the capstan and nipping the hawser. The shock of impact made every one pause for an instant, glancing anxiously forward, before he went on with his work.

Eli looked doubtfully back at the slowly closing schooner. He wondered suddenly, there in the midst of chaos, if Paulding was pursuing the right tactic. The commodore seemed to be warning the other off, while *Owanee* fought her grounding and the fire ship. But mightn't it have been better to act helpless and distracted, to lure her in and then smash her, quickly, like a fly landing on a tasty morsel, only to be slapped? But the flag officer ought to know which was the best strategy. Oughtn't he?

A sheet of fire glowed between the staysails. Full light now, and the sun heaved itself into view like a livid great hot-air balloon above the dispersing fog, the gradually revealing coast of Tidewater Virginia. Not the rolling hills above the Potomac but flat land, edged by brown marsh and backed with the greening of spring on oak and maple and pine. Hot smoke blew through the rigging, shrouding him in a wavering cloud of heated air. He coughed, wincing with the pain but barely feeling it, more intent on the crackle of flames and the yelling of the fire party, the thump-clack of the fire pump and the whish and rush of water out across the deck.

A white flash many times brighter than the rising sun was succeeded by a chorus of screams and shouts. An opaque cloud of ivory smoke burst through the mass of halyards and sails, sulphuric and biting, and a sheet of flame ten times as great as before began to glare from forward. It seemed to be moving toward him, like the steady advance of a brush fire. A tide of men came running aft, pushing aside the gunners, who still stood to their posts.

He made up his mind. He shaded his eyes and estimated range and bearing and jumped down to the deck. He shouted at the nearest gunner on the starboard side, —Three points aft of the bow, ten degrees elevation, ready, *fire.*

The gun boomed out and recoiled, its tons of oak and metal smashing into the legs of a sailor when it went off. The man fell, screaming shrilly. The tail side-tackle men stepped off the line, picked him up, carried him out of the way of working the gun, and fell back in on the tackle.

He ran forward, into the smoke, and gave the same order to the gun captains forward. He fell over the hose, he couldn't see in the glare and the smoke, and the air was so hot his throat closed on it and then he couldn't breathe either, and he fell on hands and knees to the deck.

The rigging was on fire above him. The sheets of flame he'd seen from aft were the jibs taking flame, great masses of blazing canvas writhing and fighting as if in the grip of fiery demons. The heat was so intense he couldn't lift his head. Things fell out of the flames: burning lengths of tarred hemp, fluttering scraps of blackening canvas. A buntline block slammed into the deck not a yard from his skull, so hard it left a finger-deep scar in the wet planking.

He reached back and yanked his coat up over his head, burning the backs of his hands, but with his face shielded he could peer into the heart of the furnace. Where a few dark figures stood yet, playing the water cone from the hose over the hell around them, over the flame that came up from under their boots. Beyond them the hulk, no doubt packed with combustibles for its final voyage, glared yellow-white as an immense candle flame.

A body lay beside him. It looked strangely small, and dark, almost like a midget Negro. It was little Billy Ripley, still in his bell-legged sailor-stitched uniform. His outstretched hands were black. Then Eli saw his streaming eyes had deceived him again. Billy had no hands. The boy's outflung arms ended in burned-off stumps. His face was black because the grinning skull had been blasted of flesh and charred to carbon by the explosion of the powder bag he'd been carrying.

Numb with horror, he tried to crawl forward. The deck bubbled with pine pitch, oozing out of the depths of the planks. It stuck like a hellish burning syrup to his knees and hands. The pain should have been indescribable, but he didn't feel it. He crawled for the moving shapes ahead. They moved with terrible speed, silhouetted in flame, like demon imps at work in the midst of the inferno. He glimpsed one figure that gesticulated angrily, pointing here and there as it directed the work.

A screech from above like a descending shell. He threw back his head, blinking in the glare, and saw something bright rushing down like the descent of Glory. It seemed to fall slowly at first, toppling over, and then crashed down over the forecastle, wiping everything on it from sight in a fiery shower of sparks and flame.

When he looked again the gesticulating figure was gone, buried beneath a heap of broken spar and canvas. The flames had been momentarily doused by their fall, but they were already leaping up again.

—Mr. Duycker, he croaked. But there was no answer, no movement, no sound, save the crackling rapid speech of the flames.

As the burning ship drifted down on them, Hanks had asked the gun captain twice if he should fire. Both times he'd been cursed into silence.

Now Archbold and the rest of number one's gun crew had retreated.

Alone on the deserted foredeck, he put his shoulder to the carriage and inch by inch bulled it around till it bore on the mass of flames drifting steadily down on them. He spun the elevating screw to full depression. It still wasn't pointing where he wanted it. The other ship was too close. He wanted to send the shell through her water line. But at last he stepped back and lifted himself on his toes and pulled. The lanyard tightened, the hammer tripped, and flashsmoke blasted his face as five tons of cast-iron Dahlgren crashed backward, brought to a stop by the compressors inches short of flying off its carriage.

Then he looked aloft and saw what was coming down on him; and he too ran, covering his head with his arms against the descent of fire.

———

Eli retreated, crawling backward till the deck felt cooler under his hands. The men who'd rushed aft had reconsidered once they'd reached the stern, and come in range of the colts and curses of the petty officers. They were dragging up a second hose from below, *Owanee*'s last, as far as he knew. The portable fire pump was set up on the lee quarter, and men were getting started on the handles.

Rob Schuyler was standing with his hands resting on the horse block, looking forward. Eli yelled, —The fire ship's still up there. We can't put the fire out as long as she's alongside.

The marine shouted, —Couldn't Nick fend her off?

—He was up there when the fore-topmast came down.

—My God, said Schuyler. —This is a hell of a fix.

—We've got to back her off somehow. Either that or she's going up. He looked aft, to where the hawser stretched back to the flagship. Then saw the gunner, Hanks, waiting for him with his arms dangling.

—Mr. Eaker?

—Yes, Hanks? What is it?

—You want me to run the guns aft?

He frowned. —Run them aft? What do you mean?

—We can slip the tackle on the thirty-twos and run them all back toward the stern.

He was opening his mouth to ask what for, when he understood. Shifting weight aft would lift the forefoot, seesaw the bow up out of the mud. —That's a damn good idea, Hanks. Eddowes!

The midshipman wheeled instantly. —Sir?

—I'm casting free the guns and running them aft. Get all the quarter boats into the water. We'll order all hands into them, then try the engines astern again. He added, —If the flames get much farther aft they'll be in the magazine. We need to get everyone clear before that happens.

He got a brisk "Aye aye" and a salute. As Eddowes turned away the quartermaster stepped into his place. —Signal that to the flagship sir?

—Correct, Rapp, hoist that signal, then get into the boats with the rest.

Rapp saluted too, as had Eddowes, and Eli had touched his own cap back before he realized what it meant, that salute. Why Hanks, too, had come to him.

Schuyler was a lieutenant. But he wasn't a naval officer.

With Duycker dead, Eli was the senior line officer aboard.

Saving *Owanee* was up to him.

He was willing to try, but he didn't see much of a chance. Despite streams of water playing over her, the roaring hell of the fire ship showed no signs of slackening. On the credit side, though, a glance aloft told him that with the fall of topmast and t'gallants, the flames aloft had played out. Once a burning line or sail dropped it no longer communicated fire to the rest. The mainmast was scorched and the furled bundle of the mains'l was smoldering, but they weren't actually on fire, so far as he could see.

He ran forward over the smoking littered deck and told the blackened men on the fire nozzles to forget the boat, to play their hoses on *Owanee*'s side. Her thick oak sheathing was smoldering.

Eddowes, returned from the boat falls: —See any of the forward stays, sir?

—I think they're gone. If those flames come aft, the mainmast will go next.

—I'm worried about the magazine.

—I am too, George. I am too.

A rumbling within the smoke, and like a battering ram at full charge the muzzle of the aftermost thirty-two-pounder suddenly emerged. Twelve men dug their toes in behind it, powering a fearsome Jaganath that grated onward until with a shout from Hanks it thundered on pilotless and slammed into the after bulwark with an impact that shook the hull. The men turned and ran back into the smoke.

A heavy slow fusillade pulled his attention astern again. A shining cloud surrounded *Cumberland*. Eleven. Twelve. Measured as a salute.

It was a deliberate, aimed cannonado. Paulding was firing at the schooner, which had, Eli saw, passed to windward and was now slipping along the eastern bank of the river toward Norfolk. A long shot for the thirty-twos the old sailing sloop carried twelve on a broadside. Even without the glass he could see the misses leap up on the river's emerald sward like jumping fishes. The sloop had all sail set and was running before the wind, showing them her heels. Now he could see the flag she flaunted, the broad white-and-red stripes, the circlet of stars.

A rumble like Rip Van Winkle's bowling goblins, and a second gun came hurtling aft out of the smoke. Was it his imagination, or was the deck taking on a slant? He went to the speaking tube. —Mr. Hubbard? Are you there?

—Who's that?

—Eaker. I'm senior left on deck. We are aground and on fire forward. We are hauling all our gun weight astern. I want you to let your steam pressure build. Then when I give you bells, I must have all the power you can give.

—You're asking for a busted boiler, Eli.

—Your job's to give me steam, Theo. Mine is to get us off this shoal before this fire gets to the magazine.

The engineer hesitated, then said grimly that he understood.

Eli capped the tube and glanced aloft. Spanker set and sheeted in. Staysails set. About all they could expect from aloft. A third gun came rumbling aft. But the flames were gaining.

His eyes lingered on *Owanee*'s flag, smoke-stained and worn thin by the wind and sun, but the flaming stripes and deep blue field still bright in the dawning light.

—Sir, quarter boats in the water at short stay. Dr. Steele and the wounded are boarding.

—Very well, Mr. Eddowes. Quartermaster! The log and the signal book, into the boats. The chronometer too. One more gun, and we shall try her full astern.

A last thirty-two came grinding out of the smoke. Eli signaled Hanks to give over and abandon ship. The smoke blew aft, thicker and more choking by the minute. He tried not to think about whether it was already below, racing through the passageway toward the magazine.

He'd thought he didn't care about dying. He knew now he did. No matter for how much longer, he wanted to live.

But if he had to die, better here than coughing his life out in some upstairs room. Better here than under his father's tyranny. Better here, shoulder to shoulder with men he respected and maybe by now somehow even loved, fighting under the flag for the free and indivisible Union it had always stood for.

—Mr. Eddowes, he shouted. —All hands into the boats.

He looked around the deck one last time. Deserted now, save for the debris forward, and beneath it Duycker and his fire crew, the small body of Billy Ripley. The topmen were down, and Schuyler had brought his sharpshooters down with them. He looked aft. The hawser was out of the water, a rain of drops falling from it as the growing tension wrung its fibers. As he watched a few more feet of it rose from the river. *Cumberland,* yards braced around and sails aback, was doing her part.

He put a hand out and rang the bell.

Twenty feet down and eighty feet forward, Theo Hubbard bent retching in a smoky haze, blindly pitching coal into the roaring maw of the furnace. The ventilators were sucking the smoke down from topside. He couldn't cut them off or the fires would die. MacNail lay on the deck plates, coughing helplessly. Steam hissed from the patched piping, a high-pitched, dangerous whistle. The temperature by the fire-room thermometer was a hundred and forty.

The boiling silver thread in the steam gauge stood at eighteen pounds. Far higher than he should have let it go. Far higher than he could depend on it to hold. He expected any moment to die in a blast of steam as the salt-rotten, hastily patched boiler let go in a cataclysm of fury compared to which a shell burst was a Fourth of July cracker.

His arms sagged, and slowed, and finally the shovel dropped

from his hands and clanged to the gratings. He couldn't lift another bladeful.

Staring at the gauge, dragging vomit and saliva off his blistered lips with a greasy sleeve, he looked squarely at that approaching death, and found that it did not matter.

It didn't matter because after it came nothing. He did not believe in souls, or heaven, or obsequious pleas to invisible, capricious gods. Man was an animal, a little higher than the rest, but still an animal like those from whose loins over unimaginable ages he had clawed and climbed through a savage struggle for existence into the mastery and the kingdom of the earth. He wasn't afraid to die. A little pain, and then nothingness. No heaven. No hell. He was only sorry he'd never see the future, that better world to come science and progress would bring. And sorry too he'd never kiss that girl now, the one he'd dreamed of meeting in Paris.

Then he heard the bell, faint through the clangor and the ringing in his ears. He had the reversing gear thrown in already. He grabbed a rag, put both hands on the steam valve, and with a silent curse at the idiots topside, in full expectation of imminent death, twisted it savagely and with all his strength all the way over to full.

Eli couldn't see the schooner anymore. It had done its work and slipped away into the glitter of dawn. The fire was his only enemy now. The whole bow was blazing, visible only when the wind parted the smoke. The screw was beginning to churn the water again.

He looked over the side, at the muddy tide curling and swirling by. If they didn't get her off now, he'd have to leave her. She'd burn and explode where she lay, and his first command would be his last.

He understood something else then. Not just that he wanted to live. Not just that he wanted life, and Araminta, and whatever else the remainder of his existence held. He wanted those things desperately. But as much as he wanted them, he wasn't going to leave his ship.

He was going to stay. As long as it took to save her.

—Get into the boats, he told the few who remained. Eddowes. Rapp. Schuyler. They stared back, mouths open. —That is an order, he screamed, and after a moment, an exchange of glances, they trotted for the Jacob's ladder.

He stood alone then, knowing that Hubbard only was still with him at the other end of the bell rope. He listened to the mad pounding of the engines, battering themselves to pieces below his feet. He waited to know his fate.

The next time he looked aft the hawser had gone slack. His shoulders sagged. The flagship had given up. Beat though the screw might, like an ice cream churn gone mad, it could not pull them off alone. He saw the men in the boats were pulling at the oars. He'd ordered them to cast off, but they hadn't. Just pushed off far enough to bring their tending lines and painters taut, and put their backs to their oars for their ship.

Then he felt the deck move, very slowly, a rise and then a fall.

It slowly dawned on him that they were under way again. The hawser had gone slack from the sloop's movement aft, not from slacking of the haul. *Cumberland* was noticeably nearer. *Owanee* was gaining speed, backing hard to port now.

He seized the bell rope and rang one bell ahead, and reached for the wheel spokes and spun it as rapidly as he had strength to do. The ship's burning bow slowed, hesitated, then gradually reversed direction. She drifted in the stream, smoking and aflame, and limped slowly and feebly round like a demagnetized compass needle to point north.

Jerrett's apprehensive face showed at the top of the ladder. —Back aboard, sir?

He nodded, and the boy swung up on deck. The rest of the crew followed, running to their positions on the pumps and sand buckets. He saw the hulk fifty yards away, turning slowly as it burned. The tide was carrying it away.

It was another hour before they had the fire under control, by dint of smothering it with the sails, man-killing work at the fire pumps, and as a last resort hacking away and throwing overboard burning woodwork and top-furnishing with fire axes; and yet another of jury-rigging before he was able to make steady way through the water again. In all that time not a sail passed on the flat shining mirror of Hampton Roads.

PART V

New York, April 30, 1861.

———◆———

THE AFTERIMAGE

———◆———

THE last day of April was warm and sunny as summer's height. Eli stood on the quarterdeck, fighting exhaustion as the deck gang finished making up the lines.

Brooklyn again, and the familiar granite of the navy yard seawall after a six-day passage. *Owanee* had limped north with a jury-rigged foremast, her scorched hull laved by the Gulf Stream. He'd sailed her easy, unwilling to stress fire-weakened stays and spliced shrouds. But that morning the headlands of Rockaway and Coney had heaved over the horizon, and now they were safe. Safe in harbor; safe at home.

Thurston touched his cap and reported lines made up aft. Eli returned a nod, reflecting as the youngster turned away how he'd changed during these few days, from a callow skylarking lad into a dependable deck officer. But the sloop's passageways and cabins seemed deserted. So many faces missing. Some he'd never see again. Others, if he did, would be the enemy now. Hard to remember how blithely they'd left this same pier side, so much had changed since.

Then he remembered his own changed fate, and leaned forward to sweep his gaze the length of the ship. Not to keep, but for a short space of time his own. He coughed. He felt feverish, and very tired. He and Thurston and Eddowes had had to do all the navigation, all the watch standing, and he'd spent most of his nights on deck. To go below, to sink into his bunk . . . it was a vain hope, but even the thought of it made his eyelids so heavy he had to jerk them open again.

Rapp cleared his throat discreetly, and Eli straightened. The quartermaster had been at his side through the makeshift repairs at Fortress Monroe, offering a deferential word of advice where necessary. Just as the sailmaker and the carpenter and the second boatswain had been there with diplomatically phrased suggestions. He remembered how the whole crew had rowed to help her off the shoal, stayed and put their backs to it without orders, even against orders, when they could have been blown into atoms in the next moment. The petty officer said, —Did you intend to call on the yard commander, sir? To report our arrival?

—I suppose I should. That'll be dress uniform? Sword? Gloves?

—I'd suggest full dress, yes sir. You might want to take the log along, in case they raise any questions.

—Thanks, Rapp. I'll do that.

He was in his cabin changing when Hubbard tapped at his door. Inviting him in, Eli remembered the smutty boy who'd jostled him in the passageway his first day aboard. The engineer was just as sooty today, but what had seemed like ill breeding then he knew now was just single-minded concentration. Theo reminded him about requesting a berth for repairs, and to ask about the new engines. Eli asked him to come along with him to see the yard commander, and Theo said he'd be happy to, just give him a second to wash up.

The interview was brief but not pleasant. The yard commander cross-examined him about the burning of the Norfolk yard and his engagement with the secessionists. He seemed to consider *Owanee*'s grounding Eli's fault, and began a lecture on prudent seamanship in coastal waters. Hubbard derailed it with the question of new engines and boilers. The commandant said he was sorry, but *Owanee*'s machinery had been reassigned to one of Isherwood's new gunboats a-building. Whereupon Theo pointed out respectfully that even in the best of circumstances, the new construction would not be ready for engines in three months, whereas the sloop could put to sea immediately upon installation. He said he would be glad to make the proper representation to the chief constructor.

Eli sat back, content to let Hubbard fight that duel. He was a volunteer, after all. He was surprised the captain had not remarked on this yet.

The yard commander cleared his throat. —Well, sir, you argue your point convincingly. It is true I am under considerable pressure to furnish vessels for this infernal blockade. I will place the matter before Mr. Isherwood's bureau, as you suggest. He turned to Eli. —Mr. Eaker. Commander Andrew Jackson Morriss has been ordered to command of *Owanee*. You will remain aboard as acting executive officer. Morriss will be arriving in a week. That should give you time to touch up your paint and ready your crew for inspection.

—I think I'll put their time into getting her ready to sail and fight, sir. Since we find ourselves at war.

The old man looked skeptical. —I do not think there will be much left of the rebellion after the army moves on Richmond.

Theo said, flinching a bit and sitting up, —On Richmond, sir? Richmond, Virginia?

—Exactly so; the Confederates are moving their capital there, it seems. There is talk of an expedition up the James, to nab all these traitors at one fell swoop. So I would not count on hostilities lasting too long, gentlemen.

Dismissed, outside again, Eli stood drawing on his gloves. He could smell Manhattan, could see its pall of coal smoke even on this sunny day.

And all at once an immense eagerness swept over him. He had almost forgotten. She would be waiting impatiently for him. The one he had not valued as he should. The one whose cares and yearnings, now, would be as his own, whose feet would follow whatever path they found ahead together. He took a deep breath and lifted his head, conscious of an immense impatient avidity. He'd come so close to losing everything. But thanks to an old man's sacrifice, he had one more chance.

He asked Hubbard to tell everyone about the new captain, that they'd have a week to get ready. Then left him on the steps, staring after him as he walked rapidly uphill, toward the gate.

The conversation on the horsecar was of the president's call-up, and how swiftly it was being answered. His salt-spattered uniform drew admiring glances. He sat quietly, looking out as the streets passed. Then he was there, and he pulled the bell and jumped down. He stood for a moment in front of the house, then went up the steps.

—Mr. Eli! Parkinson's florid face gaped at him. The usually immaculately barbered white whiskers were uncombed. He smiled, slapping the butler on the back.

Then the smile chilled on his lips. He looked at the black wreath in the servant's hands. At the black dress of the downstairs maid, who looked at him with astonishment and then dropped her eyes and resumed hanging crepe over the mirror. He turned on the man. —What's going on here, Parkinson?

—Your father's upstairs, sir, the butler said gently. —It would be best if you heard it from him.

He stared for a moment more, then went for the stairs. He took them two at a time, saber hammering into the carved balustrade.

The door to his father's study was closed. He hesitated outside it, remembering when intruding had meant a frown, a punishment, deprivation of some sweet or dessert; worst of all the empty cold withdrawal of paternal approval. He took a deep breath. Whatever this news was, he didn't want to know it. But loss and mortality could not be avoided in this life. He knew that now at least: that the worst had to be faced; that evasion or indifference alike led only to more folly and more misfortune.

He knocked, turned the knob, and went in.

Micah sat in a wing chair in his silk dressing gown and bed slippers. A glass and decanter were set beside him. The gas was unlit and the drapes drawn, but a coal-fire snapped in the hearth. Fine stubble gleamed in its copper light as he turned his head. —Elisha. My boy. You are home.

—Father. What is it? Whom are we mourning?

Micah pointed wearily across the room. Eli's gaze followed, to stop at a mud-stained skein of black lace draped before the fire.

—Tell me what happened, he said, and his own voice sounded faraway and unimportant, a negligible squeak amid the engine pounding of a mechanical and nihilvolent universe that created and destroyed without purpose or remorse, endlessly birthing beings and then smashing them shrieking back into nothingness with tremendous pain, burning them into faceless char, over and over and over.

—She stepped off the Hudson Ferry. A waterman found her shawl.

Eli had to sit. He rubbed his face and stared at his father.

—Are they sure it was her? Someone actually saw her go into the water?

—The Metropolitans tell me she was seen boarding the ferry. Micah reached for the glass. —I can't image why she should do such a thing. I've always provided for her, as if she was my own daughter. She was family. That was enough for me.

Eli sat. Numbly at first, letting the flame occupy his mind. But then through the paralysis he began to feel. He was not sure precisely what he felt; but part of it was something not very different from a killing rage. He remembered what Micah had said in Washington, about the inheritance. Then he recalled Araminta's telegram, the curious phrase that had puzzled him then and still did.

He said slowly, —Father, what did you do to her?

Very gradually Micah frowned, though his eyes, both their eyes, stayed locked on the fire. It was as if each were alone in the room, musing aloud to the Gothic lambrequins. —What did I do to her.

What did I *do* to *her*? What do you mean by that? All her life I've only tried to take care of her.

—Then why did she leave?

—Leave? She never left. What are you talking about, boy?

Eli gripped the arms of his chair. His own voice sounded strange to him; unwontedly calm, considering the storm in his heart. He tried again. —Didn't she go to the Childs? She telegraphed me that she had.

—Ah, so you were both plotting against me? That is interesting.

—I asked you a question, Father.

—Mind your tongue, boy! The answer is no. She went nowhere. Her duty was here with us. She knew that.

His father's tone would have turned him to jelly once. He recognized that dimly, but it was not important. He still couldn't believe this. She *couldn't* be dead. She was in her room, dressing up in front of the mirror. Practicing her elocution. He seemed to hear the echo of a Schubert lied linger still beyond the crackle of the flames. But then the rage rose again and he leaned forward and said, —She wrote me something I didn't understand. That she didn't owe you a ward's duty, or a niece's. That there was a reason. Do you know what that reason might be?

Micah said angrily, —What lying fancy is this? She had everything she wanted. Riding lessons, her horse. The house to supervise, and plenty of help, though now that maid's run off somewhere—

He said, —She wanted to act.

—Don't be ridiculous, boy. Would you marry an actress? Would any respectable man? Do you let a child drink from a dirty puddle in the street because it is thirsty?

—She wanted to act, and she wanted her inheritance. She wanted to be free, Father. We wouldn't let her go. No, wait. I did. But you wouldn't. You wanted her money; but even with it, you still wouldn't let her go.

His father slammed his hand flat on the table. —That is quite enough. I hope you don't vomit forth this sort of uncleanness to others.

—And her income? Her inheritance?

—I really had not thought of it. But since you bring the matter up, she died intestate. The Van Velsor money will remain with Eaker and Callowell. With the family. Just as it should be.

The fire crackled. At last his father sank back. He added quietly, —Well, let us not have harsh words. You're upset, and I don't blame you. Have a drink, it helps. He pointed to the decanter, and his voice hardened again. —I see you're still in a naval uniform. Go to your room and take it off at once.

He got to his feet. —I can't stay here anymore.

—Ah. You've reported to your regiment?

—No. But I can't continue in this house. Or with a monster like you.

Micah said sardonically, —Well, well, this is astonishing. And how do you intend to live? As the lilies of the field?

—I'm making my own way now.

—I doubt you can for long, Elisha. You weren't cut out for the rough-and-tumble of the world. Rather more, on your mother's pattern. Not an ignoble soul; but weak; tragically weak. And even if you could stand in the bear-pit, why should you? You're an Eaker. You have a long start on the rest.

He said, —Yes, I am an Eaker. And for that reason, perhaps I owe someone an apology. The world, perhaps. The Deity. Or maybe just those chained souls your father's ships brought here.

—You disown your ancestors?

—I disown their acts. And therefore, I suppose, I should disown the fruits of their acts.

Micah did not respond. He poured more brandy, and this time Eli noted that his hand trembled so that the decanter rang against crystal with a single fine high note like a tiny knell.

And at that single portent of weakness he realized he no longer feared his father. He had faced iron and flame, and knew he would die; and the place in his heart where that terror of this old man had lived was gone. He got to his feet and shouted, hearing his voice shake with anger and sorrow and terror, —Why did she do this, Father? For one final time. Between us. In this room. What did she mean?

Micah stared into the fire. For a little time it was the only sound in the room. Till he murmured, —She imagined I had taken liberties with her. As a child.

—Did you?

—No. Never. It was a fantasy, a dream. Something she made up, so that she could hate me. I don't understand why.

He looked down at his father. He said slowly, —I would have believed her. If she had told me.

Micah lurched to his feet, shouting about ingratitude, about lack of faith and the duty of a child. He snatched up a heavy cane from beside the chair, and drew it up to strike.

And without thought or reflection or intent Eli stepped back a step and drew his sword, clearing the scabbard swift and clean, just as he'd practiced in all the boarding drills, and the blade met the down-descending staff and struck it across the room. It landed in a hollow clatter. The old man staggered back, aghast and stammering, to fetch up with his back to the fireplace.

—You have lifted your hand against your father.

He'd never seen Micah look so old. When the shouting stopped he said again, —I can't stay here. I'm leaving.

—Don't leave, Elisha. Don't let a lie poison you. You need my help.

Eli turned at the door. He could barely speak, his voice quivered so. For a moment, standing before the fire, he'd wanted to run his father through, to pierce him and watch his heart's blood drain away.

—You're wrong about me. And I'm going to prove it. I'll make my own way. And I'll never come back to this Godforsaken house.

His father said harshly, recovering himself, —You're damning yourself, Elisha. You want to deny me? Deny your family, what makes you what you are? Is that it? Go, then. Go to hell! Go to the dogs! But if you leave, I no longer have a son.

—And I no longer have a father.

Outside, evening was falling. A band played not far away. Men pressed past, talking excitedly of war. Alone in the crowd, shaking in the aftermath of passion, he let the tears go. They ran down his cheeks, and the wind sucked the heat from them and turned them to salt. He walked rapidly downhill, toward the river. Away from his youth; from his faith in a benevolent Deity; away from his doomed love, gone now forever, one with the passing waves.

Weeping and coughing, he walked blindly toward the waiting sea.

ABOUT THE AUTHOR

DAVID POYER's twenty previous novels, including *Thunder on the Mountain, The Med, The Gulf, The Circle, The Passage, Tomahawk,* and *China Sea,* have won him millions of readers around the world. His nautical fiction has been required reading in the Literature of the Sea course at the United States Naval Academy, along with that of Conrad, Melville, and Wouk. He lives on Virginia's Eastern Shore with his wife and daughter, who sometimes sail with him researching his locales aboard his sloop, *Frankly Scarlett.*

Visit David Poyer's Web site at www.poyer.com.